Alderauge

Fernsby's War Book 2

J.C. Jarvis

WHERRY ROAD PRESS

Get a FREE Book!

Before John Howard found sanctuary on the streets of Henry VIII's London, Andrew Cullane formed a small band of outlawed survivors called the Underlings. Discover their fight for life for free when you join J.C. Jarvis's newsletter at jcjarvis.com/cullane

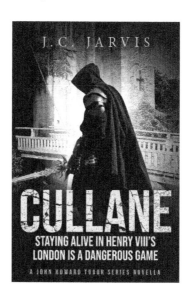

To my wife, Glenda, who is my biggest supporter and my bedrock. Without her support and encouragement none of this would ever have happened.

My editor, Melanie Underwood, who patiently and expertly wove her magic through the pages of the manuscript and turned it into the thrilling book you see today. The deft touch and the care she poured into each page has made the book far better than it could have ever been on its own.

My cover designer, Jane Dixon-Smith, who far exceeds my expectations with the masterpieces she creates every time we work together. Jane is a true master of her art, and I am truly grateful to be able to work with her.

WHERRY ROAD PRESS

Alderauge

Print ISBN: 979-8-9883912-2-7

Fernsby's War Series Book 2

© 2023 by J.C Jarvis

Edited by https://melanieunderwood.co.uk/

Cover Design by http://www.jdsmith-design.com/

Foreword

Welcome to the second novel in the Fernsby's War Series, which takes the reader on a historical adventure set in the dark days of WW2.

Early on in my research, I made the decision to write my books in modern (British) English. All my novels are UK centric, so it made sense to write the story using the correct spelling from that region.

Alderauge continues the story of Michael Fernsby, a young man who was forced to grow up quickly after the dramatic events of Ryskamp, the first book in the series.

Although more experienced than he was in Ryskamp, Michael retains the spirit of his youth, and I tried to convey that through the first-hand descriptions he gives us as he progresses through the adventure.

Because of his past experiences, some of the things he witnesses are intentionally vague because he either doesn't know what they are ,or that was how he remembered them.

For instance, one of the vehicles he comes across frequently is described *as he remembers it*, so I have explained what it is here so the reader will know what he is talking about.

As you will discover in the pages of the novel, the unusually described vehicle was in reality a VW Kübelwagen, and a basic search of the internet will reveal why Michael would describe the vehicle in the manner that he does.

The one thing I didn't change was history itself. Any authentic events I describe are as historically accurate as possible, and when using real characters from history, I didn't have them doing anything they would have found impossible to do.

I hope you enjoy the epic adventures of Michael Fernsby and Alderauge . . .

J.C.Jarvis

Alderauge

By J.C. Jarvis

Chapter One

Dortmund, August 30, 1934

Eleven-year-old Max Braun waved goodbye to his aunt Ingrid at the gates of his new school, her worried eyes never leaving him as he turned to go. This was his third week, and so far, all he had done was sit in a classroom, isolated in a realm he could not hear, and stare at the silent world outside the window.

Across the street, three massive flags billowed, each one etched with the sharp and terrifying symbol of the swastika against a bold red background. The banners seemed to dance, entrancing Max, pulling him into a world he'd glimpsed but never fully understood.

He'd watched the parades, mesmerised by the marching soldiers, their crisp uniforms, and the thunderous applause he'd seen but never heard. Yet Aunt Ingrid's face would consistently tense up, her hands gesturing rapidly to distract him.

Why didn't she like the parades? Max often wondered, his mind drifting back to the enormous rally in Dortmund two weeks prior.

The entire city had come alive, thrumming with a vibrant energy that Max could feel deep within. He'd begged Aunt Ingrid to let him watch, his hands moving frantically to express his excitement. But she refused, her face pale, her signs more forceful than he'd ever seen before.

Oh well, he mused, returning his attention to the classroom. She's just worried about me.

In this quiet space, none of the teachers knew sign language, leaving Max's world even more silent. He knew no other way to communicate with them, not like he did at home with Aunt Ingrid. They often had deep, meaningful conversations lasting deep into the night, their hands painting pictures in the dimly lit room.

Miss Alber was nice though, and Max went out of his way to say good morning to her every day. He knew she didn't understand what his hands were saying, but the warm smile she returned made him feel good, and that was all that counted.

While some of the other kids were given mathematics and German language tasks, Max and his new friend Clara were free to do as they pleased. Clara was deaf too, and they had quickly become close friends. Her hands moved with grace and confidence, and Max felt comfortable in her presence.

Clara was around the same age, but she was already a few centimetres taller than Max, who thought she looked pretty, with her hair pulled back into a neat braid. Max was short and skinny, and his dark curly hair hung over his glasses, which he had to keep swiping to the side.

"I'm not short. It's you that is a giant!" he loved to tease her, their laughter silent, but shared.

Clara picked things up much faster than Max, and he understood why. His aunt Ingrid patiently explained that his mother struggled during his birth, and his brain was cut off from precious oxygen while he was making his entrance into the world. Aunt Ingrid said that made him special, and he always giggled when she told him that.

Clara was patient, and she explained things with her hands in ways he could understand.

Max loved Clara, and he dreamt of marrying her someday and living in a castle high in the mountains, their hands forever intertwined.

Halfway through the morning, Max and Clara were enjoying their normal routine of guessing what the other had seen out of the window when a tall, official-looking man dressed smartly in a suit and tie entered the room. His eyes were hard, his mouth set in a straight line. A shiver ran down Max's spine.

He whispered something to Miss Alber, who then turned and pointed at Max. She waved her hand to summon him to the front of the class with a look of alarm on her face. The atmosphere in the room chilled, and Max felt his heart beating hot under the collar of his shirt.

"What do they want with me?" His hands worked furiously, gesturing to Clara, who shrugged, her eyes wide with concern.

The tall man looked down, and Max watched his lips move. He turned to Clara, whose face had gone pale.

"He wants to know if you are Max Braun," her hands replied, her movements slow and deliberate.

Max smiled and nodded, trying to communicate that he was. Inside, however, an icy fear was beginning to take hold.

The tall man's eyes narrowed, and he grabbed Max roughly by his shirt collar. Max stiffened, his smile disappearing, replaced with panic and fear. The room seemed to spin, the faces of his classmates blurring as he was dragged towards the door, his silent screams filling the room with terror.

The rest was a whirlwind of emotion: Clara's face as she tried to follow, the biting of the hand that was suffocating him, the woods tempting him with escape, and then the sharp pain followed by darkness.

Max woke up with blood running down his face from the heavy blow he'd just received. He looked up to see a male teacher lift Clara into the air and carry her back inside the school. His heart sank as he watched the door close behind her, his body racked with sobs.

Three men hurled him into the back of a vehicle, and as they drove away, Max looked on, leaving behind all he had ever known. His hands froze, his dreams in ruins.

Chapter Two

M **unich, September 1, 1934**
Thunderous clapping filled the auditorium after the esteemed guest finished his speech. Rows of uniformed men and stern-faced scholars, rigid as statues, leapt to their feet, their hands crashing together in fervent appreciation.

The celebrated doctor milked the applause, bowing his head to all corners of the assembled Nazi elite and medical scholars.

Tall and imposing, with a sharp angular face and piercing eyes, sixty-four-year-old Doctor Friedrich Halmer was used to powerful men clinging to his every word. He was, after all, the world's leading expert in eugenics.

Stepping off the podium, Halmer searched the faces for his good friend and mentor, and the only man perhaps more universally recognised than he was: Doctor Ernst Rüdin, the director of the Kaiser Wilhelm Institute of Genealogy and Demography in Berlin.

With his silver, swept-back hair and small, equally silver goatee beard, he wasn't hard to find.

5

The recognised voice of the Nazi's psychiatric genetics and Racial Hygiene programme, Rüdin had travelled all the way from Berlin to listen to Halmer speak, and from the look on his face, it had been a journey worth taking.

As the two colleagues embraced, an approaching SS officer interrupted them. The blood-red armband and black swastika seemed to glare from his uniform, echoing the flags that adorned the auditorium.

"Wonderful speech, Friedrich," Rüdin said, ignoring the intruder. "The dignitaries hung onto every word. Together, we will clear the Fatherland of the unworthy, and the Führer will reward us handsomely for it."

Halmer ran his fingers through his thick, silver-grey hair. "I hope so, Ernst, but right now I'd settle for higher funding for my facility here in Munich. I'm in dire need of more equipment, and experienced hands to operate it if I am to expand the eugenics programme as we discussed at our last meeting."

"Looking at the men lining up to greet you, I don't think that will be a problem." Rüdin shifted his gaze to show the line forming behind the two men.

Halmer's smile was cut short by the SS man's interruption. "Excuse me, sir," he said with a hint of urgency. "I'm sorry to bother you, but there are three men outside who have news of great importance. They told me it couldn't wait."

Agitated, Halmer turned to Rüdin. "Would you do me the honours?" he snapped, waving his arm at the distinguished men lined up to speak to him. "I won't be long."

"I would be honoured." Rüdin's face broke into a wide grin as he broke away and stretched his right hand out in front of him. "General Falkenberg, so nice to see you again."

"This had better be important," Halmer muttered to the

SS officer leading the way towards the exit door at the opposite end of the auditorium.

"I'm assured it is, sir."

Three smartly dressed men wearing civilian suits waited until the SS officer closed the door behind them.

"That will be all," one of them said.

The guard nodded and left them alone with Halmer.

Halmer tapped his foot impatiently. "Well?" he demanded, irritation creeping into his voice.

"We have him, sir. We've located the boy, as you requested. He's in our custody awaiting your instructions."

Friedrich Halmer's eyes narrowed, a glimmer of cold satisfaction seeping through. The news, a culmination of years of patient waiting, settled within him like a triumph.

"You have him?" he asked, his voice barely above a whisper.

The men nodded.

"Good. Take him to my office at the research facility and wait there for me." His voice was firm, betraying no emotion, but his hands trembled ever so slightly as he turned away.

"Very good, sir." The Gestapo men left in single file, leaving Doctor Halmer alone with his thoughts.

Eleven years. Eleven years I've waited for this, and now I have him. A faint smile curled on his cruel, thin lips.

An hour later, and with the promise of further funding ringing in his ears, Doctor Halmer was finally alone with Rüdin.

"What was so important that you had to be dragged away from your speech?" Rüdin asked. "By the look on your face, it was good news. I don't think I've ever seen you looking so content, and I am sure it isn't all because of the funding promises you just received."

"You're very astute, as always, Ernst. It was, indeed, good news."

"Well? Am I allowed to share in your good fortune? Or is it a state secret?"

Halmer playfully tapped his friend's shoulder. "They've got him, Ernst. After all these years, the Gestapo finally found him."

Rüdin's thick eyebrows furrowed. "They found your grandson?"

"He's on the way to my facility as we speak. I've waited eleven years for this, and now I finally have him."

Rüdin let out a low whistle. "No wonder you look so happy. I know you've been worried about having a defective child in your bloodline, and I know you have spent years trying to hide it from the Reich Ministry of the Interior. What about the mother? Is she going to pose any problems for you?"

"I tried to stop my son from marrying the deaf girl. I warned him it would cause problems for all of us in the years ahead. My research proved it, and I tried to show him, but he wouldn't listen."

Doctor Halmer ran his hand through his hair for the umpteenth time, a glimpse of regret and frustration showing through the mask of satisfaction.

"The child they had was always going to be unworthy. I warned him, but the woman had a powerful hold over him. When he died in that terrible automobile accident, I wanted to end it all then but she hid the child and changed his name. I always worried that one day it would come back to haunt me, so I had Kriminaldirektor Kreise secretly search for him. He never gives up, and I knew that if anyone could find my unworthy offspring, Kreise was the man who would do it. He didn't let me down, and now we have him."

"Do you know where the deaf woman is? She might be a problem for you."

Halmer's face darkened. "She's in Freising, cavorting with a Jew. She'll protest when she discovers I have him, but I'll deny it, and there's nothing she can do about it. Her day of reckoning is coming, and I can't wait to see it. She caused my family much heartache, and my dear Elsa left me because of her and her unworthy child. Gerda Yung will not be a problem. I'll deal with her when I have to."

"What are you going to do with the child?" Rüdin asked, his voice barely rising above a hoarse whisper.

"I'm going to do what I should have done eleven years ago when he was a newborn. He's life undeserving and he will be treated as such."

Halmer's eyes gleamed as he tightly gripped Rüdin's hand, a triumphant smile playing on their lips as they went their separate ways, each consumed by their dark plans.

Ernst Rüdin went to his hotel room. Friedrich Halmer headed for his secret research facility on the outskirts of Munich.

He had work to do.

Chapter Three

S andwich, Kent, May 4, 1939
The incessant patter of heavy rain against the window formed a melancholic symphony that filled the silent room. Eighteen-year-old Michael Fernsby stood alone by the window of his second-floor bedroom, his gaze lost in the sodden lush green expanse of the acre-sized Fernsby estate on New Street.

The rhythmic downpour washed away any illusion of peace and tranquillity, and his reflection in the glass stared back, drenched in desolation. His face, pale and worn, mirrored the turmoil within that threatened to engulf him.

To the world, he was the young Fernsby heir, the survivor, but within the walls of his soul, he felt like a haunted fugitive, trapped by the horrific memories of his recent past.

The rain's droplets, striking the windowpane, resonated in his ears like an accusing voice, each one echoing the pain of the brother he'd left behind, the woman he'd loved and lost, and whose family he'd probably destroyed.

The relentless tapping gnawed at his conscience, an

unending reminder that he was here, alive and breathing, while those he cherished most were either dead or suffering at the hands of the Nazis.

A shadow fell across the room as the door creaked open. Michael didn't turn; he didn't need to. The familiar scent of his father's Blenheim Bouquet cologne spoke volumes.

Ever since Michael returned from Germany without David, his father, Gerald Fernsby, had grown quiet, his once lively eyes dimmed with shared guilt. The cheerful and talkative man had become a shell, his words now few and deliberate, his voice guarded as though fearing his only surviving son might misinterpret them and rush off on some reckless revenge mission.

"Warhurst has prepared the car, Michael. It's time." Gerald's voice, once strong and confident, was barely more than a whisper.

Michael's gaze lingered on the green landscape outside for a moment before turning to face his father. Each step towards him felt heavy, like a slow march towards a reckoning with his own guilt. As a tribute to his lost brother, he wore one of David's old suits – a gesture that made Gerald's eyes well up with unshed tears.

At the doorway, Gerald stopped his son and embraced him tightly. "This is not your fault, Michael," he stammered, his voice cracking. "You have to stop blaming yourself. If I hadn't insisted on going to Germany to rescue Frank and Herbert, none of this would have happened. The guilt is mine, not yours."

Michael's eyes, filled with sorrow, met his father's. "Nice try, Father, but it won't work. I killed David, and I'll have to live with it for the rest of my life."

He turned away, glancing into the full-length mirror. The deep lines under his dark brown eyes bore witness to sleepless nights, and his black hair, once meticulously styled to impress the girls, now lay flat and lifeless. The reflection he saw was not the young man he used to be, but a broken survivor, haunted by choices and loss.

A small crowd of dignitaries and friends joined the Fernsby's at the graveyard they'd used for centuries just outside London. The quiet resting place was transformed into a sodden, sombre tableau of mourning.

His mother, Dorothy Fernsby, was a portrait of dignified sorrow, her face pale and calm, her tears already shed.

Judith, approaching her fifteenth birthday and teetering on the brink of a world she was yet to comprehend, clung to their black Labrador, Lucy, whom she had insisted on taking with her.

And then, standing alone, was Michael's grandmother, Giselle Fernsby, or Gigi, as she was better known. Her eyebrows knit tightly, and her lips formed a thin line. Her stern German features hid the turmoil that Michael sensed within, and he moved to stand beside her as the proceedings began.

The echo of the priest's words barely registered as Michael's mind wandered back to Germany, to the cold, harsh winter, and to Mina.

Her face was still etched vividly in his mind, her long blonde hair falling gently over her shoulders, and the deep blue eyes that had melted his heart the moment he first saw them. He could still feel the warmth of her touch, the urgency in her voice, the bravery in her actions, and the fragrance of her scarf that he wore around his neck.

Her bravery hung heavy on his heart, a weight that no

amount of time could lighten. His fists involuntarily clenched as he thought of what the Nazis might have done to her for helping their enemy escape.

Warhurst, the stalwart butler who had known them since they were children, stood close. His hand rested on Michael's shoulder, a solid presence amidst the turbulent sea of his emotions. "Master Michael," he murmured, his voice filled with empathy, "both your brother and Miss Mina, they'd have wanted you to live."

Michael reached up and squeezed Warhurst's hand. "Thank you," was all his constricted throat would allow him to say.

The empty casket resonated with the hollowness inside him. A life lived with guilt was not much of a life at all, but it was his burden, for those he had lost, and for those he had left behind.

The sound of earth covering the empty coffin echoed in his ears. A grave for a hero who wasn't there. A hero Michael vowed to bring home one day and give him the burial he deserved.

This was a symbolic funeral. The real one would have to wait until Michael could bring David home from the temporary grave where he lay on the outskirts of a small town in Bavaria.

As the rain washed away his silent tears, he whispered goodbye to his lost brother and the past that haunted him. Amidst the downpour, he made a silent vow to fight, to honour those who were gone, to survive, and to keep their memories alive.

The heavy rain ensured the graveyard cleared quickly, which suited Michael down to the ground. The last thing he wanted was pity from people while they murmured their condolences.

As the Fernsbys filed out, Michael noticed a tall figure standing under an umbrella watching him. The man looked to be in his early sixties, wearing round glasses that seemed too small for his face.

His father appeared to know him because he stopped to shake his hand and exchange a few words, but what caught Michael's attention was the fact that all the time the two men were speaking, the stranger's eyes never wavered from Michael. It was as though he was watching every move he was making.

Michael shrugged. He'd spent enough time in London with the security services during his debriefing sessions to recognise the air of a man who belonged in that environment.

He'd told the men in suits everything that had happened a thousand times over, and there was nothing else he could tell them.

As far as he was concerned, it was over, but if that was the case, then why was this man here, watching him, during the ceremonial burial of his brother?

Michael shrugged and ignored the man as he walked past.

Chapter Four

Dinner the following evening was a sombre affair. The Fernsby family sat in silence, the grating sound of cutlery scraping against plates the only thing that disturbed the stillness of the room.

Michael watched as his father picked at his food with his fork. Although only forty-one, recent events in Germany had etched lines of worry and sorrow into his once-jovial face. Where Michael and David once teased their father's portly midriff, months of barely eating had left his waistline shrunken and his face drawn.

His greying hair was thin and brittle, and the bald spot had grown to cover most of the top of his head. But what hurt Michael the most was the dull look in his eyes, a void that had replaced the spark of life. It was as if his spirit had evaporated the day he'd discovered his eldest son's fate, leaving him in a limbo of waiting for heart issues to put him out of his misery.

Michael sighed deeply, closing his eyes. The fork in his left hand trembled over his plate, a reflection of his own lost appetite since the failed mission to rescue his uncle and great-grandfather from the Nazis.

His mother, Dorothy, stared into emptiness, a hollow look mirroring her husband's desolation. Although three years Gerald's senior, until recently she had radiated youth. But now her hair, which used to bounce in time with the latest styles, hung lifelessly to her shoulders, as neglected as Michael had ever seen.

Occasionally, Michael caught her throwing accusatory glares towards Gigi, who ignored them and stared straight ahead. Gigi, the German grandmother he and David loved immensely, had persuaded them to go to Germany after the events of Kristallnacht, or the Night of Broken Glass, the previous November.

It was she who'd poisoned Gerald to stop him from going, accidentally causing his heart attack. Michael nodded with understood acceptance as to why his mother despised Gigi and had thrown her out of the Fernsby home after the truth came out.

She was only here now because of the symbolic funeral, and she would leave for London in the morning. Her hair, once remarkably free of grey for a sixty-four-year-old, now exhibited a disconcerting mix of brown turning to grey. It aged her in a way that unsettled Michael more than he thought it should.

Even Judith sat silent. His normally ebullient sister sat directly opposite, her eyes dulled. Her soft, innocent eyes seemed to shimmer with unshed tears.

She looked as though she were holding back a storm of grief, and Michael knew this period of mourning had to end. The time for grieving was over. It was time to heal, to move forward.

David would have wanted it no other way.

Cutlery clattering onto the table broke the simmering silence. Startled faces turned to Michael as he rose to his feet, his body taut with tension.

"Enough," he said, his voice firm but trembling with barely contained emotion. "The mourning has gone on long enough, and it's time we moved on. Do you think this is what David would have wanted? For us to be miserable, and at each other's throats for the rest of our lives? No, of course he wouldn't, and I don't either."

The atmosphere crackled with unease and friction. Dorothy's eyes widened in disbelief, while even Gigi's composure faltered, her face reflecting surprise at his sudden outburst.

"I have been back four months, and although it's been hard for all of us, none of you have any idea what I had to go through to get back here. I will carry the guilt of what I did for the rest of my life, but..."

Michael's voice broke, tears welling up, his hands clenched as he fought to control his emotions. The room fell silent, the air heavy with unspoken words, as he placed his hands on the dining table and took deep, ragged breaths.

"This is killing me inside, and I'll never get over it. Although that wasn't David's proper funeral, it's all we've got for now. I made a vow over the coffin that I would live the best life I could in his honour, and I vowed I would somehow avenge his death and bring his body home."

Michael stared around the dining table. "I promised him I would make sure this family didn't tear itself apart because of what happened, and I'll be damned if I'm not going to live up to those promises."

In that moment, months of pent-up anguish burst forth, and for the first time since January, Michael felt something beyond guilt. Even if it was only anger mixed with remorse, it was something.

Gerald's voice was low, fraught with uncertainty. "What would you have us do? Carry on as though nothing happened?"

"No, of course not, and you know that's not what I'm saying. But we've got to stop blaming each other. With the exceptions of Judith and Mum, all of us are guilty."

"Some more than others," Dorothy snapped, her eyes blazing as she glared at her mother-in-law.

Michael countered her anger with resolve. "Then aim your anger at me. If I hadn't ignored David and run back up the fire escape, he wouldn't have been shot. And if I hadn't insisted on going in the first place, he'd be sitting here right now, laughing alongside us. Don't you see? We're tearing each other apart at a time when we need each other to heal. It's what David would have wanted, and it's as sure as hell what I want."

He stood in front of his family, feeling exposed and raw. The words came spilling out in a torrent of guilt, pain, and determination. "I'm laying my emotions on the table in front of you all to show you how I'm hurting, and how I feel so guilty for David's death. Not to mention what I might have done to Mina and her family for helping me escape. Please, for all our sakes, let's put the animosity aside and settle our differences once and for all."

"I'm not sure I can do that," his mother's voice was a whisper, her eyes fixed on Gigi, filled with a mixture of pain and accusation. "She used the lives of our family for her own selfishness, and that's unforgivable."

"Then you'll lose both your sons and not just one." Michael looked deep into his mother's eyes. "I can't take any more of this. A piece of me dies every day without David and Mina, but for their sakes, I vow to regroup and start over, and for David's sake, I implore you to do the same. I need a place to heal, and if it isn't here, then I shall find a place elsewhere, far away from you."

"Are you giving us an ultimatum?" Dorothy asked.

"He's right." Gerald leapt to his feet. "We've mourned long enough. The family business is struggling because of my neglect, and my family is breaking apart because we can't forgive each other. Dorothy, please find it in your heart to forgive, for if you don't, it will destroy us all."

Tears tumbled down Dorothy's cheeks. "I can't," she said, her voice hoarse and barely audible.

"I'll leave in the morning, and you won't have to see me again," Gigi said. "Perhaps then, this family can heal."

"No!" Gerald thundered. "Michael is right. We have to end this here and now."

"I love you, Mum, but stop being so selfish. Please."

All heads turned to Judith, who had until now never spoken a word out of turn to anyone about the incident. "If you don't stop, I'm going to live with my aunt Bessie. Or Michael, if he'll take me with him."

Dorothy's clouded eyes looked at Michael. "How?" was all she could muster.

"We start with honesty."

Chapter Five

After dinner, the family retired to the sitting room for coffee and cocktails. Michael, Gigi, and Judith sat on the large, dark leather couch, whose ornate, almost circular arms seemed, to Michael at least, to be oversized in relation to the rest of the couch.

The large cushions were low to the ground, and there was plenty of room for three adults to sit without crowding each other.

A dark oak coffee table, carved with intricate designs and polished to a rich glow, stood as a barrier between Michael, Gigi, and Judith on the couch, and Gerald and Dorothy, who sat opposite in matching single chairs.

Dorothy looked uncomfortable, but they'd all agreed to reset and start again, if only to prevent Michael from carrying out his threat of leaving.

Gerald's eyes swept across the room, lingering on each face before settling on Michael. "I suppose, as head of the family, it's down to me to start," he said, his voice betraying a hint of uncertainty as if challenging someone to disagree.

Michael made a half-hearted attempt at a smile. His

father looked like he'd rather be doing just about anything else other than revealing his inner truths for all to hear.

He knew because he felt the same. But for the sake of the family, it had to be done.

Here. Now.

Gerald cleared his throat. "The last few months have been the most difficult times of our lives. It reminds me of those dark days during the Great War when my father died at the Somme, but this time it's harder. There's something about losing a child that's impossible to comprehend until it happens to you."

Michael rubbed his temples and closed his eyes, fighting hard to hold back the convulsions forming in his gut.

He glanced at Gigi, whose eyes were distant, lost in a memory. "Now you know how Gigi must be feeling," he said softly, his voice catching. "She's buried her brother, her husband, and now she's lost her father, son, and grandson all at the same time. I know what she did was wrong, but her heart was breaking."

Dorothy's gaze bore into Gigi with a fiery intensity, but as she continued to hold Gigi's gaze, something shifted. Michael watched as her eyes lost some of their hardness, her lips parting slightly as she inhaled a deep, calming breath. Her shoulders relaxed, and for the first time in months, a glimmer of understanding passed between them.

"Please, allow me. I have directed my anger at Gigi ever since I found out she lied to me about your and David's whereabouts. She sent you there knowing full well the danger she was putting you in. When she admitted to poisoning Gerald, well, that was it for me. I despised you for it." She glared once again at Gigi, who stared back, expressionless, and emotionless, masking her feelings as she'd always done.

"Can you—?" Gigi started.

"Let me finish. You went against everything this family ever stood for. Even when we were divided and fighting on different sides of the war, we didn't lie to each other and send our children off to risk their lives for our own selfish reasons. We stuck together through thick and thin, and we came out of the war stronger and more united than ever."

"You may have felt that way," Gigi said, her voice trembling. She looked down, gathering her thoughts before meeting Dorothy's eyes. "My husband died in that war, and my brother too, on the other side. Do you have any idea how that felt?" Her voice broke, and she swallowed hard. "My father disowned me for expecting Frank out of wedlock, and my mother died right after the war. I lost everything."

She stopped to look around the room, her normally stoic features lined with pain.

And guilt. Michael would recognise that look anywhere.

"When my son, Frank, moved to Germany to work with my father, I hoped it would lead to us rebuilding our relationship, and as stubborn as the old fool was, it worked. Or at least it was starting to. The Nazis and their anti-Jewish policies made it harder and harder for them, and when I began receiving letters pleading for help from my son, I couldn't take it anymore."

Gigi reached for her wine glass and took a long sip.

"With my father, it was like I was losing him all over again, and the thought of losing Frank was unbearable. The actions I took were desperate and impulsive. I never imagined harm would come to the boys. That I allowed it to happen is something I'll never forgive myself for. I understand Dorothy's anger, and if our roles were reversed, I can't say I'd feel any different."

The room fell into a heavy, palpable silence that seemed to hang in the air. Judith's hand found Michael's, their fingers intertwining. He glanced at her, and in her eyes, he found the comfort and support he so desperately needed. It was a small, unspoken reassurance that they would get through this together.

All eyes fell on Dorothy, and Michael's heart skipped a beat as he watched tears rolling down her cheeks, softly falling onto her pink blouse.

"I never looked at it that way," Dorothy said, her voice barely more than a whisper. She paused, her eyes downcast as she wrestled with the pain and anger that twisted inside her. "I guess we've all been selfish. But David's death, Gerald's heart attack — they are wounds that won't heal. I don't know if I can ever forgive you."

She paused again and looked hard at her mother-in-law.

"I'm willing to try again for the sake of my family. David wouldn't want us tearing ourselves apart over this, and for his sake, above all others, I'm willing to try again. So please don't leave, Giselle. Please stay and let's rebuild our family bond because I fear we will need each other before this is all over."

Gigi smiled, and for the first time in four months, a little warmth entered the cold, sombre atmosphere of the Fernsby family home.

The weight of the past seemed to lift slightly from the room. Michael sighed and gripped Judith's hand, and she smiled back at him.

"I'm glad we got that sorted," he said, his voice softer. "Now, if we're being completely honest with each other, there are some things I need to know that have been bothering me ever since David and I went to Germany."

Chapter Six

E veryone in the room turned their gaze to Michael as he straightened in his seat, his grip tightening around Judith's hand for support. He glanced at Gigi, noting the tired lines on her face that had noticeably deepened over the last few months.

"Gigi," he began, his voice firm yet gentle. "I have many questions, but one stands out in particular. What do you know about Gerda Yung? I never understood why she gave her life for us in Munich. She could have left the apartment and taken us to France herself if she'd wanted to. What drove her to hate the Nazis so much that she'd give her life so easily?"

A subtle twitch of Gigi's brow was the only indication that Michael's words had startled her. "That is a story from long ago," she murmured, casting her gaze down at her folded hands in her lap.

"It's a difficult tale to recount, one that I've kept close to my heart for many years. Frank and I had deep conversations about what happened to her, and he swore me to secrecy about it. I guess now she's dead, he won't mind me telling you her story," she said, her voice barely more than a whisper.

Nobody moved or uttered a word. After an extended pause, Gigi sighed before continuing.

"I've never told anyone this before, but Gerda... she was more than just a secretary to Frank. They loved each other deeply, and she was fiercely loyal to our family."

She paused again, swallowing hard. "Gerda was born with a hearing defect that made her a point of ridicule all her life, especially during her school years in Bielefeld. When she met Otto, he was kind and understanding, and they fell in love. She was young, in her early twenties, when they met."

"Gerda told me she'd been married," Michael said. "She said he died in a vehicle accident in twenty-five, and she moved to Freising to escape the memories. That's when she found a job working for Uncle Frank, and their romance blossomed."

Michael stared at his grandmother. "I get all that, but it's a massive leap from working for someone, even if they were lovers, to giving your life for his nephews, me and David, who she'd only just met. There's got to be more to the story."

"There is, and if you let me finish, I'll tell you."

"Sorry," Michael muttered.

"If that's what Gerda told you, then she missed the most important part out, which I understand because Frank told me she never spoke about it to anyone. He only found out after they began talking about marriage."

Gigi cleared her throat. "Gerda married Otto in twenty-one, and they moved to Munich to get a fresh start after he received a job offer he couldn't refuse. Everything went well, and their life together was good, but it all changed in 1923 after Gerda gave birth to their son, Paul."

"Gerda had a son?" Michael's eyes widened. "She never told me that."

"I'm not surprised. As far as I'm aware, Frank was the only person who knew, outside of their families. And therein lay the problem."

"What do you mean?" Gerald jumped into the conversation. "Frank and I were close, but he never told me any of this."

"Like I said, he was sworn to secrecy, and he respected Gerda's wishes."

"So, what happened?" Michael asked. "What was the problem? Surely having a child is a happy moment?"

"Normally, yes. But Germany is currently not a great place to be if you're not a pure-blooded Aryan. You know, because you've seen it with your own eyes."

"But Gerda wasn't Jewish." Michael waved his hand in the air. "She told me that herself."

"No, but the Nazis don't just victimise Jews. Tell me, Michael, have you ever heard of the eugenics programme?" Gigi closed her eyes and blinked hard.

"Eugenics?" Michael repeated. "No, why should I?"

"Eugenics is the excuse the Nazis use to target people with disabilities, as well as other things," Gerald answered before Gigi could say anything. "I'm guessing Paul was born deaf, like Gerda?"

Gigi nodded. "They call them genetically undesirable, and unworthy of life."

Michael's eyes widened. "They killed a young child because he was deaf? Surely not even the Nazis would—"

"Worse," Gigi interrupted, a pained expression on her face. "It gets much worse."

"How can it get worse than that?" Dorothy asked, hanging onto Gigi's words as everyone in the room was.

"Otto's father was Friedrich Halmer. He holds a prominent position in the Nazi Party, and he has a lot of influence because he's one of the senior physicians leading the eugenics programme."

Gigi looked at her grandson. "In short, he's at the head of the eugenics programme in Nazi Germany."

The silence was deafening.

"What happened?" Gerald gently probed his mother.

"From what Frank told me, the child caused severe problems within Otto's family. His father couldn't have an undesirable in his bloodline, and he wanted Gerda and Otto to hand Paul over to him. They refused, of course, and even his wife left him."

"I don't blame them," Judith said. "These people are horrible."

"That, I can attest to," Michael mumbled.

"When Otto died, Halmer went after Paul even harder, and Gerda was worried he'd use his influence to take him from her. So, she moved from Munich to Freising, where she changed her name back to her maiden name of Gerda Yung and started working for the Guttmann Department Store as a secretary for Frank."

"What happened to Paul?" Michael asked.

"I'm getting to that. Gerda was farsighted enough to see what was coming, and when the Nazis grabbed power in 1933, they proved her right. Hitler and his cohorts embraced the eugenics ideology, and Friedrich Halmer, along with his close friends, quickly rose in both stature and influence."

"Go on," Michael prompted.

Gigi's eyes narrowed, and she tapped her finger against the armrest, waiting for Michael to let her continue.

"After she sold her house, Gigi did something so brave..." Gigi's voice cracked, and she took a moment to compose herself before continuing.

"She knew Halmer would never stop trying to take Paul away from her, and she also knew that if Hitler ever managed the unthinkable and took control of Germany, then he would have the influence and power he needed to take him. So, she took a decision that would destroy most mothers, and for this reason alone, Gerda Yung deserves all the respect anyone could ever give her."

"What did she do?" Judith asked, her voice a mere whisper.

"She changed his name to Max Braun and handed him to a relative to raise in Dortmund. They proved Gerda correct, and after Hitler grabbed power, Halmer's star was brighter than ever. He used that power to pursue Paul before anyone in the Nazi hierarchy found out about his undesirable offspring."

"Did he find him?" Judith asked, clutching at her dress.

Gigi nodded, her eyes downcast. "Yes," she said. "From what Frank told me, the Gestapo discovered where he was sometime around 1934. They grabbed him from school and took him to Halmer's medical facility in Munich. Gerda tried many times to find out what had happened to him, but all attempts were rebuffed."

Gigi swallowed hard. "Although they never knew for sure, Gerda believed Halmer murdered his own grandson sometime around the summer of 1934."

Silence descended on the room, and Gigi could almost touch the feelings of compassion and sorrow.

"No wonder she hated the Nazis so much," Michael

said after a long pause. "That explains everything. She helped the Jews escape, not only because Papa Herbert was Jewish, but because that was her way of getting back at her father-in-law."

"You are exactly right," Gigi said. "And that is why Gerda has earned our deepest respect and admiration."

"What happened to Halmer?" Gerald asked. "Was he ever brought to task for murdering his grandson?"

Gigi shook her head. "As far as I know, he's still the head of the eugenics programme. I don't know anything else about him at all."

"He deserves to die." Michael jumped up and stormed out of the room, leaving everyone else behind to reflect on the inhumane savagery Friedrich Halmer displayed to an innocent child and his loving mother.

His own grandchild.

Chapter Seven

After dinner the next evening, everyone except Judith, who'd taken Lucy for a walk, reconvened in the sitting room. Warhurst served coffee and brandy and left them to their private conversations.

Yesterday's shocking revelations had turned the family's world upside down. Throughout dinner, the conversation had been polite, superficial, forced even, with Gerda's secret story an open wound in their collective consciousness.

But the tense silence told Michael there was more to come.

His father seemed unusually pensive, his face pale, the lines around his eyes deeper and more pronounced. Brief, meaningful glances exchanged with Gigi only intensified the uneasy atmosphere. Eventually, he cleared his throat, and all eyes turned to him, wondering what the next revelation was going to be, and hoping it wasn't as emotionally charged as the previous one.

"Last night was shocking to us all," Gerald began, his voice breaking with emotion. "My mother revealed Gerda's shocking truth to us. As far as I'm concerned, she was the bravest woman I have ever known, and we will never forget her."

"Amen." Michael clasped his hands together and bowed his head. "The Nazis will pay for what they did to her."

"There's more that we need to discuss," Gerald said, his voice trembling with something Michael couldn't quite place. "We, that is, Gigi, have a family secret that's been hidden from the world for over a hundred years. It's time it came out in the open."

The room went still.

"What are you talking about, Gerald?" Dorothy asked. "What other family secrets are you holding from us? After last night, I can't take much more."

"I know, darling, and I am sorry." Gerald's voice was raw with regret. "I only found out about it myself last November, after Kristallnacht, and I was sworn to secrecy. Before then, I swear I knew nothing about this."

"We're listening," Michael said. "Surely it can't be as profound as Gerda's story last night."

"As sad, surely not, but as profound? I'm afraid it is," Gigi said.

Dorothy groaned. "I can't take any more of these family secrets. Whatever it is, get it out, and there'd better not be anything else after this. I'm serious, Gerald."

"I know, and this is why I agonised over telling you. But I decided there will be no more secrets, so right or wrong, I'm telling you now. And I promise that as far as I know, there is nothing else after this." Gerald shot a glance at Gigi, who nodded gently before opening her mouth to speak.

"You might find this hard to believe," she began. "But I swear it's all true. An ancestor of the Guttmanns found himself in America after the War of Independence."

"That was in the seventeen hundreds!" Michael exclaimed. "What has that got to do with us?"

"My ancestor was close friends with a man named Ephraim Brasher. Have you ever heard of him?"

Michael frowned. "No, should we?"

"Never heard of him," Dorothy said.

"Neither had I until last November," Gerald added.

"Brasher was a renowned gold and silversmith, and was said to be a friend of George Washington himself." Gigi looked around at the faces staring back at her across the sitting room.

She switched from broken English to her native German, which they could all speak fluently. "This is where it might get a little unbelievable, so it's best if I speak in my native tongue, so there is no misunderstanding."

Heads nodded in agreement.

"Amongst other things, Brasher made a series of seven gold doubloons in seventeen ninety-seven." Gigi's voice lowered, adding weight to her words. "This is important because they were minted at a time when the United States didn't have a standardised currency."

The room seemed to hold its breath. Dorothy's eyes widened, her face taut with curiosity. "You have one of these?" she finally blurted out. "They must be priceless."

Gerald shook his head, his eyes sombre. "No, we don't have one of them. But if we did..." he trailed off, looking at each face around the table. "They are as rare as they are valuable. I'm not sure about priceless, but they are worth a king's ransom."

"If you don't have one, why are you telling us about them?" Michael asked.

"Because what we have is even better." Gigi's eyes

sparkled, and for the first time in months, Michael could see the excitement raging behind them.

"Even better?" Michael raised his eyebrows.

"The seven original doubloons are all accounted for, and they are some of the most valuable coins on earth," Gigi continued. "As far as history is concerned, seven is all Brasher made, and they are all stamped with his initials and the year 1797."

Gigi paused for dramatic effect.

"Hidden from the world, Brasher made an eighth doubloon, minted at the exact same time and to the exact same specifications and markings. He made it as a gift to his best friend, my ancestor, who protected it with his life. Over the years, the doubloon made its way to Germany, where it remained with the Guttmann family until it ended up in Freising with my father. It would have gone to my brother had he survived the Great War."

Michael whistled loudly. "Are you saying you are in possession of a gold doubloon that is worth ungodly amounts of money that nobody even knows exists?"

"Almost," Gigi answered. "The doubloon is worth more than the original seven because it's in pristine condition, and as it is unknown to the world, its history makes it even more collectable. The only problem is that I don't have it."

"Where is it then?" Michael asked.

"It's in Germany."

Dorothy gasped, her hand flying to her mouth as the realisation hit her. She cast her husband a terse look. "That's why you were so adamant you wanted to go to Germany. You weren't trying to rescue Frank and Herbert at all – you were going for the coin, weren't you?"

Gerald touched his wife's arm with his hand. "No, Dorothy, you are reading this wrong. When I declared my intent on rescuing Frank and Herbert, I knew nothing about the doubloon, I swear. Mother didn't tell me about it until I was planning the trip over there."

"Are you telling me the truth, Gerald?" Dorothy glared right at him.

"Do you think I'd have sold the shipping business to the Stourcliffes if I'd known about the doubloon? I'd rather sell my soul than sell anything to those parasites."

"Fair point." His wife believed him.

"So, why are you only telling us all this now?" Michael asked. "If you'd told us earlier, David and I could have got it while we were over there."

"David knew." Gigi looked at the floor.

"David knew?" Dorothy's neck snapped upwards. "Is that what got him killed?"

"No," Gigi shook her head. "The boys fled Freising almost as soon as they got there, so David wouldn't have had time to look for it."

"I don't understand," Michael said. "You told David, but neither of you bothered to tell me about it? I could have helped him get it if I'd known."

"That's exactly why I told David and not you," Gigi countered. "I'm sorry, Michael, but you are stubborn and hard-headed. You race in before thinking things through, and David agreed with me that the doubloon wasn't worth risking your lives over, which we knew you would, had you known about it."

"Nice to be trusted," Michael glared at his grand-mother. "I still don't understand though. Why are you telling us this now?"

"Because we need that doubloon if this family is to survive the coming war." Gerald slumped his shoulders. "The breweries are failing, and we are losing money hand over fist. The doubloon was our chance to save the family business and secure our future. I'm afraid that chance has now gone, and I'll be forced to sell. I've already put the word out, and I refused an offer from Stourcliffe."

"Stourcliffe wants to buy our breweries?" Michael asked, his face turning a deep red. "Why? He doesn't know anything about the business. He'd just turn right around and sell it for a profit, and then taunt us for the rest of our lives."

"Which is exactly why I refused to sell it to him."

"How serious is it?" Michael asked.

"Not serious enough to go back to Germany for," Gerald spoke firmly. "The doubloon is safe for now, and we'll retrieve it after this is all over. Until then, I'll go to the banks with cap in hand and beg them to help us. I'm sure they will at least listen."

"Where is it?" Michael asked.

"Somewhere where it is safe," Gerald repeated. "I'm not telling you, because you are not going for it. We lost one son the last time, and we are not losing you as well. We'll get it when it's safe to do so, and not a moment before."

A heavy silence settled in the room. The weight of this new revelation bore down on Michael, seeping under his skin to his very bones. His mind spun with a torrent of thoughts, but one stood out clearly amidst the tumult.

He had to go back to Germany. He had to save the family once again, but this time he couldn't fail.

And there was another reason, one he hadn't admitted to himself until now. Not out loud, at least. He needed to see Mina, the girl he'd loved and lost in Germany. He needed to see what had happened to her and her family after his escape. His heart ached at the thought of her, adding another layer of urgency to his decision.

He realised that he'd been searching for a reason to carry on living ever since he'd returned to England in January a broken man. He needed something to aim for, to live for, even to die for.

And now he had it. The Fernsby family was in danger, and it was up to him to ensure their survival.

Chapter Eight

That night, Michael tossed and turned in his bed, his mind a whirl of images, memories, and fears. The quiet of his bedroom, usually a sanctuary, now echoed with the ghosts of his past.

Ghosts of Germany.

His decision to return tortured him, each minute detail of the dangerous plan infiltrating his dreams and twisting them into nightmares. He'd killed men over there, and very nearly been killed himself. He'd escaped by the skin of his teeth, and the thought of returning was a heavy, gnawing dread in the pit of his stomach.

Yet he knew he had to go back.

He had to save his family from disaster, and he had to see Mina. He yearned to see her again, to understand what had happened to her and her family. The thought of her alone, in danger, was a persistent ache that refused to fade.

The memories of his failure with David were fresh wounds that bled raw guilt. He wanted – no, he had – to make amends.

These thoughts hammered into his brain, morphing into

a splitting headache. Above all was the crushing guilt that it was his fault. None of it would have happened if he'd listened to David and stayed in England.

In the dead of night, doubts seeped in. Thoughts of the treacherous journey back to the enemy's lair, the faces of the men he'd killed, the danger he was walking into — they all came crashing down and overwhelmed him.

His resolve wavered, but the prospect of not doing anything, of merely sitting around and grieving, was unbearable. He had to do something, even if it was reckless.

The next evening, after dinner, the tension hung thick in the air. It had been there since David's death, but tonight it was almost tangible. The knowledge of his decision weighed on him like a secret he needed to release.

He needed to confess before fear broke him.

"I have something to say," he blurted out, words tumbling over themselves. "I've been up all night wrestling with this."

His voice trailed off as he fought to control his emotions.

"I failed. I failed everyone I ever loved, and it gnaws at me every day. First David, and then I endangered Mina and her family, even though they were just innocent farmers. And I failed you, all of you."

He scanned the room, taking in the grief-stricken faces.

"I'm so sorry," he choked, his voice cracking.

"Michael, it's not your—" his mother began, but he cut her off.

"I'm going back. I have to save this family, get the coin, and beg Mina's forgiveness."

His announcement was met with shock and immediate protest.

"No, Michael," Dorothy cried. "We've lost David. We can't lose you too."

Gerald, pale and strained, tried reasoning. "There's too much risk, son."

Gigi chimed in, "Don't be naïve. The Nazis invaded Czechoslovakia in March, and they won't stop until the entire world is at war. You're talking of strolling back in there to apologise to a girl you barely met, and to find a coin that might not even be there."

"Think about what you are saying, Michael," Dorothy added. "For the love of God, please think about how crazy it sounds. By the end of this, thousands, maybe millions, will die. We won't be the only ones who suffer a loss, but I'll bet nobody else's son is charging into Germany on a suicide mission."

Their arguments were harsh, perhaps even valid. They were afraid, and Michael felt an urgent need to lay his soul bare before them.

"I need to make amends. I failed, and I want – hell, no, I need, to make up for it."

His confession was met with silence, a silence filled with understanding and sympathy, but also firm resolve.

"Michael," Gerald said finally, his voice shaking. "Promise us you won't do anything rash or stupid."

"You can't do this." Gigi pointed her finger at Dorothy, who sat silently fidgeting in her chair. "Look what you are doing to your mother."

"Promise me, Michael." Gerald insisted.

Michael looked at his family, the pain and worry etched on their faces. He nodded. "I promise," he said, even though he knew his decision hadn't changed.

He had to go back to Germany, for his family, for Mina, for David. But most importantly, for himself.

Chapter Nine

The dawn was still a mere suggestion, a gentle greying of the night sky, when Michael stepped out into the brisk morning air. He stood there for a moment, looking out to the dusky horizon, before stripping off his sweater and throwing it onto the porch.

It wasn't the cool morning temperature that warmed his cheeks, but a fire fuelled by haunting memories and imminent perils. The recurring nightmares, the ghosts of regrets, and the looming return to the fray of war gnawed at his spirit.

Tying the laces of his well-worn running shoes, he took a deep breath and began his morning routine, pushing his body to its limits in the hopes of finding some peace and respite.

Michael had always been an avid runner, using it as an escape from his thoughts. The rhythmic thump of his footfalls on the sandy roads acted as a metronome, setting the tempo for his inner turmoil.

He ran towards the sea, reaching the English Channel at Sandwich Bay, before turning north and running along the tracks and trails around the manicured fairways of Royal St George's Golf Club, a favourite of his father's, in happier times.

He ran for miles on end, through fields and across wooden bridges, his breath coming out in ragged gasps, his heart pounding fiercely in his chest.

Sweat dripped from his brow, matting his hair, and soaking his vest. The pain in his lungs and the fire in his muscles were a sweet distraction, a tangible agony that momentarily eclipsed the torment that plagued his mind.

He continued northward, following the shoreline until he reached Prince's Golf Club, before turning back inland, crossing the River Stour, and then looping back towards home.

By the time the horizon warmed with the hues of sunrise, Michael's body screamed for respite. Yet he pushed on, driven by a desperate need for exhaustion and peace. The intensity of his training had escalated, a physical manifestation of the mental and emotional battles he fought daily.

He wasn't a soldier, at least not yet, but he knew no other way to prepare for battle. But this battle was different. This wasn't a battlefield strewn with trenches, barbed wire, and hostile enemy lines. This was a deeply personal battle, confronting his guilt and fears.

Each morning, as the sun emerged, he ran, trying to outrun the haunting image of David's last moments, and the feel of his dying brother's weight in his arms.

And, whenever weariness threatened, the memory of Mina, her golden hair shimmering in the morning light by the barn entrance at Ryskamp, spurred him on.

Thoughts of the confrontation with his family, their fearful and pleading expressions, reminded him of the controversial decision he'd made. Despite the risks, he felt bound by promises made to loved ones, both present and departed.

As the last traces of night faded, replaced by the golden glow of dawn, Michael slowed down. He was breathless; his body ached, his mind spent. He'd run until his lungs screamed for mercy, until his legs gave out under him, and until the memories blurred into a meaningless jumble. But he felt no relief, no peace.

Instead, he felt a strange sense of satisfaction. Not because he believed he'd outrun his demons, but because it helped him make it through another day, another session of punishing physical exertion that matched the turmoil of his mind. Because he had put in the work necessary to face whatever lay ahead of him.

With a heavy sigh, he dropped to the ground, lying flat on his back. His chest heaved as he gasped for breath, his body screaming in protest.

But his mind was quiet. It was as if the exertion had momentarily drowned out the cacophony of guilt, regret, and fear. This, he realised, was the peace he'd been chasing. A peace earned through sheer will and physical exhaustion.

He lay there, under the slowly brightening sky, relishing the peace, the silence. The sun peeked over the horizon, casting long, slender shadows. Its gentle rays warmed his sweat-cooled skin, offering a soothing balm to his tired body. He closed his eyes, his mind replaying the events of the previous night, and his resolve hardened.

No matter what, he would find out where the gold doubloon was hidden and go back to Germany. Whether it was now or after the coming conflict, he didn't care.

He would face his past, and he would confront the

demons that haunted him. For his family, for Mina, and for David. And, most importantly, for himself.

Only then could he hope to find lasting peace. Only then could he hope to finally outrun the demons, not just when he was running, but in his mind as well.

Michael's run was more than a physical routine; it was a ritual, a penance, a minor victory over the darkness that enveloped him. Each stride was a testament to his resolve, each breath a silent prayer for forgiveness, strength and courage.

As he finally rose to his feet, his body protesting with every movement, Michael felt a newfound determination. They had met his decision with shock and protest, but he was more convinced than ever that it was the right thing to do. He'd made a promise, and he intended to keep it.

But first, he had to prepare. He had to be ready, physically and mentally. And so, with that in mind, he set off for another lap around the golf course, his stride strong, his resolve unbroken.

As he disappeared into the morning light, the echoes of his footfalls lingered, a testament to his resilience, and a promise to his family. It was a defiant challenge to the demons that dared to chase him.

Today, Michael was a changed man. He was not just running. He was preparing to fight.

Chapter Ten

K riminaldirektor Albert Kreise sat in the cold, austere office at the Gestapo headquarters in Munich, the radio softly playing Wagner in the background. Tall at over six feet, the forty-one-year-old career law enforcement officer rubbed his tired eyes with his hands.

It had been a long day, and he was looking forward to going home to his swanky apartment in the upscale area of Bogenhausen on the east side of the city. The apartment had once belonged to a prominent Jewish business-man, but Kreise had removed him on Kristallnacht and sent him to Dachau. He'd taken over the apartment shortly after.

The elegant grandeur of the former Wittelsbacher Palais, where his office overlooked Brienner Strasse, one of the four royal avenues that dated back to the reign of Maxi-milian 1 Joseph of Bavaria in 1812, stood in stark contrast to the grim circumstances that filled his thoughts.

Michael Fernsby.

That name was the only blemish on an otherwise perfect career record, and it had been a relentless spectre that hovered over him ever since the British spy's daring escape over the Christmas period.

Germany had promised its people that they would apprehend the spy, but the Reich had failed, and that failure reflected badly on the entire Nazi apparatus, particularly on Kreise. He had been in charge, and it was his failure that had caused the regime's embarrassment.

Until Fernsby, Kreise had never failed the Reich, and it was on the back of his successes that Himmler and Heydrich had singled him out for a transfer to the Sicherheitsdienst, or SD as it was commonly known, which was the intelligence wing of the SS, in the coming restructuring of the departments.

Michael Fernsby. I hate that name.

The sudden arrival of his secretary interrupted his sombre musings, her face pale and taut with anxiety. "Kriminaldirektor Kreise, Obergruppenführer Heydrich is here to see you," she announced.

A prickle of unease ran down his spine. Reinhard Heydrich, Chief of the Reich Security Police and the SD, was not a man to pay social visits. He must be here about Michael Fernsby.

Kreise nodded to the secretary, and a moment later, the imposing figure of Heydrich strode into the room. Kreise immediately felt the room's temperature drop by a few degrees.

"Kreise," Heydrich greeted, his tone cold and laden with barely concealed impatience. Kreise quickly rose, standing to attention.

"Obergruppenführer Heydrich," he returned the greeting, his voice attempting to hold its steadiness. He threw out his arm in the Nazi salute. "Heil Hitler."

"Heil Hitler," Heydrich replied. "Sit, Kreise."

A tense silence followed as Heydrich settled opposite Kreise. "Your failure with Fernsby... it's become quite the talk, hasn't it?" he began, his gaze chilling.

Kreise swallowed hard. "I understand the implications, Obergruppenführer Heydrich. It won't happen again."

Heydrich leant forward, his piercing eyes never leaving Kreise's face. "It's more than implications, Kreise. It's about the faith of our people and the reputation of our Reich. We need to rectify this. And you," he pointed at Kreise, "will play a part."

Kreise felt a twinge of surprise. "What sort of part, Obergruppenführer Heydrich?"

Heydrich leant forward, his eyes holding a dangerous glint. "We need to restore faith in the Reich. We need a victory. And that victory will come with the death of Michael Fernsby."

Kreise stiffened. "You want to kill him?"

"We're going to make it look like an accident," Heydrich continued, disregarding Kreise's reaction. "We'll deny any involvement, of course. But the news of the spy's death will echo across Germany, and it will restore the faith of the people in us."

"And my role in this?" Kreise asked, a wave of apprehension washing over him.

"You will be the face of this operation, Kreise," Heydrich responded, his voice firm and authoritative. "You will assure the people that justice has been served; that the Reich is competent, strong, and not to be crossed. Do you understand?"

"Yes, Obergruppenführer Heydrich," Kreise answered, his heart pounding in his chest.

"Good." Heydrich stood up, his eyes locking onto

Kreise's one last time. "Remember, Kreise, your transfer to the SD hangs in the balance. The Reich depends on you."

"When will this be happening, Obergruppenführer Heydrich? Do I need to prepare anything first?"

"You will be notified."

As Heydrich exited the room, Kreise was left alone with his thoughts. The challenge was enormous, and the stakes were even higher. But failure was not an option. He could not fail Heydrich or the Reich again. He would prove that he was worthy of the trust placed in him.

Chapter Eleven

A s Michael returned from his morning run, he caught sight of the postman walking away from the open front door of their home on New Street. Warhurst stood in the open doorway, staring after the postman as he retreated towards the road.

"You're early," Michael commented as they passed each other at the entrance to the Fernsby estate.

"I had an urgent one for your father, Mr Fernsby," the young postman answered. "I hope it isn't bad news." The postman gave Michael a sympathetic look and hurried away, adjusting the bag of mail on his shoulder as he turned.

After the local press ran the story of Michael's incredible adventure in February, everybody in the neighbourhood knew what had happened. As a result, he received sympathetic looks whenever anyone recognised him, and he'd lost count of the number of times older, well-intentioned people told him their stories of loss from the Great War. As grateful as he was for their kind thoughts, all he wanted was to be left alone.

The guilt was his alone, and he wasn't worthy enough to share it with anyone, especially well-meaning strangers who had enough problems of their own to deal with.

Warhurst held the door open long enough for Michael to enter, and he took the telegram from Warhurst's outstretched hand as he walked past.

It was addressed to Gerald Fernsby, so Michael hurried to his father's private study, a room filled with the familiar scent of aged leather and old books, to give it to him.

As he handed it over, he sensed that whatever it was; it wasn't good news. No words passed between them as the telegram exchanged hands. Instead, a sombre exchange of looks was enough.

His biggest fear was that someone would discover where he'd buried David, and then move his remains to a place that would make it impossible to find him after the war.

The Fernsbys didn't receive many telegrams, but when they did, Michael always held his breath in fear that it revealed the truth about David's temporary grave.

Michael watched his father close his eyes and take a deep breath after he'd read the brief message.

"Well? What does it say?"

Gerald held out his hand, offering the telegram to his son. Michael's breath hitched as he scanned the words for any mention of David's grave, and he was relieved to find it didn't.

But it wasn't good news.

TO: GERALD FERNSBY
FROM: ROBERT HATHAWAY,
Gerald,
Regret to inform, our old companion in arms, Edouard

Abreo, met with tragic accident. Home in Hoenheim, France, claimed by fire. Abreo did not survive.

French authorities reported no suspicions of foul play. Believed to be a tragic drunken accident.

Great loss. Abreo's mastery of his craft was invaluable during our service. Respectful condolences to you and yours.

Stay strong. Remember, discretion is our continued duty to our friend and country.

Hathaway.

STOP END MESSAGE STOP

Michael looked up at his father, his fists clenched. "Abreo is dead?"

"It wasn't an accident." Gerald looked at the ground.

"How do you know that? The telegram clearly states the authorities didn't suspect foul play."

Gerald's mind drifted back to a frosty night in a tavern in Lille during the war. While everyone else drowned their sorrows, Abreo sipped water, explaining how alcohol had taken his father from him. After that, he'd vowed never to touch the stuff.

"Abreo was teetotal," he said. "That's why Hathaway worded it like that. He knew I'd pick up on it. Abreo hated alcohol because of what it had done to his father, so if alcohol was involved, then it wasn't an accident."

"Do you think the Nazis did it?" Michael asked, his face pale. "Surely, they wouldn't dare risk killing a French national in his own country? That could mean war if the French found out they'd done it."

"I don't know, Michael. I'm not saying the Nazis are responsible, but I'm damned sure Abreo didn't die because of a drunken accident."

"What does that mean to us?" Michael asked, although

he already knew the answer. He'd never dreamt that they might be in danger of reprisals in England. He thought his family was safe.

"It means we have to be careful."

Chapter Twelve

Four days later, Michael and Gerald left the Fernsby home for their regular Tuesday afternoon game of tennis. This had been a longstanding tradition in the Fernsby family going back years, and Michael looked forward to it every week.

David had been an avid tennis player, Michael not so much. He enjoyed running, so he'd left the tennis matches to David and his father.

Now that David was gone, Michael felt an obligation to step in, and he'd become quite fond of the old game, even if he was a novice at it. He could see the pleasure it brought to his father, and that alone was worth the weekly beatings he received at the hands of a much more skilled player.

The high afternoon sun cast a long shadow of the Riley Autovia on the gravelled driveway of the Fernsby estate as Gerald steered the vehicle towards the local tennis club. Normally, Warhurst would be at the wheel, but on Tuesdays, Gerald drove himself. He loved the power and the handling of the luxury limousine, and he enjoyed listening to the one hundred horsepower, eight-cylinder engine as it purred along the roads of Sandwich, Kent.

Michael sat in the passenger seat, his fingers fidgeting with the hem of his white tennis shorts. The telegram from Hathaway was still fresh in his mind, and the gravity of the situation was sinking in.

Like his father, he agreed that Abreo's death was no accident. Although soon to be illegal with the coming Wartime Broadcasting Order, Michael frequently listened to long wave radio broadcasts from Germany, especially from Bavaria.

This last week, he'd heard broadcasts praising the drunken death of a French master forger who'd helped the British spies, David and Michael Fernsby, enter Germany illegally the previous winter.

An interview with a Gestapo chief called Albert Kreise was repeated over and over, and he stated that the weight of history was on the side of the Nazis, which was proven by this act of divine intervention against anyone that opposed Adolf Hitler.

What this broadcast told Michael was that the Nazis had been behind the murder of Edouard Abreo, and his stomach churned at the thought of them celebrating yet another innocent death.

The roar of the Autovia's engine filled the peaceful afternoon air, and Michael relaxed in the plush leather seats, watching the picturesque landscape of the English countryside flash by the windows. Despite his inner turmoil, Michael found a moment of peace in the familiar surroundings.

As they approached an intersection, he spotted a vehicle speeding towards them from a side street through the corner of his eye. He barely had time to shout a warning before it smashed into the driver's side of the Autovia.

Michael's breath got stuck in his throat as the world spun around him. With a sickening crunch, it pushed the car several feet before it rolled over. But just before it did, the passenger door flew open, and he was flung from the vehicle, landing a few yards away in the grass at the side of the road.

He blacked out momentarily, and when he stirred to consciousness, his senses were askew. Sounds seemed muffled, as if he were underwater, and the bright sunlight stung his eyes. The world wobbled beneath him, and for a confused moment, he felt he was back in another accident from not too long ago.

That accident in Germany had resulted in broken ribs and a chance meeting with the most beautiful girl he'd ever seen.

But this one was different. In that one, he'd been driving, and it had been his carelessness that had led to the accident. His head swam and his ears rang as he tried to sit up, gasping for breath.

He felt his ribs to make sure they weren't broken again. For a moment, he just sat there, dazed, as people gathered around the wreckage of the Autovia.

"Someone, call an ambulance!" a woman shrieked.

"Is he alright?" another voice asked, pointing at Michael's bloodied form.

There were murmurs and gasps, the crowd's anxiety mirroring his own.

He struggled to his feet, blood pouring down his head from what felt like a nasty wound on his scalp. His ribs twinged, but they didn't feel like they were crushed again like they had been in Germany.

Michael ran to the Autovia, and his heart dropped when he saw his father's limp body upside down, wedged between the steering wheel and the crushed door.

"Dad!" he yelled, pushing people out of the way in his frenzy. He threw himself to the ground and slid towards the shattered side window.

"Dad, can you hear me?"

Silence.

Panicking now, Michael tugged on the shattered driver's door, but it wouldn't budge. He looked around for anything that might help as leverage, and it was then he saw the vehicle that had struck them at high speed.

The impact had caused the vehicle to veer to the left, where it embedded itself in a tree. Both front doors were wide open, and Michael could see fresh blood on the road around the driver's door.

There was no sign of the driver, and as hard as he looked, he couldn't see anyone through the gathered crowds that looked even remotely injured.

He turned his focus back towards his father, who still hadn't made any sound or movement. Michael pushed his fingers into Gerald's neck to feel his carotid artery, to see if he felt a pulse.

He let out a yell of relief when he felt one. Faint, but he felt one.

The clattering of sirens filled the void in his ears, and shortly after, emergency vehicles of all shapes and sizes filled the road. Fire trucks stopped alongside ambulances, and the policemen got to work cordoning off the area, making space so the medical teams could get to work.

Hands grabbed at him, pulling him back from the wreckage.

"Let me go!" Michael shouted, trying to break free.

But more hands joined in, forcing him down onto a stretcher. He fought, he sobbed, and he yelled, but to no avail. Strong, and yet somehow soothing hands held him, and the next thing he knew, he was being driven away from the scene towards the local hospital.

Chapter Thirteen

Michael's head throbbed as the sunlight streamed through the windows of the Kent and Canterbury Hospital. His vision swam as he took in the sterile surroundings – the white-washed walls, the crisp sheets, the hustle and bustle of the nurses taking care of the patients.

The unmistakable smell of Dettol filled his nostrils. The smell of the antiseptic was so strong that it overpowered every other scent in the room, immediately transporting him back to his childhood when scraped knees and minor cuts were treated with the same potent solution. It was a scent of cleanliness and care, but also a stark reminder of the pain that often preceded its use.

He was in a ward with at least twenty other poor souls, each with varying degrees of non-life-threatening injuries. Three nurses worked the floor, and even through the fog of his injured head, Michael had sympathy for the overworked, and probably underpaid, saviours of the night, as he called them.

His mind was still processing the events of the previous day, and he constantly replayed it over and over in his mind.

It had happened so fast, and there wasn't much he could remember other than seeing a blur approaching from a side street at speed.

What the hell happened? Was someone trying to kill us? Or was it an out-of-control vehicle we were unlucky enough to be in the way of?

Visions of his father's limp body hanging upside down in the Autovia swamped his battered mind, and he yelled for the nurse as he struggled to sit up.

"Where's my father?" he croaked. "Is he alright?"

"I don't know, Michael, I'm sorry." The pretty young nurse with emerald-green eyes and a kind smile held a glass of water to his lips. "You need to ask the doctor when he makes his rounds this morning. Please drink some water and lie down. You had a nasty bump to the head, and we want to make sure you are alright."

"I'm fine," Michael spoke gruffly. "I just want to know how my father is and get out of here."

"We'll let you out when the doctor says you can leave," the nurse said firmly. "Now please, do as you're told and drink some water."

Michael scowled and took the glass from the nurse. Ten minutes later, he was drifting off to sleep when someone shook his arm.

His mother and grandmother stood over him, their faces pale with worry. It was an all too familiar look he'd seen on their faces recently, especially his mother's, and it broke his heart to see her looking like that again.

"Michael," Dorothy exclaimed, grabbing his hand. "Oh, thank God you're alright."

Michael tried to smile but found his face was too swollen. Gigi followed, her wise eyes searching his face. "You gave us quite a fright, young man."

"I seem to be good at that, don't I?" Michael squeezed his mother's hand. "Don't worry, Mum, I'm fine, and I'll be out of here today if they'll let me. How's Dad? Have you seen him? Where is he? Is he here?"

"Whoa, Michael, slow down." Dorothy's soothing voice calmed the rising anxiety in Michael's chest. "He's here, in a private room. You know your father. He has to have the finest they can offer."

Michael gave a weak smile. "How is he?"

Visions once again flooded back of Gerald Fernsby hanging upside down in the wreckage, with Michael trying frantically to rescue him before powerful arms pulled him aside and took him away.

"I won't lie. He's in a bad way." Dorothy gently squeezed his hand. "They're still assessing his injuries, but he's got a fractured femur, a broken hip, broken shoulder, and several broken ribs. On top of that, he suffered a severe concussion. The surgeons told me they won't operate because of his heart condition, so they're looking at using traction and splints."

Dorothy's voice cracked, and her eyes filled with tears. "I'm really worried about him, Michael. He's not allowed visitors, but they promised to let me know as soon as they've finished their diagnosis."

She reached for Michael's hand and squeezed tightly. "The doctors told me that if he survives, he'll probably be in the hospital for months, and the chances are that he'll never be the same once he gets out."

Dorothy bowed her head and sobbed. Gigi rubbed her shoulders, and Michael felt the moisture on his arm as tears fell from her face.

"I couldn't save him." Michael's eyes clouded. "Mum, I couldn't save him."

"Oh, Michael. From what I heard, you fought tooth and nail to get him out of the car, and it took five strong men to pull you away so the emergency crews could get to him. You did all you could, and then some."

"I couldn't get him out," Michael repeated.

"He's in the best hands," Gigi said. "Your father might not be as sprightly as he once was, but he's still strong, and he'll recover from this. You concentrate on yourself and worry about your father once you're out of here."

"I'm fine," Michael said. "I'll be out today if they let me."

"There's the doctor." Dorothy looked towards the doorway of the ward. "I'll be right back."

Dorothy left to speak to the doctor, leaving Michael and Gigi alone.

"It wasn't an accident," Gigi spoke softly. "That car rammed you intentionally."

"That's my sentiments too," Michael responded. "I've been over and over it in my mind, and there's no way it could have been anything other than deliberate. The vehicle flew out of that side street so fast and aimed right at us. I don't remember much, but I do remember that."

Gigi took her grandson's hand in hers and her eyes misted, another moment of rare emotion from the normally stoic Giselle Fernsby.

"After what happened to Abreo, I think it's retaliation from the Nazis. They're getting back at you for escaping and making them look bad. They designed it to look like an accident so they can deny it. I'm worried, Michael. I'm worried they will kill you. We've lost enough of our family already, and we can't lose anyone else."

"We'll be alright, Gigi," Michael assured her. "I promise."

"Don't promise what you can't keep. They're coming for you, Michael, whether you want to admit it or not."

Before he could answer, two policemen in uniform entered the ward. After a brief conversation, the nurse pointed at Michael's bed. The two policemen approached.

One was a sergeant and was obviously in charge. He had salt and pepper hair, and the other was a younger man, not much older than Michael, with cheeks that still showed the flush of youth.

"We're here to ask a few questions about the accident, son," the older officer started, his tone gentle but serious.

"I don't remember much."

"We're trying to piece together what happened, but we appreciate that there might not be much you can add for us."

"All I remember is seeing a vehicle through the corner of my eye speeding towards us out of that side road. Whoever was driving made no attempt to slow down, and the next thing I knew, it smashed into us. Everything after that is a blur."

The older officer nodded his understanding of Michael's recollections.

"There were plenty of witnesses who saw the whole thing, and they corroborate what you remember. Tell me, do you know of any reason someone would want to do this to either you or your father?"

"I can think of plenty of reasons," Gigi cut in. "You do know who we are, I assume?"

The officer nodded his head again. "I do, and that is why I am asking. You're the one who went to Germany to rescue his family and ended up in a shootout with the Nazis, right? Your story was all over the newspapers."

"There's your reason this happened, Sergeant," Gigi said.

"You're blaming the Germans for this?" the older officer asked. His younger companion smiled at his superior.

"I am, and with good reason," Gigi remained firm.

"Let me tell you what we know so far," the officer said. "The vehicle was stolen in London three days prior to the accident. We think it was going to be used in a robbery somewhere in Canterbury, and for some reason, the driver lost control and crashed into you instead."

"The vehicle was stolen?" Michael asked. "Surely that tells you enough to know they did this deliberately. What about the driver? I saw a pool of blood at the side of the vehicle, so the driver must have been injured. Have you arrested him yet?"

"No," the officer shook his head. "We're monitoring all the hospitals in the area, and if anyone checks in with any injuries, we'll be on it in a flash. As of now, we don't have any clue who was driving, as whoever it was ran away in the confusion."

"They may not admit it, but the Nazis did this," Gigi reiterated.

"We don't think so," the older officer said. "All the evidence we've gathered indicates that it was a robbery in the making that went wrong, and unless we get any evidence to the contrary, that's the line of inquiry we are going to take."

"Is that your opinion?" Gigi asked. "Or have you been directed to say that by your superiors?"

"It's okay, Gigi." Michael could see the red glow from the officer's cheeks. "The officers are only doing their jobs. If that's what the evidence suggests, then who are we to question it?"

"If there's nothing else you can add, then we'll be in

touch," the officer said. "We wish you and your father a speedy recovery."

Once the officers left, Gigi spoke. "This doesn't sit right with me, Michael," she said in a low voice, her gaze steady. "They're covering it up."

"Agreed. It's probably come from high above, especially after Abreo got killed. They are trying to avoid an international incident with Germany."

"That's exactly what they're doing," Gigi agreed. "This wasn't an accident. This is tied to Abreo's death."

"What can we do about it?" Michael asked. "The short answer is nothing."

"This incident will be forgotten." Gigi stared ahead as though she were deep in thought. "War is coming, and there will be much bigger problems for both countries to face. We'll be alright, Michael."

"I hope so because I feel as helpless as a hamster on a spinning wheel right now."

Dorothy returned from her conversations with the doctors and the policemen. "They are keeping you tonight to monitor the head wound, and you may be allowed to go home tomorrow if everything is alright."

"That's nice. I want to go home."

As the day waned into the night, updates on Gerald's condition trickled in. Although Dorothy wasn't allowed to see him, the doctors and nurses kept her up to date with his situation.

Aside from the injuries already reported, they found no further issues. He was awake and alert, but his injuries had set his heart off again, and the doctors worried he might be at risk of another heart attack.

They would keep him in hospital for an undetermined amount of time – potentially months – so they could monitor him and assist in his recovery. Dorothy had already rented a house in Canterbury so she could be close, and she wanted Michael to stay with her once they discharged him.

But Michael had other plans. Plans that did not include staying in a rented house in Canterbury.

Chapter Fourteen

After two weeks of recovery, Michael was on the mend. Much to his mother's dislike, he chose to recover at home in Sandwich, where he was surrounded by familiarity and family.

Gigi and Judith, as well as Lucy, kept him busy, and trusty old Warhurst made sure he was well taken care of.

Even as his wounds healed, Michael felt the heavy weight of responsibility. The police visits had finally ceased, but Gigi's words hung in the air like a heavy smog.

This was no random accident.

His father's life was hanging in the balance, and the incident had brought back memories of his previous encounter with the Nazis.

He resumed running as soon as the gash in his head had stopped leaking blood whenever he exerted himself. At first, Warhurst accompanied him on the early morning runs to make sure he was alright, but even though Warhurst had been a world-class runner in his day, he could no longer keep up with the younger, driven man in his care, and after a couple of days he'd given up, telling Michael to be careful and not to fall.

Michael was glad of the solitude, and he pushed himself more and more as his body recovered from the aches and pains of the accident.

Accident. Who am I kidding? That was no accident.

The hospital was less than twenty miles from Sandwich, and Michael drove Gigi and Judith to see Dorothy every couple of days. They even got to see Gerald occasionally, and although he was critical, they all hoped for a miracle.

On this particular morning, Michael left for his run earlier than normal. A heavy fog had rolled in from the sea, bringing visibility down to less than fifty feet. Michael loved running when the fog rolled in, because he felt isolated and alone, lost in the safety of his own little world.

He ran his usual route towards the sea, before turning north to run through Royal Saint George's Golf Club and then heading into the isolation of Prince's Golf Club.

The poor weather meant that nobody would be on the links this day, especially as it was barely breaking dawn as he ran up the narrow lane in the middle of the course.

As he turned inland to head for home, a rustle off to his left stopped him in his tracks. The visibility was too poor to see much, but with memories of the recent attack fresh in his mind, Michael clung hold of the truncheon he'd carried with him at all times since his release from the hospital.

He sensed, more than saw, that someone – or something – was ahead of him, and he stepped to his right to put more distance between himself and whoever it was.

After a few intense moments of listening, Michael spoke up. "I know you're there, so come out and show yourself."

More rustling as someone approached. Michael tightened his grip on the truncheon. "That's close enough. Stop right there."

A figure began to emerge from the fog and the half-light of the early morning dawn.

"Who are you, and what do you want?"

The all-too-familiar feelings of fear and excitement caused the hairs on the back of Michael's neck to rise. Rapid visions of his epic escape through the Black Forest tumbled through his mind, and he shivered in the crisp, foggy morning.

A shadowy figure emerged through the mists, and Michael squinted to see if they were alone. As the figure emerged, Michael stepped towards it.

"Stop. That's close enough. I asked who you are and why are you here. I won't ask again."

"Stand down, Fernsby. I mean you no harm."

Michael had never heard this voice before. Whoever it was sounded educated, and yet not aristocratic, like his father. He also sounded like a man who was used to being obeyed.

"I asked who you are. Don't take another step forward until you reveal yourself."

The figure of a man emerged from the mists.

I've seen this man before, but where?

Michael racked his brain trying to remember where he'd seen this face before.

The man was tall and wore a long grey raincoat. There was nothing unusual about that, but the round glasses on his head that seemed too small for his face looked awfully familiar.

Then it hit him. "You were at David's funeral! I saw you in the rain, talking to my father."

"Very observant of you. I was, indeed, at the faux funeral of your sadly departed brother."

"Why are you here, and what do you want with me?"

Michael stared at the grey man standing before him as he got closer. "Who are you? And how do you know my father?"

"Please allow me to introduce myself. My name, although you have probably never heard of me, is Lieutenant Colonel Claude Dansey, and I know your father because our paths crossed during the Great War."

"You're military intelligence?"

"I am."

"Why didn't I see you during all my debriefs? As far as I'm aware, I saw every one of you after I returned home from Germany."

"Not all of us, and certainly not those of us in the higher positions of the Secret Intelligence Service."

"You're SIS?" Michael asked suspiciously. He was intrigued because he'd seen his father speaking to this man, so he knew he was legitimate.

But what does he want with me? It must be about the accident. He knows it was the Nazis.

"I'm the assistant chief of SIS, and as such, you wouldn't have seen me during your debriefs. But rest assured that I read your file before meeting with you here this morning."

"This isn't a meeting. It's an ambush. A meeting is a prearranged point of contact agreed upon by two or more parties. I didn't agree to any of this."

"Your file said you were hard-headed, and it wasn't wrong, was it?"

"Why are you here, Dansey? Obviously, you didn't want anyone to know about it, or you wouldn't have picked the worst morning possible in the most remote part of my morning run."

"You are an astute young man. I'll get straight to the point, seeing as you seem to prefer a more direct method of communication."

"Please do."

"What just happened to you wasn't an accident."

"I already knew that. Tell me something I don't know."

"It was planned at the very top of the Nazi hierarchy. You embarrassed them when you escaped, and it made the German population lose faith in the regime, or at least, that's how Heydrich saw it."

"Reinhard Heydrich?"

"The one and only."

"What did he have to do with my escape? Surely, I wasn't important enough to bother someone like him?"

"It was his officers you evaded, and it reflected badly on him. He took it personally when you escaped, especially after the Nazis had been all over the German radio and newsreels, telling everyone that the Gestapo would capture you at any moment. It was an epic failure for them, and they didn't take it well."

"So, Heydrich sent someone all the way here to kill me and make it look like an accident?"

"Yes."

"Did they kill Abreo as well?"

"Yes."

"Why are you telling me this? It isn't like there's anything I can do about it, is there?"

"That may not be entirely true."

"What are you saying?"

"As assistant chief, I'm privy to sensitive information. Information that sometimes finds its way into the hands of our adversaries. Our intelligence services operate in passport offices around the world, something that is well known to all our enemies. The Sicherheitsdienst, or SD, if you know who they are, have infiltrated our resources in Europe, and sometimes we have operations that require the utmost secrecy, which is why we operate different departments within the SIS."

"I know who the SD are. They are the intelligence wing of the SS. What does any of this have to do with me?"

"We sometimes have delicate operations that need to be carried out by motivated men who have demonstrated courage, tenacity, and resilience in the field. Men such as these are hard to find, and when I find one, I want them to work for us. You are one such man, Fernsby, and I want you to come work for us."

"You want me to work for the British government? Doing what, exactly? I don't know anything about spying or the Secret Intelligence Service. My father was an intelligence officer, not me. I'm a Cambridge University student, or at least I was until Stourcliffe had me expelled last year."

"I know all about that, and once the coming war is over, I might be able to help you get reinstated, if that's what you wanted to do."

"What do you want from me? Spell it out."

"Not here. All I want from you right now is an indication that you would be willing to work clandestinely for the British government. In return, I offer you the chance to get back at the Nazis for what they've done to you and your family."

"Is it dangerous?"

"Extremely."

"Will I die?"

"Possibly, although if you follow orders, it's not likely to happen."

"What do I need to do?"

"I need you to show up at this address one week from Monday at eight in the morning. Ask for room 317, and it is there that all will be revealed."

Dansey handed Michael a folded note.

"One week from Monday."

Lieutenant Colonel Dansey disappeared back into the mists from whence he came.

Chapter Fifteen

Tension filled the air as the clock ticked towards eight o'clock. All eyes were on the red light above the doorway that would momentarily turn green, signalling that the broadcast to the German people was live.

The tension rose as the second hand swept towards the appointed hour. At exactly eight o'clock, a loud buzzer went off and the red light turned to green. All eyes turned to the overweight, balding man waiting to deliver the most important speech of his life.

It was important because none other than Joseph Goebbels himself had chosen him to introduce his illustrious guest live on air in front of the entire nation.

Sweat beaded on his forehead, and his heart raced. But Klaus Becker had been here before, and he wasn't about to fail the Reich Minister of Propaganda when he needed him the most.

He chose me! I was the one he chose.

Becker soothed his racing heart with those words as he leant into the microphone. As the soft hum of the airwaves filled the studio, he cleared his throat and began to read his speech.

"Good evening, my fellow Germans. This is Klaus Becker, your faithful servant, guiding you through the radio waves. Welcome to tonight's broadcast of Deutschland Aktuell, the voice of our powerful Reich. We stand together, sharing our triumphs and challenges, united under the banner of our glorious Führer."

Becker continued, his voice resonating with pride. "Here on Deutschland Aktuell, we bring you the most important news and updates from The Fatherland. This program is not just a testament to our triumphs but also serves as a beacon of truth, strength, and unity. We are the voice of the Reich, a platform for our collective dreams and aspirations. Tonight, as always, we strive to enlighten, educate, and guide you, as we remain forever loyal to our beloved Führer and his invincible destiny."

"Ladies and gentlemen, tonight we have a very special guest with us. A man who needs little introduction. A man whose dedication and relentless pursuit of justice has been a beacon of hope in these troubling times."

Becker paused, letting his words hang in the air. The silence was punctuated by the steady crackle of the radio.

"I present to you, Kriminaldirektor Albert Kreise." His voice, filled with a reverence that matched the man's stature, echoed across Germany. "A dedicated servant of the Reich who needs no introduction for those who have followed the news of the notorious British spy, Michael Fernsby."

He continued. "Kriminaldirektor Kreise is the man who relentlessly pursued Fernsby after his murderous spree over the Christmas period. Fernsby, as we all know, has committed heinous crimes against our great nation, murdering four of our brave Gestapo officers in Munich, and at least three loyal Wehrmacht soldiers who were simply doing their duty."

Becker's voice dipped, mirroring the nation's sorrow at the losses. After a moment, he resumed. "Kriminaldirektor Kreise pursued him night and day, tirelessly risking his own life in the process. His pursuit is a shining testament to our unyielding resolve. A resolve that places the Reich above our own lives."

The studio filled with a respectful silence. Becker, with a final nod of acknowledgement to his guest, continued. "Tonight, we are honoured to have him with us, to hear from him about his tireless efforts, and his views on the tragic story of the British spy, Michael Fernsby. Ladies and gentlemen, I give you Kriminaldirektor Albert Kreise."

With the introduction complete, there was a soft rustle of papers as Kriminaldirektor Albert Kreise took to the microphone. The room held its breath as Kreise's firm, unwavering voice filled the silence.

"My fellow Germans," he began, his voice strong and resonating with authority. "Today, I come before you with news that brings closure to a wound that has gnawed at the heart of our great nation for too long. Michael Fernsby, the British spy who caused great harm to the Reich, is dead."

A hushed silence filled the room as Kreise allowed the gravity of the news to sink in.

"Fernsby, as you all know, has been a thorn in our side. He escaped our custody, murdering four of our brave Gestapo officers, and at least three loyal Wehrmacht soldiers during his flight," Kreise continued, his tone solemn as he reminded the listeners of Fernsby's crimes.

"He travelled here with his brother, who was killed in Munich by one of our courageous officers before Michael Fernsby brutally cut them down in cold blood."

"Michael Fernsby's death brings an end to the relentless pursuit that followed his escape over the Christmas period. It brings justice to the families of our comrades who fell in the line of duty. It carries a message to all who dare bring harm to the Reich: We will not rest until justice is served."

The studio was silent, the weight of the news settling upon the listeners.

"His demise," Kreise continued after a measured pause, "occurred under tragic circumstances. Our sources indicate an unfortunate automobile accident while driving recklessly on the roads of southern England. Whatever the circumstances, justice has been served with the death of this dangerous spy."

Kreise paused, his voice softening. "Our thoughts and prayers go out to the families of our fallen comrades, and to those who were affected by Fernsby's actions. Tonight, we mourn the loss of our own, and we stand strong and united, remembering that the Reich is ever vigilant, ever righteous."

The room filled with a charged silence as Kreise's words washed over the masses. A reminder of the resolve of the Reich, a promise of justice served, and a tribute to those who had fallen – all delivered in the strong, authoritative voice of Kriminaldirektor Albert Kreise.

"Heil Hitler!" Kreise rose and shouted the words into the microphone before walking away.

"Sir, we've received reports that Fernsby might be alive," Kreise's driver and fellow Gestapo agent whispered as he left the room. "He's injured, but he survived the accident. His father is clinging to life, but it appears Fernsby himself survived."

"Our narrative is what matters now," Kreise snapped. "Not English reports that are nothing but false propaganda."

"Yes, sir." The driver opened the rear door of the vehicle for his superior officer.

In the solitude of his bedroom in Kent, Michael Fernsby listened to the faint hum of the vacuum-tube radio. The sound quality was less than perfect, but the chilling words of Kriminaldirektor Albert Kreise echoed loud and clear through the static: His own name, a death announcement.

It was surreal to be a living ghost, to hear one's own eulogy broadcast to the world. He slumped into a worn armchair by the side of his bed, the radio's message washing over him in waves of disbelief. Could they really believe he was dead? Or was this a ploy to flush him out?

His mind churned with a thousand thoughts, muddled and tangled. The mission he'd briefly discussed with Dansey during his early morning run loomed large in his thoughts. If the Nazis truly thought he was dead, could this, in some twisted way, be to his advantage? Could he strike from the shadows where they least expected?

Suddenly, an image of Mina flashed before his eyes, a piercing memory of a woman of such courage that her bravery still took his breath away. He remembered the softness of her eyes, her quiet strength when she'd risked everything to save his life in Germany.

His heart ached at the thought of her, possibly alone and in danger because of him. The thought of what the Nazis might have done to her was unbearable.

In the silent room, a decision took root in his heart. His fists clenched, and a new resolve took shape. He was no phantom; he was flesh and blood. Dansey's challenge, whatever it was, would be accepted.

There was a score to settle, not just for himself, but for Mina, David, and now his father too. He would strike back at the Nazis, not as the dead man they thought him to be, but as Michael Fernsby, a living, breathing embodiment of their worst fear. He felt an unfamiliar, raw determination take hold. Yes, they had struck a blow, but he was far from defeated.

Chapter Sixteen

VCC Imports, Bush House. Room 317.
Is this a joke?

That was the only piece of information written on the piece of paper Michael clutched firmly in his hand as he exited the taxicab on the Strand in London.

It was mid-June, and the British summer was in full swing. Men wore light-coloured cotton or linen suits, and the ladies wore skirts or dresses made from rayon or cotton.

The mood was upbeat, which was more to do with the weather than the bleak political outlook being pressed upon the nation by forward-thinking men such as Winston Churchill, who had been warning the country for years that Hitler's threats should be taken seriously.

Michael paid the taxi driver, took in a gulp of air, and walked up the steps to the impressive building that had once been described as the most expensive in the world.

An international symbol of diplomacy, Bush House today held a far more personal significance for Michael. It was here, inside the heart of the British establishment, that he would finally step into a world of danger and subterfuge.

Dansey's offer intrigued him, but underpinning his intrigue was his desire to do something, no matter how insignificant, to get back at the Nazis for what they had done to his family.

And Mina.

Michael could not get her out of his mind, and the vision of her and her family suffering at the hands of the Gestapo and the SS kept him awake at night.

Shaking the thoughts from his mind, Michael sought room number 317.

After identifying himself to the receptionist, who spent far too long looking at the manifest for the day's visitors, he was disappointed to find himself in a sparse room, filled only with the aroma of pipe smoke and the faint hum of a radio. A small desk sat underneath the window, with one chair on either side.

Michael sat and waited. For some reason, he'd expected the assistant chief of Britain's Secret Intelligence Service to have a plush office filled with ornate, antique furniture, and men and women running around carrying Britain's best-kept secrets.

Or worst kept, if Dansey was to be believed when it came to the passport offices he'd mentioned during their brief meeting.

Around thirty minutes later, Dansey walked in and sat opposite Michael. He studied his features for a few moments and then sat back, crossing his hands. Michael thought he looked very much at home amid the understated bureaucracy.

"I hope you are feeling better after your unfortunate ordeal?" he inquired, although Michael could tell from the look on his face that he couldn't have cared less about the well-being of his family's health.

"I'm doing much better, sir. Thank you for asking."

"And your father? How is he doing?"

"Not so well, unfortunately. He's critically ill and suffering from several broken bones. It's going to be a long road to recovery for him, I'm afraid."

"I'm sorry to hear that. Tell me, have you given any more thought to our conversation last week?"

"I have, and I'm interested. I wouldn't be here if I wasn't."

"I'm glad we're not wasting each other's time. I have a mission for you."

"What will I be doing?" He stared at Dansey. "And why me, exactly?"

"Your German is impeccable, and I've seen how you react under pressure. There's an instinct in you that can't be learnt. This makes you perfect for the operation we have in mind for you."

"Which is? I don't mean to be rude, sir, but you haven't told me anything yet."

Dansey leant forward in his chair and placed his elbows on the desk. "Not a single word of what we discuss can be uttered outside these walls. Do I make myself clear?"

"Perfectly, sir."

"I want you to go to Germany and make contact with a high-ranking SD officer seeking to defect. Once contact is established, I want you to assist in his escape."

A stunned silence filled the room. Dansey looked at Michael as if he'd just asked him to nip to the corner shop to buy a loaf of bread, but to Michael, what he was asking was crazy.

The details might have been vague and incomplete, but the implications were enormous.

"The Nazis mentioned me in a radio broadcast last week." Michael lowered his eyes. "Someone named Kreise told the German people that I was killed in the accident. That proves they were behind it, and they must really want me dead."

Dansey remained silent. His eyes pierced through Michael as if he was reading his soul.

"Do they really believe I'm dead? Or is it a ploy to lure me into something more sinister? Whatever it is, I want revenge for what they've done to my family, and I'll do whatever you want if it means I get to hurt them back a little."

Dansey sat back and touched his fingertips together. "I heard the broadcast, and I don't believe for one moment they think you are dead. They'll know you survived, but the German people don't know that, and it restores their faith in the Nazis if they think they got to you over here. It's propaganda, Fernsby, nothing more."

Michael nodded his head slowly in agreement.

"I can't stress enough how sensitive this operation is." Dansey's stare bored through Michael like an out-of-control dentist's drill. "Secrecy is paramount because if the Nazis find out what we're doing, many good men could die. The information we can glean if this is successful could alter the outcome of the coming war. And I'm not exaggerating. It truly is that important."

"Then why don't you send an experienced operative? Someone who knows what they're doing? This is way beyond anything I'm capable of."

"You underestimate yourself, Fernsby. You've already shown that you possess the exact qualities required to pull this off. And in any case, I'm not asking you to do anything extraordinary. All I want you to do is make contact and get him across the border. After that, we'll take over, and you'll be in the clear."

"That's it?" Michael's voice rose several notches. "You want me to waltz back into Germany, a place where I'm either dead or public enemy number one, and smuggle a high-ranking Nazi out of the country?"

"In a nutshell, yes, that's what I'm asking you do to. I think you are the perfect candidate for such a task, and I know you will not fail me."

"You do know that I tried this before, don't you?" Michael glared at Dansey. "David and I went to Germany to do just that – rescue our family and get them out of Germany. We failed, and my brother died as a result. Not to mention several more good people who died trying to help us."

"I've read your file, and I know what happened. This one is different because the man you are going to assist is a willing participant who has good reason to want to exit Germany."

"You still haven't explained why you can't use an experienced operative. Why send me, an inexperienced kid, to do something so important?"

"I already told you why. We believe the very organisation this man works for has infiltrated the SIS. He refuses to use the standard channels or any of our regular people because they're probably already known to the Nazis."

Michael sighed. "Who is it, and how do I get him out?"

"His name is unimportant, but the how is extremely sensitive. Are you still interested in working for us?"

Michael nodded.

"I need a verbal agreement."

"Yes, sir. I want to work for you."

"In that case, wait here."

Dansey rose from his desk and left the room. A few minutes later, the secretary scurried in with a handful of forms in her hands.

"Read these and sign," she ordered. "It's the Official Secrets Act, and by signing, we will hold you accountable should you ever violate the terms and conditions."

"Can I at least read it first?" Michael asked as the secretary thrust a pen into his hand.

"Yes, but you'd better hurry. Colonel Dansey is a very busy man, and he doesn't have all day to spend with you."

Michael felt the sting of the rebuff as she left the room. He had time to read the first paragraph before the door opened again, and Dansey returned, carrying a folder.

"Have you signed it yet?" he asked.

"I'm reading it, sir. I want to know what I'm signing."

"You're signing the Official Secrets Act so I can give you secret information. Without it, you won't ever be able to work anywhere, but especially for organisations such as ours."

Michael hesitated, the weight of the decision pressing on him. Memories of past failures, his brother, and the looming threat of the Nazis flashed before him. Taking a deep breath, he finally penned his signature, sealing his fate. As he pushed the papers over the desk towards Dansey, another set was thrust his way.

"What's these?"

"You want to be a member of SIS? If so, sign them. From today, you are assigned to Section V, Unit 317, which is a department of the Secret Intelligence Service. Your salary is four hundred pounds per year. We pay monthly, and you will report directly to my assistant, who will reveal himself to you in due course. If that's agreeable, then sign. I don't have all day."

"Unit 317? That's the room number I'm in."

"Precisely. The unit was conceived in this very room."

"Why that unit? What's so special about this room?"

"My assistant will tell you everything you need to know. Now sign the bloody form so we can get on with it."

"Four hundred pounds a year?" Michael ignored him. "That's a lot of money. You must be desperate if you'll pay me, a failed university student, that much money."

"As I said, you have certain skills that are not teachable. Those skills are valuable, and we pay what they are worth. Now, either sign it or get out of here."

Michael signed.

Silence fell over the office after Michael signed his name. By signing, he'd now become a member of the Secret Intelligence Service, Unit 317 of Section V, whatever that meant. It was a commitment, a vow of silence and duty. He took a moment to allow that to sink in.

Dansey placed the document to the side and handed the folder to Michael. "Read and study this after I've gone. You have until four, at which point my secretary will collect it from you."

"Then what happens?"

"It's all in the folder. I'm afraid time is of the essence with this. You will be trained, but we only have a brief window for this to happen. Therefore, you will receive two weeks of training, one week for weapons and explosives, and the other for intelligence gathering and communication."

"Just two weeks? How much can I learn in two weeks?"

"It's not ideal, I know, but for what you have to do, it's more than enough. You've already demonstrated your prowess, so this will be a refresher, with a few new things thrown in."

"When does it start?"

"You have one day to get your affairs in order, and you will report for training the day after tomorrow. You leave for Germany three weeks from today, and if all goes well, you'll be back in less than a week."

"I've heard that before." Michael ran his hands through his hair.

Dansey paused as he headed for the door. "Failure here, Fernsby, isn't just about this mission. If we don't pull this off, it could be the first domino to fall in a series of events we cannot control. The entire course of this looming war may change. It's vital you don't tell a soul about what you're doing, and when you get back, you report directly to my assistant. Is that clear?"

"Perfectly clear, sir."

Michael looked at his watch. It was ten thirty.

Chapter Seventeen

Dansey's words echoed around in Michael's mind. Over and over, he asked himself if he could do this. Going back to Germany and exacting revenge had been a good idea when he was full of anger, running along the misty trails of Sandwich. Now he was facing reality, it didn't seem like such a good idea after all.

Give over. I have to see if Mina is alright, and I have to get the doubloon and bring it back for Mum and Dad. And I have to hurt them, even if it's only a little.

Michael's mind drifted momentarily to the doubloon. He'd not given much thought to it until now. The idea of retrieving it and being the saviour of the Fernsby family had appealed to his ego, especially after the terrible losses they had suffered, but now he actually had a chance to do it.

Where is it? I don't even know that, and if Gigi won't tell me, then there's no point going.

He dragged his mind back to the folder on the desk in front of him. He didn't have long if he only had until four to study it.

He emptied the contents onto the aged oak desk, its

surface scarred from decades of use. The room carried the scent of old leather and musty papers, the remnants of countless classified discussions these walls had witnessed over the years. Overhead, the soft hum of an old ceiling fan provided a gentle, rhythmic soundtrack, punctuated only by the distant murmurs of conversations from other rooms. The golden glow from the desk lamp cast a warm hue over the documents as Michael spread them out before him. Among the sparse contents was a black-and-white photograph, its edges slightly curled, and two sheets of crisply typed paper. He adjusted the collar of his shirt, feeling the weight of the room's stifling atmosphere, and took a deep breath, preparing to commit every detail to memory over the next few hours.

The photograph depicted a tall, thin man who looked to be in his mid-thirties. Well dressed in a suit and tie, the man had short black hair combed back over his head. His ears protruded a bit more than average and his nose stood straight but prominent on his face. He looked serious, but other than that, there was nothing remarkable about the man who would cause a major fallout in the Nazi ranks if they could pull this off.

The first file was typed on official headed paper and contained the man's name: SS Oberführer Gustav Adler.

The remainder of the document was redacted, leaving Michael in no doubt as to what he could and couldn't know about this operation.

The second file was not on headed paper, but the words in capital letters spread out across the top caught his attention:

TOP SECRET EYES ONLY

He picked up the file and studied it like he was studying for an exam at Cambridge.

The words on the top of the file reminded Michael of the veil of secrecy surrounding the intelligence services, and with his interest piqued, he read further, taking in as much as he could on the first reading.

Gustav Adler holds the rank of SS Oberführer, which is a senior rank in the Nazi hierarchy. A member of the feared Sicherheitsdienst, Adler has access to sensitive information that would be useful to the British should hostilities break out in the coming months.

The operative will communicate with Adler via a dead letter box (DLB), the details of which are in a separate file.

The operative will leave a letter addressed to his dearest Gertrude at the assigned place. The body of the letter will be written in a style to match that of a man writing to his girlfriend. He will be sure to include the following:

Date he leaves the note at the DLB.

The fact that he misses the girl, and although times are difficult, he can't wait to see her again.

He is to use the initials DMF.

The operative is to monitor the DLB daily for five straight days. If, on the fifth day, there is no response, the operator is to assume the operation is compromised and must exit immediately as planned.

Assuming a response is forthcoming, Adler will leave a note in reply, telling the operator that he misses him too and will suggest a meeting place, which will be in code. We will provide the cipher before departure.

Once deciphered, the operative will leave another note at the secondary DLB only known to SIS to inform HQ that the operation is on.

The operative will meet Adler at the agreed time/place and drive him to Venlo in Holland, where another member of Unit 317 will relieve him of the package.

Operative will then make his way back to Britain via commercial means as previously arranged and report directly to Colonel Z

END

Michael shook the folder, and another, smaller note that he'd missed fell onto the table. It was folded in half, and when he unfolded it, a hand-drawn map revealed itself.

It depicted the Englisher Garten (English Garden) park in Munich. A narrow track called Gysslingstrasse ran parallel to the river Isar. Another river or stream named Eisbach – Michael couldn't tell from the map – flowed between the Isar and the track.

An offshoot track turned right towards the river close to the end of Gysslingstrasse, which turned sharp right itself before ending at a series of buildings.

The offshoot track ran a short way until it ended between two buildings that were marked as currently unused on the map. Behind the building to the right of the track that ran parallel to the Eisbach was a stone wall that looked to be a few feet high if the map was drawn to plan.

An arrow pointed to the second stone from the left on the very bottom, telling Michael this was to be the location of the DLB he was to use with Adler.

There was nothing regarding the second DLB that was for communicating with SIS, so he put that to the back of his mind for now, as he was sure they'd give it to him before he left.

Michael spent the next few hours studying the information provided, and by four in the afternoon, he had it memorised deep into his brain.

The secretary opened the door at exactly four and gathered the files without saying a word. As she left, she held the door open for Michael to follow.

As he walked past her desk, she stopped him and handed over a sealed envelope.

"Your travel documents for the day after tomorrow. You'll need those."

And with that, the meeting was over. Michael stepped back into the warm London air, now an agent of British intelligence. The decision had been made. Now it was time for action.

Chapter Eighteen

Michael and Judith drove straight to Canterbury at first light the next morning. Gigi remained in Sandwich to take care of some family business on Gerald's behalf.

As soon as he saw his mother at the house she'd rented, he threw his arms around her neck and hugged her tightly.

"Michael, really!" Dorothy Fernsby pulled back and gazed into her son's eyes. "What's got into you? I only saw you two days ago."

"Mum, please sit down. There's something I have to tell you that won't wait."

Dorothy sat, her face pale. "You're not running off to Germany again. I won't allow it."

Michael sighed and closed his eyes for a brief second. "Mum, things have changed since the accident. I didn't tell you because I didn't want to worry you, but now I have no choice."

Dorothy glared at her son, unmoving, her face a picture of fear and anger. "If Gigi has talked you into going back there, I swear I'll kill her myself," she said eventually.

Judith sat next to her mother. "Why don't you tell us where you went yesterday?" she said. "I asked him, but he wouldn't tell me."

Michael pursed his lips and spoke rapidly, trying to get it over with as fast as he could.

"Do you remember a man wearing glasses, standing underneath an umbrella talking to Dad after David's funeral?"

Dorothy shook her head. "So many emotions were too raw that day, I never noticed anything. I don't even remember the drive home. I was too upset."

"That's understandable. I would have forgotten as well if I hadn't seen the same man on one of my early morning runs a couple of weeks ago."

"You saw the same man? Who is he?" Dorothy looked crestfallen as if she knew what Michael was about to tell her.

"I was dreading telling you about this because I know how upsetting it must be for you, especially after all we've been through recently. And with Dad..." Michael's voice trailed off as he choked on his words.

He took a deep breath and cleared his throat before continuing.

"Look, war is coming whether we like it or not. I can stay here and wait until I'm called up along with everyone else, or I can take action now. I chose to take action now."

"No, Michael, you're all we have left. You can't leave." Judith looked close to tears. "Think about what this will do to Mum, especially while Dad's in the hospital."

"I know, Judith, and don't think I haven't considered that. But, either way, I'll be called up soon. At least this way I get a choice in what I'll be doing in the coming war."

"What exactly will you be doing?" Dorothy's voice was monotone and flat.

"The man I saw on my run. The same man Dad was talking to at David's funeral. He's—"

"Military intelligence," Dorothy finished the sentence for him. "I remember seeing him now. He and your father knew each other during the Great War."

Michael nodded. "We met in London yesterday, and he asked me to join his organisation. I signed the Official Secrets Act so I'm afraid I can't tell you anymore."

Dorothy gulped. "I knew this day would come as soon as I saw Hitler ranting on the newsreels. Except I thought it would be both you and David leaving, not just you."

She threw her hands to her face and leant forward. "I knew it was coming, but not now. Not while your father is so ill. Can't you tell them to hold off until he's home, at least?"

Michael shook his head. "I'm sorry, Mum. That's not possible."

"When?" she couldn't force the rest of the sentence out of her mouth.

Michael sighed. "Tomorrow morning."

"Tomorrow morning?" Judith repeated, jumping out of her chair. "Michael, that's too soon."

"I know. I'm sorry."

"Do what you need to do, son. Just know that both your father and myself are proud of you. I wish I could talk you out of it, but I know I can't. Soon, every mother will be waving their sons goodbye, all because of that raving lunatic in Berlin. Just promise me you won't be going back to Germany again. At least not until our army is marching through their streets in victory."

"I don't know what they'll have me doing," Michael lied. "I'll probably be sitting in an office somewhere in

London listening to German radio and newsreels. Don't worry, Mum, I'll be safe."

Dorothy looked at her son with a distant gaze, her spirit shattered by the cruel blows life had dealt her. Seeing her like this broke Michael's heart.

"I love you, Mum, and I'll write as soon as I can. I promise."

He rose to leave, thankful to have got that out of the way.

"Where are you going?" Judith asked.

"I'm going to the hospital to say goodbye to Dad."

"Visiting time isn't until two," Judith said. "They won't let you see him."

"They will when I tell them I'm being deployed tomorrow morning."

"I'm staying with Mum until Warhurst comes for me at the weekend," Judith said.

"Good, she'll appreciate that. Warhurst will take care of Lucy, so you don't need to worry about her."

"Michael..." Dorothy rose to her feet and held her son. "Please take care of yourself, and don't be a hero. I need you. Our family needs you. Do you hear?" Tears streamed down her face.

"I hear you, and I promise I won't do anything stupid." It took everything he had to hold himself together. "I love you, Mum."

"I love you too."

Michael pulled away and walked out of the door. He didn't look back because if he did, he'd never leave.

After a brief conversation with the nurses, they allowed Michael five minutes with his father. He'd got over the initial shock of seeing him strapped up to all kinds of medical paraphernalia, including a full-length cast covering his left leg.

Gerald looked as though he'd aged over a decade since the accident, and Michael found it hard to look at him.

This is all my fault. All of it. If I hadn't insisted on going to Germany, none of it would have happened. David would be here, and Dad wouldn't be at death's door in the hospital. Mum won't ever recover from this, and every time I look at her, I blame myself for everything she's lost.

He forced himself away from his dark thoughts and touched his father's right leg gently.

"Father, it's me, Michael. I've come to see you." He contemplated not telling him, but he knew he had to. His father would want to hear it from him and not third-hand from his mother.

Gerald opened his bloodshot eyes and blinked at the sunlight streaming through the window.

"Michael," he said hoarsely.

"Hi, Dad. How are you doing?"

"Just fine. I'll be out of here in no time."

Michael smiled. He knew that wasn't going to happen.

"Dad, I only have five minutes, so I have something to tell you." He took his father's right hand in his. His left arm was in a cast.

"Do you remember that man you spoke to at David's funeral?"

Gerald looked confused as if he didn't remember.

Michael leant forward and whispered in his ear. "Claude Dansey."

Gerald's eyes shot open. "Dansey," was all he could say.

Michael nodded. "I'm working for him now. I leave tomorrow, but I'll be back soon, and when I am, I want to see you out of here and walking around just like you used to. Do you hear?"

In a moment Michael would never forget, his father

reached up and gently wiped away the tears that dropped from Michael's eyes with his hand. They shared an unspoken bond that only a father and son could, and Michael's heart burst open.

For a minute, he couldn't see or speak. Gerald, too, had tears that drenched his pillow, and they held onto each other for several moments. Eventually, Michael pulled away and backed out towards the doorway.

"Be careful, son. Come back to us." Michael knew it took everything his father had to speak to him, and that made him feel even worse.

"I promise, Dad. Just get better, okay?"

After one last look, Michael was out of the door and headed back to the family home in Sandwich. He had one final, very important task to complete before he left for training the next morning.

Chapter Nineteen

Gigi sat in the dimly lit sitting room, the glow from the afternoon sun casting long shadows on the walls. Papers related to the Fernsby family brewing empire sprawled across the ornate wooden table, each document a testament to a legacy on the brink of collapse.

She looked up when Michael entered the room.

"You're back early. I expected you to at least stay the night with your mother."

"I can't. I have to leave tomorrow."

"Leave? Where?"

"Gigi, I'm joining the war effort, and I'm working for the same people that Dad worked for in the Great War."

Gigi put down the papers and stared at her grandson. "You've joined British intelligence? What on earth for?"

"We all know war is coming, and I'll be called up soon in any case. At least this way I get to choose where I serve."

"Fair enough, as long as you stay in Britain and don't go gallivanting off on any dangerous missions."

"Gigi?" Michael bit his bottom lip. "There's something I need to know."

His heart raced, a drumbeat of anxiety and determination. All the way from Canterbury, he'd replayed this conversation in his mind, perfecting each word. Yet, standing before her now, his carefully chosen words evaporated, leaving a lump in his throat.

"I'm waiting?" Gigi raised her eyebrows.

"I can't say much, and you're not allowed to ask questions. And whatever you do, neither Mum nor Dad can know about any of this. Do you understand?"

"What are you trying to say, Michael?"

"There's a chance I might end up back in Germany again, and I thought that while I'm there, I'd have the chance to look for that doubloon you told me about. I need to know what it looks like and where you've hidden it."

Gigi's eyes almost popped out of her head. "You're going back to Germany? You realise that would be suicide, don't you? They let you get away once, but they won't allow it a second time. Think of Gerald and Dorothy. Don't you think they've lost enough already?"

"Yes, but this time I will be on official business and not running around like a headless chicken. I can't talk about it, Gigi, so just tell me about the Brasher Doubloon."

"The family business is in a bad way." Gigi threw her hands towards the papers scattered all around her. "Without some kind of intervention, we'll lose it all. The banks are unwilling to loan us any more money, so selling up is the only choice we have left."

"Unless you find that doubloon and bring it back here," she added.

Michael said nothing.

"I swore to your mother I wouldn't tell you anything about it, and I won't break her heart a second time. So, here's what I'll do. I'll tell you what it looks like. But I won't tell you where my father said he hid it before that fateful night when the streets echoed with screams and shattered glass. Kristallnacht, they called it, the night my father and my son disappeared off the face of the earth."

Michael flinched, feeling the pain alongside her. "How will I know where to find it then?"

Gigi paused, her fingers brushing against Michael's face —a tender gesture of a grandmother's love. "I made a vow to never speak of its location, but promises can be flexible. While words might betray, a drawing can guide."

Michael smiled.

Chapter Twenty

The Small Arms School Corps (SASC) in Hythe, Kent, seemed like an entirely different universe from the vibrant, chaotic London streets that Michael had been on only a few days earlier.

Perched in quietude away from prying eyes, the establishment was a physical manifestation of stringent discipline and methodical order.

Upon his arrival, Michael found himself instantly guided to a secluded wing, assigned a room, and taken to an induction meeting with two other men.

They were assigned M, N, and P, and were not allowed to refer to each other as anything other than those monikers.

Michael was M.

He assumed the others were there for similar reasons, but they were banned from discussing anything about themselves or their missions. As far as they were concerned, they were ghosts that passed in the night.

Their instructors were men of fortitude, characterised by their piercing eyes and an aura of superiority that commanded immediate respect.

The luxury of leisure or acclimatisation was absent. The moment he dropped his baggage, they directed Michael to a bleak, confined room. Two instructors sat under the pallid glow of an overhead light, their figures framed by a table laden with a plethora of documents. These papers were hauntingly familiar – the exact replicas of the ones he had been tasked to pore over days earlier in the heart of London.

The instructors fixed him with intense, scrutinising glares that were both uncomfortable and yet challenging. If anything, it made Michael rise to the task and meet them head-on. He straightened his posture and stared back at them, his face a mask of self-confidence.

"Fernsby," one of them began in a tone that cut through the room's chill, "Let's get straight to the point. What intel do you have on the SD officer assigned for extraction?"

"His name is Gustav Adler, and he's an Oberführer in the Sicherheitsdienst. He wants to defect to Britain, and I'm going there to get him out."

The instructors switched languages to German and fired rapid questions at Michael. He knew it was a test, and he wasn't about to fail.

For the next forty-five minutes, the room transformed into a battlefield of wits, their volley of questions and his responses echoing in the tight confines. Relief washed over him as he navigated the grilling with total recall, a testament to the level with which he'd memorised every facet of the mission.

At least what he knew so far.

The three young men sat together around a bare wooden table during dinner. Michael got his first proper look at them and noticed they were both somewhere in their mid-twenties, which was a few years older than he was.

"N, P." He acknowledged his compatriots.

The two men nodded back without speaking, and the awkward silence continued throughout dinner. Michael was glad when it was over.

His bedroom was as sparse as everywhere else. All it contained was a single bed that was about as comfortable as sleeping on a rock, and a small desk with a wooden chair. An overhead light hung from the ceiling that barely illuminated the room.

"Welcome home," he spoke out loud. "What have I got myself into?"

With the break of dawn, a rigorous training regime unfurled. The day started with a five-mile run, which Michael was more than prepared for.

He took comfort in seeing the two older boys struggle to keep up, and although they all stayed together, he could see it annoyed them that the younger man was faster and fitter than they both were.

As the week moved on, Michael fell into the routine of it all. He enjoyed the physical aspects more and more, and every day his confidence grew that he'd made the right choice.

Every morning, his body protested the brutal wake-up call, his muscles screaming in objection as he forced himself out of bed. The physical toll of the training was evident: blisters formed a painful constellation on his hands from gripping the Walther PPK too tightly and hours of drills.

The days were filled with firearms training, explosive handling, and escape and evasion strategies. The instructors pushed him to the boundaries of his physical endurance and mental resilience, and although he'd never admit it during the daytime, when he was alone in his room at night, he was forced to acknowledge the intensity of his ordeal.

His skin bore bruises in varying shades of purple and blue, evidence of the countless times he'd been thrown to the ground during hand-to-hand combat training, or where he'd struck an obstacle during evasion exercises. Each bruise was a stark reminder of a lesson learnt, a move miscalculated, or a strategy that needed refining. His feet, already hardened by miles of running on roads and trails, were now calloused and sore, bearing the brunt of miles of running with a heavy pack that hurt his back and his knees.

Beyond the evident physical injuries, there was the exhaustion that weighed on him – an ever-present, heavy blanket that threatened to smother his determination. Meals became functional, devoured for sustenance rather than enjoyment. His nights were restless, punctuated by dreams where he fumbled missions, or was pursued endlessly by shadowy figures.

The mental fatigue was harder to quantify, but equally debilitating. Days filled with strategy, language lessons, and rapid-fire questioning meant his brain was constantly whirring, even when he desperately needed rest. At times, the lines between training and reality blurred. During breaks, he'd find himself scanning his environment for potential threats, or plotting escape routes subconsciously, his mind conditioned to always be alert.

Yet, amidst this brutal routine, there were moments of triumph. The first time he disassembled and reassembled his Walther PPK blindfolded in the dark. The afternoon he managed to evade his instructors during an impromptu manhunt. These victories, no matter how minor, were the balm that soothed his battered body and spirit, propelling him to face another gruelling day.

Still, he was cognisant that these trials were merely the tip of the iceberg compared to the challenges that lay ahead.

Along with N and P, he learnt the basics of creating explosives, and although he wasn't expecting to use them anytime soon, the subject was interesting enough.

Despite the physically and mentally taxing sessions, by the end of the week, Michael could see a marked enhancement in his capabilities. The Walther PPK felt natural, the self-defence moves more reflexive, and the evasion techniques akin to a well-practised dance routine.

On his last day at SASC, a fresh set of documents were presented to him. It detailed his next destination – Bletchley Park in Buckinghamshire, where he was to report for extended training and additional instructions.

As he walked away from SASC, fatigue clung to him like a second skin, but it was offset by a newfound determination burning within.

Michael was acutely aware of his novice status in this covert world, yet he was equally cognisant of the transformation he had undergone from the grief-stricken young man who stepped into Bush House a few weeks earlier.

He was being shaped into a weapon, hardened by the furnace of discipline and resolve. With each day that passed, his resolve to counteract the Nazis was only growing, fuelling his determination, and propelling him forward.

Chapter Twenty-One

The secluded secrecy of Bletchley Park in Buckinghamshire was worlds apart from the rigorous physical discipline of the SASC. Surrounded by a shroud of trees, the once-stately mansion now served as a secretive hub of clandestine pre-war activity.

In stark contrast to the SASC, the atmosphere here felt restrained, almost academic. As Michael arrived, he was met at the gates by a group of three men who introduced themselves as members of section V, SIS.

Their soft-spoken, erudite demeanours were a striking departure from the robust instructors he had known in Kent.

As in Hythe, they led him to a section of wooden blocks that were as stark and functional as the ones at SASC. The biggest difference was on this occasion, he was alone.

He wondered where N and P had gone, but wherever it was, they weren't at Bletchley Park.

Not in this block, anyway.

He sat on his bed, the firm mattress pressing against him, waiting for the next phase of his rapid training programme. The faint scent of polished wood and old paper permeated the room, creating an atmosphere of studious anticipation.

The silent isolation enveloped him, only broken by the soft padding of footsteps on the gravel path outside and the sporadic whispers of people walking by. Their voices, muffled by the walls, seemed to merge with the distant chirping of a lone bird.

The whole feeling at Bletchley Park was noticeably different from the testosterone-charged atmosphere at SASC. Here, it was more cerebral, and it reminded Michael of the solemn halls of Cambridge University and the clever men and women who studied and worked there.

Eventually, someone came for him. A middle-aged, stiff-looking man, his back ramrod straight, marched into the hut and stood in front of Michael, who rose to greet him.

"Fernsby, I presume? My name is Major Tremaine. Come with me."

Michael sighed and followed him to a secluded corner to the left of the sprawling mansion that had once been a grand home.

Major T, as Michael silently christened him, led him inside a wooden hut. The floorboards creaked underfoot, releasing a slightly musty, earthy scent. As Michael's eyes adjusted to the dimmer light, he caught sight of the secretary from London, her figure outlined by the soft glow of a desk lamp, her eyes fixed intently on him.

"Good morning, gentlemen," the secretary said, as aloof as she'd been in London. "I'll take it from here, Major."

The officer nodded and left.

"I'm Maureen Ingram and I'll be taking care of you while you're here. You may call me Miss Ingram."

"Good morning, Miss Ingram," Michael answered. "It's wonderful to see your smiling face again."

"We're not here to have fun, Mr Fernsby." Maureen Ingram didn't appreciate the joke. "Follow me."

She led him down a corridor to an office at the far end of the hut, where another officer sat behind a desk.

This man had a rounder face and was somewhere in his early thirties. His light brown hair was cut short, and his bright blue eyes held a warmth and familiarity that made Michael feel as though they were best friends, which was strange seeing as they had only just met.

After Miss Ingram exited the room, the new officer indicated for Michael to sit down.

"As you can see, we're much more laid back here than you would have experienced at SASC. Here, our weapon of choice is the pen, rather than the cruder ones you have just been subjected to."

More laid back? If it got any more secret, they'd order me to forget my own name.

Michael didn't know what to say, so he remained silent. He considered responding with a flippant remark, but somehow, he didn't think it would go down well.

"You're here to learn about an entirely different kind of war: coded letters, hidden messages, double meanings, and such like. Training like this normally takes months, but the colonel wants you done and gone in a week. It's crazy if you ask me."

"I couldn't agree more."

"My name is Captain Sanders, and I will be your liaison officer. I'm sure the colonel briefed you, but you are now a member of Unit 317, Section V, or just three-one-seven, as it's better known, which is a covert operations unit that carries out deniable missions, often behind enemy lines.

The very existence of this unit is top secret, and you are forbidden to breathe a word about it to anyone outside the unit. You will report to me, and only me. Do I make myself clear?"

"Very clear."

"Should you need to reach out to us during the mission, it is myself or Miss Ingram who will monitor your correspondence, and it will be us who greet you when you return to England."

"Why can't I use a wireless set?" Michael asked. "Surely it would be better than leaving a paper trail hidden in a wall somewhere."

"Colonel Dansey doesn't like to use radio frequencies. All too often, the enemy is listening in alongside us. So no, you'll be using a series of dead letter boxes to communicate with us."

"I'm glad we cleared that up then."

"Displaying a little sarcasm, are we, Fernsby?"

"No, sir, wouldn't dream of it, sir."

Captain Sanders cocked his head at Michael and broke out into a wide smile. "I think we are going to have fun together, you and me. Training starts at 06.00 hours sharp. Meet me here and don't be late."

"Before I go, I have a question," Michael said. "What else goes on here at Bletchley Park? I see people walking around with hushed voices everywhere. Are they all part of three-one-seven?"

"No. There are people here from all the different branches of the services," Captain Sanders said.

"Why? What are they doing here?"

"They're an advanced team from the Government Code and Cipher School, who are setting up an operational base here. We'll be moving to a new location in the next few weeks."

"What do they do?"

"Don't ask any more questions."

"Yes, sir, sorry."

"One more thing," Sanders said. "Colonel Dansey likes to be known as Colonel Z, so from now on, that is how we refer to him."

"Colonel Z?" Michael asked.

"Don't ask."

Chapter Twenty-Two

The following morning, Captain Sanders led Michael to another room at the far end of 317's hut.

"This is where you will be based for the duration of your time here, so get familiar with it."

Michael looked around the room. There wasn't much to get familiar with. A desk with a chair on one side, which is where he sat facing the door. Two more chairs sat on the opposite side of the desk.

A filing cabinet sat in the corner by the window, and apart from an overhead hanging light, that was it.

Sanders handed Michael a file and sat in one of the two chairs facing him.

"From now on, we speak only German in this room. I'm told you are fluent in the language, so that shouldn't be a problem for you."

"Not at all, sir," Michael replied in German. "I've spoken it all my life. I'm sure you know my grandmother is German, and she taught us from an early age, and made sure we were all fluent in it."

"We had you vetted. We know all about you."

Michael glared at the captain.

"What did you expect?" Sanders asked. "This isn't a game, Fernsby. In our line of work, lives are on the line, and we had to make sure there weren't any skeletons in your cupboards. You came back clean."

Sanders shot Michael a sideways glance. "The file in front of you should be familiar. Colonel Z showed it to you in London and asked you to memorise it."

Michael opened the file and recognised it immediately. The words 'TOP SECRET EYES ONLY' gave it away instantly, and he didn't need to read the rest to know what it said.

Sanders took the file and read it out loud.

"Gustav Adler holds the rank of Oberführer, which is a senior rank in the Nazi hierarchy. A member of the feared Sicherheitsdienst, Adler has access to extremely sensitive information that would be useful to the British, should hostilities break out in the coming months.

"The operative will communicate with Adler via a dead letter box (DLB), the details of which are in a separate file.

"The operative will leave a letter addressed to his dearest Gertrude at the assigned place. The body of the letter will be written in a style to match that of a man writing to his girlfriend. He will be sure to include the following:

"Date he leaves the note at the DLB.

"The fact that he misses the girl, and although times are difficult, he can't wait to see her again.

"He is to use the initials DMF.

"The operative is to monitor the DLB daily for five straight days. If, on the fifth day, there is no response, the operator is to assume the operation is compromised and must exit immediately as planned.

"Assuming a response is forthcoming, Adler will leave a note in reply telling the operator that he misses him too and will suggest a meeting place, which will be in code. We will provide the cipher before departure.

"Once deciphered, the operative will leave another note at the secondary DLB only known to SIS to inform HQ that the operation is on.

"The operative will meet Adler at the agreed time/place and drive him to Venlo in Holland, where another member of Unit 317 will relieve him of the package.

"Operative will then make his way back to Britain via commercial means as previously arranged and report directly to Colonel Z.

END"

Sanders placed the file on the desk and looked at Michael.

"I hope you followed Colonel Z's instructions and memorised it because that document is what this entire week's training is going to be based on."

Michael nodded. "I know it."

"So, you know what Adler looks like, and you know how and where you are to contact him."

"Yes, sir."

"Remember, Fernsby, this operation is of vital importance to the coming war effort, and you cannot fail. I am here for you and I'm going to do all I can to make this successful and get you home safely."

"Thank you."

Sanders was true to his word and they spent the rest of the week breaking down every aspect of the file so that, by the end, Michael would know exactly what he was doing.

The training was meticulous, nuanced, and intense. Every word, every phrase, every punctuation mark could be a veiled piece of information or a crucial directive, and he listened to Sanders as if his life depended on it, which it did.

With each passing day, the weight of his duty, and the complexity of the task bore down heavily on Michael's shoulders, and the more he immersed himself in the programme, the more daunting it became.

A fire burned in the pit of his stomach, because he realised that this was the way he could get back at the Nazis for what they'd done to his family. And Mina.

They went over the locations of the DLBs and the words he was to use in the exchanges with Adler. Finally, Sanders gave him the location of the DLB for communicating with SIS.

"Be careful with this one, and only use it when you have something definite to report. It's the ancient Frauenkirche church in Munich. When you walk in, you will see several huge pillars holding it up. Walk down the pews to the row where the second pillar rises to the roof. On the side facing the altar where it is hidden from view of the entrance, the stone on the bottom is loose. Pull it out and place your message there."

"Is it easy to find?"

"You can't miss it. The church towers are visible from almost everywhere."

The last part of his training centred around what to do if things went wrong, and his exit back to England. Sanders handed Michael another top-secret file.

During the exchange with Adler in Venlo, the agent receiving Adler will hand over a new set of documents that identify the operative as the son of a British diplomat in India. He is returning home after a holiday in Holland and is to use the Night Ferry from Paris to London.

If the operation goes wrong, the operative is to get out of

Germany by using the emergency documents he will find in the SIS DLB. Leave a message stating the relationship with Gertrude is over for SIS. The operative is to leave Germany with the new identification papers and make his way to Paris, where he is to take the Night Ferry, as mentioned previously.

On the last day, Sanders handed Michael a passport in the name of Lars Hohenberg, a Swiss national. "This is your new identity, so study it and learn everything about him. You need to know every school he went to, who his friends and family are, and even what his favourite foods are."

"I know. I've done this before."

"You leave RAF Biggin Hill at 05.00 hours on July third. The RAF will fly you to Paris, and the remainder of the journey will be by train. Tomorrow, you will report to London for your last instructions from Colonel Z, and after that, you will have three days to absorb everything you've learnt these last two weeks."

"Thank you, Captain Sanders. I've learnt a lot from you, and I hope to see you again when this operation is over."

"Be careful, for Z has given you a dangerous mission, especially for your first one. However, you are resourceful and brave, and you have every attribute to pull this off and hit the Nazis where it hurts."

"I'll do my best, sir."

The two men shook hands.

Chapter Twenty-Three

As Michael stepped into Bush House, he heard the distant echo of leather-soled shoes on marble, punctuating the murmured conversations of officials and officers.

The scent of polished wood and old books wafted through the corridors, overlaid with a faint tinge of tobacco smoke and the earthy aroma of the recent rain that had dampened the exterior of the building.

A distant telephone rang intermittently, always followed by a hasty answer, reminding Michael of the urgency of whatever secrets were being discussed.

He had come a long way since the first time he'd set foot in this building, filled with grief and determination. Now, he was a trained operative, ready to embark on a mission that could potentially tip the scales in Britain's favour.

Well, a partially trained operative at least.

Maureen Ingram greeted him with a half-smile, which Michael took as an improvement from the last time they'd met. She ushered him into Dansey's office, where the seasoned spymaster awaited.

Captain Sanders, standing off to the side, nodded at

Michael in a show of support before excusing himself to wait outside with the secretary.

"Fernsby, come in." Colonel Z beckoned him forward, his voice filled with a mixture of seriousness and encouragement. "Sit down."

Michael took a seat, his eyes fixed on Dansey as he prepared himself for the final briefing. This was the moment he had been working towards, the culmination of his two weeks of training and preparation.

Regardless of how little training he'd received, Michael knew he was ready. The most important skill he possessed wasn't anything SIS had taught him this past fortnight – it was the skill between his ears that he'd already discovered and mastered.

It was his resilience and bravery under extreme situations that had alerted Dansey to him in the first place. It was his driven focus to do whatever it took to complete his tasks and get home, and it was his commitment and loyalty to both his country and his family that mattered most.

Any other training he'd received was just mere details. Important ones for sure, but just details. He knew there would come a time during this mission when he'd have to improvise, and that is why he believed Dansey had chosen him. Plus, he knew how much he hated the Nazis.

Dansey's voice pulled him back from his thoughts.

"I want to impress upon you the significance of this mission," Z began, his voice low and steady. "Gustav Adler is a valuable asset, a high-ranking member of the SD who has indicated his desire to defect. His knowledge and insights can be invaluable to our cause. It's imperative we ensure his safe extraction from Germany."

"I understand, sir."

Dansey paused for a moment, letting the weight of his words sink in before continuing.

"There's more," he added, his tone becoming sombre. "We've received word that Adler won't be travelling alone. He's bringing his wife and nephew with him. The young boy, his nephew, suffers from cerebral palsy, and Adler fears that if the Nazis discover the boy's condition, his life will be in grave danger."

Michael's heart sank at the mention of the disabled child. He knew all too well the horrors the Nazis inflicted on those they deemed unfit or undesirable.

Gigi's words at the dinner table echoed in his brain: *Gerda believed the Nazi doctor murdered his own grandson.*

The Nazi doctor killed his own flesh and blood just because he was deaf. The blood boiled inside Michael's body. *Who does that?*

With those words, the urgency of the mission intensified, and it became even more personal, if that was possible.

"I understand, sir," Michael rushed his reply. "I'll make sure they all get out safely."

Dansey nodded, his gaze fixed on Michael with a mix of respect and expectation. "I have faith in you, Fernsby. You've proven yourself in the heat of battle, and the reports I received from your training officers all speak highly of you. I believe you're ready for this."

Dansey handed Michael an updated file containing additional information and instructions crucial to the mission's success.

"Study this carefully," Dansey advised, his eyes searching Michael's for confirmation. "Time is of the essence, and lives are at stake."

Michael nodded, his focus on the file in his hands. He

knew what needed to be done, and he was ready to face the challenges that lay ahead.

As the meeting concluded, Michael exited Dansey's office and found himself face to face with the next group of three men waiting to meet with the spy chief.

Two had their backs to Michael as he exited Dansey's office, but the third looked at Michael with piercing eyes that seemed to bore right through him.

Michael shuddered as he felt the man's eyes probing his soul, and he blinked rapidly to rid himself of the awkward feelings they evoked.

The man had a trim build, and his receding hairline did nothing to take the focus away from his glare. He had a grey moustache and ears that were too big for his head. Michael put him around fifty years of age, and whatever else he was, he was a man who was used to being obeyed.

"Good morning, sir." Michael nodded his head towards the man, who nodded back but didn't say a word. Instead, he marched into Dansey's office as if he were superior to everyone else present.

The two other men spun around, and Michael's blood ran cold as soon as he saw their faces. The younger of the two was the same age as Michael, and as they locked eyes, the hatred and disdain on the younger man's face was palpable.

Michael was staring into the faces of Robert Stourcliffe and his hated son, Robert Junior, the sworn enemies of the Fernsby family.

Chapter Twenty-Four

Sir Robert Stourcliffe Senior was a shipping magnate, and he held the distinction of being Britain's wealthiest man. Unfortunately, that title didn't bring with it a drop of empathy or humility.

The Stourcliffes were the most pompous, stuck-up aristocrats Michael had ever had the misfortune to meet.

"Fernsby!" the younger Stourcliffe sneered, speaking with a poshness that Michael thought belonged back in the Tudor age when Henry VIII and Queen Elizabeth I ruled the land.

"What on earth are they doing, allowing riff-raff like you in here? Did your dog run off, and you came here looking for it?" Stourcliffe scoffed in his aristocratic, upper-crust accent.

"Stourcliffe. What an unpleasant surprise, meeting you here."

Captain Sanders stood by Maureen Ingram's side with a wry smile on his face, which Michael caught through the corner of his eye. Something told him that Sanders had been expecting this meeting, and he seemed to be enjoying the fireworks.

The older Stourcliffe glared at Michael, and he couldn't help noticing how similar they looked. Both stood over six feet tall, and both wore gold-rimmed glasses that probably cost more than an average man's annual salary.

They were both renowned for their running prowess, although Stourcliffe Senior had gained significant weight as he'd aged. Robert Junior was trim and athletic and used to hold several records for running at Cambridge until Michael had taken them from him the previous year.

"How's the dog you stole from me?" Stourcliffe Junior sneered. "Have you killed it yet with your incompetence?"

"Lucy is faring very well, thank you. She's looking so much better now she's actually being cared for, unlike when you kicked her and starved the poor thing to death."

Stourcliffe's face turned scarlet. "What are you doing, since the dean threw you out of Cambridge?" he retorted.

"I'm doing fine. Tell me, how's the nose doing?" Michael asked. "I hope it's still broken."

Michael was referring to the incident that had got him expelled from Cambridge the year before when he'd broken Stourcliffe's nose for kicking the dog he'd been abusing. Michael took the dog from him, named it Lucy, and gave it to Judith to take care of.

"More to the point, how's the family business doing?" Stourcliffe Senior spoke up. "I hear your useless father has run it into the ground, just like he did with the shipping business your family used to own. I do hope the poor chap is recovering after the accident. It would be a shame to lose both your father and your brother in such a short space of time."

It was Michael's turn to turn scarlet. He felt his face

burning hot, and he clenched his fists by his side. His fury surged, and his patience was wearing thin. He couldn't bear another moment of Stourcliffe's taunting.

Robert Junior snorted, laughing out loud. "Not very good at keeping hold of things, are you, Fernsby? You can't even keep hold of your own brother."

Michael stepped forward, but Captain Sanders got between them.

"That's quite enough," he ordered.

"I hope that silver spoon isn't stuck in your throats," Michael snarled. "Because if I hear one more word from either of you, I'm going to knock them down there so far, they'll need to be removed from your arses."

The menacing look on Michael's face made the Stourcliffes back away. Neither said a word.

"Lord Stourcliffe, if you please." Dansey stood in his doorway with a look of restrained amusement on his face. He smiled at Michael as the two aristocrats entered the room.

"What is that imbecile doing here?" Stourcliffe Senior demanded as the door closed. "Don't tell me you are working with the Fernsby boy? You know how incompetent their whole family is."

Michael didn't hear Dansey's response because he closed the door before he spoke.

"Don't let that pompous old fool bother you," Sanders said. "He treats everyone like that, although he does seem to save his worst for your family."

Michael was shaking. He took a deep breath, trying to calm down.

"Don't tell me they are working with SIS? If so, I'm out."

"Calm down, son. You're not working with the Stourcliffes. As far as I know, Dansey and the chief are talking to them about their ships, that's all."

"Who was that other man with them?" Michael asked, trying to divert his mind from the thought of smacking either Stourcliffe in the snout.

"You didn't recognise him? That is Sir Stewart Menzies, director of military intelligence. The current head of SIS is seriously ill and Menzies is in the running to take over, although Colonel Dansey might have a say in that. You'd be well advised to remember him in the future."

"Yes, I will. Thank you."

"You'd better leave before the meeting ends and the Stourcliffes come out," Sanders guided Michael by the arm towards the exit. "I would hate for their blue blood to be spilled in this office."

Michael sighed. Right now, there was nothing more he'd like to do than take out all his frustrations on Stourcliffe's obnoxious beak.

But he didn't.

After a brief stop at home to say goodbye to Gigi and Judith, Michael stopped in Canterbury to see his parents one more time before he left.

Although nobody had mentioned it, he knew he could very well be setting off on a one-way mission, and there was a very good chance he wouldn't make it out alive.

Not a second time.

His mother wasn't at the house she'd rented, so Michael drove to the hospital to see his father. As the nurse showed him in, he found his mother sitting by the bed holding his right hand and praying with him.

Michael held back and waited in the doorway. He closed his eyes and allowed the words to soothe his troubled soul, and when he opened his eyes, he felt as if a burden had lifted from him.

It may have been a temporary reprieve, but at this point, he'd take every little thing he could get.

"Hello, Mum." Michael picked his mother up and twirled her around as she rose to greet him.

"Put me down!" she smiled. "I'm glad to see you, Michael." Her eyes filled as the look on his face told her that this was it. This was the day he was leaving her again.

Michael reached forward and grasped his father's right hand. His left arm was still in a cast, as was his left leg, but from what he'd gleaned from Gigi, they were going to be placing the leg in traction as soon as the cast came off.

"You're looking good," Michael lied. "They'll make a handsome man out of you yet."

Gerald Fernsby smiled. "It's good to see you, son. I'm glad you are fully healed."

"I was lucky. It was you that took the full force, not me. All I got was a bump on the head."

"Do you know if they've caught the culprit who did this to us yet?" his father asked.

Michael shook his head. "The police are still searching, but I doubt we'll ever find out who did it."

He knew his father didn't believe the official story any more than he did, but he wasn't going to get into that right now.

"So, how's work going? Have they assigned you a desk yet?" his father coughed, and Michael could see the obvious pain and discomfort he must be in.

"Actually, yes." If his parents wanted to believe he was

safe behind a desk somewhere in London, then he would not be the one who broke their hearts.

"I'm leaving right now, and I'll be gone for a while. I'll try to telephone, but you know how it is. Don't worry if I don't, because I'm safe. Even Hitler can't get to me where I'm going to be working."

"That's a relief at least," his mother said. "Hopefully this will all blow over and you'll be home before you know it."

"I hope so, Mum, but it isn't looking that way right now. I will be home soon though, and I want to see Dad walking again when I'm back." He looked at his father, who gave him the thumbs-up sign.

"Please take care of yourself, and make sure you eat properly," his mother fussed.

"I will," Michael smiled.

The guilt of deceiving his parents was choking him but the truth sounded even worse. After all they'd been through, his mum especially, she would have a nervous breakdown if she knew where he was really going.

"One last thing before you go," Gerald reached out for Michael, who sat beside his stricken father.

"I called my solicitor last week, and he's coming to see me. I'm changing my will so that everything I have goes to you when I die. You will be the owner of the house, the business, and everything I possess, except for a few things I am leaving for Dorothy and the others."

Michael felt a lump forming in his throat. "You didn't need to do that, Dad. You're going to be around for a long time yet."

"After what's happened these last few months, anything is possible. Life is fleeting, and we've all suffered terrible loss. This is just prudent, that's all."

"You'll probably outlive me."

If only he knew, he wouldn't be so quick to sign over his business to me.

Michael couldn't look him in the eye, but he couldn't disappoint him either. "I love you, Dad, and I promise I won't let you down."

"When you come back for a few days, I'll call him so we can go over everything together."

"I'm in no rush, Dad. Like I said, I want you around for at least another thirty years."

"Thirty years?" Dorothy laughed. "I hardly doubt we'll last that long."

After one last hug, Michael walked alone along the long, dark corridors of the hospital. It felt like he was walking the plank on a pirate ship towards his inevitable demise as he fell off the end.

Hitler be damned.

Chapter Twenty-Five

The stuffy darkness of an early July morning cloaked RAF Biggin Hill as Michael arrived, beads of perspiration forming on his brow in the clingy, warm air. Captain Sanders stood by the Avro Anson, his face a mask of serious concern. The time had come for Michael to embark on his perilous journey into the heart of Nazi Germany.

"Fernsby," Sanders greeted him, his voice carrying a mix of solemnity and encouragement. "This is it. Remember everything we trained you for. Trust your instincts and stay focused. What you're about to do is vital for king and country, and we know you won't let us down."

"I'll try not to." Michael used bravado to mask the knots that had formed in his stomach. All thoughts of going back to see Mina, finding the coin that could save the Fernsby fortune, and making sure David lay undisturbed, didn't seem like such a great idea now he was here.

I'm not going for myself, remember? I'm doing this for my country.

That didn't work either.

Michael nodded at Sanders, the weight of his mission

making him sweat even more. He closed his eyes as the visions of the accident replayed in his mind. The explosion of metal as the vehicle rammed into the side of the Autovia made him shudder, and his anger grew as he remembered the Nazi driver running away as his father hung upside down, broken and unconscious.

A surge of determination coursed through him, fuelled by the accident and the memory of David's sacrifice. And Gerda Yung's bravery. He couldn't afford to fail, not this time.

"I won't let you down, Captain," Michael replied, his voice firm. "I'll do whatever it takes to bring Adler and his family to Britain."

Sanders clasped his shoulder, his grip strong and reassuring. "I know you will. Remember, you're not alone. We'll be monitoring the dead letter boxes and providing support whenever we can. Stay vigilant and be cautious. Good luck."

With those last words, Michael turned his attention to the silhouette of the Avro Anson that was waiting silently in the pre-dawn moonlight to whisk him off to France.

The hairs on the back of his neck stood up as he approached the twin-engine aircraft. He'd never flown in an airplane before, and all thoughts of his mission momentarily fell away as he was overcome with anticipation and excitement.

The aircraft looked sleek and streamlined in the moonlight. Its propellers stood motionless as the engines awaited the commands of the pilot, who knew nothing of the mission or the passenger he would transport across the English Channel.

He climbed a metal ladder and entered the interior through a door halfway down the body. The large cockpit could seat the pilot, four crew members, and around four passengers from the look of it.

The smell of aviation fuel stung Michael's nostrils as he took his seat in the compact interior. Creature comforts were clearly secondary to the function of getting the job done, but Michael didn't mind. If there was one part of this mission he had been looking forward to, it was this, and he would not allow the lack of comfort to affect his upbeat mood before he left England.

Perhaps for the last time.

Stop it!

The large window wrapped around the cockpit, and would afford Michael splendid views once daylight broke over the skies. Lost in thought, the crackle of the intercom made him jump as the radio operator tested his equipment.

The engine roared to life, and the Avro Anson sputtered into action. Gradually at first, but then gaining momentum, Michael loved every second as the force of the acceleration pressed him firmly against his seat.

As the airplane lifted off the ground, reality hit, and Michael felt alone and isolated.

When dawn broke over the horizon, Michael watched the English countryside as it sprawled out before him in all its glory. Soon, England's green and pleasant lands gave way to a sea of blue as they crossed the Channel towards France and the hated enemy on the other side of the River Rhine.

Chapter Twenty-Six

After landing on the outskirts of Paris, Michael caught a train for the next leg of his long journey. Lyon lay in the eastern part of France, around fifty miles from the Swiss border, and he whiled away the eight-hour slog by watching the French countryside whizz past the window in his half-empty carriage.

He was on his own, and his heart beat in time with the sound of the train on the tracks as it pulsed its way southeast.

This was no pleasure ride, and his mind soon turned to the real reason he was here. He went over and over the mission, dissecting it from every possible angle.

Every scenario had been considered during his time with Captain Sanders, and they had left no stone unturned. Or had they? Michael never mentioned his other, more personal family goals to Sanders, because he knew he'd be ordered to stand down if he did.

He didn't know how he was going to find the time to do what he needed to do, but he would. Somehow, he would.

In Lyon, Michael changed trains and boarded the first-class carriage to Basel, Switzerland. He would arrive at six thirty the following morning, so he planned on resting and getting as much sleep as he could before the final, most dangerous part of his journey began: crossing the border into Germany.

In Basel, he changed platforms and boarded his last train for the six-hour journey to Munich. His stomach churned as he took his seat, and he readied his papers for the inevitable grilling he'd receive at the border.

The closer he got, the more fidgety and nervous he became. He'd been over his story a million times, and he knew the SIS would have used the best forgers available, so that didn't concern him too much.

What did were the memories. They crushed him under the weight of what he was about to do. Even after all the preparation in the world, he was still worried that something would go wrong.

What if they recognise me? I'll be arrested and killed the moment the Gestapo get their hands on me.

Forty-five minutes later, the train ground to a halt in Rheinfelden. Like it or not, Michael was now back in Germany, and his nightmares were about to begin.

Armed soldiers entered the train and began checking everyone's papers. Michael sweated, and his hands shook as the stern-faced young man barked at him for his identification papers.

He tried to look indifferent, but he knew his face was a mask of guilt and fear, and try as he may, he couldn't stop.

"Lars Hohenberg, what are you doing in Germany?" the soldier studied the Swiss national's passport.

"My mother is German, and she lives in Munich. I'm going to stay with her for two weeks during the summer holidays."

"What is her name?"

"Her name is Greta Hohenberg."

"Where does she live?"

"She lives at number forty-four, Osterwaldstrasse, close to the Englischer Garten."

"What is her profession?"

Do you want her life story?

"She is a typist for a law firm. I'm sorry, I don't remember which one."

The soldier studied Michael's papers for what seemed an age, and he kept looking up at his face before studying some more. Michael's stomach was in knots, and he knew there would be no escape if the soldier didn't believe him.

Eventually, the soldier thrust the papers back at Michael and went to the next passenger without saying a word. Michael took a deep breath to control his heartbeat that was rattling out of his chest.

I'm in! I've done it.

Chapter Twenty-Seven

With the most dangerous part behind him, Michael relaxed the rest of the way to Munich. His anxiety reared again as the train approached the Bahnhof.

As he exited, he looked for his contact. It was a role he'd played over and over in Bletchley, and he knew every emotion, and every line he was supposed to give.

A woman in her forties, wearing a knee-length black skirt and a white, full-sleeved blouse, peered around the disembarking passengers as if looking for someone. Michael paid close attention to her demeanour and when he saw her wave her right hand in the air and then scratch the left side of her nose, he knew he had the right person.

"Mother!" he yelled, walking towards her swiftly. It felt strange calling someone other than Dorothy Fernsby his mother, but it worked for the situation he was in.

"Lars! Darling Lars!" the woman hurried towards him, looking every bit the joyful mother about to enjoy a family reunion.

The woman was around the same age as Dorothy. Her brown hair was pinned back underneath a red hat, and she looked to be small, around five and a half feet tall. If she was playacting as a mother and a typist who had just left work to greet her son, she was doing a wonderful job.

"Mother, how great to see you." Michael's German was flawless, and anyone listening in wouldn't think twice about what was unfolding.

"How was your journey? Oh, darling, you must be tired. Come, let's go home where you can tell me all about it."

The woman linked arms with Michael and led him to a black vehicle that Michael recognised instantly. He stopped short and took a sharp intake of breath when he saw it.

"Is something wrong?" the lady asked.

"No, I just have memories of a vehicle just like this one."

It was a black Opel Kadett, just like the one he'd smashed into a tree before he'd stumbled into Ryskamp and met Mina a few months earlier.

"It's not far to get home. Just a few kilometres."

Once inside the vehicle, the woman's demeanour changed. "How was the journey over here?" she asked in English. She had a distinct German accent, but her English was good.

"Uneventful, I'm happy to report."

"Good. Remember, no names and no details. The less we know about each other, the safer it is."

"Understood."

Captain Sanders had warned Michael over and over, not to mention a word about the reason he was there to anyone, including the woman who would pretend to be his mother. All he knew was that she was a resistance operator who worked against the Nazis.

That's all I need to know.

Michael fell silent while the woman drove to her home on Osterwaldstrasse.

"I rent two rooms on the bottom floor. Be careful what you say, because a Nazi lives above us. We speak only German in the house, and we don't mention anything about your reasons for being here."

"Understood."

"If there's something you need to know, ask me to go for a walk with you. We'll discuss it as we walk around the English Gardens that are close to the house."

Michael nodded. Sanders had told him all this before he'd left.

Once he'd settled into the house and his new mother had fed him, no doubt entertaining the Nazi living upstairs with loud dialogue from an excited mother seeing her son, Michael retired to the room she had prepared for him.

He sat at the desk and looked around the barren room. All it had was a bed, a chair, and a wooden desk that had several loose pages of blank paper and a pen sitting on top.

A box of envelopes sat beside a lamp on the desk, and that was it. There was nothing else he either needed or desired. All he wanted now was to get it done with and get out of Germany.

Not until after I do what I came for.

He still hadn't worked out how he was going to get away for a couple of days, but he'd cross that bridge when it came. He was hoping for a day or two between making contact with Adler and making the escape, and that was when he'd go if he could.

Even though he was tired, he sat at the desk and turned on the lamp. He grabbed a piece of paper and began to write the best (and only) love letter he'd ever written. Except the practice ones in Bletchley, but they didn't count.

Tuesday, July 4, 1939

My dearest Gertrude,

The weight of the nights since we last saw one another feels much heavier than I ever imagined. Every sunset that separates us adds to the longing that keeps my heart restless. I find myself looking up at the stars and wondering if, at that same moment, you might be gazing upon them too, bridging the distance between us, if only in thought.

The silence around me is filled with echoes of our shared laughter, and our whispered secrets. It's a cruel reminder of the emptiness that has settled since your departure. How I yearn to hear your voice again, to see the familiar spark in your eyes, and to share in the warmth of your smile.

I find solace in memories of our stolen moments – soft glances, shared dreams, the gentle touch of your hand. They have become my refuge in these trying times.

I'm holding onto the hope that this separation is temporary, that soon we will be reunited to fill our days with the shared joys and dreams that we've come to cherish. Until then, I treasure each memory, each whispered promise of a future together.

Take care, my dear. Remember our dreams, for they tether my heart to yours. Let me know when fate can be kind enough to bring us together once more.

Yours, now and always,

DMF

Michael put the pen down and read the make-believe love letter. He realised it wasn't Gertrude he'd written it to. It was Mina. He closed his eyes and allowed her image to consume him for a moment before collecting himself and returning to reality.

The following morning, Michael went for a stroll around the English Gardens, conveniently situated a short walk from the rented rooms he shared with his new mother. It was a glorious morning, and plenty of people were out enjoying the early morning sunshine.

He crossed two streams and headed for a narrow road that dissected the gardens running parallel to the River Isar. He nodded to himself when he noticed a street sign telling him he had reached Gysslingstrasse.

He crossed the road and walked towards the river. A few people were enjoying a picnic breakfast to his right, but he ignored them and concentrated his focus on the two buildings on either side of the lane.

He veered towards the one on the right and saw the three-foot-high wall behind it, close to the river. Why it was there, he had no idea, but he didn't care. He looked at the position of the stones on the bottom and quickly scanned the surrounding area. Satisfied, he walked past and enjoyed the rest of his morning stroll.

As he walked past the two couples picnicking on the grass, one man made eye contact with him. It was only for a moment, but it was enough to make the hairs on the back of Michael's neck stand up and make him feel uncomfortable.

The young man stood up and watched him walk by. Michael pretended he hadn't seen him, but he was watching from the corner of his eye.

The man was tall and slender and looked as if he was in good physical shape. He had short-cropped blond hair, and although he was wearing casual civilian clothing, Michael had no doubt he served in the Nazi apparatus in some official capacity.

Perhaps he's Wehrmacht, and he's home on leave. Or he's SS, and he's a guard at Dachau.

Dark thoughts ran through Michael's head as he

wandered past them. He turned when a female voice spoke up and broke the tension.

"Karl, it's your turn. Please sit down."

The group was playing some kind of board game, but Michael wondered if Karl was on some kind of watch duty, looking out for anyone who appeared out of place.

Or he's looking for anyone he thinks might be Jewish.

Michael's suspicions were confirmed a few minutes later when he walked past a sign near the entrance to the park.

Juden Verboten

No Jews allowed.

With his blood boiling, Michael made his way back to the rooms he shared with his new mother. He'd be back for another walk later that day.

Chapter Twenty-Eight

L ate in the afternoon, Michael and Mother went for a walk in the English Gardens. They had a picnic on the grass by the river under the shade of a tree.

Michael excused himself to go find a public convenience, and as soon as he was out of sight, he turned and headed for the wall behind the building he'd visited earlier.

Making sure nobody was watching, Michael pretended to kneel and tie his shoelace in front of the wall. He pulled on the second stone from the left, and it came loose fairly easily. He felt behind to make sure nobody else was using it, and satisfied, he quickly placed his sealed envelope in the gap and replaced the stone.

After one more look to make sure he hadn't been seen, he stood up and went back to the picnic. They stayed until almost dusk, and with the park about to close, they left and headed home.

Nobody had disturbed the DLB, and with the first hurdle of his operation safely over, he turned his attention to the next phase.

Every afternoon for the next four days, Michael would walk around the English Gardens. Fortunately, they were large, and he could take a different route every day so he wouldn't look suspicious.

Every day, right before the park closed, he would tie his shoelaces, or he'd sit against the wall for a break from the summer heat.

On the second day, his heart raced when he discovered the letter had been taken. Either Adler had it, which was what he hoped, or some other person had found it and he was about to be arrested.

His legs quivered as he walked back to his room, and he found it difficult to sleep. Every noise he heard reminded him of how the Gestapo had treated Gerda and her friends just a few short miles away from where he now lay, and he imagined armed officers storming the rented rooms to arrest him.

Every sense he possessed was heightened the next day when he entered the park. The hairs on his neck and arms stood tall as electricity coursed through his veins. His back shuddered, and he fought the overwhelming desire to constantly spin around to make sure nobody was behind him and about to grab him.

When he knelt in front of the wall, he was convinced that everyone in the park was staring at him, and he took long gulps of air to keep himself calm and focused on the task.

By the fourth day, he relaxed a bit. If he was walking into a trap, surely they wouldn't keep waiting. They would arrest him as soon as they found out about the DLB, so with that little piece of comfort in mind, he approached the stone wall.

He knew something was different the moment he moved the stone. It wasn't sitting in the same position he'd left it the previous day. Although minuscule, Michael had purposely left one corner ever so slightly out of alignment.

Now it was perfectly in place, which told him someone had messed with the stone since his last visit the previous evening.

He reached behind and pulled out a sealed envelope. He had a quick look and saw that it wasn't addressed to anyone. He quickly replaced the stone and was glad to be done with the park and the wall. If he'd done this many more times, someone would have noticed, and all their plans would have been for nothing.

He walked home as fast as he could without arousing suspicion, and as soon as he closed the door to his room, he tore open the letter. Spreading it out on the desk, he read the missive.

Saturday, July 8, 1939.

DMF,

Thank you for finding me after all these years. I cannot tell you how I have longed to see you again and to share the blue skies of our beautiful countryside together.

I am busy, and as much as I want to see you, I'm afraid I am delayed. Please accept my sincere apologies.

If you can wait for me, I propose we meet seven days hence, at the place we always used to enjoy in our college days. Let's meet at the Greenway at 10 pm where we can reminisce and drink the night away.

Always yours,

Gertrude.

Michael took the book he'd brought from Bletchley that he'd been reading and opened it on the appropriate pages as he'd had them drilled into his head by Sanders.

The book, written by the Nazis as a propaganda ploy, was about a man who rediscovered himself after the events of the Great War. He wandered around aimlessly until the words of the Führer reached his ears. From that moment on, he was a changed man, saved only by the Nazis and their fearless leader, Adolf Hitler.

Michael hated the book, and he was glad he could be done with it after decoding the letter sent by Adler.

At least I hope it was Adler who sent it.

He counted the words in the letter and wrote down the ones he needed.

College, greenway, reminisce.

Michael searched for the words on the pages he'd seared into his brain in the wooden hut in Bletchley Park.

Ludwig, Docen, cul-de-sac.

Adler wants to meet in a cul-de-sac, but where? At the junction of Ludwig and Docen?

Michael poured over street maps of Munich, and by 3 am, he'd found it. He rubbed his tired eyes and slammed the book shut with the location hidden inside. SS Oberführer Gustav Adler wants to meet in the cul-de-sac on Docen-strasse, which sits off the junction of Ludwigfelder Strasse, at 10 pm seven days from today.

July 15th.

The location was perfect. It was close to a railway line, where parked rail carriages made it possible to hide and escape on foot if things went wrong. It was on the route out of Munich, and although Adler wouldn't know where Michael was taking him, it made sense to meet on the outskirts of the city. There would be less chance of road-blocks, and they would have access to quiet country roads that would lead them out of Germany.

Hopefully.

Michael closed his weary eyes and fell into a restless sleep. The easy part was over, and danger was literally around every corner from now on.

Chapter Twenty-Nine

S anders had been right. The two towers of the twelfth-century Frauenkirche church stood out like beacons in the night. They were impossible to miss, and Michael used them to guide him to his next destination.

Upon entering the hallowed space, a wave of chilled air enveloped him. The silence inside was profound, broken only by the distant echoing drip of melted candle wax hitting the stone floor. Faint whispers — remnants of old prayers, or was it the wind playing tricks? — seemed to float through the cavernous expanse. Michael paused for a moment to absorb the serenity that contrasted so sharply with the turmoil outside.

He marvelled at the ornately carved ceiling so high above his head, and the long rows of pews leading to the raised altar with the magnificent stained-glass windows that stood as testament to the great master builders of the past.

The biggest thing that stood out to Michael wasn't the sheer magnificence of the place, although that could never be underestimated.

No, it wasn't that. It was the calm serenity the walls

seemed to project onto him the moment he walked through the door. It was like somehow it knew how tumultuous and incendiary it was outside, and it reached out to wrap its arms around him and comfort him.

Shaking himself free of the emotions and the majesty of his surroundings, Michael got to work. He acted like a tourist for a few minutes, pretending to study the many archaeological wonders on display, but in reality, he was watching for signs that anyone was watching him.

After a fifteen-minute tour of the church, which he could have happily extended to several hours in different circumstances, he made his way back towards the main doors.

When he reached the second of the huge cylindrical pillars holding up the roof on the right-hand side as one would look from the doors, he stopped and sat on the pew in front of it, facing the altar.

He closed his eyes for a moment and prayed, all the while listening intently for any signs of noise close to him.

There weren't any, and happy he was free from prying eyes, he dropped to his knees as if in prayer. A gap in the pews exposed the great pillar, and Michael felt around the stone base where it faced the front of the church.

One stone felt loose, and he pulled on it until it fell away in his hand. After another look to make sure he wasn't being watched, Michael stretched out his arm and reached inside.

His hand clasped around a soft leather pouch, and he pulled it out. He exchanged it for the letter he'd written to Sanders and 317, telling them the operation was a go on July fifteenth.

He replaced the stone and left the church, making sure to take a different way back to the rooms he shared with

Mother, as he'd come to call her; even when he wasn't with her, which was most of the time.

Safely inside his room, Michael emptied the contents of the pouch onto his desk. It didn't contain much, just a piece of paper with the words 'ONLY TO BE USED IN AN EMERGENCY' written across it in black ink. It also contained a new set of identification papers, and an envelope containing Reichsmarks, Swiss francs and some French francs. Ironically, there weren't any Dutch guilders, so Michael assumed he'd get those during the exchange with Adler at the Dutch border.

The identification papers were in the name of Erich Weber, another Swiss national, who was a bank clerk just starting on his career journey.

Michael sat back and studied his life story, which he'd need if things went wrong. He understood the reasoning behind the choice of Swiss passports:

He spoke fluent German, and that is the national language in Switzerland. Movement around Europe in the current climate would be easier and less fretful if he held a Swiss passport over a German one, where he would probably be treated with fear and suspicion everywhere he went.

Michael studied the identification papers until his eyes burned and he was seeing double. He glanced at his watch and noticed it was four in the morning.

He put the papers under his pillow and fell into another restless sleep.

Chapter Thirty

Kriminaldirektor Albert Kreise sat behind his desk, putting the finishing touches to his report on their recent capture of a small group of troublemakers who distributed leaflets and pamphlets spreading lies about the Nazi Party.

His door opened, which annoyed him greatly when he was trying to concentrate. "What have I told you about coming in here when the door is closed?" he snapped, thinking his secretary had just barged in like she was prone to do.

"I didn't think I needed an invitation, Kreise."

Kreise immediately shot out of his chair. He'd recognise that voice anywhere. "Please forgive me, Obergruppen-führer Heydrich. I thought it was my secretary."

"You mistook me for your secretary?" Heydrich's tone was quiet and yet somehow intimidating.

"I apologise, Obergruppenführer Heydrich. It won't happen again."

Kreise stood tall and looked into the cold eyes of the

Blond Beast, as Heydrich had come to be known within Nazi circles.

Not that anyone ever dared call him that.

"Heil Hitler," Kreise screamed, shoving his right arm in the air in the Nazi salute.

Heydrich nodded and sat down.

"What brings you here this afternoon, Obergruppen-führer Heydrich?" No matter how many times Kreise saw Heydrich – and the closer his transfer to the SD became, the more he seemed to see him – he could never feel comfortable in his presence. It was as though a dark cloud of fear and ruthless intimidation followed Kreise wherever he went.

"I would have been more than happy to travel to Berlin if you needed me," Kreise added.

"I'm aware of that, Kreise, and if I need you in Berlin, I'll send for you."

"Yes, Obergruppenführer."

"What we have to discuss is very sensitive, and Berlin has eyes and ears everywhere."

"Yes, sir."

"I heard your radio broadcast. It was very good."

"Thank you, Obergruppenführer Heydrich. I think I reassured the German people that right prevailed. Fernsby got what he deserved, and we showed the people that the Reich always prevails."

"Except Fernsby isn't dead. He's not even injured."

Kreise already knew that, but he decided to play along and pretend he didn't know.

"What? But, sir, the intelligence we received from the SD confirmed Fernsby died in the automobile accident."

"They told you what you needed to know."

"But I went on national radio and told the German people Fernsby was dead."

"And that is what they will continue to believe, Kreise. You did a great job convincing them of it."

Kreise bowed his head. He wasn't about to argue with the most ruthless man he'd ever met.

"What can I do for you, Obergruppenführer Heydrich?"

"Fernsby might have got away from the accident unscathed," Heydrich continued. "But his father wasn't so lucky. He lies in a hospital bed with serious injuries from which he may never fully recover."

"Such a shame," Kreise answered.

Heydrich's cold eyes bore into Kreise. "You can be very cold when you want to be, Albert, which is why I'm here today."

Heydrich sat back and placed his hands behind his neck. "I have a new task for you. One that is very sensitive to the Reich. Succeed, and I give you my personal guarantee I will approve your transfer."

Kreise sat silent, waiting for Heydrich to explain why he was there.

"We have sources that penetrate deep into the British Secret Intelligence Service. We know everything they are doing, often even before their agents themselves know about it."

"I'm sure you do, Obergruppenführer Heydrich. The SD is the best in the world at intelligence gathering." Kreise wondered what any of this had to do with him.

"We recently discovered that a top-ranking member of the SD – my SD – is trying to defect to the British. And do you know how we found out?"

Heydrich glared at Kreise, his cold eyes cutting right through him. Again, Kreise said nothing.

"We found out from our source over there. Can you believe that? Not a single SD operative has a clue about this, so they're not as efficient as I'd like them to be, are they, Kreise?"

"No, sir. Apparently not."

"We know exactly who the traitor is, and how he is going to defect." Heydrich's lips curled into a thin smile. "I want you to catch him in the act with his accomplices."

"Gladly, sir. What will become of the traitor?"

Heydrich paused for dramatic effect. "He'll be killed. Quietly, of course, but not until he's told us everything he knows about his traitorous actions."

Kreise bowed his head. He knew the importance of what Heydrich was asking him to do.

"You must complete this operation with the utmost secrecy. Do I make myself clear?"

"Very clear, sir. Nobody outside of the men I task to carry out the operation will ever know."

"Don't fail me, Kreise."

"I won't fail you, Obergruppenführer Heydrich."

He meant it.

"Stand by for your orders." Heydrich tossed a file across the desk. Then he rose from his chair and strode out of the door.

After Heydrich's departure, the weight of his presence lingered in the room, heavy and oppressive. Kreise sank back into his chair, his fingers gripping the edge of the desk.

A whirlwind of fear and anxiety tore through him, not least because he was venturing into the lion's den on Heydrich's orders, where even the tiniest misstep could be deadly. But beneath it all simmered a thread of excitement.

This was a chance, a real chance, to ascend the ranks and gain the respect and recognition he yearned for. The consequences of failure were unimaginably dire.

He took a shaky breath, trying to steady his racing heart. This was the challenge of his career, a task handed to him by one of the most fearsome figures in the Reich. The risk was monumental, but so was the reward. Kreise knew he had to gather his strength and determination, for in the game he was about to play, hesitation could be fatal.

Chapter Thirty-One

Michael rose early the next morning. He rubbed the sleep from his eyes and joined Mother in the tiny kitchen for some toast with butter and jam.

"Good morning, son," Mother played the game. "Did you sleep well?"

"Not well enough," Michael replied, still tired from his late night.

"Let's go for a walk around the park," Michael aimed his index finger at the room above, where the resident Nazi lived. "It's a beautiful morning, and it would be a shame to waste it."

Mother nodded, understanding.

"What is it?" she asked once they had crossed into the park. "Is there anything you need?"

"I need to leave for a few days and I need your vehicle," Michael said bluntly.

"Alright," Mother answered, seemingly unfazed by it all. "What's the cover story?"

"I'm going to visit some old school friends before I go

home to Switzerland. You don't know exactly where, because I have friends scattered all around this area."

"It's a bit thin, but hopefully we won't be scrutinised too much. When will you be back?"

"No more than three or four days. Then it will be all over and you can go back to your normal life."

"Normal life?" Mother laughed. "You don't know the first thing about me, and it's a good thing you don't. This has been a welcome break, let me tell you."

Michael had grown fond of Mother over the last few days. Whoever she was in her real life, she was playing this role to perfection. She'd provided Michael with everything he'd needed, which admittedly wasn't much, but he'd found comfort in her company, and that was worth its weight in gold.

"You're probably right," he answered. "Although in another world, I think we could have been friends, you and I."

"I'd like to think so," Mother replied, smiling at her son as a group of kids passed by with a football.

"Take these now so our friend upstairs won't know you've gone anywhere until it's too late. I don't trust anyone, especially the Nazi above our heads."

Michael took the keys to the Opel from Mother's outstretched hand. "You've done this before, haven't you?" he asked.

"What? Played Mother with a complete stranger? Heavens no, boy."

"I didn't mean that. I meant you've played this spy game before."

Mother smiled and closed her eyes. "More than you know," she said softly.

Michael could see the pain behind her eyes, and he

dropped the subject before it could go any further.

Back at the house, Michael gathered his things together and threw them into a rucksack he'd bought, along with a few provisions the day before on the way back from Frauenkirche.

He waved at Mother and slipped out the door.

"Be back in a few days," he whispered as he passed by her.

Mother nodded and closed the door behind him. Michael threw his rucksack into the rear of the vehicle and gunned the engine. The sound took him back to that fateful day in Glatten a few months earlier, when the Nazis pursued him after he'd turned away from a roadblock.

They'd followed him, and Michael, an inexperienced driver, crashed his vehicle into a tree. He'd ended up with three broken ribs that only recently had healed.

The Opel Kadett he'd been driving was the same as the one he now sat in. Even down to the black exterior, it was identical. Michael felt a wave of déjà vu as his hands caressed the steering wheel.

His mind wandered to Mina and her family, and he felt pangs of remorse as he thought about what he'd put them through.

If it hadn't been for the accident, I'd never have met Mina, so the broken ribs were worth it. But then, if I hadn't crashed into Mina's life the way I did, she would have been able to live a normal life, safe from the Nazis.

Visions of Alwin Lutz, the local Nazi leader's young son, swam through his mind. The image had never been far from the surface, and now it burst through in all its blood and gore.

The vision was always the same: Alwin was lying dead on the floor of the barn after Mina had shot him, pools of blood swirling and mixing with the strands of hay and loose chicken feed on the ground.

As the memories that had been seared into his brain after a thousand replays poured out, Michael took small comfort in the fact that he'd been able to calm Mina down enough to make her realise that the only way out for all of her family was to blame the British spy, Michael Fernsby.

So they did. Michael took the blame, and he ran for the border. By the time the Nazis arrived on the scene, Michael was long gone, running through the Black Forest on his way to France.

His unanswered prayers ever since were that the Nazis had believed Mina and allowed her to live.

He shook his head and pulled smoothly out into the street. He'd driven a lot since the winter, and he was a much more experienced driver now.

No more kangaroo petrol!

He smiled at the memory of David's words as he'd juddered and jerked Gerda's vehicle out of Munich the last time he'd been here.

His mind cleared as he drove the route he'd carefully memorised over the previous days. It wasn't long before he approached the edge of the city and the promise of the open roads beyond.

His heart sank as he rounded a curve in the road. The vehicles ahead had slowed to a stop, and a swarm of uniformed men surrounded them, manning a roadblock.

His heart pounded and his hands trembled as he reached for his papers. He made sure he'd tucked his rucksack under the seat and out of sight from prying eyes. Then he said a silent prayer and rolled down his window.

"Good morning," he said cheerfully.

"Papers."

Chapter Thirty-Two

M ichael handed his papers over to the stern-faced young soldier. Two more stood behind with loaded rifles at the ready. There would be no miraculous escape today if things didn't go well.

The young soldier studied the papers for what seemed like a long time and he frequently looked up to compare the picture to Michael's face.

"Where are you going?"

"I'm going to Nuremberg to visit my old school friends," Michael lied and hoped his shaky voice didn't give him away. Just in case, he gripped the handle of the Walther PPK behind the door, out of sight of the Nazi guard.

"Very well." The soldier handed Michael his papers and stepped back. Michael heaved a sigh of relief and drove forward, the hairs on the back of his neck standing up in the expectation that he'd hear a shout from behind, ordering him to stop.

It didn't come, and he soon found himself on the outskirts of Munich. A quick check behind told him that his fears weren't entirely without merit. Even though the soldiers had allowed him through the roadblock, the blue vehicle behind him had been there since the centre of Munich.

Please, not again.

He slowly sped up, watching the blue vehicle a few hundred yards behind. He turned left and then right. Then he acted like he was lost and did a U-turn. The man driving the blue vehicle didn't even glance at him as they crossed paths.

Michael berated himself for being so paranoid, but then he reminded himself of where he was, and what was at stake if he failed.

To be completely sure, he made several more turns and direction changes, until, by the end, he was completely lost. All his carefully memorised plans had gone out of the window.

At least now he knew he wasn't being followed, and that alone was worth getting lost for. He drove north into the sunlit morning until he picked up a sign for Erding.

I know where I am!

His heart ached as he recognised the roads he'd driven on just one time before, on that bleak winter's day he'd never forget.

He recognised the country lane from the map he'd drawn in January on the Night Train as he sped back home to England. It looked so different in the glow of the warm sun. Grass grew where before it had been mud, and if it wasn't for the three trees that caught his eye, he would have missed it altogether.

Michael slowed to a halt at the junction of the narrow lane, his hands twitching on the steering wheel. He couldn't keep his legs still underneath him.

Here he was, reunited with his brother, his hero. Was

he still here? Had the locals found his grave and reported it to the Nazis? Had they moved him to an unmarked grave somewhere where Michael would never find him?

All these thoughts and more ran through his mind as he drove the vehicle slowly down the lane. He could barely look at the cluster of trees as he drove past.

The area looked undisturbed, and daisies and other pretty flowers grew along with the grass around the trees. Michael took a deep breath and brought the vehicle to a stop close to the river and out of sight of the lane.

Dark memories of that stormy morning when he'd jumped into the freezing water to wash the blood and dirt from his weary body came flooding back, and he found it hard to hold himself together.

He walked up to the trees and touched the farthest tree on the left. Then he fell to his knees. The topsoil was over-grown with grass, and the small branch he'd stuck into the earth had fallen over, but it was still there.

It's still there!

David's grave was intact. Nobody had found it, and in the serene summer sun, it looked for all the world like it had never been disturbed. Michael had often wondered how he'd react when he saw it again, but now he knew.

All the emotions that had bubbled inside him over the past months burst into the open and Michael sobbed for all he was worth. His chest heaved, and he couldn't see for the tears that filled his eyes.

He placed his hands above David's body and spoke as if he was still alive.

"David, I'm here," he said between deep breaths. "I promised I'd be back for you, and I am. Please be patient and remain here, safe and sound, until the coming war is over. Then I promise that if I'm still alive, I'll come back for you and take you home."

He replaced the small branch into the earth and stood over his brother's temporary resting place.

"Gigi and Judith are doing well, and you'll be happy to know that Lucy runs around like a lunatic. Judith loves her, and she takes great care of her."

He paused to gain control of himself. "Mum was devastated, as I'm sure you know, and Dad was too. After you died, he neglected the business, and now it's failing. He's having to sell it before we go bankrupt, but I might be able to do something about that. Do you remember the gold doubloon that Gigi told you to find? Well, now I know about it, and I'm going to find it. I wish you'd told me because together we could have found it."

He listened as the wind rustled the grass beneath his feet. The branches swayed gently above his head and Michael smiled. It was as though David was showing his approval for him being here and updating him on family affairs.

"Unfortunately, Dad and I had an automobile accident. Well, it wasn't an accident at all. The Nazis wanted me dead, and they drove a vehicle directly at us. Dad took the full brunt of it and he's seriously ill in hospital."

He paused for a moment as the lump returned to his throat.

"I suppose you're wondering why I'm here again. Well, you might not believe it, but I work for the British Secret Intelligence Service! I know it sounds stupid, but it's true. Dansey himself recruited me for a job over here, but I had to see you. I had to make sure you're alright and still resting peacefully."

He fell to his knees again and clasped his hands

together. "A priest risked his life to help me and I met a really brave and beautiful girl called Mina. I want to marry her, David. I just wish you were here to live your life with me."

His voice cracked and he found it hard to swallow. Once again, tears flowed down his face, landing on the green grass covering David's mortal remains.

"I'm so sorry, David. I should have listened to you and I should have never forced you to come here. I'll never forgive myself for what happened and I'd happily trade places if I could."

He knelt for several minutes, rocking back and forth, unable to speak or even think. Finally, without warning, the words David had been very familiar with rolled out of his lips.

Our Father, who art in heaven,
hallowed be thy name;
thy kingdom come;
thy will be done;
on earth as it is in heaven.
Give us this day our daily bread.
And forgive us our trespasses,
as we forgive those who trespass against us.
And lead us not into temptation;
but deliver us from evil.
For thine is the kingdom,
the power and the glory,
for ever and ever.
Amen.

He fell silent, listening to the gentle breeze as it carried away his words. For some reason, he felt better, his heart lighter. He rose to his feet and looked one more time at the spot where David's head lay several feet below.

"Rest in peace, brother. I'll be back, I promise. But now I have work to do."

A new resolve gripped Michael as he turned and walked back to the vehicle. His last words to David repeated in his brain and they strengthened his resolve. It was as though David had risen from the grave and reassured him that everything would be alright.

Rest in peace, brother. I'll be back, I promise. But now I have work to do.

Chapter Thirty-Three

The next stop on Michael's whistle tour was his great-grandfather's house in Freising. Well, the shed behind the house to be exact. If what Gigi had told him was true, it should be easy to find the coin and get out of the area before anyone recognised him.

As Michael reflected on what had happened there, his thoughts turned to the Pallotti Church, where Father Eise had shown remarkable courage by offering him shelter during the perilous days of the Nazi manhunt.

The priest's selfless actions had not only saved his life but had left an indelible mark on his heart. A wave of gratitude washed over him, and he couldn't help but long to pay the priest a visit, where he could pay homage to the man who had risked everything for him.

The risks to both of them were too great, so Michael decided it was better to be cautious and not let anyone know he was back in Freising.

The drive took around forty minutes and he slowed as he crossed the River Isar. Once again, memories of the previous winter ran through his mind, stabbing at his heart like icy daggers digging into his soul.

This was where his great-grandfather, Herbert Guttmann, had run a successful department store that had been in the family for generations. His Uncle Frank had moved from England to work with him after the Great War, and together they had taken the Guttmann Department Store to the heights of economic success.

But Herbert Guttmann was a Jew, and after the violence of Kristallnacht the previous November, the Fernsbys had lost contact with their German family. By the time Michael and David arrived in Freising to rescue them, it was too late. They had been arrested and taken to Dachau Concentration Camp, never to be heard from again.

Are they still alive? I like to think so. Where there's faith, there is hope, and that is what I'm going to cling to.

Freising, with its rolling hills and grassy meadows, was one of the most eye-catching places he'd ever seen, and he couldn't imagine a more serene place to live.

Michael shook away the memories as he drove slowly past the white-painted home that had once belonged to his great-grandfather.

The three-storey house stood before him, unchanged from the last time he had laid eyes on it. It was the place where he and David first met Gerda.

Similar to the department store, the house had a notable feature that caught his attention. A rounded turret-like structure adorned the right-hand corner of the second floor, reminiscent of the medieval turret in the department store. Two small windows, one facing the front and the other on the side, bathed the room within with natural light. Michael presumed it had been Herbert's private quarters.

On this day, a large swastika flew from the top of the

turret, signifying that the house was now in the hands of the Nazis. Gerda had told them the mayor of Freising had claimed it and from the look of it, he'd made himself at home in the Guttmanns' house.

Michael's blood boiled at the thought of the Nazi mayor enjoying his great-grandfather's home, but there was nothing he could do about it. He just hoped the mayor hadn't looked too hard at the discarded, broken office equipment in the shed in the back garden.

Or thrown it away.

Trees sheltered the rear and side of the house, which offered any would-be burglar sanctuary from prying eyes. That is, any burglar stupid enough to break into the Nazi leader's home, knowing the consequences would be terrible if they were caught.

The small open courtyard at the front stood as Michael remembered it, and he smiled at the memory of him and David stumbling over each other in the snow when Gerda surprised them by carrying a large box out to her vehicle.

Satisfied with his reconnaissance, Michael drove away so as not to arouse anyone's suspicions. He drove about three miles outside town and parked the vehicle on the side of a narrow lane in the middle of the thick woods.

Then he waited until dark.

He ate and drank from the provisions he'd brought from Munich, and he whiled away the hours remembering the good times he and David had enjoyed with Gerda before it all went wrong.

Finally, after the sun sank, and the moon filled the cloudless sky, it was time. He took out the black metal flashlight he'd obtained from the priest the last time he'd been in Freising and turned it over in his hands.

Images of Father Eise's kindly features flashed

through his mind. He smiled at the memory of his glasses which looked tiny beneath his prominent forehead. Most of all though, he felt grateful for the help he'd received, even though it had placed the priest in great personal danger.

The flashlight was about the size of his hand, and he held it by the leather strap attached to the rear. He turned the switch on the flashlight's bottom casing, and a flood of bright light instantly blinded him.

He aimed it towards the ground and played with the three sliders on the front casing. The first one turned the light red, and this was the one he chose. It preserved his night vision and made it far less bright than the white flood-light he'd had it on a moment ago.

The familiar feeling of butterflies dancing in his stomach wouldn't go away as he began walking towards the house by the Isar. He took deep, nervous breaths, and shook his shoulders to rid himself of the fear that was gripping him.

It didn't work. He had too many terrible memories.

It was around nine thirty when he arrived at the street by the side of the Guttmann house. He hid in the trees and watched for the next fifteen minutes, glad of the gentle summer breeze. The last time he'd been here, it had been freezing.

No vehicles were present, and Michael reasoned that if the mayor was home, there would be at least one, if not more.

No lights were visible from inside, and Michael was glad nobody was home. He left the cover of the trees and quickly jumped over the six-foot-high fence into the back-yard of the house.

He hid behind a row of bushes and watched for any

signs of life. The PPK was in his pocket, but using it was the last thing he wanted to do.

No lights came on, and the evening remained still and calm. Michael rose and made his way to the white-painted shed close to the rear fence. He tried the door, but it was locked. He tried the window, but that, too, was locked.

He picked up a stone from around the flowerbed and pulled out a spare sock from his pocket. He'd been prepared for this, and he wanted to make as little sound as possible.

Knowing what he was about to do would give away the fact that someone had dared break into the mayor's shed, Michael had one last walk around it to see if there was any other way of getting inside.

There wasn't.

Luckily, the window was on the opposite side of the house, and the neighbours were far enough away that they wouldn't hear the muffled thud of the glass being shattered by the sock-covered stone.

He smashed the glass and reached inside to open the window far enough to squeeze through. Then he sat on a pile of sacks under the window and listened.

If I'm going to be caught, it's going to be now.

He held the handle of the Walther just in case.

The evening remained calm, so he stood up and turned on the flashlight. Now he was safe from prying eyes, he switched the slider back to bright white and shone it around the shed.

The possibility of the mayor clearing it out, or even worse, finding the coin, loomed large in Michael's mind, but he had to be certain. He would never get the chance to look for it again, so it was now or never.

The shed was full of garden implements and outdoor chairs, and most of it looked to be new and unused. Herbert was renowned for his love of antiques, and Gigi had assured him that even his garden equipment was dated and out of touch with the twentieth century.

All of this seemed to be the mayor's stuff. Michael pulled back sacks and covers, and he opened boxes. He looked on the shelf, but there was nothing that resembled what he was looking for.

He stood in the dimly lit shed, his heart sinking as he surveyed the scene before him. Although this wasn't the only reason he was here, he had travelled across countries, defied danger, and risked everything to find the hidden family heirloom that was supposed to be safeguarded here. Yet, it was nowhere to be found. The weight of disappointment settled heavily upon his shoulders and his mind raced with the consequences of failure.

With each passing second, the enormity of the situation became clearer. His family's fate rested on the recovery of the coin. Their failing business, already on the brink of collapse, relied on him finding it to secure their financial stability. The thought of telling Gigi and his father that he had returned empty-handed filled him with a sense of dread.

How would he break the news that he'd failed yet again to save his family? How could he bear the disappointment in their eyes, knowing that their hopes for a brighter future had crumbled? The burden of their impending hardship lay squarely on his shoulders and the weight threatened to crush him.

He sat on the sacks for a few minutes to allow himself time to calm down. Everything he'd done had been geared towards the moment he triumphantly returned with the secret doubloon, and once again he had failed them in the moment of their greatest need. After the emotion of seeing

David's resting place earlier, Michael's mental state couldn't take any more.

He sat and buried his head in his hands.

As he exited the shed, darkness surrounded him, mirroring the bleakness that enveloped his spirit. His steps felt heavy, each one carrying the weight of perceived failure. He had hoped against hope to uncover the Brasher Doubloon, but all he saw now was an uncertain future for his proud family.

It was over, or at least this part of his mission was. Now he had to put this to the back of his mind, as he still had other vital work to attend to. As sad as it was, he had to find a way to mask his disappointment.

I'm earning four hundred pounds a year. That should be enough to keep the house at least. We may lose the business but we can keep the house.

Feeling better after that revelation, Michael trudged back to the Opel. He forced himself to focus on the next phase of his mission: Mina.

Chapter Thirty-Four

Michael's spirits lifted as he thought of seeing Mina again. He settled down in the back seat of the Opel and closed his eyes. A glance at his watch told him it was one thirty, so he had several hours before it was daylight. He'd use that time to get some much-needed rest.

Mina's long blonde hair shone like golden silk, cascading down her back and capturing the radiance of the sun perfectly through the open door of the barn at her farm close to Glatten.

She smiled, and Michael felt electric bolts coursing through his body as their hands touched. His heart melted as she looked longingly at him, her deep blue eyes baring his very soul to the outside world.

She laughed at his silly jokes as they fed the chickens, and after the eggs had been collected, they lay together in the hayloft, enjoying both the morning sun and each other's company.

He reached over and swept her into his arms. The taste of her kiss, sweet and tender, danced upon his lips, turning him to mush. He rose to his knees and took her hand in his.

"Mina?" A powerful surge swept through him, and it was a feeling he never wanted to stop.

"Yes?"

"Will you—?"

"Yes!" she shouted, cutting off his question. "Yes, I'll marry you."

They kissed again, and they fell back onto the soft hay.

A loud rap on the window of the Opel dragged Michael from his dream. Confused, he squinted in the darkness, trying to get his bearings. Thinking he had been dreaming again, he closed his eyes.

Another rap, this time louder and more forceful. A loud, gruff voice broke the solitude of the forest. "You in there. Get out here now!"

Michael's heart jolted and he felt for the Walther PPK tucked underneath his leg. Three flashlights shone through the windows, and he knew he'd have no chance in a fire-fight. He rolled the weapon onto the floor and pushed it under the driver's seat.

"I'm coming." Michael grabbed his shoes and opened the door, stepping out with his hands held high.

"Who are you and what are you doing here?" a voice barked at him.

All three flashlights shone in his eyes, making it impossible for him to see who his adversaries were.

"I'm Lars Hohenberg and I am here to visit my mother during the summer holidays."

"Papers."

"They're in the vehicle," Michael pointed to the Opel. "Can I get them?"

"Hurry."

Michael's mind raced as he fumbled in the glove box. He took a moment to compose himself and devise a plausible explanation for why he was parked in the middle of nowhere.

A hand roughly snatched the papers, and the faceless man turned his flashlight towards them.

"What are you doing out here?" another asked.

He took a deep, steadying breath. "It's a little embarrassing, actually. I was supposed to meet a girl but she stood me up. I was too tired to drive back to Munich tonight, so I was just resting until daylight."

"You're from Switzerland?" the man with his papers barked.

"Yes, sir. As I said, I'm visiting my mother in Munich. I met this girl down there, and she told me to meet her here. As you can see, she never showed up."

One of the men stood behind him and sniggered. Michael hoped that was a good sign.

"Where were you last night?"

"I was here, waiting for the girl."

"Where else did you go?" the man's voice seemed a little more menacing now.

"I didn't go anywhere else. I came straight here so I wouldn't get lost. She didn't show up, so I fell asleep."

"Show me your socks."

"What?"

"You heard me. Show me your socks."

Realisation dawned on Michael. He'd forgotten to retrieve the sock from the stone he'd used to smash the window and the Nazi mayor must be up in arms because someone had broken into his shed. Michael pulled his trousers up to his shins, revealing a pair of socks on his feet.

"What was the girl's name you were seeing?" the man passed the papers back to Michael, his tone a little softer.

"Mina." Michael gave the first name that entered his head.

"Where is she from?"

"I don't know, somewhere in Freising, but that's all I know."

"Looks like she stood you up."

"I know." Michael smirked at the men, hoping for a little sympathy.

"If you're still here in the morning, I'm taking you in."

"Yes, sir, I'll be gone, I promise."

The three policemen went back to their vehicle, and soon Michael was alone in the solitude of darkness again. He knew he'd been lucky that regular policemen had found him and not the Gestapo because it would have been a whole different story if it had been them.

He spent the rest of the dark hours sitting by the side of the vehicle, and as soon as he could see well enough, he took the emergency identification papers he'd taken from the dead letterbox in Frauenkirche and stuffed them as far under the seat as he could. He shuddered at the thought of what would have happened if they'd searched the vehicle and found them.

By the time the sun was rising, Michael was on his way to Ryskamp, the farm Mina and her family called home.

Chapter Thirty-Five

M ost of the roads were quiet, and it wasn't until he was close to Stuttgart that he encountered another roadblock. He told them the same story, that he was visiting an old school friend who'd moved to Glatten, and they allowed him to pass without incident.

He restocked his supply of food and snacks in the general store in Glatten. The swastika flying on the flagpole outside made his stomach churn and he all but slammed the Reichsmarks onto the counter when the Aryan who now ran it took his order.

Like the Guttmanns, the Glatten General Store had been owned by a Jewish family – in this case, Mina's best friend, Anna. Or at least it had been until Kristallnacht when the Nazis seized it from them.

Jews were no longer allowed to own shops or stores in Germany, and Michael choked on the sandwich he'd bought when he thought of the suffering the Nazis had caused.

Had caused? Are causing.

The fifteen-minute drive to Ryskamp was the most

nerve-wracking time Michael could ever remember having. Even his daring escape through the Black Forest the previous winter hadn't been this bad.

He struggled to control his feet, and he almost crashed into a horse and cart before he overtook it on a country lane. The farmer shook his fist at Michael, who smiled and waved in response.

He'd managed to get hold of a larger-scale map of the area and he used it to navigate the tiny lanes that skirted around the edges of the Black Forest.

He was close now and his heart juddered like an out-of-control train as he steered the Opel into the thick, dark void that was the Black Forest. Memories of almost freezing to death, dogs frothing and barking, and angry young men relentlessly hunting him down flashed through his mind and he blinked hard to get them out of his head.

The lane came to a junction with another, wider one. If his calculations were correct, there should be another lane a few hundred yards farther down, and if this was true, he was in the right place.

With his heart pounding, he drove slowly, holding his breath, hoping he'd taken the right roads.

He had. The next junction came at him from out of the trees and Michael stopped to catch his breath. He turned around and parked the vehicle on the narrow lane between the trees where it would be hard to discover.

He checked to see if anyone casually driving past could see it and, happy that they couldn't, he locked the doors and headed for the clearing he knew was half a mile or so ahead of him on the edge of the forest.

The rear of the farmhouse came into view as he cleared the trees and he stopped to gather himself. He was literally shaking all over and try as he may, he couldn't stop himself.

What had become of Mina and her family after his dramatic escape? Did the Nazis believe their story that Michael had shot Alwin? Or were they now either dead or languishing in a concentration camp, filled with hate for the Englishman who had ruined their lives?

Not knowing what to expect, Michael crept up to the edge of the trees and used them as cover to get as near the front of the farm as possible. He saw the sign, Ryskamp, painted on the side of the gate, and everything looked the same as it had the last time he'd been here seven months earlier.

Almost.

This time, there was a large swastika flapping in the breeze above the farmhouse. Michael knew Mina's father, Tim Postner, would never allow that to happen, so the Nazis must have taken over the farm after Alwin died.

Gulping for air, Michael melted back into the forest. Once he was clear from the edge, he sat and thrust his head into his hands.

What did I do? Did I kill the girl I love? And her family too?

He forced back the bile that was forming at the rear of his throat, and he rose to his feet. As he'd done in December, he skirted around to the rear of the farm, where he saw the barn with the large grey roof.

Clinging to the side of the building, he remained wary of any dogs, but none were present. He found the barn doors and slid inside as quickly as possible.

It took a moment for his eyes to adjust to the dull light and when they did, he was met with a sight he'd long held in his memory. The barn looked exactly the same, with chickens running around loose on the straw-covered ground. The hayloft was full of bales of hay, and the ladder stood tall, ready to be used.

His eyes focused on the spot where Mina had shot Alwin and he paused for a moment. As sad as it was that Alwin lost his life, Michael was more concerned about the consequences to Mina and her family.

He was about to leave and head back to the forest until after dark when he heard voices approaching. He checked his watch and blew out his cheeks. It was late afternoon and it was time to feed the animals.

He ran for the hayloft and climbed up the ladder as fast as he could, covering himself with straw just in time before the doors opened.

Expecting to see Nazis as the new owners, Michael had his finger on the Walther PPK. As much as he wanted to kill them for what they'd done to Mina, he knew he couldn't do anything unless forced to. His primary mission was too important, and he wasn't even supposed to be here. Whatever the Nazis had done to Mina, it was he who was responsible. He was the one who had got her into all this.

The barn door opened, and Michael's jaw dropped. Senta strolled in, singing and chatting as though she didn't have a care in the world.

Senta was Mina's younger sister and she was the spitting image of her. Long blonde hair grew down past her shoulders, and her face reminded Michael so much of Mina that he almost gasped when she walked in.

Then he saw her.

Chapter Thirty-Six

As Mina trailed through the barn doors behind Senta, Michael caught sight of her. The moment was so intense that he stopped breathing, his breath lodged somewhere between anticipation and surprise.

There she was, her presence even more enchanting than the memories that had kept him company for so long. Her beauty, magnified in the late afternoon sunshine, struck him with such intensity that he was overwhelmed and entirely spellbound. He had to stop himself from calling out her name.

A wave of relief washed over him when he saw her radiant smile and the pure joy in her eyes.

She's alright!

It was as if it suddenly lifted a heavy burden off his shoulders. The Postner family appeared unharmed by the repercussions he'd feared his escape would cause. He couldn't quite believe it and he was struck with an overwhelming sense of surprise and gratitude.

Never had he been so glad to be proven wrong and his heart pounded with a mix of relief and joy. For the first time in months, he found himself sharing Mina's and Senta's carefree smiles and laughter.

After the disappointment of not finding the Brasher Doubloon, this was just the medicine he needed.

He watched, mesmerised, as Mina went about her afternoon chores of cleaning out the stalls and feeding the animals. He fixated on her, his eyes never leaving her.

Hidden among the hay, he mulled over how to attract her attention without raising alarm. *Could the Nazis have seized the farm? Were they in control of it?*

The presence of the swastika flag fluttering over the farmhouse seemed to suggest as much and he knew he needed to be cautious, no matter how much he wanted to call out her name.

Something was different, and he had to know what it was before he could reveal himself to her. He lay, pondering different ways of how he could reach out to her when her voice reached up from underneath the hayloft. His jaw tightened, and he almost swallowed his tongue when he heard her. It was the voice of an angel.

"We're nearly done here, Senta," she said, bending down to pick up a few loose eggs the chickens had laid. "Why don't you take these to the house before they get broken? I'll fill up the water trough and I'll be there in a minute."

Senta agreed, taking the eggs from her sister. From his vantage point in the loft, Michael swore that if Senta was a couple of years older, they'd be twins.

He watched from under the hay as Senta left the barn, leaving Mina all alone beneath him. This was his moment. Taking a deep breath, he sat up and said hoarsely, "Mina."

He wanted to say so much more, but he couldn't find

the words. Mina stood still, her back to him. He noticed her body go stiff, then slowly she started to turn around.

"Mina," he said softly, "It's me, Michael. Don't be afraid."

She turned around, and the surprised look on her face was something Michael would never forget. He knew he was the last person she was expecting to see and yet, her surprise seemed to be a happy one.

"Michael? Is it really you?"

"Yes," he said, climbing down the ladder.

"Mina," he half whispered, half sobbed as she ran towards him.

Michael spread his arms and closed his eyes as they embraced. Every feeling he had for her exploded right there, in the middle of the barn, and for a brief moment, it felt like time stood still.

"Mina. I've missed you so much."

Mina quietly wept and then pulled back to look into his eyes. "Michael, I can't believe it's really you. Why are you here?"

"I came to Germany for other reasons," he explained. "But there was no way I could be here and not see you. I was scared for you, Mina. I thought the Nazis might have hurt you and your family after everything that happened."

Mina pinched his arm to make sure he was real. She shook her head from side to side.

"So, what happened?" he asked. "Did they believe your story?"

"I don't like talking about it," she replied. "But yes, Alwin's father, Dieter Lutz, was furious when he found out, and he sent the entire army after you. We were sure they were going to kill you and I listened to the radio and read the newspapers every day. All they talked about was the

British spy who was running away through the Black Forest."

She hit his chest with her hands. "But you did it, Michael, you escaped."

Michael smiled. "So, what happened next? Why is the swastika flying on the farmhouse?"

"There was an inquiry led by Dieter Lutz. At first, he didn't believe us, and he wanted the Gestapo to arrest my father. But after we showed them where you'd been hiding, and how you'd been taking the eggs and chickens, he changed his mind."

Michael clasped her hand, enjoying how it felt in his hands.

"I cried and showed great remorse for Alwin. I told Herr Lutz how much I was going to miss him and that we had discussed maybe having a future together."

Michael scowled and he could see her enjoying the jealousy stamped all over his face.

"I lied, of course, but he believed me."

"You'd better have been," Michael said playfully.

"My father told him we'd heard a gunshot from the barn, and when we ran down here, we found Alwin lying dead in the middle of it."

"You still haven't told me how the swastika came to be flying on the farmhouse."

"I'm getting to that. Everyone believed the British spy had killed Alwin, so Dieter Lutz and the Nazis turned their attention to the Black Forest, which is where they presumed you'd gone."

"Correctly, of course," she added.

"So, how—?"

Mina placed her fingers over Michael's mouth to shush him, and the sensation of her fingers touching his lips sent uncontrollable sensations running down his spine.

"Dieter Lutz is the leader of the Nazi Party in this region and in return for being model citizens, he gave us first access to fuel and other essential farming supplies. We've never done so well, Michael, and it's all because of you."

Her eyes clouded and she looked towards the ground.

"Then why do you look so sad?"

"Because none of it ever happened. At least not in the way the Nazis believe it did. I killed Alwin and I have nightmares almost every night. I'll never forgive myself, even though I know that what I did was the right thing."

Michael cradled her hand. "I know exactly how you feel and, trust me, the nightmares won't ever go away. All you can do is tell yourself that you did the right thing, and over time, hopefully, they'll fade."

"There's something else." Mina looked up at Michael, and he could see the pain in her features.

"After it calmed down, Alwin's brother, Karl, started showing up at the farm on the pretext that he was making sure we weren't being persecuted by the resistance."

Michael held her gaze and shared her pain.

"I kept telling him we were fine but he wouldn't listen. His father made sure that as model citizens, we needed to fly that stupid flag from the farmhouse, and he put it up there himself. We daren't take it down."

"I understand. There's no telling what he'd do if you did."

"Karl is in the SS and they scare me. They scare everyone."

"Quite right too. They scare me as well."

"He made advances to Senta." Mina's eyes filled with tears.

"He did what?" Anger rose in Michael's chest. "I hope your father stopped him, SS or not."

"Father never knew. I stopped him." Tears tumbled down her face.

"What did you do?" Michael's body tensed.

"He threatened our family, Michael..." Mina's voice broke, tears streaming down her face. "And I... I had to protect them."

"What did you do?" Michael asked again gently.

"I allowed his advances on me. I made him promise to leave my family, especially Senta, alone, if I didn't resist him."

She sobbed on Michael's shoulder. "I'm sorry, Michael. I'm so sorry."

Michael's breath caught in his chest. Blood boiled inside his body and yet his heart yearned to comfort her.

He held her tight, sharing her grief and shame. "It's not your fault, Mina, so don't blame yourself. You love your family and he knew you'd do anything to protect them. This is all him, not you."

Mina sobbed.

"He'll pay for what he's done." Michael's face turned deep red. "If it's the last thing I ever do, he will pay."

"I won't blame you if you don't want me anymore," she said between sobs.

"Mina," Michael's voice cracked, pulling her close. "Karl's a monster. I love you more than anything in this world."

"You forgive me?" she asked.

"Of course I do, silly." Michael pulled back and wiped the tears from her face. "If anything, it makes me love you even more. The war hasn't even started yet and all I want is for it to be over so we can be together."

They shared a moment's silence.

"Do what you need to do to keep yourself and your family safe. This will be over soon and Karl Lutz will pay. I promise you that. He will pay, Mina."

Michael had never meant a spoken word more than he did at this moment.

"He'll be here soon and I have to go."

"I need to leave too. If I see him, I might not be able to control myself."

They kissed one more time and as she was closing the barn door behind herself, she halted. The sound of an approaching motor vehicle disturbed the peacefulness and they both knew it could only be one person.

"He's here," she said, visibly stunned.

"Go, Mina. I'll get out of here as soon as the coast is clear."

She looked at him one more time before leaving the barn.

"Karl," Michael heard her through the half-open wooden doors. He fought the urge to race out and confront the young Nazi. Instead, he climbed back up the ladder and waited for an opportunity to leave.

Chapter Thirty-Seven

Late afternoon shadows wrapped themselves around Mina, casting her shadow deep into the barn. Michael found a position on the edge of the hayloft where he could watch what was happening and remain hidden.

"Mina, it's so good to see you again."

Michael watched, his body breaking into a hot flush as a young man in his early twenties came into view and swept Mina into his arms. His sweaty fists clenched when he saw him kiss Mina on the lips, and it took everything he had not to reveal himself and beat the living daylights out of him.

The young man was tall, athletic, and had short cropped blond hair – a perfect Nazi, Michael mused to himself. His features looked strikingly familiar, and Michael was sure he'd seen him before somewhere, though for the life of him, he couldn't remember where.

Don't be stupid. I couldn't possibly have seen him before.

"Let me help you," Karl said.

"I'm finished in there," Mina steered Karl away from the barn. She threw a final glance towards the hayloft before linking arms with Karl and steering him towards the farmhouse.

"How is Munich?" she asked, obviously distracting Karl from the barn.

Michael cringed and ground his teeth as he heard them laughing and giggling, their voices fading as they walked away from him.

He lay in the hay, fighting his inner jealousy until well after dark. He wasn't sure what to do as he was torn between waiting to see Mina again and getting out of the way before Karl discovered him.

If that happened, it would be a disaster. Not only for him and Mina's family, but for Gustav Adler, the British government, and possibly even the fate of Europe itself. His life wouldn't be worth living if the Nazis discovered him hiding in Mina's barn.

His insides were tearing him apart. Half of him relished the memory of Mina rushing to him, the smell of her fragrance, and the way she kissed him.

But the other half was full of pure envy and resentment. The image of Karl kissing her replayed over and over in his mind, driving his tortured mind crazy. He'd never met Karl before, but right now, he despised him more than anybody else on the planet.

After what seemed like hours, the sound of a vehicle's engine roaring to life dragged Michael from his dark thoughts.

He's leaving. Finally.

As darkness descended, he lay still, hidden under the hay, and he felt a weight lift from his shoulders as he heard the vehicle moving farther and farther away.

Now what do I do? Do I leave now while I have the chance? Or do I risk staying to see Mina one more time?

He'd just about decided to leave when he heard footsteps scurrying towards the barn.

"Michael," Mina hissed in the darkness, "Are you still here?"

"Yes."

"Come down here."

Michael did as he was told and was greeted by Mina carrying a plate of food. She smiled and even in the half-darkness, his heart melted.

"My father doesn't know you're here, so hurry and eat this. Michael, it's so good to see you."

"How do you put up with him?" Michael asked, jealousy rearing its head again.

Mina pulled a face. "I go along with it for the sake of Senta and my family. He's in the SS, Michael, and they can wreak so much harm if they so desire. He took advantage of us after Alwin's death and I don't want to make it any more difficult for my father than I already have. So, I go along with it. I hate him."

"I understand," Michael lied.

"No, you don't," she said. "You're the one I love, Michael. Please remember that."

Michael reached out to her and trembled as he placed his arms around her. "I have to leave soon, Mina, and I don't know when I'll see you again, but just know that I love you and I will be back for you."

"There's something else I want to tell you," Mina said, guiding Michael to a corner of the barn where it was dark, away from the door.

"What is it? Please don't tell me you're marrying Karl."

"No!" she exclaimed. "I'd rather die than let that happen. Fortunately, he's leaving in the morning to report back for duty in Munich."

"So, what is it then?"

"After you left, and we realised we weren't going to be punished for Alwin's death, we all, every one of us, felt ashamed for not standing up to the Nazis."

"But you couldn't," Michael replied. "Anyone that lifts a finger against them ends up arrested by the Gestapo. And you all know what happens if they get involved. You couldn't do anything, Mina."

"But we could," Mina replied. "We stood by and did nothing when my best friend Anna and her father had their store in Glatten smashed and taken from them. Luckily, they escaped to Belgium, but what about all the others? We know people who have just disappeared and we've heard rumours of a camp in Dachau where they're taking the Jews. What's happening to them? Nobody knows. And yet we stood by and did nothing."

"There's nothing you can do," Michael said.

"But there is," Mina replied firmly. "You showed us the way. You, an Englishman, showed more bravery than we ever did, and we felt ashamed. After you'd gone and the Alwin situation died down, we got together as a family and decided we had to do something."

"What did you do?" Michael asked, taking Mina's hand in his. He stroked it gently, enjoying the shock waves it sent through his body.

"We got together with some other people we know who despise the Nazis as much as we do. Together, we formed a group that helps Jews escape Germany. So far, we've helped over a dozen families get out of Germany."

"Blimey." Michael's head snapped back in surprise. "How? You need to be careful because they'll kill you if they find out."

"We know," Mina said, "And it's got close sometimes,

especially as Karl rarely announces his visits. Sometimes we have Jews hiding when he comes here. He's almost caught us a few times."

"So, how do you do it?" Michael asked again.

"Other families help the Jews from all over the country, and some of them end up here in Ryskamp for a few days while we make arrangements to smuggle them over the border."

"That's brave."

"My father created a safe space at the farm where they can hide for a few days while we make the arrangements. Someone else comes to take them over the border. We don't know where or how, and that's a good thing, because the less we know, the safer it is for everybody."

Michael held her hand, feeling an even stronger pull towards her. "You are a brave girl, Mina. All of you are, but especially you. Not only are you helping Jews escape, but you also have to deal with Karl."

Mina gazed into Michael's eyes. "That's another reason I'm doing it. It's my way of getting back at Karl and his father for what they've done to us. We are doing something, Michael. Not every German is sitting back, watching the Nazis destroy our world."

"I'm so proud of you," Michael said. "You're doing a wonderful thing. But please be careful, Mina. I've already lost my brother and I couldn't stand the thought of losing you too."

"It was you who gave us the idea." Mina brushed his face with her hand. "It was you that came all the way to Germany to rescue your family from the Nazis. And even though you failed, at least you tried. Saving Jewish lives is the least we can do, at least until Hitler is stopped."

"I don't know when that's going to be," Michael said, trembling at her touch. "The war is coming, and it's close."

"I know," Mina said, "I'm frightened. We're all frightened. Hitler is going to kill us all."

"I'm going to have to fight against Germany," Michael said softly. "But this will end and, God willing, we will prevail and defeat the Nazis. I don't know how long it will take but I promise you this: As long as I have breath in my body, I will fight, not only for my country and the freedom of the world, but also for you, for your freedom, and your family's freedom."

"I love you, Michael."

"I love you too, Mina."

"I'll wait for you." Her voice broke. Michael gently wiped her eyes with his hands and then held her tight.

"Please do," he said, "Because I promise that as long as I'm alive, I'm coming back for you."

They kissed passionately one last time. And then Michael was gone.

Chapter Thirty-Eight

For the second night running, Michael spent the night on the back seat of the Opel. This time, he hid in the trees on the edge of the Black Forest a mile or so away from Ryskamp.

Sleep was hard to come by, and all he could think of was Karl forcing himself onto Mina. His blood boiled and on more than one occasion, he had to stop himself from marching to Lutz's house and confronting him.

He was glad when the sun rose so he could see well enough to drive without headlights. He consoled himself on the long drive back to Munich with memories of Mina, and how her touch turned him into a giddy mess.

As much as he wanted to destroy Karl Lutz, he'd already caused plenty of strife to his family by killing, at least in their minds, Alwin. He hoped that by the end of the coming hostilities, Karl and the rest of his SS brethren were dead.

The drive back to Munich was uneventful, the roads to the city quiet. Michael was grateful that, for once, he didn't run into any roadblocks.

Apart from when he was driving through towns, the only vehicles he'd seen had been military ones. A few of the bathtub-type vehicles that had caused him so many nightmares the previous winter passed in the opposite direction and their appearance turned him cold, momentarily taking his mind away from Mina and Karl.

It was late afternoon by the time he rolled into Munich. Upon entering the ground floor of the house Mother rented, he found her waiting for him in the small sitting area. She raised her eyebrows when he walked in.

"Did you have a good time?" she asked.

"A good time?" Michael asked.

"Where did you go?"

"I thought we'd agreed to ask no questions, tell no lies." Michael felt uncomfortable.

Does she know I've been somewhere I wasn't supposed to be? Does she know I've taken precious time away from the vital tasks that lie ahead of us?

"We did. I'm just making sure you're all right."

"I'm perfectly fine," Michael replied gruffly.

He went to his room and closed the door. The last thing he needed right now were questions about where he'd been. He was relieved that David's grave had been intact, and he'd carry the memories of Mina's soft touch with him for the rest of his life. But the rest of it had been a disaster.

He'd failed to find the doubloon that would have saved his family from economic ruin, and he'd witnessed the pain on Mina's face as Karl Lutz had forced his way into her life.

The hardest thing was knowing there was nothing he could do about it. The SS were notorious and were feared everywhere they went. Even though it pained him to admit it, Mina was doing the right thing to preserve both her and her family's safety. He tore his mind away from his dark thoughts and turned his attention to the important tasks that lay ahead.

Getting Adler safely out of Germany was his only priority and from now on, he would give it his full focus.

The next morning, Michael checked the drop location in the wall of the English Gardens. He was relieved to find it empty, which meant that the operation was still on.

In the afternoon, he went to the Frauenkirche and checked the secret DLB belonging to the SIS. It, too, was empty, meaning there were no last-minute instructions for him to follow.

He spent the evening having a quiet dinner with Mother. As the clock ticked, she locked eyes with him and grasped his hand over the table.

"Don't ask how, but I know what you must do tomorrow. So please be careful and keep your focus on what's important. The SS and the Gestapo are ruthless and they will torture you beyond recognition if they catch you. We will not meet again after this evening, but I wish you all the best for the future. I hope that when the war comes, and it is coming, I hope the Allies defeat the Nazis, and bring peace back to my country," she said.

"Thank you," Michael closed his eyes. "I know what's at stake and I won't let you or anybody else down."

He opened his eyes and stared at the brave middle-aged resistance fighter sitting across from him.

"You need to be careful as well. I doubt the Gestapo would treat you any differently just because you're a woman. In fact, I know they won't because I saw what they did first-hand to our female friends last year. I hope our paths cross again, but if not, I hope you survive the coming war and can return to the life you had before."

Mother snorted.

Chapter Thirty-Nine

Time seemed to stand still. The clock on the wall moved so slowly that Michael was convinced it was broken. He played the coming events over and over in his mind, making sure he knew the outcome of every possible scenario.

His biggest hope was that he'd meet Adler and his family at the designated place and that everything would go smoothly. He'd been on tenterhooks ever since he'd taken the mission and he couldn't wait to be safely over the border where he could hand him over to someone else.

Late in the evening, he was surprised when Mother knocked on his door and entered, carrying a package in her hand. "This is for you," she said, holding it out to him. "It's something we use here in Germany when we don't want things to be found and I thought it might be useful for you on this mission."

"What is it?" Michael asked.

"Look and see."

Michael took the package from her and discovered a

new black rucksack similar to the one he already owned. "What's this for?" he asked. "I already have one."

"Not one like that, you don't," she replied.

"What do you mean?" he asked.

"Let me show you."

Mother spent the next ten minutes showing him three secret compartments hidden in the rucksack. It had a false bottom and two secret pockets built into the walls.

"These will be difficult for anyone to find other than a trained agent searching for such things. It's useful for storing identification papers or anything that you don't want prying eyes to see, should you be stopped and searched," she explained.

"Thank you," Michael said.

He emptied the contents of his regular rucksack onto the bed and sorted through them. He took the emergency set of false papers he'd recovered from the SIS drop at Frauenkirche and hid them in one of the side compartments. The rest he left for later, should he need it.

When he was alone again, Michael lay back on the bed and rested his eyes.

Who knows when I'll get to sleep again?

And yet, try as he may, sleep wouldn't come. Every little detail replayed over and over in his mind as he tried to find a solution to every scenario he might face in the coming days.

One thing that kept cropping up was how Mother knew about his mission. As far as he was aware, she hadn't been told anything, so how did she know? Was she bluffing? If so, why?

He trusted her and not for a moment did he suspect her of being a Nazi spy, but it bothered him all the same.

As the minutes ticked by, Michael felt the tension rising in the pit of his stomach. He struggled to remain calm, his mind never far from the fear of capture. He was under no illusions about what he was about to undertake; it was the most dangerous thing he'd ever done.

Escaping through the Black Forest was one thing, but helping a senior member of the Sicherheitsdienst escape the clutches of the SS was a whole different ball game and it was one that could, and most likely would, end in his own painful demise.

As evening approached, he went back into the kitchen and sat across the table from Mother in total silence, his face pale and gaunt. Finally, with the clock ticking past eight thirty, he spoke.

"It's time."

Mother nodded and without uttering another word, she rose from her chair and headed for the door.

Michael grabbed his new rucksack and triple-checked everything for the thousandth time. He took one last look around the house and followed Mother out of the door.

He was ready.

The twenty-minute drive towards the drop-off point was taken in silence, the understanding between them unspoken and yet somehow necessary.

Michael directed Mother to drop him off half a mile from the meeting point, on the opposite side of the railway tracks. The very real possibility that he was being lured into a trap was foremost in his mind and he needed to make visual contact with the area before advancing.

If it was a trap, the Gestapo wouldn't be looking for them there and Mother could drive away unnoticed. After she stopped, Michael reached over and kissed her gently on her cheek.

"Thank you, Mother. Thank you for everything. I hope we meet again but if not, I will never forget you."

Mother squeezed his hand and wished him good luck. Michael closed the door softly so as not to make any noise. Then he waited in a bush until Mother's taillights disappeared from view.

Suddenly, feeling very alone and isolated, Michael doubted himself and his ability to complete the task at hand.

Stop it! I did this before and that was with no training. At least this time I know what I'm letting myself in for.

He waited ten more minutes until he was sure Mother had left the area. Then he made his way over the fields towards the railway tracks and the rendezvous point with Gustav Adler.

Several rail cars stood between Michael and the meet zone and he found a decent spot underneath one of them while he got a good look at the surrounding area.

He was still early, and after watching for fifteen minutes, he made his move. Crossing the tracks, he crouched low and ran swiftly towards the safety of the vegetation on the opposite side.

After another extended period where he watched and listened, he dashed through the short, lightly wooded area, where he reached a road.

He crouched behind a tree close to the road, and for the first time, he got a clear view of Docenstrasse and the cul-de-sac where he would meet Adler in less than an hour.

He patiently watched for a long time, glad of the training he'd received at Bletchley Park. He listened for any unusual sounds and for any parked vehicles that looked out of place.

Nothing seemed out of the ordinary, so with less than ten minutes remaining, and with his blood pressure rising, he ran across the street to a small, wooded area facing the cul-de-sac.

He now had a clear view of the entire meet zone. If anything was going to go down, this was where it would happen.

At precisely 10 pm, a set of headlights turned off the main street onto Docenstrasse. Michael held his breath, his gut doing somersaults as he watched the approaching vehicle turn into the cul-de-sac. The vehicle turned around, reversed into the rear right corner, and killed the headlights. The engine followed immediately after, and everything fell silent.

Michael watched and waited, looking for any sign of enemy activity. When there wasn't any, he closed his eyes, looked up to the heavens, and said a silent prayer.

He left the cover of the trees and crossed the short field. Skirting around the opposite side of the cul-de-sac, he approached the vehicle from behind a set of trees that hid him from view.

A few minutes later, he made his move. Emerging from the trees, he rapped on the driver's window with the flat of his hand so as not to make much noise. His pistol was in his hand, raised and ready to use.

The driver slowly wound down the window and Michael shone his flashlight directly into his eyes, blinding him, and giving him no chance to see his face.

He'd studied the photograph of Adler so many times that he knew every line and crease of his face. If this man was SS Oberführer Gustav Adler, he would know it.

It was.

"You're younger than I expected," Adler spoke in perfect English.

"You're older than I expected," Michael replied in perfect German.

Without another word, Adler slid out of the vehicle and

got in again on the passenger side. Michael climbed into the driver's seat and took a deep breath. Then he gunned the engine.

"We pick up my wife and nephew in Ingolstadt. I'll tell you where to go when we get there," Adler instructed.

"Ingolstadt?"

"It's north of here. It might be out of your way, but that's where they are, and that's where we're going to meet them."

This man's used to giving orders.

"Ingolstadt, it is then."

Not wanting to hang around, he stole a glance at the map. He knew the route to Venlo like the back of his hand and he knew exactly where Ingolstadt was. It was directly on the way to Venlo.

"Move," Adler ordered.

Chapter Forty

The drive out of Munich was done in complete silence, both men lost in their thoughts. Adler stared out of the passenger window, while Michael concentrated on the road and their surroundings.

Although he knew this was a pivotal moment in the early days of the approaching war, Michael hadn't realised how jittery he would feel in the presence of the senior SS intelligence officer. Who knew what evil deeds Adler had done in the name of the SD?

At the thought of the SS, Michael's attention turned to Karl Lutz and his advances towards Mina and Senta. He gripped the steering wheel tightly, making the whites of his knuckles stand out in the darkness.

The city lights faded, and the concrete fell away. Adler finally turned and faced the front. Michael noticed he was carrying a large briefcase, which he gripped tightly and held close to his chest.

Whatever was in there, Michael knew it was of great importance to both SIS and the Nazis. That, and the fact that a senior SD Officer had never before defected, was the reason Adler was being given the red-carpet treatment in his planned defection.

"You seem very young for such a responsible task." Adler finally broke the tense atmosphere.

"I'm sorry if my age bothers you," Michael answered. "But I assure you, I'm the best they have available at this moment in time."

He refused to address Adler by his Nazi rank, SS Ober-führer. In fact, he'd decided he wouldn't show him any respect at all. Not after what he'd seen the Gestapo and the SS do.

As far as he was concerned, the SS and the SD were enemies that needed defeating, and none of them, not even those who were defecting, deserved any respect.

"I know many brave young men who are suited to positions that defy their years," Adler said. "But I doubt any of them would be chosen for something as important as my defection."

Important to you or the British?

Michael knew the answer, but he couldn't bring himself to admit it.

Forty-five minutes into their journey, Adler spoke again.

"I know who you are. I recognise your face."

"Good for you," Michael said. "Many people in Germany know who I am. And if they knew I was here, it's likely that I'd be in more danger than you are right now."

"That's doubtful, but I get your point," Adler said. "You're Michael Fernsby, aren't you?"

"You can call me Gertrude," he replied.

Adler smirked.

"It seems I underestimated you, Fernsby. What you pulled off last winter was nothing less than miraculous. Heydrich himself was fuming over your escape."

"He'd be fuming even more if he knew I was back in Germany."

"Did you know he placed one of our top Gestapo commanders in charge of your capture?" Adler asked.

"I suppose I should be honoured," Michael answered.

"His name is Albert Kreise, and he should not be underestimated. If he even gets a whiff of you being in Germany again, he won't rest until he's detained you. It's become a personal mission of his to make sure you never set foot in Germany again."

"It looks like he failed," Michael said.

For some reason, this man rubbed him up the wrong way. He seemed decent enough, but then Michael knew better.

The two men fell quiet, and about fifteen minutes later, Adler broke the silence.

"We will shortly approach the River Danube. That's our indicator that we're entering Ingolstadt. We're heading for St Moritz Church, and I'll give you directions after we cross the river."

"We're picking up your wife and stepson?"

"Yes," Adler said. "I suppose you've read my file, and know why I'm defecting?"

Michael nodded. "I know the official story but that doesn't mean it's the truth, does it?" he asked in an accusatory tone.

"I don't blame you for being sceptical. I suspect everyone I meet for the foreseeable future will have good reason to be dubious. After all, nobody in the SD has ever defected before. I'm the first, and although it will be a good coup for the British, the Nazis will be beside themselves with anger and fear over what I may reveal."

"The Nazis?" Michael asked. "I'm sorry, Oberführer

Adler, but let's not mince our words here. You're a Nazi too, are you not?"

"I understand why you don't like the SS," Adler said. "I've read your file and I know why you came here last November. Your great-grandfather and your uncle were taken to Dachau on Kristallnacht, and you came here to rescue them. You were too late and you probably still don't know what became of them."

Michael remained silent. Something told him this man knew the fate of his family.

"I don't know what happened to them if that's what you're thinking," Adler said. "All I know is they were taken to Dachau. What happens there never reaches my desk. And with the concentration camps, I make it my business for it not to be my business."

Michael scowled. He didn't believe him, but there was no point arguing about it.

"The Nazi hierarchy favours certain doctors," Adler continued, almost to himself. "They strongly believe in the eugenics programme. Do you know what that is, Michael?"

Michael nodded. "Unfortunately, I do, and it's disgusting."

"I agree," Adler said. "And I have a personal interest in this area because my nephew, who I've taken care of since he was a young boy, has cerebral palsy. I know the doctors would kill him if they knew where he was. I'm doing this for him, not for myself, and certainly not because I hate Germany."

Michael said nothing, but on that one point, he didn't blame him.

"All you have to do is get us over the border," Adler said. "Where are you taking us?"

"I'm not at liberty to say," Michael replied. "You'll see

when you get there."

They crossed the Danube in silence. As they approached the other side, the looming shadows of a road-block materialised in the dim light. Instinctively, Michael slowed the car, his grip tightening around the steering wheel.

He looked to Adler for guidance. Adler's face didn't show the faintest hint of concern. He pulled out his ID, holding it in his hand, ready.

"Drive slowly, but don't stop until they ask you to," Adler said, his voice suddenly cold.

A pair of guards stepped into the light, their uniforms sharply contrasting against the dark night. One of them, a young man, probably in his early twenties, gestured for them to halt.

Michael stopped the car, his heart pounding. The young guard peered into the car, first at Michael and then at Adler. His gaze lingered suspiciously on Michael for a moment longer than was comfortable. Michael resisted the urge to shift under his scrutiny.

Without a word, Adler handed over his ID through the window. The guard took it hesitantly, inspecting it under the dim glow of a nearby lantern. His brow furrowed. He looked at Adler, then back at the ID, cross-referencing every detail.

From a nearby post, another guard, older and with a more imposing stature, called out, "What's the holdup?"

The younger guard turned and held up Adler's ID for him to see. The older guard approached and the two exchanged a few whispered words. Michael couldn't make out what they were saying, but he felt a knot form in his stomach. What if they were recognised? Or worse, detained?

After what felt like an eternity but was probably only a minute, the older guard handed the ID back to Adler, nodding curtly. "My apologies, Oberführer," he said, with a note of reverence in his voice.

The younger guard, now looking slightly embarrassed, quickly stepped back, signalling for them to proceed. "Safe travels, sir," he muttered.

As they drove away, Michael let out the breath he hadn't realised he was holding. Adler leaned back, smug satisfaction on his face.

"That was close," Michael whispered.

Adler gave Michael turn-by-turn directions until he told him to stop outside an old church that, like others he'd seen in southern Germany, had two distinct towers. Even though it was dark, he could make out the fact that they were large and shaped differently. One had a spiked tower, and the other had what looked, in the night sky, like a dome on top.

Michael loved old buildings, and in better times, he would have loved to explore this old church. As it was, he stayed in the car and waited while Adler got out and went inside.

A few minutes later, he came out with a woman, who looked at least a decade younger than him, and a young boy who limped and whose hands seemed deformed.

Michael immediately felt sorry for the young man and his resolve to get them to safety intensified.

How can the Nazis justify hurting innocent young boys and girls like this?

His heart ached, and he wanted to reach out to reassure the boy. But he remained silent and waited for the two new passengers to get into the rear seats.

Michael drove out of Ingolstadt and headed towards the Dutch border.

Chapter Forty-One

The atmosphere was tense as they turned left and right along the streets of Ingolstadt. Adler kept a lookout to see if they'd been followed. His wife and nephew sat huddled together in the back seat, silent and afraid.

Michael gripped the steering wheel tightly, the whites of his knuckles showing as he steered the vehicle, following the directions barked at him by Adler. Finally, the tension lifted as they cleared the town.

"Did anybody see you?" Adler turned to his wife.

"No," she said.

"Did you take the precautions, like I said?" he asked.

"Yes, we went over it a dozen times or more," she replied. "We did exactly what you told us to do."

"And you didn't tell anybody where we were going?"

"No." She shook her head. "And I'll never forgive you for that. My mother and sister are going to be worried sick, wondering what's happened to us."

"Maria, you just stayed with her for a week," Adler snapped.

"And I hated every minute," Maria Adler replied. "Do

you know how hard it was? Being with them, knowing that I would never see them again? And I couldn't tell them anything."

"You'll see each other when the war is over," Adler said.

He turned to the boy, who sat clinging to Maria. "How are you, young Heinrich?"

"I'm scared," the boy said, slurring his words as he spoke. "Where are we going?"

"We're going somewhere safe," Adler said. "Somewhere where the doctors won't harm you."

Michael's heart broke at the thought of all the children who needed help but weren't as lucky as Heinrich Adler.

Adler noticeably relaxed as the towns fell away. Even Michael, who had been more worried than he dared let on when they picked up the two passengers, thought they might have a chance.

It was a long drive to Venlo, around three hundred and sixty miles by Michael's reckoning. And even with no road-blocks or problems the Nazis may cause, it would take them several hours to get there. Nobody could relax until they crossed into Holland.

Twenty minutes into their journey, they approached a sign for a town called Stammham. Everything seemed to go smoothly and the roads were quiet and empty of traffic.

Michael came to a stop at a crossroads. He checked left and right. All was clear, so he pulled forward.

Then all hell broke loose.

Chaos reigned as headlights suddenly came at them from all four directions. Blinded, Michael instinctively went for the brakes.

"Drive!" Adler ordered. "It's a trap."

Michael's training and survival instincts kicked in and he floored the accelerator pedal. He picked up speed rapidly, and he sped past the two vehicles on either side of the road facing him.

Two more vehicles gave pursuit from behind, and Michael jammed his foot as far to the floor as it would go.

Heinrich whimpered in the backseat and Michael felt incredibly sorry for him as he heard Adler's wife comforting him and telling him that everything would be all right.

Michael thought he might just get away from them when he approached a junction with another minor road. More vehicles turned on their headlights, and several men ran onto the road with weapons raised.

Michael veered to the right, knocking one man into the air like a rag doll. There was no time for sympathy, and even if there were, he wouldn't have any. These men were likely Gestapo and he knew exactly what they'd do to him if they caught him.

He left the road and sped around a vehicle that was trying to cut them off. Adler's heavy Mercedes was at an angle, and for a moment Michael thought it might tip over.

He corrected it and got around one car before another rammed the rear driver's-side wheel just past the junction. The Mercedes spun around until it faced the way it had just driven.

Shouts came from several men racing towards them. They were less than five hundred yards away, and Michael knew they were doomed.

"They knew we were coming," Adler said. "Someone betrayed us."

"Here, take this." Adler threw the briefcase at Michael. "It contains everything the British need to know about what's going on over here. There's a map in the rear pouch that directs you to a hidden vehicle in Ingolstadt. Take it and get out of here."

Michael went to put the Mercedes back in gear and drive towards the onrushing armed men.

"No!" Adler roared. "They'll kill us all. It's over. Now go, while you still can. Run!"

"What about you?" Michael asked, getting ready to jump out of the vehicle.

"I'm not leaving him." Adler nodded his head towards Heinrich, who sobbed uncontrollably in the back seat.

"He can come with us," Michael pleaded, but Adler cut him off.

"You know he can't. Get out of here and help the Allies end this ungodly regime."

Michael threw one last sorrowful look at Heinrich and dropped to the ground outside the Mercedes.

"What did we do?" he heard Heinrich whimper from the back seat.

"You two stay in the vehicle," Adler ordered. "You've done nothing wrong and are just following my orders. I'll make a deal with them to keep you safe."

Michael half crawled, half knelt as he dived into the bushes at the side of the road. He pulled the Walther PPK from his pocket and turned to face the enemy.

Adler threw open the passenger door and stood in the middle of the road, his arms in the air.

A loud voice screamed out from a vehicle that sped past the running men, who were almost at the Mercedes. "You are surrounded. Stop where you are and get on the ground. Spread your hands and legs and don't move."

Michael pulled the briefcase into his body and rolled onto his stomach. Holding the PPK in front of him, he held his breath and waited. He'd be cut down if he ran, so there was no other option.

Fight or die.

Six men swarmed around Adler, three of them laying the boot to his face and ribs, screaming at him, calling him a traitor. Two others headed towards the bushes where Michael lay. One man stood off to the side, carefully watching everything as it unfolded.

The two men crashed through the bushes. Michael waited, an easy target for anyone who found him.

Kill or be killed!

He fired off four rounds, two double taps into each man. They fell, mere feet from where he lay.

Michael instantly spun around and faced the road. Hearing the shouts of the other agents, probably Gestapo, he rapidly reloaded, silently thanking himself for taking his weapons training seriously.

Two more Gestapo agents ran towards their fallen comrades and both times, Michael dropped them with double taps. That left just two more. One who had stayed with the stricken Adler, and the other, the man who seemed in charge, who stood watching.

"Kreise," the man next to Adler shouted. "Do you want me to go after him?"

"No. Get Adler and the passengers and take them back to Munich. Whoever that is, he won't get far. This area will be swarming with men soon and there's nowhere for him to hide," the leader ordered.

Kreise! That was the man Adler had spoken about on their drive from Munich. His voice was the one he'd heard over the radio, spreading the news of his untimely death.

Kreise! Was he here for me or Adler? Or both of us?

The wail of approaching sirens cut through the silence, and the sound of vehicles approaching at speed got louder as they closed in on the grizzly scene.

With the two remaining Gestapo men distracted,

Michael had one last look through the bushes at Adler, who was on his feet and in handcuffs. Heinrich and Maria stood next to him, also in handcuffs.

"Doctor Halmer will be delighted to meet you," Kreise sneered at Heinrich. "He's particularly interested in... unique children like you."

Heinrich sobbed and struggled, resisting for all he was worth. Kreise silenced him with the butt of his weapon.

Michael's heart broke and he made a silent vow to somehow avenge what he'd just witnessed.

He stood and ran into the darkness as a deluge of vehicles clattered down the road towards Adler and his family.

Chapter Forty-Two

Michael ran for his life. He ran for Heinrich's life, and even though he wouldn't admit it, he ran for Adler's life as well. What he had just witnessed wasn't the uncaring image he had of the SS, but that of a doting uncle trying to save his nephew.

Every thud of his heart reverberated with the vision of what he'd just seen, driving his legs to move faster, to not give up.

Clutching the briefcase, he ran through fields and hedges, over country lanes, and around buildings.

Now and again, he'd see sirens on the roads and cars driving slowly, searching for him. He saw a few of the bathtub-looking vehicles with searchlights that had plagued his life near the border with France during his escape the previous winter.

Now, of course, he knew they were Volkswagen Kübelwagen's but he still preferred to call them bathtubs.

Sweat clung to his skin, making his shirt stick to his back, the sultry summer air doing little to cool him. His mouth felt dry and itchy and he needed fluid.

He took a moment to go through his rucksack for the water bottle he knew was in there, and cursed himself when he realised he'd left it on the front seat of Adler's Mercedes.

Even though it slowed him down, he kept off the roads. Mindful of his need for liquid, he kept a lookout for any streams as he ran towards Ingolstadt and the vehicle Adler had secretly left there.

What for? Michael didn't know, but he was glad he had.

He ran through trees and farmyards. Occasionally, an angry farm dog would chase after him and on two occasions he barely escaped over a fence without getting bitten.

Daylight comes early in the summer and Michael didn't have the luxury of darkness for much longer. He wasn't sure how much farther he had to go, as his map was useless in the middle of a dark field.

He estimated the run to Ingolstadt would take around three hours, but by his reckoning, dawn was a lot nearer than Ingolstadt was. Not wanting to be caught out in daylight, he raised his pace and ran faster.

Thirty minutes later, an exhausted Michael stumbled upon a stream and he gulped mouthfuls of the life-giving liquid down his throat. He ducked his head and shoulders into the water to cool off, and when he'd had his fill, he sat under a tree to rest for a few minutes.

Using the red setting on his flashlight, Michael removed the identification papers identifying him as Lars Hohenberg. Then he hid them in one of the empty secret compartments in his rucksack.

Lars Hohenberg was dead.

From now on, he'd be Erich Weber, the man in the identification papers he'd found hidden in the SIS DLB in the Frauenkirche church.

He opened the pouch on the rear of the briefcase and

removed a folded sheet of paper. An address was scribbled on it: 17 Zuccallistrasse.

On the rear of the paper was a rough map, directing its owner on how to get there. Adler had drawn directions using the river as a guide, which was a good thing because it gave Michael a fighting chance of finding it without having to stop to ask someone, which wasn't a good idea in Hitler's Germany.

If he kept going south, sooner or later he'd hit the river. From there, he'd use the rough map and find Zuccallistrasse. He rose to his feet, took one more long drink of water, and set off again in a race against the oncoming dawn.

Sirens, and vehicles of all shapes and sizes sped up and down the roads that he either crossed or followed for a short while.

There was no doubt that the military would be called out and roadblocks would be everywhere. By daybreak, they would lock the entire area down, and not even a mouse would get in or out.

Michael had to assume that Adler would eventually crack and tell Kreise who he was, but he estimated he would have at least twenty-four hours before that happened, if not longer.

The lights of what Michael presumed was Ingolstadt shone in the distance. As the first strands of dawn were breaking in the night sky, Michael knew he was close. There were more cars, more built-up areas, and a lot more chances for him to be captured.

Staying in the shadows as best he could, he navigated around buildings and crossed roads at double speed.

According to Adler's map, Zuccallistrasse was fairly close to the river, so if Michael kept going south, there was no way he could miss it.

Tension inside him rose as he entered the outskirts of town. Both military and civilian vehicles drove slowly up and down the streets and he threw himself to the ground every time he saw them.

In the distance, on the horizon where the sky meets the land, Michael watched it radiate with a soft, subtle glow that foreshadowed the sun's imminent arrival.

He quickened his step until he reached a piece of ground between a road and the river. The map showed a subtle bend, and he realised he was standing in the exact spot shown on the map.

Finally, knowing where he was, he took a deep breath and hurried against the rising tide of daylight, following the map until he found Effnerstrasse, which was clearly marked on Adler's rough map. From there, it was an easy couple of minutes to find Zuccallistrasse and number seventeen.

Michael had expected it to be a residential area, but it wasn't. Instead, it had a few industrial buildings, with number seventeen being one of the smaller ones on the bottom left-hand corner. He reached into the briefcase's pouch and retrieved the key he'd felt earlier, hoping it would unlock the doors.

It was now light enough for anyone to see him, so Michael crouched and ran around to the rear of the building. Instead of a door, this building had an iron grating secured by a padlock and chain.

Behind the iron grate was a blue door, and Michael hoped against hope that Adler's vehicle lay behind it.

With panic rising in the pit of his stomach, he tried the key in the padlock. He breathed a sigh of relief when it turned and the chains fell away.

Now for the door. He stepped forwards a few feet into the covered porch and tried the door.

It opened! It may have squeaked louder than he liked, but it opened.

A small, grimy window allowed the light to stream into the building and he saw he was inside a large, open room. So large, in fact, that it was the only room in the entire building.

On the opposite side to where he stood, which would have been at the front, facing the road, he saw it.

Adler's vehicle! It's here!

Michael backtracked and secured the iron grate with the padlock so anyone searching for him wouldn't be able to walk in without making a noise. Then he barricaded the door from the inside with a tilted chair.

Satisfied he was safe, for now at least, he approached the vehicle to see what Adler had left.

It was another Opel but this time it was a larger sedan and a model Michael had never heard of – the Kapitan.

Adler was smart because this black sedan would blend in with all the other vehicles out there and whoever drove it wouldn't stand out from the crowds.

Michael sat in the driver's seat and looked for the keys. He found them under the seat and when he gunned the engine, it sprang to life with a loud roar that echoed around the empty building.

Relieved, Michael killed the engine and turned his thoughts to what came next.

Every muscle ached, begging him to stop, while his mind swirled with a cacophony of thoughts, making it hard to focus. He was hungry and thirsty, but above all else, he was worried about how he was going to get out of Ingolstadt.

Every road would be locked down by now and there was no way he could get out without being stopped.

A heaviness settled over his eyelids, his thoughts growing murky, each one slipping away before he could grasp it. He couldn't think straight, so he lay on the back seat for a few minutes to rest and clear his head.

Chapter Forty-Three

The sun was high in the sky by the time Michael opened his eyes. He was covered in sweat, and his back stuck to the leather seats.

He flopped out of the Opel and sat on the cooler floor. He was parched, and he needed food.

Rising to his feet, he got a good look at the empty storage building. It was around one hundred feet by forty feet, which wasn't as big as it had looked earlier.

Plenty of space for a vehicle though.

He checked the vehicle for fuel and was happy to see it was full. He was even happier when he found three five-gallon cans in the rear boot space.

There was a sink that had running water in the opposite corner to the Opel, and Michael drank his fill from the tap. Revitalised, he sat on the ground against the car door and considered his options.

Limited, that's what they were.

He went over the ambush and how the Gestapo had caught them by complete surprise.

What happened? How did the Gestapo know we were

there?

All he could think of was that someone close to Adler had betrayed him.

But who?

Unless Adler had set a trap for Kreise to capture Fernsby, there was no way he could be involved in this. Michael had seen how he doted on his nephew, and in any case, when the defection was first set up between Adler and SIS, there was no way Adler, or anyone else, could have known it would be Michael they sent to rescue him. Even SIS wouldn't have known at that early stage of the planning.

So, if it wasn't Adler, then who else could it be? He was an Oberführer in the Sicherheitsdienst. He was an intelligent, well-informed man who wouldn't go around spilling his innermost secrets.

No, Adler didn't set a trap for me.

The only other person Michael could think of was Adler's wife, but why would she turn him in? Was she a staunch Nazi who believed in Hitler so much that she would sacrifice her husband and nephew? That would require total commitment to the cause.

It's possible. Who else could it be? It's that or Kreise is so good that he knew all along what was happening and waited to catch them in the act.

It had to be one of the above scenarios and content that it wasn't him they were after, he turned his attention to how he was going to escape.

His mind wandered from one possibility to the next, but none of them held up to scrutiny. Every scenario he came up with ended with him being captured or dead and neither of those options sounded appealing.

He found himself messing with the handle on the briefcase, his fingers absentmindedly twisting around it as he considered his escape plans.

He stopped and stared at the leather briefcase, suddenly realising he was potentially holding the key that could unlock victory over the Nazis in the coming war.

He tried to push the locking mechanism, but it wouldn't budge. He looked around for something to smash the lock, but couldn't find anything. As a last resort, he fished around in the rear pouch and felt his fingers clamp around another set of keys in a small pocket inside the pouch.

He pulled them out and tried them on the briefcase.

It opened!

Breathless, and with a slight feeling of trepidation, Michael pulled out a thick wad of files. He spread them out on the floor and read the file headers that were written in large, black, bold ink:

Operational Intelligence

Operational Personnel

Policy and Strategy

Eugenics Programme

European Network Contacts

Michael sat back, stunned. He knew he held in his hands information of such vital importance that the Nazis would kill for it. The British would gain an extraordinary insight into the inner workings of the Nazi regime, and it might even give them the upper hand in the coming conflict.

No wonder Dansey wanted to get his hands on Adler.

His eyes drifted towards the folder titled EUGENICS.

Doctor Halmer will be delighted to meet you.

Kreise's brutal comments to Heinrich Adler echoed in

Michael's mind. Halmer! He'd heard that name before but couldn't quite put his finger on who he was.

Then it hit him.

He was Gerda's father-in-law. The man who'd murdered his own grandson because he was deemed defective. He had been and seemingly still was, the chief Nazi doctor responsible for the eugenics programme.

Kreise's taking Heinrich to Halmer so he can kill him!

The reality of the situation struck him like a winter gust, chilling him to the core.

What kind of monster does things like this?

He sat dumbfounded, unable to wrench his mind from what Kreise and Doctor Halmer were about to do to an innocent young boy. He couldn't – no, he wouldn't – allow this inhumanity to happen, even at the risk of losing his own life.

Sanders would be furious, and rightly so. The documents he had in his possession were vital to the war effort but this boy's life meant something. It had meant something to Adler, a senior officer in the SD, and it meant something to Michael, even if he wasn't worthy of such an undertaking.

Sod it. I'll deal with Sanders if I get home. I'd never forgive myself if I ignored this and left the boy to die.

Realisation dawned on Michael. Whatever the reality of the situation in Europe, he, Michael Fernsby, was now at war with Nazi Germany. Even if Britain and her allies had yet to catch up.

He reached for the Eugenics folder and opened it.

Doctor Friedrich Halmer.

Head of Alderauge Medical Eugenics Facility, Abfanggraben, Munich.

Michael read the document, each sentence stabbing at him like a dagger to the heart.

Alderauge was a medical research facility that was supposed to be a burns unit, but in reality, it was the facility where Doctor Death, as Michael now called him, carried out his murderous procedures on innocent young children.

The file contained Halmer's personnel records on where he attended medical school and who his known associates were. He spent most of his time away from Alderauge with another doctor named Ernst Rüdin, who ran the Nazi eugenics programme from Berlin.

Michael retched when he read a document that told how Halmer had murdered his own grandson, Paul Halmer, in 1934, for being defective.

Gerda's son! Here it is in black and white. Proof that Halmer killed Gerda's son because he was handicapped.

Michael's eyes clouded, and for a moment he couldn't see through the mist. *It's all true. It's right here in this file.*

He studied photos of the ageing doctor and committed his image to memory. Then he slammed the file shut and threw it with the other ones back into the briefcase.

He'd seen enough.

Chapter Forty-Four

Michael was starving by the time darkness descended over Ingolstadt. He waited until after midnight before creeping out of his hiding place.

The town was asleep under a canopy of stars, the streets drenched in shadow with only the faint glow of distant lampposts offering respite. Ingolstadt's heartbeat was a soft murmur, occasionally interrupted by the distant bark of a dog or the whistle of the night wind.

He was searching for a shop that sold food. Anything would do, just something to stop his mind from focusing on his stomach.

He kept to the back alleys behind the shops and houses until his nostrils picked up the intoxicating aroma of freshly baked bread. Well, maybe not freshly baked. It might be a day or so old, but the unmistakable smell was like honey to a bee.

The lingering smell invaded his senses, and he followed his nose to the rear of a corner shop. It was almost pitch black, which suited Michael for what he was about to do.

Using the same trick he'd used on the shed in Freising,

Michael took a deep breath, removed his sock, and smashed the window. He replaced his sock and climbed in. The dull thud pierced the quiet night, sending shards of broken glass scattering on the floor inside.

As he carefully climbed through the broken window, the jagged remains of the pane threatened to catch onto his clothes. He landed softly, but the crunch of glass beneath his boots echoed ominously in the shop's silence.

In the dim light filtering through the broken window, he could see a shelf with a few unsold loaves.

Reaching out, he picked one up, its surface slightly hardened by time. The bread felt cold and tough under his fingertips, a testament to its age, but Michael knew that its stale exterior would still protect the softer core inside.

As he grabbed more loaves, he could feel the slight give and crumble of the crust, evoking memories of better days when he had warm, fresh bread to eat.

Every sound, from the rustle of his rucksack as he stuffed the bread inside, to the distant scraping of his feet on the ground, heightened his senses. The soft cooing of pigeons on the roof occasionally interrupted the silence of the shop, reminding him that he was a trespasser in this quiet domain.

Exiting the way he entered, Michael could still feel the gritty residue of the crushed glass on the soles of his shoes. The weight of the loaves in his rucksack brought a tiny sense of victory, but it was overshadowed by the constant prickle of danger nipping at his heels.

He'd snagged five loaves, and although not very good nutritionally, it would tide him over for several days if he rationed it properly.

Long enough to do what I've got to do and get out of here.

He knew that once the break-in was reported, the

Gestapo would connect it with the escaped killer, so he had no other choice.

He had to leave Ingolstadt tonight.

Cringing at the noise the double doors made as he opened them, Michael drove the Opel Kapitan out of the storage building and killed the engine.

He didn't want to leave any trace of where he'd been in case the building belonged to a friend or acquaintance of Adler.

After closing the doors, he gunned the engine, and with his heart in his mouth, he set off on the fifty-mile trek to Munich.

He drove slowly with the headlights turned off and the window wound down. He searched every side road and bend for signs of activity, and if he saw anything, he turned and found an alternate route.

Once he'd cleared the town, he relaxed a little. He kept to the smallest back roads he could find, and he stopped often to get his bearings. The last thing he wanted was to get lost, so he carefully wound his way along country lanes barely wide enough for one vehicle, never mind two.

By lunchtime, he'd passed through several small towns and villages, each one an abject lesson in how to control the fear that rose inside him. He approached the sign for the next town and choked on the piece of bread in his mouth when he saw where he was.

Dachau.

Dachau. The home of the concentration camp where Uncle Frank and Papa Herbert had been taken after Kristallnacht.

Are they still alive?

Michael doubted it and he forced the bile back down

his throat as he thought of all the evil the Nazis were committing on their people.

If they'll do this to their own people, what will they do to the rest of Europe?

He knew they had to be stopped before they burst out from behind their borders and reaped havoc on the world.

Resisting the urge to find the concentration camp, Michael headed towards Munich and the Frauenkirche Church. He had to warn SIS that the mission was compromised and that he was using the emergency papers to get home.

Michael was now in the heart of Munich, which was the seat of Nazi power. He drove carefully so he wouldn't draw any attention and concentrated on his surroundings. He looked at every junction before approaching to make sure it wasn't blocked, and he made sure the road was clear before proceeding.

By early afternoon, he was close enough to Frauenkirche to leave the Opel and reach the church on foot. He parked the car in a safe place where it wouldn't warrant a second look and headed for the church.

His stomach churned when he stepped inside and he spent a long time scanning for anyone that looked out of place. Finally, he sighed and headed for the DLB at the base of the second pillar.

He looked at the letter he'd written one last time and checked it over for accuracy and intent.

Gertrude left me!

It's over. She resisted, but her ex-partner used her nephew against us.

I'm using the emergency method because I fear her ex-partner is going to come after me for trying to get her away from him.

Yours,

Lars Hohenberg

He took the pouch that had contained his emergency papers and slid the note inside, replacing the stone carefully.

His next stop was the English Gardens, although he stopped on the way to pay for a full tank of petrol and four sandwiches.

He parked and made his way to the house he'd shared with Mother on Osterwaldsstrasse. If she was still there, he was going to warn her to get away.

He looked for her vehicle, but it was gone. Next, he walked up to the door of the house and looked around. The door was closed and he had no way of entering. He didn't want to disturb the Nazi upstairs, so he went to the side of the house and looked through the windows.

There was no sign of Mother. He peered into the kitchen and the living area and didn't see anything. Assuming that she'd already left, which is what he'd expected, he turned and headed back to the Opel Kapitan.

He had a date with Doctor Death.

Chapter Forty-Five

Abfanggraben looked to be a narrow road on the outskirts of Munich, around seven miles from the English Gardens. Michael didn't know where the research facility called Alderauge was located, or even what it looked like, but it was somewhere on that road, and he was determined to find it.

Deep anger and resentment burned in his soul as he approached the junction of Hüllgraben and what he thought was Abfanggraben. The lane split into two around a narrow body of water, so Michael took the right-hand fork and slowly drove alongside it.

Then he realised, Abfanggraben was the name of the waterway, not the road! He neither knew nor cared what the lane was called. He just drove down it, trying to find Halmer's house of horrors.

Thick trees obscured his view but he could see the water shimmering in the afternoon sun, so he knew there couldn't be a medical facility there.

A short while later, the body of water stopped, before it continued again a few feet farther on. A narrow road occupied the gap, and even though surrounded by trees, Michael got a good view of what was behind it.

A set of heavy iron gates blocked the lane and barbed wire looped over the top of it. Armed, uniformed men patrolled the grounds, making it almost impossible to break into.

Why would a burns unit be hidden away like this with heavily armed men patrolling?

The imposing structure behind the gates looked like an old military barracks or an old prison of some sort. It had four floors, each stretching far back, with several windows on each floor.

Michael was in no doubt that this was Alderauge.

He couldn't hang around because of the guards, so he coasted for another few hundred yards until he found a thicket of trees he could pull into.

The trees provided cover all the way back to the intimidating facility, and Michael settled deep in the trees across the road from the gated entrance.

He watched and waited. Not much happened near the gates but there was activity around the entrance to the building.

Around five thirty, an official-looking vehicle pulled up to the front of the building. Michael sat up and took notice as a tall, slender man who looked to be in his sixties strolled out and climbed into the back seat.

Halmer!

He watched as a young man in a black uniform opened the door for him. As they headed for the gates, Michael bolted through the trees for his vehicle.

He watched Halmer pull through the gates and turn right towards Munich and Michael wasn't far behind as he joined the lane behind him.

Captain Sanders had given him basic training in how to tail someone, so he hung back and followed Halmer as he approached the outskirts of Munich. He wasn't hard to miss because he had one of the nicest vehicles Michael had seen in Germany. Sleek, long, and black, the Mercedes oozed power and class.

Michael sneered. *That's what inhumanity gets you in Nazi Germany.*

~

Fifteen minutes later, the Mercedes veered right onto a street flanked by grand houses, each behind courtyards more expansive than any Michael had previously encountered.

Every house was large and detached from the other houses, and small groups of trees grew between them for privacy.

I wonder which poor Jewish family had this house snatched from them, Michael wondered as the black Mercedes swept into a concrete courtyard big enough for five or more vehicles.

He slowed and watched as Halmer climbed out of the rear door, held open for him by the young man wearing the black SS uniform. He continued for another half mile, where the road ended at a field.

He turned left, and then right, a few hundred yards farther. This lane ran between the field on one side, and a railway line to his left. Like everywhere else, trees were plentiful, and when he reached another junction a half mile down the lane, he found a cluster big enough to conceal his vehicle.

He parked and headed back along the side of the railroad tracks towards the house Halmer claimed as his own.

He hid in a thick group of trees and sat on a branch where he could see over the fence into the spacious rear garden. He could also see through the gap between the houses, so he would know if the Mercedes left the property.

He waited until after dark, nibbling on his dwindling bread to stem his hunger. Images of Kreise's cruel words to Heinrich Adler drove through his anger and he used them to formulate his plans to confront Halmer.

What am I going to do? Kill him?

As much as putting a bullet between his eyes appealed, Michael knew he wasn't a cold-blooded killer. Instead, he planned to show him what he'd done and somehow force him to leave Heinrich alone.

Around eight, he heard the distinctive sound of the Mercedes and a few moments later, he watched as it glided out of the courtyard and headed towards Munich.

Surely, he isn't going to kill Heinrich right now, is he?

Anger once again consumed him and after allowing a few minutes for the Mercedes to put distance between them, he made his move.

Leaving the cover of the trees, he jumped the fence and crouched in the shadows, listening and watching for any response. When nothing materialised, he stood up and sprinted towards the back of the expansive house.

He pushed himself back against the stone, feeling its cold, rough texture against his skin, straining his ears for the slightest hint of footsteps. Listening and watching for any response, he waited a few moments and then approached the windows at the rear of the house.

They were all locked. Glancing around, he spotted a small, loose stone on the ground nearby. Picking it up, he used it to smash the glass as silently as he could, hoping fervently that nobody was home.

He held his breath and stiffened, ready to run at the slightest sound from within.

Silence.

He forced open the window and climbed inside. Then he moved the broken glass and positioned the curtains so that anyone looking in the room wouldn't notice the break-in.

Unless they moved the curtains.

He moved from room to room, searching for anything related to Alderauge and the children Halmer so cruelly murdered there. He found nothing on the ground floor, so he moved upstairs.

The bedrooms revealed nothing except Halmer's taste for expensive clothing and he was about to give up by the time he approached the last room on the upstairs floor.

Chapter Forty-Six

The room was obviously his office. A desk, empty of everything other than a small lamp, faced the door. A leather chair with the initials FH embroidered on the back-rest faced the desk.

The door was unlocked, which surprised Michael. Halmer must feel well protected and well insulated from any probing eyes. With the SS guarding him, he probably felt invincible.

A filing cabinet sat in the corner and on the floor next to it was a large wooden box. Michael tried the filing cabinet but it was locked. So, he turned his attention to the box on the floor.

The box didn't have a lock on it, and the lid opened easily. Michael knelt in front of it and shone his flashlight inside.

A dark blue or black coat – it was difficult to see what it was with the flashlight – sat on top, and Michael stiffened when he picked it up. His heart raced when he recognised it.

This was Gerda's coat! The one she wore to Munich

when she drove me and David to Sophie's apartment the previous winter.

Vivid images shot through Michael's mind of Gerda's bullet-riddled body stretched out on the floor of the apartment and he was momentarily overcome with shock. He cast the coat aside, the memories too painful to bear.

Then it got worse.

A black wallet with FF embroidered on the front in gold lettering came next.

Frank Fernsby. This is Uncle Frank's wallet! This is the box David and I helped Gerda carry to her vehicle from Papa Herbert's house in Freising. Halmer has my family's possessions!

The more he looked, the more he found. Jewellery and several items bearing the name of the Guttmann Department Store. Michael's anger rose like a dark hammer inside his chest and he was about to slam the lid shut when he noticed a black object stuffed in the corner.

Unable to see very well, he threw caution to the wind and turned on the overhead light. He reached in and pulled out the object – a black Olympia typewriter. With his palms sweating, Michael turned it over in his hands and rested it face down on the floor.

Unable to find something to loosen the screws, he ran downstairs and grabbed a kitchen knife. His heart raced when he removed the screws, one by one.

He popped off the bottom of the typewriter and held his breath. *Could this be it?*

He felt inside and his fingers clamped around a small, soft sack. Trembling now, he opened the sack and allowed a cufflink box to fall into his lap.

He opened it.

Then pulled it out.

About one inch in diameter, the gold coin was the most beautiful thing he'd ever seen.

No, second, behind Mina.

He held the coin up and examined it in the light. The intricate patterns mesmerised him and he studied it intently.

One side had an eagle holding arrows in one claw and an olive branch in the other, which Michael understood to mirror the Great Seal of the United States. From what he'd read about the descriptions of the Brasher Doubloons, the eagle represented the country's preparedness for war (arrows) and desire for peace (olive branch).

He wondered how prepared America was for the coming war.

A shield on the eagle's chest represented defence and protection.

Excitement grew inside him and his heart beat louder and louder. Everything he had read told him he was holding the mythical eighth Brasher Doubloon.

It was more or less confirmed when he saw the letters EB on the eagle's right wing.

EB. Ephraim Brasher.

This is the Brasher Doubloon. I've found it!

Latin words inscribed the edge of the coin and Michael read them out loud, glad that he'd paid attention in Latin classes at Cambridge.

UNUM E PLURIBUS.

He'd read that when he'd secretly researched the Brasher Doubloon before leaving England. Its literal translation is the motto of the United States of America: Out of many, one. From what he remembered, it was first suggested in 1776, the year America gained its independence from the British after the Revolutionary War.

He flipped the doubloon over and studied the equally impressive reverse side. It depicted the sun rising behind a series of mountains over a sea.

More words in Latin encircled the scene, and Michael read them aloud to himself.

NOVA EBORACA COLUMBIA EXCELSIOR.

Nova Eboraca Columbia is Latin for New York in America, and Excelsior means ever upwards.

The uniquely intricate skill of Brasher was incredible and Michael's hands shook as he stared at it in disbelief. His heart beat like a drum as he realised how fortunate he'd been to follow his instincts and confront Halmer.

He pictured the look on his father's face when he saw the doubloon for the first time, and he hoped it would help speed up his recovery from the accident.

After carefully replacing the doubloon in the cufflink box, Michael stowed it in his rucksack.

This isn't leaving my side until I get home. Not for anything.

He smiled to himself at the irony of what Halmer had in his possession, and yet he'd never had a clue.

Serves him right. There might be some justice in the world, after all.

Intrigued as to what else he'd find in Halmer's box of stolen treasures, he swivelled around and looked inside.

He retrieved several more items that Gerda must have kept for safekeeping after Frank Fernsby and Herbert Guttmann had been snatched from the department store and taken to Dachau the previous November.

Most were small mementos but occasionally he'd find a handwritten note from Frank, telling Gerda how precious and special she was to him.

His eyes filled when he read their tender words to each other, and he felt his face burning red when he thought of how the Nazis had so needlessly and cruelly ripped them apart.

And it all ends up in a box in Friedrich Halmer's office. A man who couldn't have cared less if he'd tried.

Michael was angry and he was about to slam the top down on the box when he saw a child's rucksack at the bottom, underneath a pile of papers belonging to his Uncle Frank.

He pulled the rucksack out of the box and studied it, dreading finding out who had once owned it, and yet already knowing the answer.

The blood in his veins ran cold when he read the name written in faded ink on the side of the rucksack:

Paul Halmer.

Gerda's son! Halmer's flesh and blood. His grandson. An innocent young boy who the Nazis deemed unworthy of life.

Gerda had done her best to conceal Paul from his grandfather but the Gestapo had found him and taken him to Alderauge. Halmer had done the rest.

Michael pulled a golden-brown teddy bear from the rucksack and clutched it to his chest. He rocked back and forth, cuddling the bear as if it were a human baby.

I might not have been able to save Paul, but I'll be damned if I won't try to save Heinrich.

Michael made a silent vow and looked towards the heavens. He put the teddy bear and the wallet in his rucksack along with the cufflink box.

A door banging below dragged him back to the reality of where he was. He glanced at his watch and gasped when he realised it was ten o'clock. He'd lost track of time during the emotional search of the box that held so many of his family's secrets.

He hurriedly threw everything back into place and turned off the overhead light. He cracked open the office door and waited patiently for the right moment to strike. After what he'd seen in the box, breaking Halmer would be an easy task.

Another hour went by, but Michael didn't care. He'd wait all night if he had to. Halmer wasn't getting away with this anymore.

With the downstairs clock striking midnight, Michael heard creaking on the stairs. He prepared to pounce the moment Halmer opened the office door, but instead, he turned the opposite way and walked to his bedroom.

Michael gave him twenty minutes to get into bed and settle down for the night. It would be easier to subdue him that way.

He left the office and tiptoed towards Halmer's bedroom.

Chapter Forty-Seven

Taking a deep breath, Michael placed his hand on the door handle and was about to enter the bedroom when a shout from behind startled him.

Spinning around, a young man wearing a black uniform bore down on him at speed. All he had time to see in the dim light was the man's fist as it crashed into his face.

Halmer's chauffeur!

Michael fell backwards, Halmer's bedroom door stopping his fall. The frenzied man attacked again, but this time, Michael was ready.

The man was about the same height, but not as muscular. Michael dodged his flying fists and landed one in the gut, knocking the wind out of his assailant.

He pushed the attacker back and as soon as he had room to move, he landed a few blows of his own. The man staggered back, his face contorted in hatred and glared at the intruder who had dared to break into the Nazi doctor's home.

"You are a dead man," the black-clad assailant

screamed. "I am SS-Sturmmann Lutz, and you are under arrest."

Michael noticed something very familiar about the blond-haired Nazi, and as they circled around weighing each other up, the realisation hit him.

"Karl Lutz!" he shouted. He couldn't help himself.

The Nazi looked at Michael in surprise. "You know me? How?"

Searing anger boiled inside Michael and without another word, he launched the most vicious attack he'd ever made. He hit Lutz from every angle possible, and he kept hitting him until he fell backwards down the stairs.

Michael didn't stop there. He went after him. He really wanted to tell him who he was and that he was taking revenge for all the things he'd done to Mina and Senta. But he remained silent, knowing that he'd have to kill Lutz if he found out who he was.

Even with all his anger, Michael couldn't just kill Lutz in cold blood, no matter how much he deserved it.

Lutz rolled down the stairs and Michael bounded after him. He might not kill him, but he was going to beat the living daylights out of him.

Lutz stood up and snatched his pistol from its holster on his belt.

"Who are you?" he screamed, wiping the blood that was running down his face and into his mouth.

Michael stood still, weighing his options. The gun changed everything.

"I said, who *are* you?" Lutz screamed again. He pointed his gun at Michael's head, but Michael didn't flinch. He was too angry.

"I won't ask ag—"

In one swift motion, Michael threw the knife he'd taken

from the kitchen at Lutz. His eyes grew wide as it embedded itself in his chest.

He fired as he fell backwards, striking the ceiling far above Michael's head. In a flash, Michael was upon him, and he snatched the gun from his hand.

"Stop!"

Michael froze.

"Stand up with your hands above your head."

Halmer couldn't have missed the commotion outside his bedroom door, and now he stood in his pyjamas pointing a weapon at Michael.

Michael rose and turned slowly. Without missing a beat, he threw himself to the side of the staircase and fired Lutz's pistol at Halmer.

Halmer juddered and staggered backwards into the wall. Michael fired again, striking Halmer in the stomach.

Halmer fell.

"Who?" Halmer struggled to speak.

Michael ran up the stairs and kicked the gun away from him. "This is for all the innocent children you've murdered."

Halmer's face looked pale in the yellow overhanging light.

"This is for Paul," Michael continued. "Do you remember him?"

Halmer stared up at Michael, confusion and pain etched on his face.

"You murdered your own grandson, you evil bastard. Then you kept his teddy bear as a souvenir."

"Don't let me die." Halmer's blood-stained hand reached for Michael.

Michael slapped it away in disgust. "You don't deserve any mercy. I'm giving you the same as you showed Paul and the countless other children you've murdered. And the same you would have shown to Heinrich Adler tomorrow morning."

"Who are you?" Halmer forced the words out.

"Where is Kreise holding Heinrich Adler?" Michael ignored Halmer's questions.

Halmer stared at Michael, his face a mixture of confusion, pain, and fear.

"I won't ask again. Where is Heinrich Adler?"

"Kreise is taking him to Alderauge at five tomorrow morning."

"What were you planning to do to him?"

Halmer shook his head. "Who are you?"

Halmer screamed as Michael thrust his thumb into the wound in his stomach. "What were you going to do to him?"

Halmer turned his pale face away but Michael grabbed him by the hair and slapped him hard across the cheek.

"Next time, I'll use the gun. Answer my question."

"He's unworthy of life. It's Rüdin's decision, not mine. I'm just carrying out his orders."

"Like you were when you murdered your own grandson?"

Halmer stared at Michael.

"You're a coward. An evil coward who preys on innocent children. You make me sick."

"Who are you?" Halmer was struggling to breathe and Michael took some satisfaction in seeing him suffer.

"You know who I am. All you Nazis know my name. You probably murdered my great-grandfather and my uncle, and you took everything from them. Gerda Yung was family. Frank Fernsby was family and Herbert Guttmann was family. Do you remember them?"

Halmer stared at Michael in disbelief. "You can't be...?"

"I'm Michael Fernsby and I'm here to avenge my family and to stop you from harming any more children, starting with Heinrich Adler."

"How?" Blood ran from Halmer's mouth and Michael knew he was close to death.

"Just die, Halmer. It's all you deserve."

A guttural scream took Michael by surprise and for the second time that evening, Karl Lutz attacked him from behind.

Blood-soaked hands wrapped around his head and Michael threw an elbow into the knife wound. Lutz screamed and clutched at his chest.

"Fernsby! I'm going to kill you."

With what must have been a herculean effort, Lutz drove himself towards Michael. He'd pulled the knife from his chest and was stabbing it at Michael's head.

Michael ducked and dived, trying to avoid the violent onslaught from the enraged Lutz. He caught Lutz's arm and twisted hard. The knife fell, and Michael smashed his elbow into Karl's blood-soaked face, sending him spinning to the floor.

Lutz reached for Halmer's gun, which had fallen near where he lay. Michael grabbed the knife and launched himself on top of Karl, plunging it under his rib cage, deep into his heart.

Karl Lutz died instantly.

Michael turned his attention back to Halmer, who was taking deep, intermittent breaths.

"I hope you rot in hell."

Michael grabbed both their pistols and headed for the bathroom. He retched and vomited for several minutes, and his hands shook as he cleaned himself up.

By the time he'd taken a clean set of clothes and as

much fresh food as he could carry, both Lutz and Halmer lay dead at the top of the stairs. All hell would break loose in the morning when they were discovered, but by then, Michael hoped to be far away from Munich.

He had just one more thing to do.

Chapter Forty-Eight

The shrill ringing from the telephone in the hallway downstairs woke Albert Kreise from a heavy sleep. He stared at the ceiling for a moment and wiped the sleep from his eyes.

Stumbling, he lurched down the stairs, pausing only to look at the clock hanging on the wall above the noisy instrument that was causing him so much annoyance.

"It's three in the morning. It'd better be important!" he yelled as he reached to answer it.

"Kreise," he answered gruffly into the mouthpiece.

At least it's stopped shrieking at me now.

"I hope I'm not disturbing you." The cold, calculated voice on the other end was one he'd recognise anywhere. Thoughts of sleep immediately fell from his brain, replaced by the fear and unease the caller instilled in him every time he heard his voice.

"Obergruppenführer Heydrich! What can I do for you at this hour of the morning?" Kreise stood to attention in the darkness. If Heydrich was calling in the middle of the night, he knew it must be important.

"I'm glad you finally answered the telephone, Kreise," Heydrich snapped impatiently.

"I'm sorry, sir. I didn't get to sleep until late. We got him, sir. We got Adler and his family."

"So I heard. What did you do with them?"

"They are at the Gestapo headquarters at Wittelsbacher Palais. My men are working on Adler and his wife as we speak, and I'm taking the boy to Halmer at five o'clock."

"Find someone else. I have another task for you."

"Sir?"

"Get someone else to take the boy to Halmer. I've just heard from my contact in Britain. It seems their Secret Intelligence Service is playing games with us, but we are going to be the ones who win."

"What do you need me to do, Obergruppenführer Heydrich?"

"Have you apprehended the man who was driving Adler yet?" Heydrich snapped again. He sounded as angry as Kreise had ever heard him, even if it was the middle of the night.

All thoughts of sleep were well and truly gone. Kreise held the telephone to his ear and concentrated on every word Heydrich uttered.

"Not yet, sir. He can't have got far, because we have every major road blocked. We'll break Adler, and when we find out who was driving him, we'll get him. He killed several of my good men, so believe me, sir, I want him as much as you do."

"I doubt that, Kreise."

Kreise stared at the telephone. "Why do you say that, Obergruppenführer Heydrich?"

"My contact in Britain told me who was assisting Adler and they assured me the information was correct."

"Who is it?" Kreise asked. "Who killed my men? Was it one of our own?"

"No. It wasn't one of our men. It was Michael Fernsby."

Kreise almost dropped the telephone. "Fernsby?" he spluttered.

"You heard me correctly. My contact has never given wrong information, and I am assured the SIS sent Fernsby to assist Adler across the border to Holland."

"Why him?" Kreise could barely believe what Heydrich was telling him. "He's not an agent for SIS. He's too inexperienced."

"Inexperienced?" Heydrich countered. "He may have lost Adler but he managed to kill several of your men and get away. And it isn't the first time he's done that, is it, Kreise?"

"No, sir. But it will be his last."

"I'm told he is operating under the name of a Swiss national called Erich Weber. We believe he will try to leave Germany via Switzerland, so I want you to take as many men as you need and find him. Do not allow him to get away. Do you understand me, Kreise?"

"Yes, Obergruppenführer Heydrich. I have my own reasons for wanting to find Fernsby, and I assure you he will not get away this time."

"Make sure of it."

Chapter Forty-Nine

By four o'clock, Michael was in position close to Alderauge. He knew he was taking an enormous risk, but he could never live with himself if he allowed the boy to die at the hands of the Nazis.

His vehicle was hidden in the trees close to Halmer's residence. Instead, he'd taken Halmer's Mercedes in the hope it was well known by anyone on patrol that evening.

He'd been proven correct because two uniformed men tried pulling him over but when they saw the swastikas and the other Nazi insignia, they'd saluted and allowed him to continue unopposed.

Now he waited down a side street off Abfanggraben. He had good vision along the narrow lane and he would see any vehicle lights that approached long before they reached his position.

He was less than a mile from Alderauge, so he knew he'd have to act quickly before the alarm was raised and reinforcements arrived.

He'd gone over a rough plan several times but brute force was the only thing he could think of.

I'm ready.

His left hand shook violently and no matter what he did, he couldn't make it stop. He knew it wasn't fear of what was about to go down because although he knew he could lose his life, he was long past the point of fearing it.

No, it wasn't that. It wasn't even the nightmares he knew would come later over the deaths of Lutz and Halmer. They would merge with the other ones he had about his brother and all the other Nazis he'd killed.

The good Lord above knew his sins and he prayed for forgiveness should he die this day. Killing people would never come easy to him, and he longed for the day when peace reigned once again in Europe.

He was shaking because he didn't want to fail. If he succeeded in nothing else during this war, he desperately wanted to save this poor innocent boy from the hands of the Nazis.

What he was going to do with him afterwards was anyone's guess, but right now, that wasn't the problem. Rescuing him from heavily armed Gestapo agents was.

As five o'clock approached, Michael felt himself getting more and more nervous. His stomach quivered and he felt nauseous. He'd already vomited everything he'd eaten and he couldn't shake the feelings of sickness that overwhelmed him.

The soft hum of an engine soon accompanied the dark outline of an approaching vehicle. Dawn's faint light edged the horizon, casting an eerie gloom. With the vehicle drawing near, Michael felt time slow to a crawl.

Banking on the hope that Kreise would deliver Heinrich alone, Michael flew into action. He started the Mercedes and waited until the vehicle was right on him before making his move.

He inhaled sharply as he thrust the accelerator to the floor. The powerful Mercedes lunged forward, smashing into the side of the oncoming car with a muffled, metallic roar.

The world momentarily turned into a cacophony of shattering glass and crumpled metal.

Silence followed.

They collided with a sickening crunch that must have been heard for miles. Michael knew he didn't have long. He tucked away his emotions and allowed ice to enter his veins.

He leapt out of the Mercedes, hoping to use the element of surprise to his advantage. It worked, because the two men in the front of the vehicle hadn't moved by the time he reached them.

Without hesitation, Michael fired off two double taps through the windshield. Both men slumped sideways.

Michael rushed to the passenger side and pulled the door open. Heinrich was on the rear seat, wailing in fear and confusion.

"Heinrich, I hope you remember me. I'm here to take you away from these men. Take my hand. We have to get away before more of them come after us."

Heinrich stared at Michael, his eyes darting all over the terrible scene.

"Don't look at them, Heinrich. Look at me. That's it. Come on."

Heinrich held out his arms, and it broke Michael's heart to see him so frightened and alone. "Those men didn't like me. They made fun of me." Heinrich slurred his words, which made Michael's heart ache even more.

"They won't hurt you anymore, I promise. But we have to move or they'll find us."

Michael picked him up and carried him to the rear seat

of the Mercedes. He shut the door behind him and ran back to the mangled wreck at the side of the road.

He pushed the two dead men back so he could get a good look at them. None of them looked like Kreise, which was a disappointment. Not wanting to waste another second, he jumped into the driver's seat of the Mercedes and drove off as fast as the wrecked vehicle would take him.

Chapter Fifty

H oping the two patrolmen weren't still trying to stop any vehicle that passed, Michael drove as fast as he dared to Halmer's death house on the outskirts of Munich. The drive was only around fifteen minutes but each one of them felt like an hour. Michael was expecting to be swarmed by angry Gestapo agents at any moment, and he could hardly breathe as he navigated his way to Halmer's courtyard.

He breathed a sigh of relief when he made it without incident. He grabbed Heinrich and took him around the side of the house to the railway tracks behind.

"It's a little way down here. Are you able to walk?"

Heinrich nodded. "Those men told me I was no use and a waste of the Führer's oxygen. They hit me and made me cry."

Michael placed an arm around the boy and pulled him close. "They were wicked men and there's more of them after us but we're going somewhere where they won't hurt you."

"Where are we going?"

"It's a surprise."

Michael hadn't a clue what to do with Heinrich Adler. He couldn't risk taking him across the border, because after what he'd done, the Gestapo would be on high alert, and Heinrich's condition would give them away in a heartbeat.

"Let's get to our vehicle and we'll decide from there," he murmured to himself.

When they approached the Opel Kapitan hidden in the trees, Michael made Heinrich lie down beside him for a few minutes while he assessed the situation. When he was sure the vehicle hadn't been compromised, he stood up and helped Heinrich to his feet.

"I'm proud of you, Heinrich," Michael said as he helped him into the vehicle. "You took on the bad men and beat them! Then you walked all this way with me. You are the bravest boy I know."

He meant it too.

Heinrich smiled. "Are we going to see Uncle Gustav?"

Michael shook his head. "I'm sorry. The bad men got him and we can't help him escape. But I've got you and that's all that counts."

He made sure the briefcase was still where he'd left it under the seat and started the engine.

Now the hard part began.

As they headed out of Munich, Michael saw a sign for Freising. A thought hit him like a cricket bat and he smiled to himself. He turned to look at Heinrich, who was sitting quietly beside him.

"I know a man who will take good care of you. He's a good man and you can trust him. Is that alright?"

Heinrich nodded.

Michael turned back to concentrate on the roads and headed for Freising. He got lost a few times because he was keeping to the small lanes and back roads. The last thing he wanted to see was a Nazi roadblock.

What would normally take under an hour took them three but Michael didn't care.

They waited on the outskirts of Freising until darkness fell over the picturesque Bavarian town. The authorities would be on full alert looking for Heinrich and he'd be easy to identify if they were seen together.

After dark, Michael left the Opel on a quiet cul-de-sac and led the young boy towards what he hoped would be a safe sanctuary. He didn't know how he'd be received, and he was sure Heinrich wouldn't be welcomed, but he had nowhere else to take him.

It was a stark choice – either Father Eise agreed to help or Heinrich would die. Surely the priest wouldn't allow that to happen?

Along the way, Michael told Heinrich stories of how Father Eise had helped him the previous winter when the bad men were after him. Heinrich giggled when he heard how Michael hid underground while the Gestapo searched for him in the church above.

The ploy worked and Heinrich remained calm during the walk to the Pallotti Church on the corner of Vimystrasse and Pallottinestrasse.

They hurried around to the rear and hid in the court-yard where Michael had said goodbye to the priest the previous Christmas. He positioned Heinrich in a tight clump of trees and held his shoulders.

"If I'm not back in an hour, you must run. Get away from here as fast as you can, and find somewhere to hide."

Heinrich nodded.

"Do you understand me, Heinrich? This is important."

He nodded again.

"Sit tight and don't make a sound. If everything goes well, I'll be back for you shortly. Are you ready?"

Heinrich fist-bumped Michael and smiled. "Ready," he said.

It hurt to leave him, but there was no other choice. He wasn't even sure if Father Eise was still at the church, and even if he was, how would he react to having a disabled boy dumped on him? Especially when the Gestapo were looking for him.

Michael walked through the narrow passage he remembered so clearly and entered an inner courtyard. He paused for a moment and then continued to a door he knew led inside the church.

He held his breath as he tried the door handle. The last thing he wanted to do was take Heinrich in through the front doors where they were an easy target for prying eyes. This was safer, but only if the door was unlocked.

It opened!

He heaved a sigh of relief as he stepped inside. Now he hoped Father Eise was in residence and that he'd be receptive to his outrageous request.

Candles burned around the church, their light casting shadows on the stone walls. Michael held his imagination in check as he watched the shadows dance in the gentle breeze caused by the open side door.

"Is someone here?" A voice shouted from the far side of the church. It was a voice Michael recognised, and he breathed a sigh of relief when he heard it.

He cautiously moved towards the sound of the voice, conscious of the fact that the priest might not be alone. His mouth broke into a wide grin when he saw he was.

"Father Eise, I bet you didn't expect to see me again, did you?"

Father Eise came into view, his features unchanged since the last time they'd met. Balding, and in his forties, a pair of round glasses that looked too small for his head sat underneath Eise's prominent forehead. More importantly, Father Eise had a kindly, welcoming look about him that immediately disarmed anyone he came into contact with.

"Who is this?" Eise got closer to get a better look at the man standing before him.

"It's me, Michael Fernsby."

Father Eise stopped dead in his tracks. Even in the dim light of the candles, Michael could see the blood drain from his face.

"Fernsby? You're supposed to be dead! What are you doing here?"

"I hate to do this to you but I need your help, Father."

"What have you done this time? And why are you back in Bavaria? And how are you alive? I heard the radio broadcast telling everyone you'd been killed in an automobile accident. Don't you realise how dangerous it is for you here?"

"I heard that broadcast and although they tried, they didn't kill me. They lied, Father Eise, just like they lie about everything else."

"You look in remarkable condition for a corpse."

"I'm sorry to bother you again but I didn't know who else to turn to."

"You need me to hide you again and help you escape? I followed you on the radio and through the newspapers last time and I was sure they'd kill you. But why are you back?"

"Haven't you heard anything on the radio?" Michael asked, assuming that what he'd done would be all over the airwaves by now.

Father Eise shook his head. "I've been listening to the radio all evening, and I haven't heard anything."

"They must be keeping a tight lid on it then, which is a good thing."

"What happened? And why are you here?"

Michael gave the priest a brief synopsis of what had happened to Adler and why he was at the church.

"It's impossible!" the priest exploded. "I cannot take a crippled boy into my care. What would I do with him? The Gestapo will be everywhere looking for him, and it's not as though he'll be hard to spot, is it?"

"I know, and I wish there was another way. I can't take him across the border, and I don't know anyone else in Germany. He is in desperate need, Father Eise. His life is on the line and he needs help more than ever before. They'll kill him if they find him."

"They'll kill me if they find him here. Have you thought of that?"

"I have, and I understand the risk you would be taking. But surely a young life is worth such a risk? Especially one that is as innocent and frail as the boy waiting outside?"

Father Eise closed his eyes and prayed.

When he opened them, he stared at Michael for a few moments. "Bring him inside. I might know a family that can care for him until we somehow get him out of Bavaria."

"Thank you, Father. I knew you wouldn't let me down."

"You leave me no choice, do you? Either I take him or he dies at the hands of the Gestapo, which he may yet still do, with me alongside him. This is the last thing I'm doing for you, so don't ask again."

"I won't, I promise."

Michael ran outside to find Heinrich and give him the good news.

Chapter Fifty-One

After a tearful goodbye and a promise to find him again after the coming war, Michael used the cover of darkness to put as much distance between himself and the area around Munich as he could.

Keeping to the side roads, he headed southwest towards the border with Switzerland. Austria was closer, but as that was under Nazi rule after the Anschluss in 1938, it wouldn't be any safer for him.

By two thirty in the morning, a tired Michael found himself near Dachau once again. He knew that once he'd cleared that, his run to the border would be fairly clear, as long as he didn't run into a roadblock.

As this was going through his mind, he noticed a vehicle pull out of a side street behind him. The vehicle gained pace, closing the gap between them. Not wanting to raise any suspicion, he resisted the urge to speed up and instead continued as if nothing had changed.

The vehicle followed for a few miles until the road opened up into the countryside. Michael knew it must be the Gestapo and he wondered why they hadn't just pulled him over.

Then it hit him. There had been complete radio silence over the Adler incident and the dead Gestapo agents. It was the same with Heinrich and the dead agents near Alderauge.

The Nazis are keeping a lid on this! They don't want it getting out that they're slaughtering handicapped children! That's why they're tailing me. They want to take me quietly. Well, they won't.

Whoever was behind him couldn't possibly know who was in the vehicle they were tailing. They'd probably been pulling over anything that moved all night long.

The vehicle closed up behind him and the next thing he knew, red lights were flashing on and off, signalling him to stop.

Panic rose inside him. *What do I do? I can't keep killing them all. Sooner or later, they'll start shooting first and asking questions later and innocent people will die because of me.*

Keeping his weapon in hand, but out of sight, he pulled over and opened the window. He prepared his papers and hoped for the best. There was nothing else he could do.

Two men in police uniforms approached. "Papiere," one of them snarled.

Michael handed over his papers.

"What is your name and where are you going?" The officer shone the bright light of his flashlight in Michael's face, momentarily blinding him.

"My name is Erich Weber and I am driving to Mindelheim to meet my uncle."

He was glad he'd looked at the map and looked at what the nearest town was called.

"Why is your uncle in Mindelheim?"

"His vehicle broke down. He called my mother and asked if I would meet him there to take him home to Munich."

"You are Swiss?"

"Yes. I'm visiting my mother who is a German national."

The policemen wrote down the details from his papers and handed them back.

"Is there anyone travelling with you?"

"No, sir. As you can see, I'm completely alone."

"Very well."

The policeman handed back his papers and left Michael alone with his thoughts. His shoulders quivered as the adrenaline swirled around his body, and he replaced the Walther PPK under his leg on the driver's seat.

He knew it wouldn't be long before the Gestapo learnt about the police stop and they'd be all over him long before he reached the border.

He had to change his plans. Fast.

He waited until the policemen were out of sight and then he spread the map out on the passenger seat. He turned right and headed north for Ulm.

It should have taken less than two hours to reach Ulm but fatigue took over, forcing him to pull over for an hour to rest his eyes. Twice he had to take alternative routes to avoid roadblocks and by the time he reached Ulm, dawn was breaking and the early morning commuters were starting their daily activities.

He parked the Opel close to the railway station and left it there. From now on, he'd be travelling by train as it was too dangerous to go by road.

On one platform, he bought a ticket to Innsbruck,

Austria, using the name of Lars Hohenberg, the original name he'd used when he entered Germany from Switzerland. The Gestapo would get wind of it and be all over it, hopefully leaving the path clear for him to head the opposite way and leave unopposed.

He changed platforms and bought another ticket, this time in the name of Erich Weber. This ticket was for Ravensburg in the south of Germany. From there, he'd purchase another ticket to Switzerland and safety.

He sat with his rucksack and the briefcase firmly in his grasp, trying for all the world to blend in and appear as if he was just another weary early morning traveller going about his business.

The train came on time, and he settled into a row of seats that he had all to himself. The conductor checked his ticket and Michael did his best not to look guilty or furtive as he handed them over for scrutiny.

The conductor had a long look, handed it back, and went about his business. Michael's chest heaved in relief and he sat back, watching and hoping that nothing would happen between here and the safety of Switzerland.

He had to change trains in Ravensburg but after that, it would be plain sailing.

He hoped.

Chapter Fifty-Two

Albert Kreise replaced the receiver on the telephone and sat back for a moment, deep in thought.

Heydrich had told him Fernsby was travelling under the name of Erich Weber, so what was Lars Hohenberg doing buying a ticket to Innsbruck?

"He's trying to throw us off," he mused aloud. He gestured to one of his men, a broad-shouldered officer standing by the door, to approach.

"Seidel, someone purchased a ticket from Ulm to Innsbruck in the name of Lars Hohenberg. That's the name Fernsby was using before meeting up with Adler. I think it's a decoy, but just in case, take Assant and get on that train. If he's there, take him."

"Dead or alive, sir?" Seidel asked.

"After what he did to Doctor Halmer, I don't care. Just get his body back to Munich."

"Jawohl, Kriminaldirektor Kreise."

Seidel snapped his feet together and thrust his arm high in the air. "Heil Hitler."

Without another word, he rushed out with Assant, leaving Kreise simmering in his thoughts.

Kreise's concentration was broken by the sharp ring of the telephone again.

"Kreise," he responded tersely.

"Kriminaldirektor, this is Oberscharführer Ernst Berndt from Ulm's Gestapo office. Rumour has it you're after a certain Erich Weber?"

A shiver of anticipation ran down Kreise's spine. "Indeed. What have you found?"

"We have a purchase under that name for the nine thirty to Ravensburg. Should I halt the train?"

Kreise thought for a split second. "No, let it continue. Just observe from a distance. Make no changes to the routine."

"Very well, Kriminaldirektor. If further assistance is needed, you know where to find me."

The urgency in the room was palpable. Kreise abruptly hung up and took a deep breath to steady himself.

"He's going to Ravensburg. It's clear as day. He's trying to reach Switzerland. We'll intercept him."

Glancing at the ornate clock hanging on the wall, Kreise's determination solidified. "We have just over an hour. Let's move." Without waiting for a response, he stormed out of the Wittelsbacher Palais, his officers close on his heels.

Chapter Fifty-Three

The rhythmic sound of the train on the tracks and the gentle rocking made Michael sleepy. He glanced around the carriage and everything looked good. Nobody was looking at him and nothing seemed out of place.

He allowed his heavy eyelids to close and drifted into an uneasy sleep. He knew he'd be grateful later in Ravensburg when he would have to be on full alert.

The train slowing down pulled him from his slumber and it took a moment to gather his senses.

We're slowing down. We must be approaching Ravensburg.

The familiar feelings of butterflies dancing in his stomach made him queasy, so he gulped down some water and took a deep breath. Hopefully, the Gestapo were chasing the train to Innsbruck and leaving this one alone, but he wasn't taking any chances.

He checked his pocket for the Walther PPK and readied himself for the final, most dangerous part of his escape from Germany. Once he reached Switzerland, it'd be plain sailing to get back home from there.

The shrill sound of a whistle from the front of the train alerted the passengers that they were about to pull into the station. Fighting back nausea, Michael joined the middle of the queue, waiting to disembark.

As he stepped off the train, another one stopped beside them, heading the opposite way. Michael tried to act as normally as possible, but he couldn't help himself from looking all around to make sure nobody was rushing towards him.

All seemed calm and he headed for the ticket office and his final brush with danger. At the last minute, he had a change of heart. Instead of buying a train ticket to Switzerland, he bought one for the brief journey to Friedrichshafen in Germany.

Friedrichshafen sat on the shores of Lake Konstanz, and ferries crossed the lake several times a day, carrying passengers to and from Switzerland. An alarm inside Michael's head told him not to cross by train and he followed his instincts as they had proven correct many times before in times of crisis.

The next train left in forty-five minutes, so he took his time and mingled with the other commuters while he slowly made his way to the platform.

A noise behind caught his interest and he turned to see what it was. The walkway between platforms was busy, and someone was hurrying in his direction, pushing people out of the way.

Fear gripped Michael, sending his pulse into a wild, frantic drumbeat. He turned and hurried towards the exit.

They've found me, but how? Nobody knows about Erich Weber, so it can't be for me.

His denial didn't work. He knew that whoever it was, they were coming for him. *Who else could it be?*

As he was about to run, he saw a woman burst through the crowd. They locked eyes, and Michael's breath caught in his throat. There, amidst the chaos, was a face he thought he'd never see again – it was as if he'd seen a ghost.

His heart, just a moment ago pounding with the rhythm of a terrified sprint, seemed to stop in his chest. The world around him fell away, leaving only the woman whose gaze held him frozen in disbelief.

It was Mother, and she was staring at him with a look of desperation he'd never seen during their short time together in Munich. He waited, not wanting to create a bigger scene than was already playing out. People were looking at them, and Michael had to do something before it got out of hand.

"Mother! What are you doing here?" he asked, shocked at the unexpected sight of her.

"I just had to see you one more time before you left," she replied, and when the crowds realised it was an impromptu family reunion, they lost interest and carried on with their lives.

Nobody in Hitler's Germany wanted any involvement with strangers. They never knew who they were dealing with and the trouble just wasn't worth it, so by and large people kept to themselves and kept their heads down.

Michael and Mother used this to their advantage and they linked arms as they hurried towards the exit.

"What's going on?" Michael asked in a low voice. "How did you find me here?"

"You are in terrible danger, Michael. I don't have time to explain but we have a friend who works at a certain telephone exchange, and she passed on some vital information that involved you."

"What happened?" Michael froze to the spot, unable to comprehend the words that Mother had just spoken.

"Someone has betrayed you, Michael. There is a traitor in your camp and until we find them, we're stopping all communication with the British. I'm getting you out of here, and then I'm going to a place the Nazis will never find me."

"Who is—?"

"There's no time to talk. We have to move." Mother pulled Michael forwards with her linked arm. "I'll tell you what I know once we get out of here."

They reached the exit, only to see a commotion going on in front of them. "We're too late," Michael said. "They're here."

"There they are!" someone yelled, pointing at Michael and Mother. "Stop them."

People panicked and shot off in all directions. Others looked at the two fugitives and went to block their way forward. Michael looked around for an escape but couldn't see one.

Three men approached from behind and two others from the front. All had guns in their hands and all were staring right at them. They left Michael in no doubt who they were after.

Knowing that a painful death was all he could expect, he silently vowed to himself that he would not be taken alive. He went to shove Mother out of the way so she could vanish into the crowds, but she beat him to it.

"Here." She thrust an envelope into his hand. "I haven't read it, so they can't force it out of me. Take it and go."

"Mother—" Michael started but was interrupted by the sudden urgency in her actions. She pulled away from Michael, her fingers wrapping around a small pistol Michael could see in her jacket pocket.

"Wait," he managed, but it was too late.

As the Gestapo agents came into view, a car backfired in

the distance. Startled by the noise, a panicked man collided with an agent, causing his gun to discharge wildly.

Mother reacted to the chaos by firing at the agent, striking him in the chest. He fell to the ground, surprise and agony etched on his face.

A second agent fired at Mother, dropping her instantly.

The crowd scattered, screams echoing off the buildings, and through the dust and confusion, Michael saw Mother collapse, a bright bloom of red spreading across her clothing. The agent's bullet had found its mark.

Their eyes met as she fell and he felt the world tilt beneath him. Even in her unintended demise, Mother had given him a chance to escape, and he would not let her sacrifice be in vain.

Why did she do that?

Women screamed and men shouted. Children cried and clung to their mothers. Fathers forced open the doors to the stranded train and were throwing their families onboard to get out of the way.

Michael shook himself and joined them. He looked at the bloodstained body of Mother, who was now being roughly handled by three angry men, and locked eyes with one of them who stood back from the melee, watching the fleeing crowds.

Kreise! Michael fought the inner urge to attack him and instead turned and entered the train carriage.

Kreise would have to wait. Right now, he had to get away and find somewhere to take stock and think about what had happened.

He squeezed through the people jamming the carriage doors and followed the few who had jumped onto the tracks between the two trains. With fewer people in the way, he hurried after them and ran down the tracks towards the rear of the other train.

He found a gap between the carriages and climbed onto the couplers that joined them together. He stepped over them and onto the platform on the other side. From there, he ran towards a low fence where the platform ended, and jumped over.

He ran for waste ground, hoping to find some way out of the labyrinthine tangle of the railway yard. His breath was ragged, echoing the staccato rhythm of his pounding heart, still reeling from the harsh reality of Mother's demise.

Why did she do that?

He didn't have time to ponder the question because the cracking of gunfire behind him sent him hurtling to the ground.

He crawled behind abandoned railway sleepers and took out his gun. Men, women and children were still scattering all around the railway station, and he could hear sirens in the distance. If he was going to get away, it had to be soon, or he'd never make it.

Three men struggled over the fence he'd just leapt over, and as one of them got a leg over the top, Michael fired at him. All he could see was Mother's mutilated body, and he was overcome with rage.

The man fell over the fence and lay still on the ground. The other two took cover on the other side of the fence. Michael used their momentary hesitation to crawl backwards towards the river he could see close by.

There was still one more, Kreise, but Michael didn't have the time to worry about him right now.

An agent jumped over the fence. Michael fired but missed. The man returned fire and threw himself to the ground. As he did so, the other man followed him over the fence.

A large building sat to Michael's right and he crawled towards it, hoping it was empty. He knew the two men wouldn't stop until they'd caught him, and there were dozens more on their way. He had to act now.

Chapter Fifty-Four

P allets stacked with lumber filled the vast warehouse, all waiting for their final distribution. Ducking behind one, Michael waited, his eyes adjusting to the dull grey light piercing the grime-streaked windows.

The hushed creaks and groans of settling wood mingled with the muted sounds of the panicked public. Behind him, a frightened parent stifled a child's cry, informing Michael he wasn't alone in the warehouse.

Two menacing silhouettes stood guard at the warehouse's large entrance, effectively blocking any hope of escape.

"We know you're in here. Come out with your hands up."

More cries and whimpers, this time off to his right.

"Please, don't shoot us. We're coming." A woman rose from behind a stack of wood to Michael's rear. Two young children clung to her, both with their tiny arms held high in the air. A lump formed in Michael's throat as they stepped forward.

The Gestapo agents shoved them roughly out of the

way. "We know you're in here, Fernsby, so come out before innocent children get hurt. You don't want that on your conscience, do you?"

Now they're trying extortion.

A man and a woman stood up next, both with their hands in the air. "We're coming. Please don't shoot."

Another family, and then an old man, stood and moved towards the entrance. Soon, only Michael would remain, and the men would bear down on him and show no mercy.

The sirens were close now and Michael knew his time was running out. It was now or never. He slid backwards, towards the rear of the warehouse.

Surely there has to be another way out of this place.

There wasn't. It was either the front entrance or a window. He wasn't going out of the window, which left only the front of the warehouse and certain death.

Do or die.

Spotting a narrow gap between the planks of a nearby pallet at the rear of the warehouse, Michael hastily shoved his briefcase and rucksack into the makeshift hideaway, ensuring they were concealed from prying eyes.

He inched towards the front, searching frantically for any other means of escape, and just as he was about to give up and go out in a blaze of glory, a reckless, wild idea formed in his mind.

Surveying his immediate surroundings, his eyes landed on a tall stack of lumber, precariously balanced on a pallet, and he knew what he had to do.

He crouched on one knee behind the pallet and took aim at one of the Gestapo agents blocking his escape. He fired, catching him in the upper chest. The agent returned fire as he fell and his comrade joined in, throwing himself to the ground and spraying the area where, moments earlier, Michael had shot from.

But he wasn't there. As soon as he'd fired, he leapt to his feet behind the dubiously stacked pile of lumber and climbed a quarter of the way up it.

With both Gestapo agents lying on the ground, Michael pushed as hard as he could, sending the massive pile of wood crashing on top of them with a loud thunderclap, the violent thud reverberating through the cavernous space of the warehouse.

He took a deep breath and broke into a sprint towards the entrance. Dust and splinters filled the air, plunging the warehouse into chaos. The sudden noise sent those still hiding in the warehouse into a renewed panic.

Michael veered off towards the left, his eyes locked on the nearby river. He could hear shouts and curses behind him as the fleeing men, women, and children scrambled over the fallen lumber but he didn't look back. The river was his only chance.

As he sprinted towards the river, an imposing figure materialised from nowhere, blocking his path.

Michael came to an abrupt halt as Kreise emerged from the shadows. A cold smile was the only hint of emotion on his otherwise stoic face. The two men locked eyes, each one sizing the other up.

"I've been waiting for this, Fernsby," Kreise sneered, casually drawing his gun and pointing it at Michael. "You've done a lot of damage to the Reich, and you murdered a very important doctor. There won't be a trial for you." His voice was icy, promising pain and retribution.

Caught between the river and the barrel of Kreise's gun, Michael feigned surrender, raising his hands slowly.

"No need to shoot, Kreise," he said, his voice steady despite the pounding of his heart.

As he spoke, his right foot subtly nudged a loose piece of lumber lying nearby, rolling it slowly in front of him. His distraction seemed to work as Kreise's gaze flickered to the movement.

Seizing the moment, Michael's instincts took over. With a surge of adrenaline, he kicked the discarded lumber with all his might, sending it hurtling toward Kreise.

Surprised, Kreise instinctively moved to dodge it, momentarily lowering his weapon.

Michael launched himself, crashing into Kreise with full force. The two men grappled, their fight a desperate struggle for survival. Michael landed a solid punch, momentarily stunning the older man.

He seized Kreise's gun and smashed the handle onto the bridge of his nose. Blood spurted all over Michael's face and arms and the sound of crunching bone sent a shiver down his spine. Kreise groaned and fell limp underneath Michael's weight.

Seizing the opportunity, he continued his mad dash towards the river. He threw himself into the murky, cold water and took in mouthfuls of river water as he sank beneath the surface.

Rising again, he allowed the current to carry him downstream. He turned and watched Kreise struggle to his feet and stand at the riverbank, staring at the expanse of water as it carried Michael away from his grasp.

Their paths would cross again, but for now, Michael had escaped him.

Chapter Fifty-Five

Soldiers with dogs would soon saturate the place and Michael knew he had to find somewhere to hide before they found him. The current of the river wasn't fast enough to outrun the angry mob searching for him, so he had to find a better alternative.

He floated past a culvert on the opposite side of the river to the warehouse, and he swam towards it, intending to leave the river and run for his life. Somewhere, anywhere, other than where he was right now.

He knew he wouldn't get very far but he had to try. Too many people had died for him to just quit and hand himself in, not that he had any intention of doing that. He knew what kind of reception he'd get if the Nazis caught him and he'd sooner go down in a blaze of glory than allow that to happen.

When he reached the riverbank, his hand brushed against rough stone. He had to look twice because whatever it was, it was submerged in undergrowth and mud.

Parting the bushes and overgrown weeds, his spirits lifted when he saw it was a circular drain. He pulled himself in and allowed the thick vegetation to fully conceal him. The drain was over a foot deep in water, so he hoped that would be enough to keep the dogs from picking up his scent.

It was dark, and he was freezing, but he was safe, at least for now. He couldn't have found a better hiding place if he'd tried and he was glad he'd taken notice of his surroundings.

He lay still, shivering from the cold. He was tired and hungry from the physical and emotional exertions but he was safe, and he'd take that any day of the week.

He huddled in the murky darkness, listening to the muffled sounds of the search party. The echoes of German commands and barking dogs grew closer before gradually fading away. The culvert provided just enough cover to conceal him from the search party.

His mind replayed everything that had happened since leaving Heinrich with Father Eise. Mother's words haunted him and clawed at his soul.

Someone has betrayed you, Michael. There is a traitor in your camp, and until we find them, we're stopping all communication with the British.

What did she mean by that? Who had betrayed him? It had to be someone in Britain or they wouldn't be cutting off communication with them.

Is that how the Nazis knew what name I was travelling under? There was no way they could have known who Erich Weber was unless someone told them. But who? Only a handful of people ever knew. And who told Mother I was using that name?

Michael played everything over and over in his mind, and slowly he realised that the most likely culprit was

Captain Sanders. He knew everything about the operation because he was the one directing it from London.

But why? Michael didn't know, but he made a silent vow that he'd find out if he survived his current predicament.

Visions of Mother falling in a pool of her own blood joined the many other images that would haunt him for the rest of his life. He didn't know how much more of this he could take. Every time someone he cared about died, a part of him died with them, none more so than David. The gaping wounds these deaths left on his soul would never heal.

What am I going to do now? He focused on his current situation, forcing Sanders and Mother to the back of his mind. He had more pressing problems to worry about right now.

How am I going to get out of this?

He'd start with the envelope Mother had pressed into his hands before she died. Whatever was in it must be important, so he'd start with that.

As night fell, he listened one more time for any signs of the enemy. Certain that he was alone, he carefully emerged from his hiding place and began the dangerous journey to retrieve the crucial documents he'd left inside the storage facility.

He hadn't heard anything for some time, and the search had moved farther down the river. Nobody in their right mind would circle back to the scene of the crime and the Nazis would have no reason to believe he would go back to the railway station or the warehouse, where so much death and destruction had taken place.

Relying on the cover of darkness, he stopped frequently to make sure he wasn't walking into a trap. It was a calm night with good visibility, which was both good and bad. It was also quite warm, which he welcomed because he'd suffered lying in the cold water inside the drainpipe.

As the warehouse came into view, he dropped to his stomach and crawled the rest of the way. He rose to his feet at the rear of the building, and inched his way around, staying on the river side of the building, out of sight of the railway station.

At the edge, near the doors that were still open, he heard a noise. Faint, but definitely human. He heard a foot or a hand scrape against wood and he knew the Nazis had left a guard on duty, just in case.

He scampered back to the rear of the building, where he'd spotted a length of rope curled up against the back wall. It was about four feet long, which was enough, and it was about three inches thick.

He picked it up and crept to the front of the building. He held the rope in his left hand and the Walther PPK in his right. Then he listened.

There it was again! Footsteps, barely discernible, but footsteps walking around the entrance. He listened hard for several minutes but it was quiet, and he didn't hear anything else.

He fell to his knees and peered around the side of the wall, hoping that whoever was guarding the building wouldn't see him. A lone soldier stood on guard, clearly disinterested. His rifle was slung over his shoulder and he stared at something in his hands rather than what was in front of him.

The soldier clearly hadn't suspected for a moment that Michael would go back to the warehouse. Why would he? Which was probably why he wasn't paying any attention to his surroundings.

He waited until the soldier turned his back on him. Still staring at whatever was in his hand, the soldier didn't see Michael approach from behind. He heard nothing until it was too late.

He spun around and Michael could see the whites of his eyes as panic set in. Michael struck him hard with the butt of his pistol and watched him collapse like a burst balloon.

Michael removed his rifle and checked him for any other weapons. He found a knife on his belt and when he looked at it in the moonlight, he noticed it had the Nazi swastika above a red and white diamond on the handle.

This was a Hitler Youth knife, so this young man was either still in it or had graduated to the regular army in recent months. Either way, he wasn't getting it back. Michael put it in his sopping wet jacket pocket and dragged the limp body into the darkness of the warehouse.

The mess he'd created when he collapsed the massive pile of lumber onto the Gestapo agents had been cleared, no doubt to rescue the bodies of the agents, and someone had stacked the wood in rough piles at the front of the building.

Michael dragged the young soldier to the wall and used the rope to tie him to a metal rod that held the wall in place. The awakened soldier was about to scream for help when Michael flashed the tip of the knife in front of his face.

"I wouldn't do that if I were you," he whispered.

He used the knife to cut the young man's shirt into a couple of strips and wrapped them around his mouth to prevent him from making any noise.

"Stay still and quiet, and I won't hurt you. If you make a fuss, I'll kill you."

The boy looked terrified and Michael hoped that would be enough and that he wouldn't have to hurt him. The soldier nodded, showing that he would comply with Michael's orders.

Michael tested the rope one more time to make sure the soldier couldn't escape and melted into the darkness of the warehouse. He waited a few moments until his eyes adjusted to the darkness, and then half felt, half saw his way to the large stack at the back of the building.

He found the pallet, and he groped around for a few minutes until he found the hole where he'd hidden his bags.

With one last look at his captive, who stared at Michael as if he were the devil himself, Michael was gone. By the time the soldier was discovered, he'd be miles away.

Chapter Fifty-Six

As Michael hiked through the darkness, the only sound accompanying him was the gentle babble of streams and the occasional rustle of leaves.

The fields and hills around him were silhouettes against the faint starlit sky. Now and then, the dark outline of a farmhouse or barn would emerge, oftentimes with the swastika hanging prominently for all to see and for Michael to fear.

Though he couldn't see it, he could feel the oppressive weight of the Nazi regime all around him, like a looming shadow in the night.

Though there were no birds to break the stillness, the distant screech of a lone owl or the croak of a frog from a nearby pond punctuated the silence.

At dawn, as the first rays of sunlight pierced the horizon, Michael neared a denser patch of woodland. During the night, he had trudged for over a mile in a shallow river, hoping to hide his scent from any dogs that might be on his trail.

As dawn approached, the melodic twittering of awakening birds echoed through the towering trees, signalling the start of a new day.

He climbed a tree and sat high in the branches, hidden by thick leaves. Once settled, he pulled off his boots and checked his aching feet.

A shudder skated down his spine as his gaze fell on their dreadful condition, the flesh puckered and tortured, reminding him of the texture of forgotten prunes. Blistered welts spread like a grotesque canvas, each a signature of agony. He turned his head and looked away.

Finally, he laid out his soaked clothing, glad at least that it wasn't the middle of winter as it had been the last time, made sure the rucksack and briefcase were secure and fell asleep.

He awoke with a start when he heard vehicles not too far from his hiding place. He groggily glanced at his watch to see what time it was.

It was nearly noon. He'd slept for six hours!

He pulled on the partially dry clothing, being careful to wipe his sore feet before covering them with damp socks and boots. He ate some of the stale sandwiches from his rucksack and settled down to look at the envelope Mother had given him before she'd died.

Mother! Visions of her falling played over and over in his mind, and he wiped his eyes several times as he tried focusing on the contents that she'd believed were so important.

The envelope contained new identity papers for a twenty-year-old German engineer from Munich called Erwin Engel. The photograph was of Michael's face.

There was nothing else in the envelope. No explanation, nothing.

Mother gave her life so I could have new identification papers to get out of Germany!

Michael clutched the papers to his chest and heaved as the bile rose in his throat. She may not have known what was in the envelope but the reason she'd died clawed at him like a dagger to his heart.

Why? I'm not worthy.

He rocked back and forth for a few minutes until he regained some control of his emotions.

You are in terrible danger, Michael. I don't have time to explain but we have a friend who works at a certain telephone exchange and she passed on some vital information that involved you.

Mother's words at the railway station burst into his mind and he went over them repeatedly.

What telephone exchange? Did they have a contact who worked at the Gestapo headquarters telephone switchboard? That would be a perfect place for a spy to work.

What did they hear?

Whatever it was, it must have included Michael's alias as Erich Weber, as well as information about the train ticket he'd purchased.

Michael wouldn't allow Mother's bravery to go unrecognised and he wouldn't let her death be for nothing. If he made it back to England, he would find out who betrayed him and make them pay for what they had done to this wonderful, brave lady.

With more questions than answers, Michael sat back against the tree and spent the rest of the day eating stale sandwiches and trying to figure out a way to escape.

It's impossible!

The Swiss border would be swarming with soldiers and Gestapo, and if one of them recognised him, it'd be over in an instant. As much as he wanted to go that way, he realised it was far too risky.

Shuddering at the prospect of making it all the way to France, Michael realised that would be his best option. He remembered the last time he'd crossed the Rhine from the Black Forest and he groaned at the prospect of doing it again.

He drifted into a restless sleep, waking continually at the slightest crack of a twig or the sound of a dog barking in the distance. Eventually, he gave up and counted his money for the umpteenth time that day.

He had more than enough to get home, but what he lacked was a plan to make it happen. No matter what scenario he came up with, it ended with his death.

Mother, Heinrich, and even Adler deserved better.

Slowly, a plan came to him. It wasn't much of one but it was better than sitting in a tree waiting to be discovered.

As risky as it was, he'd take as many trains as it took to get to Freiburg, which was near the French border. He would avoid the fast, long-distance trains, and instead take the slower local ones that stopped at every station.

This not only gave him an escape route if things went awry but it was one with potentially less scrutiny from the security forces. He would hop from town to town, posing as an engineer going to a new job. He'd work out how to cross the Rhine after he'd done the impossible in reaching Freiburg.

With his plan loosely in place, he waited until the early hours and slid down the tree. The nearest town wasn't too far away, and he could reach it by daylight if he didn't dawdle.

His feet screamed in agony the moment they touched the ground. It took several minutes for the pain to subside enough for him to walk properly, and he limped awkwardly until they loosened up.

By dawn, he was on the outskirts of a small town called Horgenzell. He knew because he'd just passed the sign a few minutes earlier. He was tired, hungry, and running out of energy.

Seeing the signs for the railway station, Michael turned towards it. He shifted down an alleyway between two rows of houses and sat under cover of trees as he took a moment's rest.

He watched as a woman hung her washing on a line outside and he waited, out of sight, for her to finish. His clothes were filthy and he needed a fresh set if he was going to get on a train without being noticed.

Once the woman went back inside her house, Michael jumped the small wooden fence and snatched a set of what looked like her husband's clothes from the line. They were still wet, but he didn't care. At least they were clean.

Two soldiers stood on the platform as Michael nervously waited for the train to a town called Krauchenwies, which was less than an hour away.

The soldiers patrolled up and down, staring at everyone as they walked past. Butterflies in his stomach made Michael feel nauseous and he struggled to keep the stale bread and hard cheese sandwich down.

One soldier stared at him, which made his stomach cramp even harder. As the soldier approached, Michael stood up and walked towards the ticket office. He made conversation with the ticket master and got a pocket timetable of the trains running from various towns in the area. He pocketed the booklet and rested his hand on the weapon in his pocket.

"You!" The soldier pointed at Michael.

Michael gulped down a lungful of air and fought off the desire to run, which took everything he had. Other commuters looked away, glad it wasn't them the soldier had singled out.

The other soldier stood close by, casually watching his comrade going about his business.

"You, show me your papers."

Michael handed his new set of papers over to the soldier, who studied them closely.

"Your name?" he barked.

"Erwin Engel."

"What are you doing here?"

"I'm an engineer working for Süddeutsche Industriewerk in Munich. We are a specialist railway equipment company that manufactures and services railway signalling equipment. They sent me to inspect them at various places on the tracks."

Sweat formed below Michael's hairline as he spoke because he knew it was a flimsy story that would be easy to disprove. He'd made it all up during his overnight walk. He knew nothing about railway switching systems and a single technical question would have shown him to be an imposter.

He glanced down at the briefcase in his left hand and caught his breath as he thought of what it contained. If the soldier asked to see inside, all hell would break loose, and once again, his chances of survival would be almost non-existent.

The soldier held the papers up against Michael, eyes scanning intently, then back to Michael's face. After what felt like an eternity, he passed them back. "Heil Hitler!" he barked, snapping his heels together.

Michael's heart raced, his mouth dry. Mustering a

semblance of calm, he replied, "Heil Hitler," the words tasting like ash in his mouth.

He was glad when the train finally arrived, and as he found his seat, he watched the two soldiers laughing together on the platform, waiting for their next victims to show up.

Chapter Fifty-Seven

An hour later, Michael was about to board another train, this time heading west. He'd chosen train journeys of less than an hour's duration, hoping the smaller Bahnhofs wouldn't attract as much attention as the larger ones.

So far, it had proven him right, and as the train approached, he packed the newly purchased food he'd bought from a nearby shop that would last several days if he was careful.

He'd also bought a new canvas satchel big enough to conceal the briefcase. The last thing he wanted was an inquisitive soldier or policeman asking what was inside it.

At eight thirty in the evening, he pulled into a small town called Löffingen. He was only around thirty miles from Freiburg, which would be another one or two train rides away.

After the altercation with the soldier earlier, nobody else had bothered him. Soldiers and policemen were evident at each stop, and at one small Bahnhof, three members of the Hitler Youth patrolled proudly in their brown shirts, black neckerchiefs, and black shorts. What stood out the most though, was the Swastika proudly displayed on their left arms.

Michael knew they were as fanatical and brainwashed as any Nazi out there and he'd kept well away from them.

Although only a short way from Freiburg, dusk was closing in and he needed somewhere to sleep for the night. Tomorrow was a vital day, and he was exhausted. He hadn't dared sleep on the trains for fear of being woken by the Gestapo and after walking all the previous night, he was done for.

He desperately wanted a bed, but he couldn't risk staying in the one hotel the little town of Löffingen possessed, just off the main street, because Nazi Germany had informants everywhere. Images of Benno Vogel, the Blockleiter, or block supervisor, of the apartments in Munich where Gerda and her friends had died rushed through his mind.

The memory of David struggling down the stairs of the fire escape after catching a stray bullet in the apartment filled him with sorrow and he shook his head to clear his thoughts.

It was too much of a risk to stay in the hotel, so he ventured outside the town for a couple of miles until he came across a farmyard. A warm hayloft sounded perfect, but two angry dogs making way too much noise chased him away.

He circled the town for another two hours, by which time it was pitch black. Heavy clouds covered the stars and he knew there was about to be a storm. He needed to get inside somewhere before he got soaked.

He approached the houses at the edge of Löffingen and noticed a few of them had a shed in their back gardens. The rain started as he tried one after the other but they were all locked.

Finally, as thunder cracked above, he found one that opened. Relieved, he stepped inside and wedged the door behind him with a garden shovel.

He found an uncomfortable space on top of some sacks and pulled out his flashlight, which he placed on the red setting. After carefully massaging his sore feet, he ate and drank some water before turning his attention to the railway schedule and what he was facing the next day.

How am I going to get over the border? I can't just walk over a bridge into France. The Nazis would be all over me.

He pondered for over an hour but he couldn't come up with a workable solution. In the end, he put it to the back of his mind until he got there. He'd worry about it then.

He settled back, using his new canvas satchel as a pillow. The documents inside the briefcase meant instant death if he were to be caught with them crossing the border. But he had no other choice. His mission had been to get Adler across the border but failing that, the documents he carried were almost as good.

Tension rose inside his chest and he forced it back by thinking of his beloved Mina. He was less than seventy miles from her yet it might as well have been a million miles for what it was worth.

As he closed his eyes, he wondered what she was doing and if she was thinking of him. He had no idea if she'd heard of the demise of Karl Lutz, and if she had, he hoped her life was easier now that he wasn't harassing her anymore.

He drifted off with memories of them lying together in

the hayloft, enjoying and exploring each other's deepest hopes and fears.

"I'm really going to marry you one day," he murmured, right before he fell into a deep sleep full of dreams of Mina and their life together on a farm in times of peace and tranquillity.

Chapter Fifty-Eight

It was daylight by the time Michael left the shed the next morning. The first train for Freiburg left at six thirty, and he wanted to be there in plenty of time so he could buy his ticket and assess the situation before climbing aboard.

Immediately upon leaving the shed, he knew something was different. It was only five forty-five and yet the roads of this small town were filled with the sounds of vehicles and the shouts of men barking out orders could be heard long before they could be seen.

Michael lay behind a row of bushes and watched a column of eight bathtub Kübelwagen's drive past him towards the Bahnhof.

Instinctively, he knew they were for him, but how? How had they found him so quickly?

A wave of relief washed over him as he saw the bath-tubs stop outside the little hotel on the main street. Swarms of armed soldiers swept inside and if he'd given in to his urge the previous night, his life would now be over.

It still will be if I don't think fast. What am I going to do? They're all over the place and there are hundreds of them. There is no way I can outrun all of them. I'm done for.

He wrapped the palm of his hand around the handle of the Walther PPK and renewed his vow to go down fighting. He knew what fate awaited him if he didn't and he'd rather die quickly in a hail of bullets than in the torture chambers of the Gestapo or SS.

He took a deep breath and took stock of his situation.

Hopeless.

Soldiers, uniformed policemen, Hitler Youth, and plain-clothed men gathered outside the hotel and when the soldiers returned from inside empty-handed, they fell in with all the others.

Barriers blockaded the streets and all traffic had been halted. From what Michael could see, the locals remained indoors, wisely keeping out of the way.

The large group of at least a hundred men fell into whispered silence and from Michael's vantage point behind the bushes, he watched as a familiar figure stepped out of the hotel and stood in front of them.

It was Kreise!

He was too far away to see but Michael hoped he was still hurting and bruised from their last encounter at the side of the river in Ravensburg. Right now, he'd take any kind of victory, no matter how small.

"Silence!" Kreise roared and the men instantly went quiet. Michael held his breath as he strained to hear what he was saying.

Kreise began shouting to the men standing in front of him.

We're searching for a young man who looks to be in his early twenties. He has short black hair and brown eyes and goes by the name of Erwin Engel.

More importantly, he is carrying a brown briefcase. It is your job to get that briefcase by any means possible.

It is vital the briefcase be recovered. Under no circumstances are you to open it once Engel is apprehended. Do I make myself clear? You are authorised to stop him by lethal force, if necessary, although we'd prefer him to be taken alive. Either way, the most important task is to get that briefcase and deliver it to me, here at the hotel.

Kreise paced up and down like a medieval king giving a final inspirational speech to his warriors before leading them into battle. Then he stopped and threw his right arm in the air, bellowing out in a full-throated roar. "Heil Hitler!"

"Heil Hitler." The roar came back at him so loud that Michael swore he saw the shingles on the hotel roof lift into the air.

He shrank into the bushes, his face pale and drawn. *How did Kreise find me so quickly? How does he know what name I'm using?"*

Confused and insecure, Michael retreated towards the outskirts of town. Almost immediately, two bathtubs turned towards him, forcing him to throw himself on the ground to keep as low a profile as he could.

Four soldiers, two on each side, scanned the area as they drove past slowly. Michael pulled his knees to his chest, so the bush covered him completely, and he held his breath. His heart beat out of his chest and it was so loud that he was sure they'd be able to hear it over the roar of the engines.

Once they'd passed, Michael scrambled to his feet and ran across the road before disappearing again into the wasteland between the houses.

Soldiers and members of the Hitler Youth were going from door to door, banging and forcing entry to search for their enemy. Michael heard shouts and screams as the villagers suffered the wrath of the Nazis as their frustration grew.

Michael crawled from bush to bush, pausing each time to make sure he hadn't been seen. When he was sure the coast was clear, he crawled further until he reached the very edge of the town. Open fields lay ahead for as far as the eye could see, but in the distance, he was sure he could make out the edge of a forest.

The sounds of vehicles and men shouting were all around him. Kreise had ordered the locals to leave their homes and assist in the search and Michael knew it was only a matter of time before he was discovered.

He checked the gun and his ammunition supply for the fiftieth time and crawled on his stomach through the fields. It was slow going, but he had no other choice.

As he crawled, the dampness of the morning dew seeped through his clothes, chilling him to the bone. Every inch he moved, the coarse texture of the earth scraped against his palms, leaving them raw.

Tiny pebbles and fragments of hard soil pressed into his flesh, leaving transient imprints. Thistles and thorns from the neglected undergrowth reached out, scratching his arms and face, drawing tiny beads of blood.

His cheek brushed against the cold, dewy grass, its wetness mingling with the sweat on his face. Each sensation, each prick and sting, was a sharp reminder of the perilous reality he was navigating.

Daylight prevailed and there was no natural cover he could aim for. He was stuck in an open field with nowhere to go and as all hope drained from his heart, he realised that this was where he was going to make his last stand.

He stopped and lay still, listening to the sound of his

heartbeat thumping against the soft ground soaked from the overnight rain. He was drenched and covered in mud, yet he didn't seem to notice. Above all else, he could feel an oncoming darkness wrapping itself around his soul and as hard as he tried, he just couldn't shake it.

Distracted, he almost missed the farmhouse off to his left, a few hundred yards away. He only noticed because he heard what appeared to be the owner and his son slam the front door on their way out. Both carried pitchforks, and he could tell from the tone of their voices they were angry.

He was sure their anger was directed at him.

Luckily, they moved in the opposite direction from where he lay in the grass, so when they were out of sight, he crawled towards it, hoping to find somewhere to hide. Or, better yet, a motorised vehicle he could use to escape.

Not that I'd get very far, but it's better than crawling through a field in full view of the entire German army.

Hoping they didn't have any dogs that would either attack him or bark loudly, he crawled to the edge of the farmhouse. Once there, he sat against the wall and looked around.

Nothing.

There was an old wooden hay cart that was no doubt pulled by a horse, but nothing mechanical that could get him away. He didn't even see a bicycle.

An idea hit him. He knew it was a risk, but the area was swarming with the enemy, and he was living on borrowed time. He crawled to the hay cart and climbed on it. Short, wooden sides around a foot or so tall hid him from prying eyes, and the old wet hay was thick enough to cover him completely.

The stench of animal dung undercut the distinct aroma of the hay. It was a scent that spoke of farm life, of days under the sun and nights under cold stars. But now, that familiar smell was masking Michael, both comforting and disgusting him.

He quickly realised that they had thrown the hay into the cart for disposal. It smelled terrible, which perversely appealed to Michael as it would probably hide his smell from the dogs he could hear straining on the ends of their chains as they searched for his scent.

He pulled the hay over him, closed his eyes, and prayed. If he could make it until nightfall, he might yet stand a chance.

Chapter Fifty-Nine

A few minutes later, the sound of rustling grass caught Michael's attention. He held his breath and listened as hard as he could.

Something isn't right!

A small hole above his face allowed him to breathe. It also enabled him to see what was directly above him, and as something glinted in the sullen, overcast sky, a flash of steel broke through the uniform greyness with an incongruous spark.

An unnatural gleam, piercing the soft curtain of the gloomy daylight, thrust down towards him, and Michael reacted in an instant. He moved and a split second later, a knife embedded itself in the wooden floor of the hay cart, where mere moments before, his head had been.

He shot up, scattering hay everywhere. He didn't have time to gather himself, because a large pair of hands wrapped themselves around his neck. His assailant squeezed and the struggle for life and breath was real.

Michael felt his face turning red and his vision blurred. He knew he didn't have long before he passed out and he grabbed the hands, trying to force them off his throat.

They didn't move. Whoever was attacking him was strong and there was no budging them. As his consciousness faded, he heard the man talking to him from above. His brain, struggling for oxygen, couldn't make out the words and as he slipped into darkness, he welcomed the feeling.

So, this is what death feels like. It isn't so bad after all.

His hands relaxed and fell away and as they did, he felt the hold on his neck tighten even further. It felt like he was in the grip of a giant snake, maybe an anaconda, or one of those massive Australian ones he couldn't recall the name of.

As he drifted towards death, his hand rested on something hard and cold. His befuddled brain struggled to work out what it was and then it came to him. It's a knife!

In one last desperate attempt to live, Michael's oxygen-starved brain searched for clarity. He grabbed the knife, ripped it out of the hay, and thrust upwards, feeling it grating against the bone and soft tissue of his would-be killer.

Warm liquid ran down Michael's arms, splashing onto his face and body. The vice-like grip relaxed and the giant hands fell away. As he gasped for air, Michael heard a thud, followed by groaning.

Life returned to Michael's body and with it came a splitting headache. Stars formed in front of his eyes as vision returned, and with it came an understanding of his predicament.

He shook himself into life and rolled out of the hay cart, looking for the man who attacked him. He found him lying in a pool of blood on the ground beside the cart.

Michael turned him over and thrust his entire weight onto his chest, knee first. He'd expected someone giant-sized but was shocked when he saw the man was no bigger than he was. What had felt like giant hands were, in fact, no different from his own, and he reflected on how the brain perceives things when it's starved of life-giving oxygen.

The knife had entered the man's chest and was so deep that Michael knew it had pierced his heart.

"You're dying," he said, his voice hoarse from the near throttling he'd received.

Even though the man had tried to kill him, Michael couldn't help but feel sorry for what he'd done. He was probably no older than he was, which made it even worse. He would have had plenty of years ahead of him if he hadn't been in this situation, right now, in a fight to the death with another young man his age.

A young man desperate to live.

The mortally wounded man was a soldier, as he wore the grey uniform of the Wehrmacht. The man grabbed Michael's arm and pulled him down.

"You're under arrest. I caught you." He coughed and blood foamed from the corners of his mouth. Michael took no pleasure in his demise.

"You did and you'll get all the glory for it."

The man smiled and relaxed his grip on Michael's arm.

"How did you find me?" Michael asked.

"You were crawling through the grass. I thought you were a dog at first but then I made out your face. I followed you and waited until you jumped into the hay cart."

"That was clever of you." Michael half meant what he was saying, but his sympathy for the enemy didn't run that far. By now, he'd recovered his senses and he wanted to know how Kreise had found him.

The soldier coughed again and more blood ran from his

mouth. Michael quickly scanned the area, ensuring they were still alone, before turning back to the dying man.

"How did you know where to look for me?" Michael's voice was low, urgent.

The soldier's eyes fluttered open, his gaze distant. "Kreise... he's everywhere. Your description... your briefcase."

"Someone saw me at the Bahnhof?"

A faint nod. "They thought you were just another traveller until Kreise's warning came through. Your description, a man with a brown briefcase."

Michael's heart raced. "So, it was just bad luck?" He aimed the words at himself more than the soldier.

The soldier managed a weak, almost rueful smile. "You could say that."

The pain in the soldier's eyes was clear but there was also a hint of pride. "You won't escape him. Kreise always gets his man. He's going to kill you."

"I know." Michael agreed with him. "What were your orders?"

"We had orders to capture or..." His voice trailed off, his energy waning.

"Or kill," Michael finished for him, his voice barely a whisper.

The soldier writhed and opened his mouth. With his last breath, he began shouting for help. Michael had no choice other than to silence him, so he covered his mouth and pressed on the knife until he fell silent forever.

Voices in the distance were getting closer and Michael assumed it was the owner and his son returning from their search. He grimaced and hated himself for what he had done, but he had no other choice.

"I'm sorry," he whispered.

Chapter Sixty

The owner of the farm slammed the door when he entered the farmhouse, no doubt annoyed at the disruption the manhunt was creating. Once the noise subsided, Michael dragged the soldier out of sight.

He stripped the body and changed into the clothes of a Wehrmacht soldier. He lost count of the times he apologised to the soldier's corpse and each item of clothing he put on felt like he was violating every ounce of decency he possessed. But he knew he had no other choice if he was to survive the day.

Once he'd changed, he looked around for somewhere to dispose of the dead soldier. After searching for a few moments, he spotted a well a few yards to his left.

Making sure the farmer wasn't watching, he dragged the soldier to the well and threw him in. He fell to his knees, said a quick prayer for his soul, and then scampered back for his old clothes.

After retrieving the satchel and his rucksack from the hay cart, he sighed, feeling awkward and out-of-place inside a dead man's clothes. He checked his map and headed for the Rhine.

The other soldiers ignored him as he passed them by, his heart pounding every time he came close to them. At all times, he gripped the PPK in his pocket, quite prepared to die rather than allow himself to be captured.

A group of motorcycles sat at the side of a road. Nobody was guarding them and the riders were nowhere to be seen. There were several makes and models and as Michael inched towards them, he racked his brains trying to remember what he'd learnt from Captain Sanders back in England.

Captain Sanders! That traitorous rat!

The thought of Sanders made Michael's blood boil. Images of Mother falling to her death because of his treachery caused his adrenaline to spike, and he forced the images from his mind before they consumed him.

Concentrate on the here and now. Worry about Sanders later.

It seemed to work and he focused on the array of motor-cycles in front of him. One of them, at the front, looked the most familiar. He recognised the DKW NZ 350 from Bletchley and was familiar enough to know its operation.

A small seat sat on top of a narrow steel frame that housed the 350cc engine. From what he remembered, it had a four-speed gearbox and twin exhaust pipes. They'd painted this one in a dull green, but the most important thing was that the key was in it.

When he looked, all the motorcycles had the keys inserted, so he had a quick look around and removed them all except the one in the DKW. He pocketed them and jumped onto the seat.

Not having much experience on a motorcycle, Michael

felt the familiar twangs rising in his stomach as he turned the key and pressed down on the foot lever to start the engine. He knew he'd have mere moments once it roared into life and any mistakes would be fatal.

The engine started, shattering the tranquil illusion of the quiet countryside. Heads turned towards the noise and Michael pressed on the gear lever with his foot. The motorcycle jerked into action and he turned and drove as fast as he could.

Men ran towards the other motorcycles parked at the side of the road. Their mouths moved but Michael couldn't tell what they were saying. What he saw though, were the men aiming their weapons at him.

He sped up and started bobbing and weaving, hoping he didn't fall off. Bullets ricocheted off the road all around him. Some pinged off the steel frame, and one even grazed his ankle, although it didn't penetrate.

He was glad when he reached a corner and rode out of sight. He was also glad he'd had the foresight to snatch the keys, otherwise, he would have been an easy target for the more experienced riders.

He drove off at full speed, barely making it around several bends. Once he'd put a few miles between them, he slowed down to a less suicidal pace.

He took different roads, turning left here and right there. He didn't have a clue where he was and all he wanted was to stay out of the way of the following horde, who by now would be mobilised and after him in force.

Assuming Kreise would call ahead to get the roads blocked, Michael didn't go near any towns or major roads. He rode for about an hour until he reached the outskirts of a small town he didn't know the name of.

Two vehicles blocked the only road that went through

the village and as he couldn't find any other way around them, he pulled off the road and rode into the middle of a group of trees. He covered the bike as best he could and skirted around the little town on foot.

From what he could glean from his map, he couldn't be more than ten miles from the Rhine, so he hid inside a thick bush and waited for nightfall.

While flat and exposed, the village was surrounded by forest. Michael hoped it was dense enough to take him all the way to the river but he knew from experience that it wasn't likely.

As darkness descended, he gathered his belongings and listened one more time for any sign of Nazi activity. The village road was still blocked because he could see the vehicles in the distance stopping everything that came through, which wasn't much because it was such a small place.

As he stepped out, he almost walked into a cyclist who had just passed him. Luckily, whoever was riding it hadn't seen him and they had sailed right past the most wanted man in Germany.

Michael berated himself for his carelessness. He'd been fortunate this time, but he needed to be more aware if he was going to make it home.

Cursing Captain Sanders one more time, Michael got away from the road and tramped through the wet fields, each step sending shards of hot pain through his damaged feet.

After a while, he reached the edge of the forest and he breathed a sigh of relief when he entered. Ever since his ordeal in the Black Forest, he'd somehow felt safer and more secure when he was surrounded by trees and wilderness. It was as though the outstretched branches felt like guardians, allowing safe passage, and guiding him to safety.

At least it was then. I hope they're as kind to me this time.

Except this time, it wasn't a forest he was in. The trees came and went, interspersed with open fields and wooden fences. Each time he climbed over them, his feet sent jolts of pain into his brain, slowing him down and making him vulnerable to his pursuers.

After an hour or more, he started seeing signs of civilisation again. Lights were visible in windows, both upstairs and down, and he found himself longing for Mina and the cosy hayloft where they'd spent their time together.

A sign on the outskirts told him he was in Schliengen. He was close, less than two miles to the river. Now it was time to turn his attention towards how he was going to get across.

I've got to get there first.

Once again, he skirted around the town, keeping his head down and staying away from the few people who were wandering down to the local beer hall. Once past the town, he headed for the river.

As he neared the river, he came upon a body of water that had a road running alongside it. He found a place to rest in the trees and pulled out his map. With his flashlight on the red setting, he looked to see where he was.

According to his map, he was standing next to a small lake that stood between a town and the Rhine. He'd made it! Now he had to work out how to get across.

The trees thickened on the other side of the lake, and from reading the map, it appeared they remained that way until they reached the riverbank. He got up to go when he heard vehicles approaching.

Not again!

More painful memories flashed by from when he'd been

attacked by a group of soldiers mere feet from the river the previous winter. He'd been lucky that time but it had forced him to take the lives of the young men who stood in his way.

He'd do anything to avoid that happening again.

He lay close to the ground as two slow-moving vehicles passed by. *At least they aren't the bathtubs that seem to haunt me every time I'm here!*

He watched the lights as they swept away the darkness and held his breath until they were out of sight. He was about to move when he heard them coming back.

The vehicles split up, one turning towards the town and the other patrolling up and down the lane.

He waited until it had gone by and ran for the trees. They were dense, which suited him perfectly. Ten minutes later, he crossed another narrow lane and then he was standing at the edge of the riverbank, staring across the darkness to the safety of France on the other side.

The river was wide and deep and although it looked calm, Michael knew it had a strong current that would sweep him away if he tried to swim across. There weren't any boats that he could see either. He was stuck, so close, and yet so far. He'd have to keep moving until he found a boat he could steal.

Lights and the sound of an engine approached down the lane. Michael threw himself into the trees and crawled out of sight. The vehicle stopped less than a hundred yards away and the men spoke to each other in the darkness.

What are they doing?

It was too dark to see properly but the men seemed to be jovial and happy. They laughed and joked together, and Michael realised they had stopped to pee.

Relieved, he let out a deep breath. A few minutes later,

they got back in the vehicle and drove off, leaving Michael alone in the darkness beside the mighty river.

For hours, he scoured the riverside, dodging Nazi patrols and navigating thickets in search of a boat.

By midnight, he was tired, hungry, and frustrated. The river gods were conspiring against him, keeping him in Germany when freedom was so close.

As the forest cleared, an industrial building loomed ahead, possibly his last chance at finding a way across. It was dark, so nobody should be working. He scouted around it, hoping to find a small craft he could use to cross the river.

Nothing.

As another patrol approached, Michael darted to the building's side, spotting a door in the shadows. It was locked, but a window was cracked open.

Is there anything inside I can use?

Intrigued, he waited until the patrol had gone, and climbed in through the window. He set his flashlight on red and looked around.

Chapter Sixty-One

Rows of pallets lined the walls from floor to ceiling and as he looked around, Michael saw he was inside a storehouse of some sort.

The pallets contained items of all kinds of shapes and sizes, but Michael stared at the empty ones as a wild idea began to take shape.

He'd build a raft!

A couple of the pallets contained fence posts and as he scouted around, he found some wire and rope.

With everything laid out, he assembled the makeshift raft. He was so engrossed in what he was doing that he never heard the footsteps approach from behind.

By the time he'd registered that he wasn't alone, it was too late. A heavy object smashed down on his head, sending him into the abyss. Explosions of stars erupted in front of his eyes and he felt himself being dragged by his feet. The next thing he knew, a rope was being tied around his ankles.

His assailant was about to tie his hands when he came around. It was like he was flying towards the light at the end of a dark tunnel and as he burst through, he squinted at the flashlight that was shining in his eyes.

The back of his head immediately ached, but he didn't have time to think about it.

"Who are you?" he asked, his voice sounding hoarse and somehow hollow in the vast warehouse.

"You're the one they're looking for," a male voice replied. "I found the briefcase. You're a traitor, and I hope the Gestapo kill you slowly and painfully."

"I'm not a traitor and it's not what you think." Michael knew it was hopeless. If he told him the truth, that he was an English spy, he'd probably save the Gestapo the job and kill him himself.

The man grabbed a piece of rope and bent down, grabbing Michael's hands.

"Who are you?" Michael asked again.

"Me? I'm just the night watchman. Now, shut up."

He clasped Michael's hands between his right arm and his torso as he wrapped the rope around his wrists. Michael felt some wiggle room and yanked his hands away before the night watchman could restrain them.

In a circular movement, Michael pulled his hands out and swept them around, striking the older man in the temple. The man wobbled, allowing Michael to strike again.

The night watchman roared and threw himself on top of Michael, who thrashed about underneath him. His bound legs made it difficult to manoeuvre but he found enough space to launch another attack with his fists.

The night watchman rained blows onto Michael's body and as he did, Michael's hands gripped the flashlight the man had dropped during the assault.

He hit him in the head as hard as he could. The night

watchman stopped his assault and made a gurgling sound. Michael struck him again.

And again.

The night watchman fell in a heap next to Michael, who struggled to untie the rope from his legs. He used it to secure his attacker to a post, and when he'd finished, he ran around the warehouse to make sure he didn't have an accomplice anywhere.

He didn't, and as Michael went back to speak to him, the night watchman started yelling and screaming at the top of his lungs. Michael crashed his foot into the man's skull, screaming alongside him as the pain in his foot shot up through his body.

The night watchman fell silent, but to be sure, Michael took his socks from him and shoved them into his mouth. Two teeth fell into his palm along with a mouthful of blood, making Michael want to vomit. He tied some rope around the man's mouth, securing the socks to make sure he remained quiet.

Even though the man was secured to a post, Michael wanted to be sure he couldn't escape, at least not until the next morning. By then, he'd be long gone and it wouldn't matter.

"I don't want to hurt you," Michael muttered. "But I won't hesitate if you give me reason to. Do you understand?"

The night watchman glared at Michael as though he were the devil himself.

"Good. Now I've got work to do."

He got to work and by three in the morning, he had a workable raft. The last thing he did was wrap the satchel and his rucksack in a piece of rubber to waterproof it as best he could. He checked the night watchman, whose face had turned different shades of purple and black after the fight. Michael felt sorry for him but there was nothing he could do about it.

"Sit tight and your colleagues will find you in the morning. I'm sorry I did this to you but you gave me no other choice."

The man hissed.

Michael checked outside to make sure the Nazi patrols weren't in the area and then dragged his makeshift raft towards the river.

He didn't know if it would work or not but he'd rather drown than face the wrath of the Gestapo or the SS.

He said a prayer and pushed the Arc, as he'd christened it, into the deceptively calm, murky waters of the River Rhine.

He sat up on the raft as it gathered pace in the middle of the wide river. Using a fence post as an oar, he paddled for all he was worth towards the other side.

The raft creaked and squeaked but it held together. The wooden posts he sat on submerged, and his clothes were soaked, but he didn't notice. All his focus was on the other side.

Two hours and several miles downstream later, Michael emerged from the Rhine. For the second time in his life, he'd crossed the mighty river into France and escaped Nazi Germany. Something told him he'd be doing this again before the war ended.

The war? For most people, it hadn't even begun yet. For Michael, it had been raging for over half a year.

He pulled the raft into the trees on the other side, gathered his almost-dry bags, and headed inland.

Chapter Sixty-Two

A week and a half later, Michael stepped off a fishing boat in Ramsgate harbour and immediately headed for the railway station.

Situated on the coast in East Kent, Michael was less than ten miles from his home in Sandwich. It took everything he had to avoid going there and his heart ached at the thought of being so close and yet so far.

It was too dangerous for his family, especially his father, who might still be in the hospital for all he knew. Until he'd taken care of the traitorous Captain Sanders, home was out of bounds.

Forcing his mind away from them, he boarded a train and headed for Cambridge, where the Fernsbys owned a home that had been in the family for decades. After David's death and Michael's expulsion from Cambridge University, the house had sat empty, an unwanted relic from a time gone by.

It was the perfect place for what Michael had in mind.

The house on Green Street was close to Trinity College. The family always had a set of keys hidden underneath an empty plant pot near the front door, and Michael was relieved to find they were still there.

As soon as he opened the door, he regretted his decision to use it. Reminders of David were everywhere and he hesitated at the sight of an old photograph on a wooden table in the living room. It was a picture of them together, taken during a summer holiday in Brighton.

Michael's fingers traced the contours of the frame, pausing at David's smiling face. He could almost hear his laughter, the way it rang out, pure and untainted, during those carefree days.

His throat tightened and he pulled the photograph close to his chest, the cold glass pressing against his cheek. For a moment, he was lost in the past, enveloped in the warmth of memories.

Another discovery halted him. There, neatly folded on David's bed, were clothes that belonged to Patricia, David's last girlfriend. A particular scarf draped over the chair caught Michael's attention. He remembered the day David excitedly showed it to him, sharing how he'd chosen it specifically for Patricia's birthday. As he held it, a tremble coursed through his hand, the fabric slipping between his fingers as emotions threatened to drown him.

His eyes clouded over and his breath became ragged. He bit his bottom lip hard, tasting the metallic sting of blood in an effort to ground himself in the present and keep from being completely consumed by grief. Pangs of guilt swept over him, and the all-too-vivid images of David dying in his arms haunted his already tortured mind.

Snap out of it. I'll avenge David by stopping Sanders.

Michael repeated the words over and over but no matter what he did, the visions were too strong. Finally, and against all the decisions he'd made on the way, he left the house. He wandered the streets, finding himself irresistibly drawn towards the Wren Library.

Its majestic architecture loomed before him, standing as a testament to the countless generations of scholars who had passed through its grand doors. The fading sunlight played upon the intricately carved stone, casting long, stretching shadows across the pristine lawns.

But it was the distant sound, drifting from beyond the library, that truly captured his attention. The gentle tolling of the bells from King's College Chapel rang through the air, their resonant notes echoing with memories of simpler times. Each chime seemed to pull at Michael's heartstrings, evoking images of David and their youthful escapades around the university.

He paused for a moment, allowing himself to be immersed in the melancholic beauty of the scene. The rhythmic tolling, combined with the serene flow of the River Cam, provided a brief respite from the tumultuous emotions that had plagued him since his return to England.

He found a familiar bench near the River Cam where he'd sat many times during his brief stay at the university. Some of his happiest memories had been made here with David, when they'd just sat and watched the ducks and other waterfowl sail by on the peaceful river, their laughter mingling with the gentle rustle of leaves and the soft ripple of the water, encapsulating a camaraderie untouched by the war's looming shadow.

Further down the riverbank, a student sat cross-legged, engrossed in a book, occasionally glancing up to enjoy the serene view. Nearby, the faint strumming of a guitar emanated from beneath a willow tree, where another student practised a soft ballad, lost in the melody.

But what caught Michael's eye was an elderly couple

strolling along the path. The man held a cane, but it was clear his primary support was the woman beside him.

Their fingers interlocked and they walked hand-in-hand, radiating a contentment that came from decades of shared experiences. They seemed without a care in the world, living completely in the moment, and he couldn't help but envy their apparent peace.

The serene scene soothed his soul and he sat for hours, absorbing the tranquillity of it all. It was a far cry from his recent experiences and it was just what he needed.

Thoughts of David mingled with happier ones of Mina and what their time together meant to him, which was everything. He imagined a world where he and Mina could live together in peace and happiness and he allowed his mind to drift along with the pace of the river Cam.

Finally, with darkness approaching, he rose from the bench and made his way back to the Fernsby residence less than half a mile away. He'd purged his soul and was glad to be back on home soil. Now it was time to get to work.

Someone has betrayed you, Michael. There is a traitor in your camp and until we find them, we're stopping all communication with the British. I'm getting you out of here and then I'm going to a place the Nazis will never find me.

Mother's final moments echoed around in his brain over and over, and he couldn't get them out of his mind. *Was it Sanders? Are you sure he is the traitor?*

It had to be. His mission had been top secret and nobody else had known anything about it, especially the dead letter boxes he'd used in Munich and the false identity they'd given him to use as a last resort.

And yet Kreise had known all about them, so it had to have been Sanders. Who else could it be?

I've made a plan, and I'm sticking to it.

The next morning, he took a train to London so he couldn't be traced to his safe house in Cambridge and entered one of the iconic red telephone boxes that were famous throughout the world.

His hands shook as he dialled the number etched in his brain. Hoping Sanders was at the office, he waited impatiently for the switchboard operator to patch him through to Sanders' private line that went directly to his desk.

Several nerve-racking moments later, a male voice Michael recognised instantly answered.

"Hello?"

"Captain Sanders, I bet you're surprised to hear from me."

"Who is this and how did you get this number?"

"Don't you recognise me, Sanders? It's Michael Fernsby."

"Fernsby?" The shock in Sander's voice was real and the line fell silent as they both gathered their thoughts.

"Fernsby? Is that really you?"

"In the flesh."

"I need to be sure. Give me the codename of the letters in the dead letter box you used to address our friend in Munich."

"Gertrude," Michael replied.

Sanders paused. "It is you. How can this be?" He genuinely did sound surprised to hear his voice.

"I assure you it is me, Captain Sanders. Were you not expecting me to call?"

"No, I thought you were dead."

Chapter Sixty-Three

A stunned silence filled the little red telephone box.

"What?" Now it was Michael's turn to be surprised.

"We can't talk on an open line," Sanders said. "We need to meet."

"Not until you tell me why you abandoned me." Michael held firm.

"It's too risky. Come in and we'll talk."

Michael scoffed. "I'm not going anywhere near your office, Sanders."

Something in Sanders' voice made Michael consider his words. "What do you mean, it's too risky?"

Did he know there was a spy in the agency? Or is he trying to lure me into a trap?

"How long have you been back in England?" Sanders shot back. "And why didn't you call me?"

"I have my reasons," Michael replied. "I don't trust you."

Sanders sighed. "Have you tried calling your family?"

Panic rose in the pit of Michael's stomach. "No, why? Has something happened to them?"

He'd assumed they would be safe as long as he stayed away from them.

"Judith is missing," Sanders spoke rapidly as if he didn't want to say the words. "Fernsby, it's imperative you come in. It's not safe for you out there."

Michael stood for a moment, the coldness of the phone box contrasting with the warmth of the day outside. He felt as if a thick fog was swirling around him, shrouding everything in confusion.

Judith.

His younger sister, with those bright hazel eyes and a contagious laugh. How could anyone want to harm her? The pain in his chest was physical, a raw and aching wound. Every step he took from this point on was for her.

Michael almost dropped the telephone that was cradled to his ear. "Judith?" was all he could say.

"She was kidnapped a week ago and whoever took her is demanding something in return. I can't say any more until you come in."

"What about the rest of my family?"

"They are safe. We put them in a safe house where they will be guarded around the clock."

Michael imagined his mother going crazy with worry and despair. Not only had she lost David but now she was facing the loss of her two other children as well. What must she think of him?

"I'm not coming in." Michael had to regain control of both himself and Captain Sanders. Thoughts whipped through his brain. "There's a bench outside the Wren Library facing the River Cam in Cambridge. Meet me there at ten tonight. Make sure you're alone or I won't show. Something is wrong, Sanders, and I'm going to fix it."

"Ten tonight. I'll be there."

"Make sure you're alone."

"I will."

Michael put the telephone down and left the red box. He wandered for over a mile, stunned beyond comprehension. He'd assumed that once he returned to England, he'd arrest or kill Sanders, and that would be it. Now he knew that wasn't happening.

Was Sanders even the traitor? He'd sounded genuinely surprised when he heard Michael's voice but that could just be a ploy to lower his suspicions and get him to come in.

He sat by the Thames and forced himself to think clearly. What did Sanders say? *Someone kidnapped Judith a week ago and whoever took her is demanding something in return.*

Michael knew exactly what they wanted and he had no doubt Sanders knew it too – the briefcase.

Now what do I do? If I hand them the briefcase, there are no guarantees they will release Judith, and all the people who died to help me get it here would have died for nothing. They will probably kill both Judith and me once they have it, so we won't be able to tell anyone what happened or who they were.

On the other hand, if I don't give it to them, they will kill Judith for sure.

A thought hit him. Sanders had intimated that he'd never heard a word from him once he arrived in Germany. That can't be true, because he'd sent word via the dead letter box in the Frauenkirche Church, and he'd kept them up to date with everything.

318

If Sanders never received it, then who did? Kreise? Had the Nazis known about it all along?

The more he thought about it, the more he realised that couldn't be true, because if Kreise had known about the dead drop, he would have arrested him at the church and never let him escape.

And then there were Mother's words. A telephone operator who worked with the resistance told her there was a spy in the SIS. How would she have known that if the Nazis had been running this all along?

No, this wasn't the work of the Nazis. This was the work of a British traitor. And the traitor was Captain Sanders.

Maybe.

The more he thought about it, the more he doubted himself. He needed more information, and there was only one other person who could provide it.

He stood up and walked a mile to another telephone box on the other side of the city. If Sanders was behind this, the original telephone box would be swarming with SIS by now.

This time he asked to be put through to the main office in Bush House. After a couple of rings, he heard the familiar voice of Maureen Ingram, the personal secretary of Captain Sanders and the only other person who knew what Michael had been doing.

"VCC imports. How may I help you?"

That was the response Michael had been expecting. VCC imports – Victoria Corporate Imports – was the alias SIS used in all correspondence from the office in Bush House. After all, she could hardly answer by saying the caller was speaking to the British intelligence services.

"Good morning, Maureen. This is Michael Fernsby and

I'm reporting in." He decided to be bold and get straight to the point.

"Fernsby?" Like Sanders before her, Maureen sounded surprised to hear his voice. Maureen might not have known every little detail of the operation, but if Sanders was in charge, Maureen was the one who organised it all.

"Yes, it is me."

"Thank goodness you are safe. We've all been worried about you. Where are you? Are you going to come in?"

"No, not for a while. I have a few things to do first."

"What do you need from me?" she asked, as efficient and to the point as ever.

"What happened to the correspondence I sent? Everything went quiet, and I found myself without support when I needed it the most. Some things are troubling me and I need to know who I can trust."

He did a bit of fishing to see if Maureen would give up anything that Sanders had left out, either deliberately or otherwise.

"Whatever correspondence you sent was given to the boss," Maureen replied. "I saw to it myself."

The cogs in Michael's head whirred quickly. If she passed them through, then it proved Sanders was the traitor.

He was about to ask about Judith when Maureen spoke up. "Have you spoken to Sanders yet?"

"No," Michael lied.

"Good. I shouldn't say this but I've had my doubts about the boss for a while. I know you brought something back with you and I can meet you somewhere to get it so that he can't get his hands on it."

A blinding light hit Michael between the eyes. How did Maureen know he had the briefcase? Not even Sanders knew that. How could they, if none of my communications had gone through to them?

"That's what I wanted to hear." He was thinking fast on his feet. "I want to come in but I don't know who to trust."

"I understand and you are doing the right thing. Where do you want to meet?"

"The Lodge at Prince's Golf Course in Sandwich. Meet me outside there at eleven tomorrow night. Be alone."

"Consider it done. I'll see you then."

"Maureen?" Michael hesitated.

"Yes?"

"Is there anything else I should know before you go?"

"No. Just keep your head down and don't contact the boss. We'll work it all out tomorrow night."

Michael stepped out of the telephone kiosk with Maureen's last words still ringing in his ears. The gravity of the situation bore down on him, the noise of the surrounding streets fading to a muffled drone.

Why hadn't she mentioned Judith? The very thought sent a shiver down his back. He replayed their conversation in his mind, searching for any subtle hint or implication about his sister. His heart raced, pounding with worry and growing trepidation.

Panic ate away at him. Was Maureen trying to shield him from some darker truth about Judith's situation? Or was her omission more sinister, suggesting her own involvement or, at the very least, that she was keeping vital information to herself?

The notion that Maureen, always so efficient and seemingly straightforward, might be embroiled in this was hard to stomach.

A surge of anger bubbled up, catching him off guard

with its force. He needed answers and every second of silence, every detail withheld, felt like a betrayal.

He clenched his fists, feeling the cold metal of the telephone kiosk against his back. The burden of responsibility weighed heavily on him; he had to be the rock, the saviour for his family, especially for Judith. But doubt was casting long shadows over everyone he once trusted.

He let out a slow breath, attempting to find a semblance of calm amongst the whirlwind of emotions. Suspicion had become his constant companion, chipping away at his trust.

Now, faced with Maureen's glaring omission, his conviction wavered. The not knowing was the worst bit; each moment of uncertainty felt like a fresh twist of the knife.

Michael knew he needed to take action, to unearth the truth for himself, but as he trudged on, every face he passed felt potentially hostile, every hushed conversation a possible conspiracy.

The weight of the unknown was immense, but it spurred him on, driving his determination to get to the bottom of things, come what may.

Chapter Sixty-Four

Michael stumbled through London's busy streets until he found a bench by the River Thames. Water helped him think clearly and above anything else, that is what he needed.

Why hadn't Maureen mentioned Judith? Was Sanders bluffing? Had Judith really been kidnapped or was that a ploy to make him hand over the briefcase?

The questions seared into his brain and he had to know for sure. He could ask Maureen, but what if she didn't know? Sanders might not have told her. Everything in the SIS was on a need-to-know basis, so if Maureen didn't need to know, then it made sense that Sanders wouldn't have told her.

But what if Judith was at home right now, playing in their back garden with their black Labrador, Lucy?

He had to know.

Michael found another telephone box and asked the switchboard operator to put him through to his home in Sandwich. He allowed it to ring for several minutes before the operator cut in and told him nobody was answering. He thanked her and asked to be put through to Sanders' private line.

This time, he answered almost immediately. "Fernsby?" he asked before Michael could even speak.

"It's Fernsby. What happened to Judith?"

"I can't tell you anything on an open line. When we meet, I'll tell you everything."

"I want to speak to my family."

"That's impossible. They are in a safe house."

"I want to speak to them or I won't come in. I know what you want but you'll never get it if I don't speak to my family."

"That's impossible, Fernsby. You know that as well as I do."

"I'm not asking, Sanders, I'm telling you. Put me through to my family right now."

"How dare you order me around? Don't you know who you're talking to?"

"I don't care if I'm talking to the king himself. I won't ask again."

The line went silent for a moment.

"I know why you want to speak with them but it's impossible."

"Then you will never get your hands on the package. I will find them, Sanders, and if they're harmed in any way, I promise I will find you, and I will kill you."

The line went silent again.

"All right, calm down, Fernsby. Let me see what I can do but this goes against all protocol, and we'll have to move them again after you've spoken to them."

"I don't care. I want to speak to them."

"Give me ten minutes and call back."

"There's one more thing," Michael's voice was icy calm and yet somehow menacing at the same time.

"What?"

"Don't tell Maureen what you are doing. Arrange it yourself. I just spoke to her and she doesn't appear to know anything about Judith. I'd like to keep it that way."

Another pause.

"Why did you call Maureen?"

"Because I don't trust you, Sanders. Someone betrayed me and I aim to find out who it is."

"Fair enough. I'd probably feel the same if I were in your shoes. But why didn't Maureen tell you about Judith? She knows about it. In fact, she was the one who arranged the safe house for them after the kidnapping."

Now it was Michael's turn to fall silent while he processed what Sanders had just told him.

"I'll call back in ten minutes. Don't involve Maureen Ingram."

He hung up and left the telephone box.

Ten minutes on the dot later, Michael called back. Three-way telephone calls were not the norm, but he knew the SIS could make it happen. Either way, he didn't care. All he wanted was to make sure his family was safe and to find out if Sanders was telling the truth or not.

"Michael, is that you?" His heart melted when he heard the distress in Dorothy Fernsby's voice. At that moment, he wanted to reach through the receiver and hold his mother as tightly as he could.

"Mum, thank God! Are you alright?"

"We're not good, Michael. Judith is missing and the government moved the rest of us to some safe house that I'm not allowed to tell you the name of. Your father is barely walking after the accident, although he's out of hospital finally."

Her voice trembled. "Where have you been, Michael? The man from the government wouldn't tell us and we've been worried sick. They won't even tell us why Judith was kidnapped."

Michael could hear her sobbing quietly on the other end of the telephone, and he felt as inadequate as he had ever felt in his life.

"Oh, Mum. I'm so sorry. This is all my fault. I can't tell you where I've been, at least not on the telephone but I promise I will once I've found Judith. How's Gigi?"

"Gigi is here. She's quiet and she's as worried as we are. This is killing us, Michael. We've already lost David and then we thought we'd lost you and Judith as well. No parent can withstand that and it's broken us. I think your father has given up the will to live."

"So have I," she added after a brief pause.

"Mum, I'm sorry." That was all Michael could think to say, which was completely inadequate, and he knew it. "I promise I'll find Judith and make this right. I'll tell you everything I'm allowed to tell you once this is over, which won't be long. Please hang on and don't give up. Believe in me and I will bring Judith home."

"Your father wants me to tell you he loves you and that he's very proud of you. He says this is not your fault, so don't blame yourself."

Don't blame myself? I'm killing the people I love the most in the world, and for what?

"I love you, Mum. You have no idea how much I've been needing to hear your voice."

Captain Sanders cut into the conversation. "I'm sorry to

break this up, but we have to disconnect the call. Operator, please disconnect the family and leave me on the line."

"Michael, we—" Dorothy spoke, but the operator cut her off.

Michael sighed. His eyes misted over, and his vision was blurry.

The line went dead. Inside the cramped confines of the telephone box, Michael felt the full weight of his world pressing down upon him. He rested his forehead against the cool, misted pane, taking a shaky breath.

A solitary tear coursed down his cheek but he quickly brushed it away. Now wasn't the time for vulnerability; he had work to do.

Drawing another steadying breath, he lifted the receiver to his ear once more.

"Your family is safe," Sanders spoke. "We're moving them to another location as we speak. They're under our protection, Fernsby, I promise."

"What happened to Judith?" Michael's voice held an edge, contrasting with the tender tone he'd used with his mother moments earlier.

"Not now. Later."

"Don't be late." Michael hung up and left the telephone box.

Chapter Sixty-Five

It might have been foolish to arrange a meeting with Sanders so close to his home in Cambridge but it was all Michael could think of. In any case, by the time his train pulled back into Cambridge station, he was almost certain that Sanders wasn't the traitor.

Almost.

His head was swimming with questions, none of which he could answer. Who had taken Judith? How? If Kreise hadn't known about the dead letter box, then what happened to the letters he'd left in there? If she knew, why hadn't Maureen Ingram told him about Judith? And why was she so adamant about meeting him and taking possession of the briefcase?

All these questions and more fizzed around in his head, driving him a little crazier each time it popped up again.

Sanders hadn't mentioned the briefcase not one time, so was he bluffing? Or was he genuinely in the dark as to what happened after Michael went into Germany?

He'd soon find out. Sanders wasn't leaving Cambridge until he'd answered all his questions and he still hadn't ruled out the possibility of drowning him in the River Cam if his answers came up short.

Listen to me, acting all tough. Sanders could probably kill me with his bare hands but I'd happily die trying.

Michael was at the meeting point hours before the scheduled time. It was still daylight when he made his first scouting trip around the area, looking for anyone or anything that looked out of place.

He sat on the bench eating a sandwich and pretending to feed the ducks. As darkness fell, he scouted the entire area one last time. He walked around the Trinity College Library, where he'd spent hour upon hour researching and reading, looking for anyone who didn't look like they belonged.

He walked back to the bench through Scholar's Lawn and peered inside the windows of the Wren Library as he went by. Everything looked normal on both sides of the river, so either Sanders was telling the truth and would come alone, or he was far superior in the spy world than he was. Either way, it was almost time to find out.

He knew Sanders would be armed and Michael himself carried his trusty German Walther PPK that had saved his life several times already, often at the expense of another life.

At ten on the dot, Michael sat on the bench, pretending to be watching the river. A flock of butterflies had taken flight in his stomach and he could barely keep still. He couldn't hear anyone approaching because his heart was banging in his chest like a bass drum.

He was as ready as he'd ever be.

Ten minutes passed and Michael was beginning to think Sanders had set him up. He was about to leave when he heard a voice behind him.

"Sit down, Fernsby, and look at the river."

Sanders! Michael did as he was told. Sanders had already outfoxed him and was probably holding a gun to the back of his head.

"I had to make sure nobody was watching us."

Sanders sat next to Michael, his voice low and his head facing the river.

"Sanders, I—" Michael started, but Sanders cut him off.

"I was really worried about you and when it went dark over there, we assumed you'd been either captured or killed. The Nazis had already announced your death months ago and we thought they'd disposed of you quietly so they could deny any knowledge."

"I have a lot of questions that I need answers to, Sanders."

"I understand. Come, walk with me." Sanders rose and set off, walking down the path at the side of the river.

Is he leading me into a trap?

Michael hesitated, which prompted Sanders to turn and face him.

"It isn't a trap, if that's what you're thinking. We have a problem, Fernsby, and together we are going to fix it."

"What happened to Judith?" Michael asked the burning question first.

"She was home alone when they took her. The rest of your family had taken your father out for an impromptu drive. Judith didn't want to go, so she stayed home with her dog, Lucy."

Michael flinched. "Go on."

"Whoever it was, they knew what they were doing. They snatched Judith, and within the hour we received a message informing us that unless you handed over the package, whatever that meant, they would kill her. As we'd assumed you were already dead, you can imagine what a surprise it was to us too."

"When was this?"

"Like I said, a week ago. Ever since then, we've been trying to find out what happened to you in Germany. Our contacts over there went dark around the same time you did, so we had no way of knowing what happened. So, tell me, what did happen? Where's Adler and what's this package the kidnappers are referring to?"

Michael stared at Sanders. If he was the traitor, he was displaying all the wrong traits. Michael doubted more and more that he was the one who had betrayed him.

He took a deep breath and decided to tell him everything.

When he finished, Sanders took a deep breath. "No wonder you didn't trust me. I wouldn't have either."

"I have so many questions, Sanders. What happened to the letters I wrote? Kreise couldn't have found them or I wouldn't be standing here today. How did Kreise find out about the false identity papers I was using to escape Germany? How did they know about Judith?"

"I wish I had the answers, but I don't. I suspect we both know the probable cause of our leak though. Maureen Ingram knew almost as much as I did, perhaps more if she knew about the dead letter box correspondence. And yet, she passed none of this to me. She knew about the briefcase when clearly, I didn't, so I think we start with her."

"Agreed. I think she's our spy and if she is, she has a lot of blood on her hands. Mainly though, I need to get Judith back. Is there anyone you can contact that would have handled the communications on this side before it came through to you?"

"Yes, and I'm already on it. I reached out to a good

friend of mine in the basement, as we call it. They handle all the communications from the field. They have logs of what came in and when and they have a record of who they passed it to, although in our case, it would have been either Maureen or myself."

"How do we handle this?" Michael asked.

"We keep it between ourselves because we don't know how deep this runs. If the SD has penetrated our department, we are in a lot of trouble."

"What do you want me to do in the meantime?"

"Meet her tomorrow night as planned. I'll be there in the shadows, waiting to pounce once you hand over the briefcase to her."

Chapter Sixty-Six

There was no sign of life anywhere. All Michael could hear was the crashing of waves on the nearby beach and the cries of seagulls as they cruised overhead.

Twilight came late at this time of year, and shadows held back the darkness as he ran quietly up the lane alongside the coast from the Royal St George's Golf Club towards Prince's, one of Sandwich's other golf clubs.

The briefcase made it difficult to get into his stride, so he slowed down and concentrated on watching for anything out of place.

Michael knew this area better than most and he used it to his advantage as he ran. The flatlands gave no natural cover for anyone to ambush him, which was why he'd chosen this particular place for his meeting with Maureen Ingram.

So far, there had been no sign of her and he wanted to be in position long before she arrived. Ironically, there was no sign of Sanders either but he knew he would be around somewhere.

Maybe this place isn't as open as I thought.

A few trees stood on the inland side of the clubhouse, so Michael hid himself in them and waited. He had a good view of the surrounding area, and as darkness fell over the landscape, he seemed to be the only living land creature for miles around.

With his watch approaching eleven, Michael stiffened as he heard a motor vehicle driving up the same lane he'd run up earlier. He tensed even more when he heard a car door closing.

Footsteps in the gravel grew softer as they walked around the seaward side of the clubhouse. Michael used that moment to climb down from his perch and follow the person making them.

Whoever was ahead of him was obviously not used to sneaking around anywhere because they were making enough noise to drown out the noisy seagulls overhead.

Michael closed the gap and, in the moonlight, he could make out a shadowy shape a few feet ahead of him. When he was six feet behind, he had them exactly where he wanted: out of sight and earshot of anyone else.

"Stop right there and reveal yourself," Michael ordered. His arm extended in front, the PPK casting an ominous shadow under the stars.

"Fernsby!" Maureen's voice was high-pitched and slightly breathless. "You scared me."

"Why do you suspect Sanders is a spy?" Michael asked bluntly, getting straight to the point. He lowered his arm and put the gun back in his pocket.

"He's been secretive and furtive ever since you left. I understand operational protocol better than most but there were things I needed in order to do my job and Captain Sanders withheld them from me, which I found rather odd."

"Like the correspondence I sent from Germany via the dead letter box?" Michael asked.

"Yes, exactly."

"Where is my family, Maureen? The house is empty and I can't find them anywhere."

"We moved them to a safe place after you disappeared. It was for their safety and they'll be allowed home once all this is over."

"All what? I was abandoned and left to die behind enemy lines. Don't you think that might be a breach of operational protocol?" Michael's voice became harsher.

"I do, but that's beyond my level of responsibility. I'm just the secretary, remember?"

"So why are you here then? Why do you think the briefcase will be safer with you than Sanders?"

"I just told you. Sanders has been acting strange since you left and I don't trust him. I'll take the briefcase above his head to Colonel Dansey. He'll know what to do with it."

"Did you inform Dansey?" Michael asked. "Why isn't he here with you? Surely something as important as what's inside that briefcase would warrant him showing up?"

"I haven't told him yet." Maureen's voice sounded squeezed and flat as if she was on the defensive.

"Why not?"

"Because I wanted to make sure you had it first. I didn't want to drag him all the way out here for nothing if you didn't have it."

Michael paused for a moment to gather himself for what he was about to accuse her of.

"Where is the briefcase?" Maureen asked. "Did you bring it?"

"It's safe. I'll hand it over when I'm certain you're not

the one who betrayed me. I'm confused, Maureen, and I don't know who to trust."

"I don't blame you. I would feel the same if I were you. Give me the briefcase, Michael, and I'll take you to Colonel Z. Then you'll know everything is alright."

"Why didn't you tell me about Judith?"

Maureen hesitated. "How do you know about her? Have you spoken to Sanders?"

"I have, and he told me about her. You left that bit out, didn't you, Maureen?"

"I didn't want to upset you any more than you already are, that's all. Give me the briefcase and everything will be sorted out, Michael."

"You seem awfully keen to get your hands on the briefcase. Why is that?"

"Because there's too much at stake for something so vital to be floating around out here. It needs to be in our custody so we can see what the Nazis are up to. With the information it contains, we might even be able to stop them before this dreadful war begins."

Michael stepped forward. "How do you know about the briefcase? Adler threw it at me during the ambush. I never mentioned it in my communications through the dead letter box, so nobody over here could have known about it. So, how do *you* know, Maureen?"

Maureen stared at Michael and even in the darkness he could feel her glare burning into his soul.

"You're a silly boy, Michael Fernsby. You're playing in a world you know nothing about. You run around thinking you're saving the world, but all you are doing is bringing the war even closer to our shores. Give me the briefcase, Fernsby. I won't ask again."

Maureen Ingram pointed a gun at Michael's head.

"I won't hesitate to shoot if you don't hand it over."

"Alright, hang on." Michael held his hands in the air. "It's over there, in the trees. I'll get it for you."

"Go, and don't try anything or I'll kill you."

Michael shuffled towards the trees and the briefcase, racking his brains trying to think of how he was going to extricate himself from this. He had severely underestimated Maureen Ingram and now he was going to pay the price for it.

As they walked, Michael stalled for time. "Why are you doing this? You know we're already at war with Germany, don't you? It might be in the shadows at the moment, but mark my words, it's about to break out into the open anytime soon."

Maureen laughed. "Hitler can't be stopped and the sooner everyone realises it, the better it will be. Britain, and the world, will realise that he was right, and it isn't the Nazis that are the problem. The Führer is the answer to the age-old problem, which is the Jews. He will eradicate them, and the world will see he was right all along."

Michael was stunned to hear a British woman speaking in this manner, especially one trusted with some of the nation's biggest secrets.

"So, you're a Nazi? I bet Sanders didn't know that when he recruited you. Britain is about to be at war and you are going to have to choose a side."

"I already have. Give me the briefcase. Now."

"We won last time and we will win again this time. Then what will you do when your precious Führer is dead and Germany is in ruins?"

Maureen scoffed. "It's different this time. The Fatherland has risen again, and this time we won't be stopped, not by Britain or anyone else."

"Why?" Michael asked. "Why are you doing this?"

"The briefcase, Fernsby. No more talking."

Michael reached the trees where he'd left the briefcase. He reached in to get it but Maureen shoved him out of the way, the gun pointed straight at his face.

"Back away. I don't trust you."

"Where is it?" Her voice rose as she thrashed about in the undergrowth.

"I'll give it to you when you tell me where Judith is. Once I have her safely in my custody, the briefcase is yours to do what you want with."

Maureen shook her head. "You might have got away with your tricks in Germany but not here. One last time, Fernsby, where is the briefcase?"

Michael knew she wasn't bluffing. As he turned towards the trees, he scanned the area for Sanders. *Where is he? Is he working in tandem with Ingram? Are they in it together?*

With no time left, Michael reached into the branches and pulled down the briefcase from where he'd left it. Holding it out in front of him, he pleaded with Maureen Ingram one more time.

The wind picked up, carrying the salt of the sea with it. Michael's voice trembled but he held Maureen's gaze. "Judith is just a child. We've lost David already. How many more lives will satisfy your allegiance to our nation's enemy?"

"She'll be released once we have the briefcase. Until then, she's staying put."

Michael knew she was lying but something else she'd said piqued his interest. "We?" he asked. "Who are you doing this with? Is Sanders in it with you?"

Maureen laughed. "Sanders? Hell no! I wouldn't trust that incompetent schoolboy to tie my shoelaces."

"Then who?"

"The people I work with will be the new rulers of Britain after the Führer stomps you into the ground. That's who I work with."

Michael racked his brain trying to work out who she was talking about but nothing came to mind.

He clutched the briefcase, refusing to let it go. "Give me Judith, and I'll hand it over."

"You have exactly five seconds to hand it over, Fernsby. If I'm not back at the safe house in the next thirty minutes, Judith will be dead, no matter what I promise here. I'll let her go once I have the case. It's your choice."

I have no choice.

Michael held out the briefcase and allowed Maureen to snatch it from him with her free hand. Her right hand held the weapon that was aimed at his head.

She backed off a few feet and tried the lock, but it wouldn't open. "Where's the key?"

"Adler didn't give it to me. He never had the time. I didn't dare open it in case it was booby-trapped, so whatever is inside must be important for you to have gone to this much trouble to get it."

"More than you'll ever know, Fernsby. Now it's time for you to die but before you do, there's something I want you to know. You see, I lied. I'm not letting Judith go. She's going to die just like you are."

Michael moved towards her but she anticipated what he was going to do, and stepped out of the way, keeping a safe distance between them. She raised her arm and aimed at Michael's heart.

Michael closed his eyes and felt the weight of his failure. *I failed my brother and now I've failed my sister. I failed everyone I tried to save.*

In the split second after he heard the weapon go off, a vision of Judith calling his name rushed through his mind.

He stopped. Something was wrong.

His eyes opened and he wasn't dead. He wasn't even hurt. Instead, Maureen Ingram was sprawled out before him, lying in a deepening pool of dark liquid.

He was stunned and as he looked around, a figure ran out of the trees towards them. Michael squinted.

It was Sanders!

With his senses returned, Michael threw himself next to Maureen and snatched the weapon from her hand. "Where's Judith? If you have any decency left inside you, tell me where she is."

Maureen's eyes flickered open and she gave Michael a twisted smile. Sanders joined them as she spoke her final words. "You are all so stupid. The wolf was at your door and all you did was open it and let him in."

"What are you talking about?" Sanders asked.

"He's coming for you and you can't even see it." She arched her back and let out a loud breath. Then she slumped to the ground.

Maureen Ingram was dead.

Chapter Sixty-Seven

Michael shook the limp body of Maureen Ingram, trying to get her to respond. "Where's Judith?" he yelled.

"She's dead, Michael." Sanders pulled Michael's arm from the traitor's corpse.

"Why did you kill her?" Michael turned his ire towards Captain Sanders. "I've got to find Judith."

"She was going to kill you. I had to save your life."

"I don't care," Michael lost control of his senses and yelled at Sanders. "You could have let her kill me and then got her to tell you where Judith is."

"You're not making any sense, Fernsby."

"Why did you kill her?" Michael slumped to the ground, holding his chest. He struggled to breathe, as if his rib cage was constricting his heart, preventing the blood from flowing through his veins. "I could have saved her."

"We still can if we hurry."

Michael didn't seem to hear Sanders' words. "She's going to die because of me, just like David and everyone else did."

"Snap out of it, Fernsby," Sanders ordered. "I know where Judith is and if we hurry, we can save her. So, stop crying about it, and let's go get her."

Michael stared up at Sanders as though he'd lost his mind. "How can you possibly know where Judith is?"

He rose to his feet and clenched his fists, blood rushing to his head as his anger rose. "Unless you are involved too?"

"Pull yourself together, or I'm leaving you here. Grab the briefcase and follow me."

Sanders strode off into the darkness through the trees towards a dirt track behind them. Michael followed, his head clearing as they picked up the pace.

"How do you know where she is?" he asked, his demeanour calm and rational, which lay in stark contrast to how he felt inside.

Sanders led the way through the trees towards what Michael knew was another dirt track several hundred yards further inland. His vehicle sat hidden behind a clump of bushes close to the track.

"I met with my friend in the basement. He's a captain in the intelligence corps, and he runs the information desk for our unit. He showed me the logs of what you sent and what we received."

"I'm guessing Maureen took it and kept it to herself?"

Sanders nodded, his head visible in the clear night sky. He paused while he opened the right-hand driver's door of the dark-coloured Austin 10.

In a brief moment of respite, Michael recognised it immediately. It was the vehicle he'd had his eye on ever since its introduction in the early thirties. With a top speed of around fifty-five miles per hour, the Austin 10 could cruise at a gentlemanly thirty-five all day and Michael had spent many an enjoyable moment

342

daydreaming about cruising around the roads of Southern England in one.

He'd planned on buying one, and at two hundred pounds, or about the price of the average yearly salary in 1939, it would have taken a sizeable chunk of his inheritance for him to afford it.

He turned his mind back to the present. Sanders was speaking and he concentrated on what he was saying.

"I'll tell you about the logs later. Right now, we have to get Judith back. After my meeting with the chap from the basement, Maureen told me she had to leave early for a dental appointment. I didn't believe her, so I followed her here, to the Kent coast."

Sanders glanced at Michael. "I followed her to a house in Deal and although I didn't see Judith, a man let her into the house. She stayed there until she left again to see you this evening. I'm guessing that Judith is being held at that house in Deal."

"I hope you're right, Sanders, or whoever has her will kill her if Maureen doesn't check in with them soon. We only have fifteen minutes left."

"We're almost there," Sanders said as he sped as fast as he could towards the coastal town less than six miles away.

"Hurry," Michael ordered.

The men fell silent, both lost in their thoughts.

"She worked for me for two years and I never suspected a thing. I'm sorry, Fernsby, this is on me."

"What did your friend in the basement tell you?" Michael ignored the half-hearted apology.

"He showed me the logs of what you sent and when. It didn't reveal the content because that was for my eyes only, but he showed me where you'd sent at least two messages. She kept them both from me."

"Did you not think to ask about them earlier? Like, when I was in trouble and needed help over there?"

Sanders shook his head. "I trusted Maureen. I had to. We worked with some of the country's top secrets and I dread to think what damage she's done to us with her treachery. I assumed you were dead, especially as the line of communication we had with Adler went dark around the same time."

"So, you just forgot about me and left me there to die?"

"That's how it works, Fernsby. You know that. There wasn't anything we could have done to get you out. You were on your own and you knew that going in."

Michael took a deep breath. Sanders slowed as they turned onto the coastal road in Deal. He took a right onto Stanley Road and Sanders nodded his head as they drove past the first house on the right. It was dark but the street-lamps gave enough light to see the front of the row of terraced houses close to the beach.

The house didn't have a front garden. The front door was right on the pavement, which fit in with all the rest of the houses they drove past.

The curtains were drawn and they could see a dim light glowing behind them.

"Are you sure she's here?" Michael asked.

"As I said, I didn't see her but this is where Maureen spent the evening before driving out to see you. At least one man was with her and there might be others. What do you want to do?"

"I'm going in. If my sister is in there, I'm getting her out. And if anyone gets in my way, I'll kill them."

"We'd like them alive so we can find out who Maureen was working with."

"That's your problem," Michael hissed. "I'm getting Judith."

Chapter Sixty-Eight

Sanders circled around and parked on the promenade in front of Stanley Road. Michael checked his pockets and placed his hand on the car door.

"I'm going in through the rear. Watch the front and if anyone runs out, you stop them by any means possible. That's the only plan I have."

Sanders shrugged. "I can't think of a better one but do you want me to go in first? It's my cock-up, after all."

"It's my sister. I'm going in."

A narrow alleyway separated the rows of houses at the rear. Unlike the front, there were no lights at the rear, and the darkness swallowed Michael as he slipped out of sight.

He checked the alley to make sure nobody was watching and jumped over the high wooden fence, dropping into the tiny backyard of the little house by the seaside.

He ran for the shadows, crouched, and waited. His heart pounded so loud that he couldn't hear anything above it and he took deep breaths to get control of himself.

Nothing seemed out of the ordinary, so he ran to the

wall at the side of the house. He hid in the darkness around the corner and listened intently.

Nothing seemed out of place. The house was quiet, in tune with the rest of the sleepy seaside town at this ungodly hour of the night.

He looked for an obvious entry point but the single back door was locked and the windows were shut tight so he couldn't see what was inside.

He looked up and saw a drainpipe on the corner of the house from the gutter above. These were common in Britain because of the rainy weather, and many a child had got in trouble for shinning up and down them, himself and David included.

With one last listen, Michael climbed the drainpipe and stopped when he got level with the upstairs window that was less than a couple of feet to his left.

He listened intently and was about to reach over and try to open it when he heard a scraping sound below. He froze, clinging to the drainpipe, his mind sharply focused on the source of the sound.

The rear door opened and two men walked out of the house into the tiny yard. Michael couldn't see much but the men looked like they could handle themselves in an altercation.

"You and Ben get the girl," one of them said in a hushed voice. "I'll get the vehicle and meet you out front."

"I still think we should give Maureen a bit longer. She's only twenty minutes late," the other one protested.

"You know the drill. We all do. We agreed we'd move the girl if Maureen wasn't back on time. No delays and no exceptions, so unless you've got any other complaints, get a hood over her head and meet me outside."

"I still think we should wait."

"Well, we're not. So, get a move on. We're taking her to London."

"London?" the other man seemed surprised. "Why there?"

"Because if she's no use to us, she's going in the Thames. We'll melt into the crowds and nobody will ever know who took her. If we leave her here, the Old Bill will be all over us."

"Fair enough."

"Good. Stop yapping and get the girl outside in five minutes."

Michael hung less than ten feet above their heads, unseen and unheard. His blood boiled at the thought of his sister being dragged outside with a hood over her head, never mind that she was to be murdered and dropped into the Thames, so these cowards could get away with it.

The lead man waited until the other was back in the house. Then he lit a cigarette and stood for a few moments, taking deep lungfuls of smoke and watching it float into the ether when he exhaled.

He looked up to observe the smoke evaporating and froze when he saw a human body hurtling out of the sky towards him. Michael used the wall to kick himself off the pipe and landed on top of the heavyset man with a quiet thud.

They both fell to the ground and Michael used the element of surprise to his advantage. He head-butted the man's nose as hard as he could, sending rivers of light through his senses as he did so.

He shook his head and quickly regained control. The man groaned beneath him, warm blood spurting from his broken nose. Michael covered his mouth so he couldn't speak and smashed him over the head with the butt of his weapon.

The man fell limp beneath him.

Michael dragged his body to the side of the house where he couldn't be seen from inside. Then he searched him for weapons and anything that would tell him who these men were.

He pulled a long, serrated knife from the man's belt but there were no forms of identification on his body that would reveal who he was or who he worked for.

To make sure he was out, Michael hit him again with the gun's butt and then put a hand onto the wall, allowing it to guide him to the front edge of the house.

He waited, poised and ready for whoever came out. He couldn't see Sanders but he knew he was there somewhere.

The front door opened and a man walked out. Behind him, another man pushed a figure with a hood over their head through the open doorway.

Judith! Her hands were tied behind her back and she stumbled on the doorstep as someone shoved her onto the street. The man in front turned and slapped her where her face would be under the hood.

"Watch where you're going, bitch!" he snarled. "Where's Tunney?" He looked up and down the road for the vehicle that was taking them to London.

Michael's blood boiled over, and as soon as he was certain that nobody else was coming out behind them, he launched himself at the man who'd slapped his sister.

The knife was in his right hand and he slammed the hilt into the man's temple, dropping him like a sack of coal. His partner spun around but before he could register what was happening, Sanders appeared out of nowhere and dropped him with a blow to the head.

Michael ran to Judith and snatched the hood from her head. Her mouth was tied and she struggled. Michael could see the whites of her eyes in the moonlight as she panicked and fought for her life.

"Judith, it's me, Michael. You're safe."

Michael's hands trembled as he gently untied the gag from Judith's mouth. A rush of emotions threatened to overwhelm him and relief washed over him as he saw recognition dawn in her terror-stricken eyes.

A deep and burning anger quickly replaced the relief at what they had put her through. His heart ached to see her in such a state and he could feel a knot of worry and guilt in the pit of his stomach. Had he arrived even a moment later, he couldn't bear to think of what might have happened.

But there was no time for that now. He had to stay focused, determined to get them both to safety. His sister needed him and he would not let her down. The adrenaline still coursing through his veins kept his mind sharp and his senses alert.

They were not out of danger yet and he knew he would have to draw on all his strength and courage to see them through. But for now, in this brief moment, he allowed himself to feel a fierce, protective love for his sister. Her life was in his hands and he would not fail her.

"Michael!" Judith threw herself into his arms, tears streaming down her face. "Is it really you? They told me you were dead and that they were going to kill me, and then Mum and Dad as well."

Hysteria took over and Michael held her close for several moments. "Everything is alright, Judith. I've got you now and you're safe. Mum and Dad are safe too."

He steered her to the wall of the house and helped her sit down. "Wait there while we take care of them," he pointed to the two unconscious men sprawled out on the footpath.

Sanders already had one of them by the scruff of the neck and was dragging him into the house. Michael grabbed the other and followed.

Once inside, he let Sanders restrain them while he went out of the back door for the other one. He wasn't there.

With the injuries Michael had inflicted on him, he couldn't have got very far. The gate leading to the alleyway was ajar, so Michael went after him.

It was too dark to follow any trail, so he turned around and went back to the house. Hearing a commotion, he ran to help Sanders subdue the two men they still had in their custody.

He stopped dead in his tracks when he entered the tiny living room that was bare except for a two-seater couch along the back wall.

Sanders was lying on the ground in a ball, protecting himself as the two men assaulted him with their feet. The third man, who Michael thought had run off, stood over them, pointing a gun towards Sanders.

Judith sat on the couch, her face pale and drained. The normally vibrant teenager looked completely defeated, as though resigned to her death in that house.

Spurred on by Judith's image, Michael sprang into life. At the last moment, the man with the gun noticed Michael had entered the room. He spun around, blood running down his forehead from a deep gash, joining with the blood from his broken nose that splashed onto the linoleum flooring.

"You," he growled.

The other two men stopped their assault on Sanders and turned their ire towards Michael. As they rushed towards him, Michael let loose with the Walther PPK he'd rapidly yanked out of his pocket.

The man with the gun fell first, a bullet smashing through his skull and ending his life instantly. The onrushing man closest to him fell next, clutching his stomach as he went down.

Judith screamed and covered her face with her hands. Michael knew it was too much for her to take in, but he had no other way of saving their lives.

The third man crashed into Michael, knocking the wind out of him as they collided. Michael's head crashed into the doorframe, sending lightning bolts of white light through his vision.

By the time he'd recovered enough to fight back, the gun had been knocked from his grip and the angry man was laying into him with both fists. Michael fell under the onslaught.

The man saw Michael's discarded weapon and he grabbed it from the floor. Michael tried reaching for the knife in his other pocket but he was too late.

"Where's the briefcase?" the man snarled. "Give it to me now or I'll blow the bitch's head off."

The wild look in the man's eyes told Michael he meant it. In his mid-thirties, his assailant looked like he'd seen his fair share of altercations in his life.

In the split second it took to raise his hands and rise to his knees, Michael noticed something unusual about the man's forehead. A healing mass of deep red filled the space between his hair and his eyes, as if it was an old wound that was infected and wasn't healing as it was supposed to.

The type of wound one might see after an automobile accident.

Michael's breath jolted in his chest. *Could this be...?*

"I won't ask again," the man growled.

"It's outside in our vehicle," Michael answered, still staring at the deep red gash on his forehead that was struggling to heal. "I'll give it to you if you let Judith go."

"Do I look like I want to negotiate?" the man asked, froth seeping from the corner of his mouth.

Michael shook his head. "I need to get it for you."

"Give me the keys and I'll get it myself."

"I don't have them, he does." Michael nodded his head towards Sanders, who was slowly getting to his knees.

The man looked around at Sanders and Michael used the split second to act. He grabbed his knife and hurled himself at the man, grabbing his hand as he got close, steering it from harm's way.

The gun went off, once again deafening everyone in the room and no doubt waking all the neighbours from their slumber across the street.

Michael plunged the knife through the man's forearm. He screamed loudly and dropped the gun to the floor. Sanders quickly gathered it and turned it on the man.

"That's enough. Stop, or I'll kill you."

The man slumped to his knees, holding his arm and looking as pale as the evening moon.

Michael grabbed the man by the back of his hair. "That scar on your forehead. Where did it come from?"

The man sneered and spat in Michael's face.

Michael tightened his grip on the man's hair. "That kind of injury had to have come from a vehicle accident. Was it you that smashed into us? Was it you who tried to kill us?"

The man sneered at Michael but said nothing.

"It *was* him," Michael glanced at Sanders. "He was the one who crashed into our Autovia."

He turned back to his captive, who was sweating from the wound to his arm. "You almost killed my father that day and now here you are, kidnapping my sister."

He snatched the man's head back and stood over him as though he were about to execute him. Sanders jumped up and held Michael's arm back.

"Easy, Michael. I know how you must be feeling but we need him alive if we're going to find out who he's working with."

Michael stood over the man for a moment before relaxing his grip and shoving him roughly to the floor. "You'd better get him to talk or I'm going to kill him myself."

Sanders prised the knife from Michael's hand and angled his head towards Judith. "Go take care of your sister."

Judith sat on the couch, her whole body shaking. Her face was as ashen as a corpse, and she stared straight ahead with a look on her face that melted Michael's heart.

He ran to her and placed his arm around her shoulders. "It's over now. You're safe."

Judith didn't respond. Instead, she just stared ahead as though his words weren't registering in her brain. Michael had seen that look before because it was exactly how both he and David had responded when the bullets flew in the Munich apartment the previous year.

"I'll watch him." Sanders spat a loose tooth from his mouth. "Go find a telephone box and call for help."

"There's no need," Michael gestured towards the window. "Listen."

Someone must have already called the police because the sounds of sirens were getting louder and louder.

Michael and Sanders threw down their weapons and held their arms in the air as the police rushed inside the blood-soaked house.

Chapter Sixty-Nine

Three days later, Michael strode into the office on Baker Street in London that 317 was using as a temporary office. The first thing he noticed was that there wasn't a secretary in sight.

Captain Sanders sat at his desk, facing the open doorway as Michael entered. "You're looking worse for wear," Michael observed, looking at the bruised and swollen black eyes that stared back at him.

"I've been worse," Sanders replied. "How's Judith?"

"She's fine. They're keeping her in the hospital for observations, which she's not too happy about, as you can imagine. She's got a round-the-clock guard, which makes her feel more secure, but all she wants to do is to go home."

"I'm sure she does, but I'm glad she's alright."

"It was close," Michael sighed, sitting down on the opposite side of the heavy oak desk to face Sanders. "If we hadn't got there when we did, I dread to think what they would have done to her."

Sanders nodded. "We have more important business to discuss, Fernsby. The powers that be in Whitehall pulled out all the stops to get the police to back off and keep it out of the newspapers. They went to even greater trouble to get the briefcase without the police opening it first."

Sanders stared at Michael through bloodshot, bruised eyes. "You can imagine their disappointment when they discovered it was empty."

Michael shrugged. "I never said there was anything in it. They, just like Maureen, took it for granted that I'd be stupid enough to bring Adler's documents to a meeting where my chances of survival were slender. It's not my fault nobody asked me before they went berserk over it."

"Berserk is a good observation. Some very powerful people are furious with you and there's been mention of arresting you for withholding information vital to the state. That's a serious accusation, Fernsby."

Michael nodded. "I know and I never intended to with-hold it. I knew someone had betrayed me and I thought it was you. Even after our meeting, I wasn't sure who I could trust and it wasn't until Maureen pulled that gun on me that I knew who it was."

"That's what I told the PM when he questioned me about it yesterday."

"The PM is involved? This has gone higher than I ever imagined. Even after the Maureen incident, I still wasn't completely convinced you weren't a part of it. Surely the top brass would know that?"

Sanders bowed his head. "That's why you haven't been arrested and charged with treason. But their patience is wearing thin. Where is it, Fernsby? We need it, and there can be no more delays. People's lives are at stake."

"Don't tell me about people's lives." Michael's face turned red. "I've seen more good people die this past year than most people in the top brass have seen in an entire lifetime. Obviously, I'll hand it over, but I don't need any of their sanctimonious bullshit."

"Easy, Fernsby. Remember who you're talking about."

"I'm sorry, but I've lost some people who were very important to me, and I don't need a lecture on it from anyone."

"Where is it?"

"I first need to know what happened after the police arrested us."

"Stop playing games, Fernsby. We need that briefcase and we need it now."

"No games. I want to know what happened and why they targeted my family. Then you can have your precious briefcase."

Sanders sighed and placed his hands behind his head. He didn't appear to have slept since they'd last met.

"Two of the three are dead. You know that because you killed them. The other, who we now know is called Geoffrey Tunney, is in a serious, but stable condition in hospital, which is where he'll stay until his arm heals."

Michael raised his eyebrows.

"He's in a different hospital from the one Judith is being treated at, if that's what's on your mind."

Michael grimaced. "He was the one who crashed into us and almost killed my father. Then he kidnapped Judith. I want to know what they have against my family."

"We're working on that. He's hard to break but we'll get it out of him."

"Are my family safe?" Michael stared at Sanders intently.

"It's over," Sanders replied. "We've broken up their cell and as far as we know, we got all of them."

"Do you know who the others were?" Michael asked.

"We know who they all are, or were. They belonged to a breakaway group of the British Union of Fascists, founded by Oswald Mosley—a prominent political figure who attempted to model his party after Mussolini's fascists in Italy. The one you shot in the head was Maureen's fiancé and he'd converted her to their cause."

"Do you know how they were working with the Nazis?" Michael asked. "Someone told them about Adler and that same person told them the name I was using to get out of Germany. Kreise knew everything, so it had to have come from someone here."

"Our initial observations are that Maureen was the conduit for the information leak to the SD. We think the group worked alone as a cell of Fascists preparing for a Nazi invasion of this country."

"Are these facts, or are they just what you think happened?" Michael looked at Sanders suspiciously. "How much information did Maureen give them?"

"We're not sure, but from what we've got from Tunney so far, she didn't tell them everything about your operation or you'd have been arrested the moment you arrived in Germany. We think the plan was for you to be captured at the same time as Adler, which wouldn't cast any suspicions on Maureen and her group of traitors over here."

"That answers a lot of questions," Michael said. "What about our wolf at the door?"

"We think Maureen was referring to herself when she said that. She sent the communications to her handler in Germany, but we don't know how. We think that whoever was receiving them was also directing her activities over here."

"So, there's nobody else involved?"

"At this early stage, it doesn't appear that way. That's what I've been told, anyway."

"Then what did Maureen mean when she said the wolf was at our door and we let him in?"

"That I don't know." Sanders slumped forward onto his desk. "I'm with you, Fernsby. I believe there is a lot more to this that we don't know about, but what I'm telling you is the official response. Whether we choose to believe it is an entirely different matter."

"What are we going to do about it?"

"What are we going to do about it?" Sanders laughed. "Unless we get more information out of Tunney, all we can do is be vigilant and hope someone slips up."

"Be vigilant and hope someone slips up?" It was Michael's turn to repeat Sanders' words. "You do realise what's at stake, don't you?"

Sanders smiled wryly. "Of course I do. What else do you want me to say?"

"That we're going to turn every stone until we find the person at the top who is the real traitor. That's what I want you to say."

"And unofficially, that's what we are going to do," Sanders said. "We wait until whoever it is makes their next move and when they do, we'll be ready."

Michael hesitated, his fingers brushing against the leather of the false briefcase as though assuring himself of its presence. He seemed to weigh his options, his gaze flickering between Sanders and the exit. Finally, he let out a slow breath, nodding his agreement.

"I'll be back later this evening."

He stared at Sanders, who stared back with eyes that carried the truth of his convictions. For the first time, Michael believed in him.

"Make sure you are alone, and for God's sake, keep what I'm giving you safe. We need to know who gets access to Adler's files and if anyone acts on them, we'll know who the traitor is."

"I'd already thought about that. We're going to have to rebuild this department from the ground up to make sure it's clean, and it begins with you, me, and Adler's briefcase."

The office was empty when Michael returned later that evening. He'd gone back to Cambridge and retrieved the real briefcase from its hiding place behind a stone wall inside the family home.

He'd avoided his family because he knew the emotional cost would be high when they reunited. He needed to have both a rational mind and a clear conscience when he finally met them face to face.

A single light shone from the office Sanders was using as a temporary home for the new Section V's 317. Michael strode in and closed the door behind him.

Tensions were high as he opened the briefcase, pulled out Adler's files and laid them on the desk before Sanders.

He watched as Sanders' eyes bulged at the sensitive, potentially war-changing documents before him. Michael spread them out so Sanders could see their contents.

Operational Intelligence

Operational Personnel

Policy and Strategy

Eugenics Programme

European Network Contacts

Sanders whistled as he thumbed through the thick files.

He paid particular attention to the file marked **European Network Contacts** and he pointed a finger at it as he spoke.

"Our answers might be right in front of us."

"My thoughts exactly."

"Thank you, Fernsby. You might not have got Adler out but you did the next best thing. This information could prove vital in the coming conflict."

"I'm glad to have done my duty, Captain. Now, if it's alright with you, I need some time off with my family."

"Take whatever time you need. We know where to find you and we'll be in touch if we need anything."

As Michael turned to leave the office, Sanders spoke again. "Thank you for all you have done, Fernsby. You are the most resourceful man I have ever met and I'm glad you're on our side."

Michael nodded and walked away, relieved to be rid of the burden of holding onto the briefcase and the secrets it contained. For a while at least, he would be plain Michael Fernsby, faithful son and brother to a family that needed time together to heal.

Chapter Seventy

The early morning steam train from London arrived on time at Sandwich station. Michael disembarked and with his rucksack slung over his shoulder, made the ten-minute walk to his family home on New Street.

He knew he should be happy and underneath, he was. But he couldn't help but feel apprehensive as he approached the large stone house with the manicured lawn and ivy-covered walls.

He stopped and had a good look at the old house, remembering happier times when he and David used to charge around without a care in the world.

Those days were long gone and it was largely down to him and his actions. He clawed at the skin on his arms, as if trying to wash away his sins, and the guilt they had brought upon him.

Get a grip.

He thought of Judith and how she had looked so lost and fragile when he'd rescued her in Deal. He gasped for breath as images of his father flashed through his mind, trapped upside down in his vehicle after the accident.

And then there were the unseen victims in all of this. His mother must have been close to death herself from the tension after all that had happened. First David, and then she would have believed both her other children were dead as well, not to mention that her husband was hanging onto life with his fingertips. Michael was surprised she hadn't suffered a heart attack from all the stress he'd caused her.

His whole body felt like it was wading through treacle as he approached the heavy oak front door. He held his hand in a fist, ready to knock, then hesitated and pulled back, unable to catch his breath. He sank to his knees and for a moment thought he would pass out as the light left his eyes.

He gasped for air and took in a large breath. A cold sweat broke out on his forehead and his skin felt clammy under his clothes.

Pull yourself together. This is supposed to be a happy time.

He stood up, wiped his face with his sleeve, and rapped on the door.

The door opened and as soon as the gap was big enough, a large black Labrador forced itself through and leapt onto Michael, knocking him to the ground in its eagerness to get to him.

"Lucy! Lucy, come here now," Warhurst's stern voice bellowed.

Lucy wasn't listening. She knew who was at the door and she loved him.

"Lucy!" Michael laughed, the tension immediately fading away as a big, wet tongue showed the unconditional love that only a dog can provide. "You've got big since the last time I saw you."

Warhurst dragged Lucy off by the collar and pushed

her back inside the house. "I apologise for the dog—" he started.

But Michael cut him off. He shocked Warhurst by throwing his arms around the tall, gangly butler's shoulders, and gave him the biggest hug he'd ever given him. Warhurst stepped back in surprise.

"Master Michael, it's so good to see you. Are you alright?" Warhurst's normally strait-laced features burst into a genuine, radiant smile.

"I'm fine, Warhurst, and much the better for seeing you."

"Come in, sir. Your family will be delighted to see you."

Michael waited in the sitting room, biding his time by looking at the family photos that adorned the walls and cabinets. He balked at the one showing him and David standing together, smiling and enjoying a not-too-long-ago summer together

He was about to sit in his favourite armchair when the door burst open and his mother charged inside.

Dorothy Fernsby looked like she'd aged a decade since Michael had last seen her. Her hair, normally perfectly coiffed, was now dishevelled and streaked with grey, her face etched with lines of worry, grief, and exhaustion.

The light in her eyes, once a vivid spark of life, seemed dimmed by the tragic losses and unending anxiety she had endured. Her entire bearing spoke of a mother weighed down by fear for her children's safety and haunted by the harsh cruelties of a world teetering on the brink of war.

Speechless, Michael grabbed her and held her close. Everything that had happened came flooding back and once again, he blubbered like a baby in his mother's arms.

"Michael, I never thought I'd see you again." Dorothy finally spoke, tears streaming down her face. "They wouldn't tell me where you were or what you were doing and I was worried sick you were back in Germany again."

"I'm so sorry for everything I've put you through." Michael regained control of himself. He'd rehearsed what he was going to say a thousand times but now he was here, it all fell apart.

Another flurry of activity at the door caught Michael's eye. Dorothy stood aside as Judith threw herself on him. "Michael! I told Mum and Dad you were alive and that you'd rescued me."

She hugged her older brother so tightly he couldn't breathe. "Careful, tiger, I can't breathe." He laughed at her and wiped the tears from her cheeks as they fell.

Judith looked as though the experience had forced her to grow up before her time. Her expression was serious, much like an adult with life's problems weighing them down. Michael wasn't surprised after all she'd been through.

Finally, Judith let go and joined her mother on the couch. Michael looked at the figure standing in the doorway and gasped as he watched a once proud man limp heavily towards him using a wooden cane for support.

"Dad!" Michael ran towards him and held him, almost knocking him over. He looked so fragile and vulnerable, a pale shadow of the man he used to be.

"I knew you'd come back to us," Gerald said. "I knew they were wrong."

Michael helped his father to the armchair and helped him sit down.

"Where have you been, Michael?" his mother asked.

Before he could answer, Gigi strode into the room. Although in her mid-sixties, Giselle Fernsby still dominated every room she entered and she looked as stern as she ever had. If anything, all the recent turmoil had made her look even sterner.

Once everyone had taken a seat, Michael got their attention and began to speak. A lump formed in his throat and he found it difficult to get the words out.

"Before I tell you what happened, please let me tell you all how sorry I am. This is my fault and all I've done is put my family in danger from the moment I set foot in Germany. I never meant for any of this to happen and I'd do anything to take it all back. I don't care what they say, I'm done working for the government. All I want is for my family to be safe and I can't do that as long as I keep doing what I'm doing."

"What have you been doing?" Gigi asked the question everyone was dying to ask.

"I can't say much, but I will tell you I had to go to places I didn't want to go and had to do things I didn't want to do. I saw things I didn't want to see and bad things happened to my family because of it. Sorry isn't enough and I hope you can find it in your hearts to forgive me."

"So you went back to Germany," Gerald said.

Michael nodded.

"What for?" Dorothy cried. "Why would they send you back there, knowing full well what happened last time?"

"The government doesn't care about that," Gerald said. "They only care about what's important to them, not to the people their actions affect."

"Who kidnapped Judith?" Dorothy asked. "And how did you find her? How did you know she was missing?"

"It's all related and that is all I can say. A group of British Nazis used her because they wanted something from me."

"Did they get it?" Gerald asked. By the look on his son's face, he already knew the answer.

"No."

"How long have you been in England and why didn't you reach out to us?" Gigi asked.

"I didn't know you were in a safe house and I didn't know about Judith until a few days ago, and that's the truth. As soon as I found out, I found her and, well, you know the rest."

"You're the bravest man I have ever known," Judith said, her eyes filling up again.

"Stop it or you'll set me off again." Michael smiled at his sister.

"Well, I'm glad you're home now," Gerald said, leaning over and coughing.

"How are you, Dad? How is the recovery going?"

"Not very well, as you can see. I'm struggling, Michael, and I don't know if I'll ever make a full recovery."

Everyone felt the sombre mood and Michael noticed they all held their heads down, as if in prayer.

When his mother looked up, her eyes were cloudy and heavy. "I'm worried about your father. I don't care if he hears this or not but he's lost his will to live. If he doesn't take better care of himself, we're going to lose him."

Tears tumbled down her cheeks and she buried her face in her hands, her gentle sobs breaking Michael's heart with each breath she took. He glanced at his father, who looked at Dorothy with an unmistakable glimmer of sorrow behind his eyes. Michael took a deep breath and addressed his father.

"I can't even begin to understand the pain and anguish you've been through. You're hurt, that's obvious, but you can't give up on us, Dad. We need you. We need you more now than ever before. You're the rock this family depends on, and we can't do it without you, especially with the shadows of war on our doorstep."

Dorothy's silent sobs grew in volume. Judith joined in and even the normally stoic Gigi looked as if she was fighting back tears. It took all he had for Michael to hold back too.

Gerald Fernsby looked at his son, the love he had for his family on full, raw display. "I'm struggling, Michael, I admit it. I've struggled ever since we lost David. The accident nearly killed me and I don't expect I'll ever fully recover physically."

"I'm sorry, Dad. I was there and I couldn't save you. It's all my fault."

"Stop taking the blame for what other people do," Gerald demanded. "The one thing I've learnt from you and David this past year is that we rise above adversity."

"You haven't done a very good job of it." Gigi joined the conversation. "Dorothy is correct. You've given up on us."

"I'm ashamed to admit it, but you're right. I have struggled more than I can ever tell you these past months and when I thought we'd lost Michael and then Judith on top of that, I couldn't cope anymore. I should have been there for you and I wasn't. I'm sorry."

The raw emotion was too much and Michael observed every one of their faces lined with pain and distress.

"There's more, Gerald. You're holding something from us and you won't tell us what it is." Dorothy said. "I've known you a long time and I know when you're keeping something from me."

Gerald bowed his head. "I swear, sometimes you know me better than I know myself. There is something I have been keeping from you. I'm embarrassed to admit that I've failed as a father, a husband, and a son. I've failed this family and the legacy that was passed down to me."

The strain of emotion lined his face and it was obvious how difficult this was for him.

"Whatever it is you think you've either done or not done, we all love you, Gerald," Dorothy stared at her husband. "You've been nothing but a good husband, father, and son all your life, so whatever it is, we know you haven't failed us."

Gerald slumped back in his chair, gave his wife of many years a long, loving stare, and opened his mouth to speak.

Chapter Seventy-One

The room fell silent. Even Lucy lay still at Michael's feet as Gerald revealed his inner fears and failures.

"You all know the family brewery business is struggling but what you don't know is the extent of it. We've lost so much money this last year that I've had to re-mortgage the house just to pay the bills. Even that hasn't been enough and now the banks are calling in their loans."

He stared at his wife. "They're taking the house, Dorothy. They're taking everything from us. The house, the business, everything."

Stunned silence filled the room. Dorothy's already pale face became even paler, something Michael thought impossible. Gigi stared at her son as if he was speaking a foreign language.

"That can't be right," Dorothy said. "Not that long ago we had a record year. You told me so yourself."

"That was before our world fell apart," Gerald answered. "Losing David changed everything. I lost the ability to concentrate and I took more and more time away from the business. Then the accident happened and I wasn't physically able to do it anymore. I should have sold it then when I had the chance."

"When?" was all Dorothy could say.

"When what?" Gerald asked. "When are they taking the house? I'm expecting to hear from them any day now. I've failed you and I'm so sorry."

Michael sprang to his feet. He'd allowed himself to get lost in the sea of emotion and had momentarily lost track of his senses.

"I've heard enough," he said.

Everyone turned their attention to him as he rummaged in his rucksack. He pulled out an item and passed it to his grandmother.

"There's something I haven't told you yet." The sorrow restricting his chest lifted and his eyes sparkled. "Things are not as bad as you think they are."

"What's this?" Gigi turned the black wallet over in her hands and gasped when she saw the letters 'FF' embroidered on the other side. She looked up at Michael, her eyes wide. "Is this...?" Her voice trailed off.

Michael smiled and nodded his head. The depression in the room lifted as everyone strained to see what Gigi held in her hands.

"I can't tell you what I was doing but when I was there, I found Friedrich Halmer, Gerda's father-in-law," Michael said, noting the complete attention his words received from his family. Even Lucy stared at him.

"He's the Nazi doctor who was involved in their ungodly eugenics programme," Gigi said. "He murdered Paul Halmer, his own grandson. I hope you killed him."

"I did something even better." Michael left out the gory details. "He had a box of Gerda's personal belongings in his office. Amongst them was Uncle Frank's wallet." He pointed at the wallet Gigi was now holding.

Tears fell from her face as she held the wallet in her trembling hands. Her normally steadfast features fell away as she held her son's wallet close to her chest.

"Frank," was all she could say, and she held the wallet to her heart.

Another stunned silence filled the room. Gerald, Frank's brother, finally broke it when he spoke up. "Was there any sign of what happened to Frank and Herbert?"

Michael shook his head. "Nothing, I'm sorry. The last I heard, they were at the concentration camp in Dachau and nobody's heard from them since."

Gigi stood and pulled Michael towards her. "You have no idea what this means to me." She buried her head in Michael's chest.

After a few moments, she gathered herself and sat down, staring at the wallet as though it were made of gold.

Michael beamed at his mother and father. "There's more."

He pulled out the golden-brown teddy bear and held it up in front of his stunned family.

"This belonged to Paul Halmer." A lump formed in Michael's throat and he struggled to release the words.

Gigi held out her hands to receive it but Michael held back. "Give me a minute and I'll give it to you."

Everyone stared at Michael with a mixture of sorrow and surprise. He pulled the stitching from the back and removed the cufflink box from inside. Then he handed the bear to Gigi, who held it to her chest and closed her eyes as if in prayer.

"Paul. May God rest your soul," she said softly.

"Amen," everyone repeated after her.

All eyes turned to Michael as the realisation of what he was about to reveal dawned on them.

"The typewriter wasn't in Papa Herbert's shed, which was where Gigi said he'd left it. I'd assumed the Nazis had found it and we'd never see it again. Nobody was more surprised than me when I found it in Halmer's house with Gerda's belongings. He had it all along and never knew it."

"You found it?" Gerald's deflated features suddenly sprang into life.

"That was inside a typewriter?" Dorothy asked, her eyes as wide as a saucer.

Michael nodded. "If this is as valuable as you say it is, we're saved." He passed the cufflink box to his father, who handled it as though he was holding the holy grail.

"The EB Brasher Doubloon," Gerald whispered. "It's beautiful."

And beautiful it was. He held it up so everyone could see the intricate designs of the sun rising over the mountains on one side, and an eagle holding an olive branch and arrows on the other.

There were gasps when Gerald pointed out the initials E.B. And the Latin words UNUM E PLURIBUS.

"Out of many, one," he said, staring at the coin. "This is it. It's real! This is the missing Brasher Doubloon. We're saved, Dorothy. This coin is worth a king's ransom, and it will ensure our family remains solvent for generations to come. It will save the business, our home, and it will take care of all of us, even our grandchildren, when they finally arrive."

He looked up at Michael in awe. "You did it, son. You saved us."

Everyone spoke at once and Gerald held up his hands. "I know I've failed you but from now on I promise to work harder than I ever have, both in my physical recovery and the business. We'll sell this coin and I'll make sure we're never in this situation again. Michael, what can I do to thank you?"

Michael took a deep breath, realising the significance of what he had achieved. His family, his legacy, was now secured. And in this profound moment, he managed a smirk.

"You already have," Michael said. "I have you and I don't need anything else. Well, except maybe one thing."

"What's that?" his father asked. "Name it and it's yours."

"I've always wanted an Austin 10."

Everyone laughed. "Consider it done," Gerald said.

After a family hug, they dispersed. Gerald retired to his study to alert the world to the existence of an eighth Brasher Doubloon and Michael went to his room and settled down to write the letter he'd been wanting to write ever since he'd returned to England.

Chapter Seventy-Two

Two weeks later, Michael stood alongside his parents and Captain Sanders in a secret ceremony in the bowels of Bush House. Colonel Dansey was present, as well as Colonel Stuart Menzies, the deputy chief of the Secret Intelligence Service, who Michael thought would conduct the ceremony.

Michael felt uncomfortable with all the attention focused on him. He'd initially wanted to decline the award but his father had talked him into it, reminding him of the benefits and prestige the award would bring him, during both the oncoming war and beyond.

On this grey summer morning, he stood there in his Sunday best, with a white shirt and matching waistcoat and tie, wanting to get it over with. He had another reason to be there today and it wasn't one Sanders and the rest would enjoy.

Michael's pulse quickened when a hushed murmur rose amongst the attendees. A side door slowly creaked open and in walked a figure whose presence no one in the room – or the world – could mistake.

It was King George VI himself!

For a moment, everything seemed to fade into the background. Michael's throat tightened, his earlier aloofness replaced by a sudden, overwhelming reverence. He caught a glimpse of his parents, their faces reflecting the same awestruck surprise.

Dressed in a resplendent military uniform adorned with numerous medals, the king approached Michael with an air of regal authority that was punctuated with unmistakable warmth. "I'm sorry the ceremony has to take place here. Top secret and all that. Usually, such honours are given at Buckingham Palace but we must maintain discretion for operations of this nature."

"I understand, Your Highness," Michael responded, offering a respectful bow. "The honour is truly mine, sir."

"The honour is mine. From what I've heard, you are quite a remarkable young man." King George smiled at Michael.

If only he knew the cost, he wouldn't be so keen to congratulate me.

"It gives me great pleasure to bestow this award on an extraordinary young man who has shown bravery and dedication to our nation beyond his years," the king started his speech.

"His outstanding courage and ingenuity belie his youth, and it is my great pleasure to make two awards today to a fine young man who has demonstrated that no matter what Adolf Hitler and his Nazis throw at us, we will prevail through the courage and commitment of young men like Michael Fernsby."

Michael glanced at his father, who looked as proud as any father could be, especially as he was in agony, standing there with his leg strapped up and barely able to walk.

"It is my great honour to bestow upon you today the rank of captain in the intelligence corps, and from now on, you will be known as Captain Michael Fernsby."

Menzies and Dansey beamed, and even Sanders smiled as Michael became his equal.

"Even greater than the bestowing of rank, it is my greatest privilege to award the Military Cross for gallantry during active operations against the enemy to Captain Michael Fernsby."

The king stepped forward and pinned the exquisite medal depicting the British Crown on each of the four sides of the cross. It was further enhanced with the purple and white striped ribbon, the purple stripe sitting in the middle of two white stripes.

King George stepped back and shook Michael's hand vigorously. "Well, done, sir. You thoroughly deserved this award and I'm glad you're on our side."

"Thank you, Your Majesty. I'm deeply honoured. Michael bowed one more time."

And he was. The letter of resignation in his pocket seemed out of place and he shelved it for another time.

Chapter Seventy-Three

Kriminaldirektor Albert Kreise strode into the interrogation room in the bowels of the Wittelsbacher Palais in Munich and surveyed the carnage laid out before him. He didn't like this part of the job, but it was a necessary requirement.

He was good at it and that was why Obergruppenführer Heydrich had chosen him specifically to do it. Not only that but he'd promised that if he cracked the prisoner, he would finally get the transfer to the Sicherheitsdienst.

Heydrich had already set the wheels in motion and upon successful completion of his latest – and final – task in his capacity as Kriminaldirektor of the Munich Gestapo, they would transfer him to the Sicherheitsdienst and assume the rank of Sturmbannführer.

That was all the motivation Kreise needed.

Untersturmführer Klaus Müller snapped his heels together and stepped back from his bloody job. With cold, slate grey eyes and a long scar down the left side of his face from a hunting accident, Kreise thought he looked every bit the hatchet man he was.

"Leave us," he snapped at the junior officer.

Müller nodded and removed the blood-soaked apron he wore over his uniform. He left the room, leaving Kreise alone with the sole prisoner in the thirty-by-twenty-five-foot torture chamber.

The prisoner was hanging by his arms from a rope tied to the ceiling. Handcuffs dug deep into the flesh on his wrists and a hook threaded through them attached to the rope that hoisted him to his tiptoes.

The man was barely recognisable, such was the beating he'd received from Müller. His eyes were swollen and closed and his face looked deformed from the bruising and swelling. His naked body was cut in a thousand places and blood dripped to the floor from the deep lacerations.

Kreise wondered how much longer Gustav Adler could hold on to life.

"It doesn't have to be like this," Kreise said, the tone of his voice softer than that of the interrogator. "You can be with your wife and nephew if you just cooperate with us. I can make that happen, Adler. Wouldn't you like that?"

Gustav Adler acted as though he hadn't heard a word Kreise had said to him.

Kreise grabbed Adler's face and squeezed. "We know everything. Your wife confessed and now she is with your nephew. What's his name? Heinrich, is that right? Anyway, they are together, waiting for you to join them."

"Lies." Adler spat the words out of his shattered mouth. Blood spurted onto Kreise's lapel, making him shiver in disgust. He stepped forward and slapped Adler hard across the face.

"I'm tired of your games. We know you were defecting to the British with a briefcase full of top-level secrets. You're nothing but a traitor, Adler, and you know what happens to them."

Adler's body hung limply, his eyes closed.

"I'm going to give you one last chance." Kreise stopped to allow the words to sink in. Adler didn't know that Fernsby had killed Doctor Halmer and rescued Heinrich and he was going to use that to his advantage.

"Heinrich needs you, Adler. He's defective and you know what that means to the Reich. I'm holding onto him but I'm under pressure to get results. I need you to tell me who your contacts were and what was inside that briefcase. If you don't, I won't be able to hold on to Heinrich and the SS will take him from me."

Adler stirred. As expected, Kreise's tactics were working. He'd sacrifice himself, perhaps even his wife, but he would never sacrifice the boy and that was his weakness.

"Doctor Halmer is waiting at Alderauge for the delivery of the boy and I'm going to send him there if you don't cooperate with me now. This is your last chance, Adler. It's either you or the boy, so what's it going to be?"

"I need proof." Adler struggled to get the words out.

"You need proof?" Kreise screamed. "I'll give you proof. Look."

He shoved a blurred photograph of a young boy into Adler's face. It wasn't Heinrich Adler. Kreise didn't know who it was but that wasn't the point. Adler's eyes were so badly damaged that he wouldn't be able to tell and that should hopefully be enough.

Adler strained to see but Kreise's assessment had been correct. Adler sighed and slumped as if resigned to his fate.

"I'm giving you one last chance, Adler. When I walk out of that door, Heinrich either lives or dies. It's up to you."

"I don't trust you."

"You have no choice. But surely even the chance of saving the boy is worth it, isn't it? I give you my word that if you tell me what I want to know, this will end for all of you. You will be released and allowed to live with your family. Under guard, of course."

Adler sighed.

"It's now or never, Adler." Kreise stamped his feet as if to emphasise the urgency.

Adler remained silent, so Kreise stomped a few more times and walked closer to the door. "I'm about to give the order to hand Heinrich over to Doctor Halmer. Right now."

He turned and placed his hand on the door handle.

"Stop!"

Kreise smiled to himself and turned around.

Got him!

"I'll tell you if you give your word Heinrich will be safe."

"I give you my word. I'll see to it personally that your injuries are treated and you may live out the rest of your life with your family."

"Alright. Cut me down and I'll tell you."

Kreise called Müller back into the room and had him take Adler down from the rope. Then he ordered him out again.

"The handcuffs remain for now."

"I need water."

Kreise forced water down Adler's parched throat, although most of it went down his chin, joining the dark brown stains on the ground.

"No more games," Kreise said, sitting opposite Adler. "Tell me what was in the folder."

"Everything I had access to was in that briefcase. I was giving them everything I had."

"Everything?"

"Yes. If they have it, the British will know all about the eugenics programme and who is behind it. They'll know who the SD agents are throughout Europe, and who their contacts are."

He gasped for air. "And they'll know our policy and strategy going forward, including our plans for Western Europe."

"Did you give them the operational intelligence folder for the hierarchy of the SD?" Kreise worded it exactly as Heydrich had instructed him to. He, himself, hadn't been authorised to see it, but Adler didn't know that.

Adler nodded.

"Is that a yes?"

"Yes," Adler confirmed.

"Who were your contacts in British intelligence?"

"I never saw anyone and that I swear to be true. I mentioned the possibility of me defecting to a business associate called Robert Stourcliffe and he passed it on to British intelligence. After that, it was all conducted through a series of dead letter boxes in the English Gardens in Munich."

"Did you know it was Fernsby who would take you across the border?"

Adler shook his head. "Not until the night we left for Venlo."

"He was taking you to Venlo in Holland? Who were you meeting there?"

"I never knew. I don't think even Fernsby knew, not until he got there, at least. Nobody was more surprised than me to see it was Fernsby. Like everyone else, I heard you on national radio telling everyone that he was dead."

"A necessary action to save the face of the Reich. You know how that works, Adler."

"Did he get away with the briefcase? Is that why you are interrogating me so viciously?"

"We're interrogating you because you are a traitor, Adler." Kreise had what he wanted and now his tone changed.

"You don't have it, do you?" A smile cracked open on Adler's torn lips.

"We have the briefcase. We wanted to confirm there was nothing else in it we didn't know about. From what you tell me, it's all there."

"I don't believe you. Fernsby got away with it, didn't he? He outfoxed you again, didn't he, Kreise?"

Kreise's face reddened. He jumped to his feet and stood over the stricken prisoner. "Fernsby is dead. For real this time. I caught him near the border at Venlo with the briefcase. Now we know we have retrieved everything, you are no longer useful to us."

"You gave me your word."

"I lied, Adler. The boy is already dead. Halmer enjoyed every moment from what I'm told. Your whore is dead too. You are a traitor, Adler, and that is what traitors deserve."

He strode out of the interrogation room and looked at Müller waiting outside.

"Kill him."

THE END.

Get a FREE Book!

Before John Howard found sanctuary on the streets of Henry VIII's London, Andrew Cullane formed a small band of outlawed survivors called the Underlings. Discover their fight for life for free when you join J.C. Jarvis's newsletter at jcjarvis.com/cullane

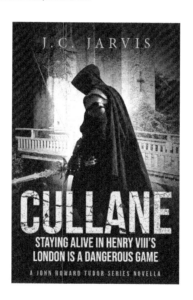

Please Leave A Review

If you loved the book and have a moment to spare, I would really appreciate a short review.

Your help in spreading the word is gratefully appreciated and reviews make a huge difference to helping new readers find the series.

Thank you!

More Books by JC Jarvis

Fernsby's War Series

Ryskamp

Alderauge

Book 3 Coming Soon

The John Howard Tudor Series

John Howard and the Underlings

John Howard and the Tudor Legacy

John Howard and the Tudor Deception

About the Author

J.C. Jarvis is the author of the breakout John Howard series.

He makes his home at www.jcjarvis.com

Email: jc@jcjarvis.com